SWIMMING POOL
SUNDAY

Also by Madeleine Wickham

The Tennis Party
A Desirable Residence

SWIMMING POOL SUNDAY

Madeleine Wickham

ST. MARTIN'S PRESS ✿ NEW YORK

A THOMAS DUNNE BOOK.
An imprint of St. Martin's Press.

SWIMMING POOL SUNDAY. Copyright © 1997 by Madeleine
Wickham. All rights reserved. Printed in the United States of
America. No part of this book may be used or reproduced in any
manner whatsoever without written permission except in the
case of brief quotations embodied in critical articles or reviews.
For information, address St. Martin's Press, 175 Fifth Avenue,
New York, N.Y. 10010.

Library of Congress Cataloging-in-Publication Data

Wickham, Madeleine.
        Swimming pool Sunday / Madeleine Wickham.
            p.   cm.
        "A Thomas Dunne book."
        ISBN 0-312-18188-4
    PR6073.I246S95   1998
    823'.914—dc21   97-33051
                          MAR 2 6 1998   CIP

First published in Great Britain by Black Swan Books, Trans-
world Publishers Ltd.

First U.S. Edition: April 1998

10   9   8   7   6   5   4   3   2   1

For Gemma and Abigail

I am grateful to Dr Stephane Duckett of
The Children's Trust, Tadworth, and to
Anna Lordon, for their expert advice.

SWIMMING POOL
SUNDAY

Chapter One

It was only May, and it was only ten o'clock in the morning. But already the sun was shining hotly, and the grass in the garden sprang warm and dry underfoot, and the breeze under Katie's cotton dress felt friendly and caressing. Katie gave a little wriggle. She felt like doing some ballet jumps, or rolling down the slope of the lawn until she landed in a heap at the bottom. But instead she had to stand, still as a rock, with elastic round her legs stretched so tightly it was going to give her red marks. She bent down and shifted the elastic slightly.

'Katie!' Amelia, who had been about to jump, stopped, and regarded her crossly. 'You mustn't move!'

'It hurts! It's too tight!' Katie bent her head round until she could catch a glimpse of the backs of her calves. She spotted a small pink line. 'Look! It's making marks on my skin!'

'Well, stand nearer the chair, then. But keep the elastic tight.' Katie gave a melodramatic sigh and shuffled nearer the chair.

They were playing with a chair because you needed three people for French skipping, and there were only two of them. Sometimes Mummy played with them, but today she was too busy, and had got cross when they asked. So they'd had to drag a chair out into the garden, and thread the elastic round its legs, just like human legs. Now it stretched, two white springy lines, a few inches above the grass. The very sight of it filled Katie with an excited anticipation. She *loved* French skipping. They played it in every single break at school; during lessons she would often put her hand into her pocket and check that the tangled mass of elastic was still safely there.

'Right.' Amelia sounded business-like. She began to jump efficiently over the taut elastic, biting her lip, and planting her feet carefully in exactly the right places. 'Jingle, jangle, centre, spangle,' she chanted. 'Jingle, jangle, out.' She jumped out without even touching the elastic.

'My go,' said Katie hopefully.

'No it isn't,' retorted Amelia. 'Don't you know how to play French skipping?'

'In my class,' said Katie, raising her eyebrows expressively, 'we play so that everybody has one go, and then it's the next person. Mrs Tully said that's the fairest way.' Amelia wasn't impressed.

'That's just for little ones,' she said. 'We play until the person makes a mistake.'

'But you'll never make a mistake!' cried Katie. She scratched the place on her leg where the elastic had been too tight.

'Yes I will, I expect,' said Amelia kindly. 'And anyway,' she added, 'at least you know it's your turn next; I don't think the chair will want to play.' Katie looked at the chair, standing benignly on the grass. She giggled.

'We could ask it,' she began. But Amelia had started jumping again.

'Jingle, jangle, centre, spangle, jingle, jangle, out.'

They had been sent out to play in the garden until their father came to pick them up. Nobody could quite remember what time he'd said he was coming. Amelia thought it was ten, and their mother thought it was ten-thirty, and Katie had been convinced it was quarter to nine, like school, and had actually stood by the door,

ready to go, until nine o'clock had come and gone and
it was obvious he was coming later.

Amelia had suggested, sensibly, that Mummy should
ring Daddy and ask him. But for some reason she didn't
want to. She never wanted to ring Daddy. It was always
Daddy who rang. He'd rung during the week, and talked
to Mummy, and said he was going to take the girls
fishing this Sunday. Fishing! Katie had never even
been fishing. They'd both got very excited and gone
down into the cellar and brought up all the nets and
buckets they could find. Amelia actually had a fishing-
rod that Grandfather had given her, and she'd
generously said that Katie could hold it with her if she
wanted. Mummy had washed out two jamjars for them,
in case there was anything small that they wanted to
bring home, and they'd chosen a chocolate bar each as
a special treat for their packed lunch.

But all of them, even Mummy, had forgotten that this
Sunday was Swimming Day at the Delaneys' house.
They *couldn't* miss the Swimming Day. Everyone was
going from the village; even people who didn't really
like swimming. Amelia briefly wondered what it must
be like, to be a person who didn't like swimming. She
simply couldn't imagine it. Everyone she knew liked
swimming: her, Katie, Mummy, even Daddy when he
was really hot.

They'd only remembered about the Swimming Day
yesterday, when they bumped into Mrs Delaney at the
shops, and she asked if they were coming, and Mummy
said that she thought this year, unfortunately, the girls
would have to miss it. Katie had nearly started crying
right there in the street. Amelia was more grown up than
that, but as soon as they were in the car, she'd asked in
a desperate voice, 'Couldn't we go to the Swimming Day
tomorrow and go fishing another time?' At first Mummy
had said no, of course not, in an angry voice. Then,
when they got home, she'd said no, but it really was a

pity. Then, later, she'd said maybe Daddy wouldn't mind. And last night, as she tucked them into bed, she'd said that as soon as Daddy arrived, she would ask him, and she thought he was sure to agree.

'Jingle, jangle, *out.*' Amelia thumped heavily onto the grass. 'I'm boiling,' she added.

'So'm I,' said Katie quickly. 'I can't *wait* to go swimming.'

'I'm going to dive straight in,' said Amelia. 'I'm not even going to feel it with my toe or anything.'

'So'm I,' said Katie again. 'I'm going to *dive* in.'

'You can't dive,' said Amelia crushingly.

'I can,' retorted Katie. 'I learned it in swimming. You sit on the side and . . .'

'That's not a proper dive.'

'It is!'

'It isn't.'

'It is!' Katie's voice rose in fury. 'It is a proper dive!' Amelia smirked silently. 'I did it the best in my class,' shrilled Katie. 'Mrs Tully said I was a little otter.'

There was a pause. Then Amelia wrinkled her nose superciliously and said, 'Yuck.'

'What?' Katie looked discomfited. 'Why is it yuck?'

'Being an otter is yuck.' Amelia looked at Katie challengingly, and Katie met Amelia's gaze silently for a moment, then she looked away. Amelia's eyes glinted.

'You don't know what an otter is, do you?' she said.

'Yes, I do!'

'What is it, then?'

Katie stared crossly at Amelia. Her mind scrambled over half-imagined pictures. Had Mrs Tully ever actually told her what an otter was? *Otter.* What did it sound like? Into her mind came an image of blue-green water; of silvery streaks of light and a lithe body shooting through the water in a perfect dive.

'It's like a flower fairy,' she said eventually. 'It's a

12

water fairy. It lives in the water and it's all blue and green.'

Amelia started to crow. 'No, it's not! Katie Kember, you don't know anything!'

'Well, what is it then?' shouted Katie angrily. Amelia brought her face up close to Katie's.

'It's an animal. It's all slithery and hairy and its feet are all webbed and slimy. That's what you are. You thought you were a water fairy!'

Katie sat down on the grass. It didn't occur to her not to believe Amelia. Amelia hardly ever made things up.

'I haven't got slimy feet,' she said, her voice trembling slightly, 'and I'm not all hairy; I've just got normal hair.' She pushed her bright brown fringe off her forehead and looked at Amelia with worried blue eyes. Amelia relented.

'No, but otters are really good at swimming,' she said. 'I expect that's what Mrs Tully meant.'

'Yes, that's what she meant,' said Katie, immensely cheered. 'I'm the best swimmer in my class, you know. Some of them still have *arm-bands.*'

'One boy in my class still has arm-bands,' said Amelia, giggling, 'and he's *nine.*'

'Nine!' echoed Katie scornfully. She was only just seven, and she'd been swimming without arm-bands since last summer.

Suddenly there was the sound of a car pulling up outside the house.

'Daddy!'

'Daddy!'

They both ran around the side of the house. There was their father getting out of the car, as tall as ever, wearing a pair of shorts and a very old-looking blue checked shirt. There was a combination of familiarity and strangeness about the sight of him which made Amelia stop momentarily in her tracks and look away. Katie pushed past her.

13

'Daddy!' she cried. Their father turned and smiled. And immediately, predictably, Katie burst into noisy, copious tears.

Louise Kember sat in her pretty kitchen and waited for Barnaby to come in. She'd heard the car pull up, heard the girls run out to greet him, and could now hear Katie's muffled sobs. It was nearly five months since Barnaby had moved out, and still Katie wept every time he arrived or left. And every time, a hand seemed to squeeze Louise's heart until fresh painful guilt filled her chest.

Hadn't she been told that it was far better for parents to separate than to stay together, arguing? In those awful few weeks over Christmas, when the rows between her and Barnaby had reached their height, when her frustrations and his suspicions had spilled over into everything they did, contaminating every gesture and giving every seemingly innocuous remark a double-edged meaning, she'd been convinced that when the split did come, it would be a relief for all of them. For her and Barnaby, certainly, but also for the girls.

Larch Tree Cottage wasn't big enough for two shouting parents and two sleeping children; more than once she and Barnaby had been interrupted mid-flow by a white-faced, white-nightied little person at the kitchen door. They would shoot accusing looks at one another as they quickly adopted soothing voices, proffered glasses of water and spoke gaily to Mr Teddy or Mrs Rabbit. And then they would inevitably both go back upstairs with whichever of the girls it was, in a self-conscious togetherness – tucking in and tiptoeing out as though they were once again the young married couple besotted with their first baby.

For a few moments the pretence would last. They would float down the stairs together in a cloud of deliberate good nature, fulfilling the image of the happy, loving, contented parents. But downstairs in the kitchen, the air would be thick with lingering, remembered jibes. The smiles would fade. Barnaby would mutter something incomprehensible about popping to The George for a quick half, and Louise would run a hot bath and weep frustratedly into the foamy water. By the time Barnaby got back she would be in bed, sometimes pretending to be asleep, sometimes sitting up, having formulated in her mind exactly what she wanted to say. But Barnaby would wave her speeches aside.

'I'm too tired, Lou,' he'd say. 'Busy day tomorrow. Can't it wait?'

'No, my life can't wait,' she once hissed back. 'It's been on hold for ten years already.' But Barnaby was already in his automatic, unseeing, unthinking, undressing and going-to-bed mode, and he didn't even reply. Louise stared at him in exasperated anger.

'Listen to me!' she screeched, forgetting the children, forgetting everything but her need to communicate. 'If you really loved me you'd listen to me!' And Barnaby looked up, baffled.

'I do love you,' he said in a low resentful voice, folding up his trousers. 'You know I love you.' And then he stopped and looked away.

And Louise looked away too. Because the truth was that she *did* know that Barnaby loved her. But knowing that Barnaby loved her was no longer enough.

Katie was sitting on the grassy bank outside the cottage next to Barnaby. His arm was round her, and she was juddering slightly, but her tears had dried up. On the other side of Barnaby was Amelia, who felt a bit like crying herself, but was far too grown up.

'That's better,' said Barnaby. He squeezed them both

15

tightly so their faces were squashed against his shirt. After a moment Katie started to wriggle.

'I can't breathe,' she gasped dramatically. Amelia said nothing. She felt safe, all squashed up against Daddy, smelling his smell and hearing his laugh. Of course, Mummy hugged them all the time, but it wasn't the same. It wasn't so . . . cosy. Her face was pressed up against a shirt button and her neck was a bit twisted, but still she could have stayed safely inside Daddy's hug all morning.

But Barnaby was letting go of them and reaching into the car.

'Here you are, you two,' he said, tossing a package into each lap. 'Vital equipment for the day.' The two girls began to unwrap their parcels and Barnaby watched, a pleased smile on his face. He'd bought each of them a present. For Katie he'd bought a small collapsible fishing-rod, and for Amelia, who already had a fishing-rod, he'd bought a smart little fishing-tackle box.

Katie unwrapped hers first. She squealed in delight and leaped up.

'Goody gum drops! A real fishing-rod! You can keep your smelly old rod, Amelia!'

But Amelia looked up from her tackle box in sudden realization, and said in dismay, 'What about going swimming?'

'What about it?' said Barnaby easily. 'I'm afraid you'll have to leave that to the fish. You might be able to paddle, though.'

'No, silly!' Katie dropped her fishing-rod on the ground and rushed over to Barnaby. 'Swimming Day, at Mrs Delaney's house! Can we go instead of fishing?'

Barnaby tried to hide his surprise.

'What! Don't you want to go fishing?'

'I want to go *swimming*,' said Katie coaxingly. 'It's so *hot*!'

By way of illustration she began to fan her legs with

the skirt of her dress. It was a familiar-looking pink and white striped dress; a cast-off of Amelia's, Barnaby abruptly realized. He had a sudden memory of a small Amelia wearing it, leaving for a birthday party, excitedly clutching a present, while an even smaller Katie jealously watched from the stairs.

'Mummy said you wouldn't mind,' offered Amelia. She tried to signal to Katie to shut up. She would make Daddy cross if she wasn't careful, and then they'd never be allowed to go swimming. 'We could go fishing next week,' she suggested. Abruptly, she remembered. 'And thank you for the lovely present,' she added.

'Yes, thank you, Daddy,' said Katie quickly. She picked up her fishing-rod and stroked it tenderly. 'For my lovely fishing-rod.' She looked up. 'But can we go swimming? Please? *Please?*'

'I don't know yet,' said Barnaby, trying to keep his temper. 'I'll go and talk to Mummy.'

Louise had begun rather self-consciously to make some coffee, waiting for the moment when Barnaby would come in. She moved gracefully around the kitchen, a careless half smile on her lips, noting with pleasure the pretty citrus-tree stencils which she had carefully painted onto the pine back door the week before. Those, and the new curtains, splashed brightly with orange and yellow flowers, had really lifted the kitchen, she thought to herself. Next she intended to stencil the bannisters, and maybe even the sitting-room. Larch Tree Cottage had, in the ten years they'd lived there, always been pretty, in a predictable old-fashioned sort of way, but Louise was now determined to transform it into something different and beautiful; something which people would look at with admiration.

As she heard Barnaby's heavy tread in the hallway, she glanced quickly around, as though to reaffirm in her mind the image which she presented. A happy, fulfilled, independent woman, at home in her own beautiful kitchen.

Nevertheless, she turned away as he got nearer, and turned on the coffee-grinder. Her hand trembled slightly as she pressed the top down, and the electrical shriek meant that she couldn't hear his greeting.

'Louise!' As she released the pressure on the coffee-grinder and the noise died down, Barnaby's voice sounded aggressively loud. Louise slowly turned. A jerk of fearful emotion rose up inside her, then almost immediately subsided.

'Hello, Barnaby,' she said in carefully modulated tones.

'What's all this nonsense about going swimming?'

As he heard his own rough voice, Barnaby knew he was playing this wrong; rushing in angrily instead of asking reasonably, but suddenly he felt very hurt. He'd planned this fishing expedition carefully; he'd been looking forward to it ever since he'd had the idea. The cheerful disregard with which his daughters had abandoned the idea wasn't their fault – they were only kids; but Louise should have been more thoughtful. An angry resentment grew inside him as he looked at her, half turned away, feathery blond fronds of hair masking her expression. Was she trying to sabotage his only time with the girls? Was she turning them against him? A raw emotional wound, deep inside him, began to throb. His breathing quickened.

Louise's head whipped round. She took in Barnaby's accusing expression and flushed slightly.

'It's not nonsense,' she said, allowing her voice to rise slightly. 'They want to go to the Delaneys' to swim.' She paused. 'I don't blame them. It's going to be a boiling hot day.'

She tipped ground coffee from the grinder into a cafetière and poured on hot water. A delicious smell filled the kitchen.

'Mummy!' Katie's piercing voice came in from the hall. 'Can we have a drink?' There was the sound of sandals clattering against floorboards, and suddenly the girls were in the kitchen.

'I'll pour them some Ribena,' said Barnaby.

'Actually,' said Louise, 'we don't have Ribena any more.' Barnaby stopped still, hand reaching towards the cupboard. 'Water will do,' added Louise.

'What's wrong with Ribena?' demanded Barnaby. He flashed a quick encouraging grin at Amelia.

'What's wrong with Ribena?' Amelia echoed.

'It's bad for your teeth,' said Louise firmly, ignoring Barnaby. 'You know that.'

'What's wrong with Ribena?' Amelia repeated, lolling against a kitchen cupboard.

'I want Ri-bee-na,' said Katie.

'I can't blame them,' said Barnaby.

'Or Tango,' said Katie, encouraged. 'Or Sprite. I *love* Sprite . . .'

'All right!' Louise shouted. There was a sudden silence. Louise scrabbled inside a jar on the work-surface.

'Go on, both of you, along to Mrs Potter's shop, and buy yourself a fizzy drink.' Katie and Amelia stared at her uncertainly. 'Go on,' repeated Louise. Her voice trembled slightly. 'Since it's such a hot day. As a treat. Stay on the grassy path and come straight back.'

'And then will we go swimming?' said Katie.

'Maybe,' said Louise. She handed some coins to Amelia. 'It depends what Daddy says.'

When they'd gone, there was silence. Louise slowly pushed down the plunger of the cafetière, lips tight. She stared down into its gleaming chrome surface for a minute, formulating words. Then she looked up.

'I would appreciate it, Barnaby,' she said deliberately, 'if you would try not to undermine *everything* I do.'

'I don't!' retorted Barnaby angrily. 'I wasn't to know

you'd suddenly taken against Ribena. How the hell was I supposed to know?' There was a pause. Louise poured the steaming coffee into mugs.

'And anyway,' added Barnaby, remembering, with a sudden resentful surge, the reason for his anger, 'I'd appreciate it if you didn't muscle in on my time with the girls.'

'I'm not! How can you say that? They're the ones who want to go swimming, not me!'

'What, so you aren't going swimming?'

'I probably will go, as a matter of fact,' said Louise, 'but I wasn't planning to take them.'

'Planning to take someone else, were you?' said Barnaby, with a sudden sneer. 'I wonder who?' Louise flushed.

'That's unfair, Barnaby.'

'It's perfectly fair!' Barnaby's voice was getting louder and louder. 'If you want to go swimming with lover boy, then I don't want to get in your way.'

Louise's eyes swivelled, before she could stop them, towards a new shiny photograph, freshly pinned up on the notice-board behind the door. Barnaby's gaze followed. His heart gave an unpleasant thud. The picture was of Louise, smiling, standing next to an elegant young man with smooth brown skin and glossy dark hair, on the steps of some grand-looking building that Barnaby didn't recognize. They were both in evening dress; Louise wore a silky blue dress that Barnaby had never seen before. The man wore a double-breasted dinner jacket; his patent-leather dress shoes were impeccably polished and his hair had a confident well-groomed sheen. As he stared, unable to move his eyes away, Barnaby's chest grew heavy with despair and loathing. He scanned the picture bitterly, as though searching for details, for clues; trying not to notice the excited happy look in Louise's face as she stood, with a strange man, in a strange place, smiling for a strange photographer.

Abruptly, he turned to Louise. 'You've had your hair cut.'

Louise, who had been expecting something more aggressive than that, looked surprised.

'Yes,' she said. Her hand moved up to her neck. 'Do you like it?'

'It makes you look . . . sexy.'

Barnaby sounded so gloomy that Louise smiled, in spite of herself.

'Isn't that good? Don't you like me looking sexy?' She was moving on to dangerous ground, but Barnaby didn't take the bait. He was staring at her with miserable blue eyes.

'You look like someone else's idea of sexy, not mine.'

Louise didn't know what to say. She took a sip of coffee. Barnaby slumped in his chair as though in sudden defeat.

For a few minutes they sat still, in almost companionable silence. Louise's thoughts gradually loosened themselves from the current situation and began to float idly around her mind like dust particles in the sunshine, bouncing quickly away whenever she inadvertently hit on anything too painful or serious. Sitting, sipping her coffee, feeling the sunshine warm on her face, she could almost forget about everything else. Meanwhile Barnaby sat, in spite of himself, blackly imagining Louise in a pair of strong dinner-jacketed arms; dancing, whirling, laughing, being happy, how *could* she?

Suddenly there was a rattling at the back door. Louise looked up. Katie was beaming in through the kitchen window, triumphantly clutching a shiny can. The door opened and Amelia bounded in.

'We had a lift,' she said breathlessly, 'from Mrs Seddon-Wilson. She said, were we going to the swimming?'

21

'And we said, yes we were, nearly,' said Katie. She danced over to Barnaby. 'Are we going, Daddy? Are we going swimming?'

'We haven't talked about it yet,' said Louise quickly.

'You *must* have!' said Katie in astonishment. 'You were talking all that time, when we went to the shop and got our drinks . . . They didn't have any Sprite,' she added sorrowfully, 'but I got Fanta.' She offered her can to Louise.

'May you open my drink for me?'

'In a minute,' said Louise, distractedly.

'Are we going swimming, Mummy?' asked Amelia anxiously. 'Mrs Seddon-Wilson said it was going to be tremendous fun.'

'*Tremendous* fun,' echoed Katie, 'and I told her about my new swimming-suit and she said it sounded lovely.'

'What about it, Barnaby?' Louise adopted a brisk businesslike voice. 'Can they go swimming?' Barnaby looked up. His face was pink.

'I think the girls and I should go fishing as planned,' he said stoutly. He looked at Katie. 'Come on, Katkin. Don't you want to use your new rod?'

'Yes, I do,' said Katie simply. 'I want to go fishing, but I want to go swimming, too.'

'But you go swimming every week at school,' said Barnaby, trying not to sound hectoring.

'I know we do, Daddy,' said Amelia, in an attempt to mollify, 'but this swimming is different. It's the Swimming Day. It only happens once a year.'

'Well, tell you what,' said Barnaby, giving her a wide smile. 'I'll speak to Hugh, and get him to invite us over to swim another day; just us. How about that?' Amelia looked down and swung her foot.

'It won't be the same,' she said in barely audible tones. Barnaby's good humour snapped.

'Why not?' he suddenly bellowed. 'Why is it so important that you go swimming today? What's wrong

22

with the lot of you?' Louise's eyes flashed.

'There's nothing wrong with the girls,' she said icily, 'just because they want to spend a nice hot day swimming with their friends.' She put a proprietorial hand on Amelia's shoulder. Amelia looked at the floor. Suddenly Katie gave a sob. 'I'll go fishing, Daddy! I'll go fishing with you! Where's my rod?' She fumbled with the back door and rushed out into the garden.

'Oh great,' said Louise curtly. 'Well, if you want to blackmail them into going with you, that's fine.'

'How dare you!' Barnaby drew an angry breath. His cheeks had flushed dark red, and his forehead had begun to glisten. 'It's nothing to do with blackmail. Katie wants to come fishing. So would Amelia, if you hadn't . . .'

'If I hadn't what?' Louise's grip tightened on Amelia's shoulder. 'If I hadn't what, Barnaby?'

Barnaby looked at the two of them, mother and daughter, and suddenly a defeated look came into his eyes. 'Nothing,' he muttered.

Then the back door opened and Katie was in the kitchen again. She was holding her rod in one hand and a piece of tangled elastic in the other. 'I nearly couldn't find my French skipping,' she said breathlessly.

'Are you sure you want to go fishing?' said Louise, ignoring Barnaby's glance.

'Yes, I'm *quite* sure,' said Katie grandly. 'And anyway, I've got my swimming-suit on under my dress, so I can go swimming with the little fishes.' Barnaby began to say something, then stopped.

'All right,' said Louise. 'Well, we'll see you later, then.' She looked at Barnaby. 'Not too late.'

Barnaby looked at Amelia. He gave her a friendly smile.

'How about you, Amelia? Want to come fishing?'

23

Amelia blushed. She looked up at Louise, then back at Barnaby.

'Not really,' she said in a small voice. 'I want to go swimming. Do you mind, Daddy?' Barnaby's cheerful expression barely faltered.

'Well,' he said slowly, 'of course I'd love you to come with us, but not if you'd rather go swimming instead. You should just do what you enjoy the most.'

'I enjoy *fishing* the most,' announced Katie, brandishing her rod. 'I hate nasty old swimming.'

'You love swimming,' objected Louise.

'Not any more,' retorted Katie. She looked up at Barnaby. 'Me and Daddy hate swimming, don't we, Daddy?' Louise's lips tightened.

'Well, Katie,' she said, 'you're a big girl now, you can make your own decision. I just hope you don't regret it.'

'What's regret?' asked Katie immediately.

'It's to look back on something you've done,' said Barnaby, 'and wish you hadn't done it. You won't do that, will you, Katkin?' But Katie wasn't listening. She had begun to do her birdcage dance around the kitchen, using the fishing-rod instead of her birdcage. As she danced, she began to hum the tune.

'We won't regret going swimming,' said Amelia bravely. 'Will we, Mummy?'

'No,' said Louise, 'I shouldn't think we will. Katie, stop dancing, and go with Daddy.' Katie stopped, foot still pointed out.

'I don't regret going fishing,' she said.

'You haven't been yet,' pointed out Amelia.

'So what?' said Katie, rudely.

'Come on,' said Barnaby, impatiently. 'Go and get in the car, Katie.' He grinned briefly at Amelia. 'I'll see you this evening,' he said, 'and we'll tell each other about our day.'

When he had left the kitchen, Amelia's chin began to wobble. She suddenly felt very unsure of herself. The kitchen seemed empty and silent now that Daddy and Katie had gone, and she wasn't sure that she'd made the right decision. She looked up at Mummy for a comforting glance, but Mummy was staring at something on the notice-board. Amelia followed her gaze. It was a photograph of Mummy and Cassian.

'Is Cassian coming swimming, Mummy?' she asked, falteringly. Louise's head whipped round.

'No!' she said. Then, at the sight of Amelia's anxious face, her voice softened. 'No,' she repeated, 'he's in London.'

'Oh.' Amelia wasn't quite sure why, but this piece of news made her feel a bit better about going swimming with Mummy instead of fishing with Daddy. 'Oh,' she said again. Louise suddenly smiled.

'So we'll have a lovely day, just the two of us,' she said, 'swimming and getting brown. Mummy and Amelia. What do you think?'

Into Amelia's mind appeared a blissful image of a blue swimming-pool glittering in the sunlight, herself floating effortlessly in the middle of it. She looked happily up at Louise.

'I think, yes please,' she said.

'Well, go and get your things, then,' said Louise brightly. 'We want to make all we can out of the day.'

Amelia clattered out of the kitchen and thudded up the narrow cottage stairs. And Louise followed at a more leisurely pace, humming gaily to herself and wondering which sun-hat she should take with her, and trying as hard as she could to dispel from her mind the lingering image of Barnaby's indignant, angry, wounded face.

Chapter Two

Hugh and Ursula Delaney had first opened their swimming-pool for charity more than twenty years ago, when their two sons were children and the people at Melbrook Place – the largest house in the village – were refusing to hold a village fête. Devenish House, the Delaneys' own house, was not in quite the same league as Melbrook Place, but it was the second biggest house in the village – and it had a swimming-pool.

The first Swimming Day had been on a blisteringly hot day, at a time when the nearest public swimming-bath was thirty miles away in Braybury, full of chlorine, and housed in an unpleasantly green-tiled building. Parents and children alike, unused to the luxury of an outside heated pool, had thrown themselves into the blue water like joyous seals, tumbling and splashing with the determination of those who know they have a limited amount of time for pleasure. Pictures of the occasion in the Delaneys' photograph album showed women and men in baggy pre-Lycra swimming-suits emblazoned with orange flowers and purple swirls, leaping from the diving-board, or floating on their backs, or sitting round the side of the pool, legs dangling in the depths, unwilling to relinquish the water for a moment. And all around them – in the water, under the water, jumping and diving and ducking and shrieking – were the children. Some, unable to swim, clutched in fearful delight to the edge of the pool, while parents coaxed them further in, others floated in pleasurable torpor, buoyed up by shiny rubber rings and arm-bands. Some had proper bathing-suits; many did not. Many had never been swimming before in their lives.

In the two decades since then everything had changed. The people of Melbrook now benefited from a shiny new leisure centre in nearby Linningford, complete with indoor and outdoor pools, Jacuzzi, steam-room and sauna. All the children of the village could swim as a matter of course. The appeal of a simple swimming-pool – by now rather old, and with no accompanying exercise bikes or health bar – had rather diminished. Meanwhile, new people had moved into Melbrook Place and declared themselves more than happy to reintroduce a Melbrook Place fête. There was really no need for the Swimming Day to happen any more.

But the people of Melbrook were both loyal and conservative. When Hugh and Ursula had tentatively suggested, six or seven years ago, that the Swimming Days had outlived their function, there had been a general outcry. People whom Hugh and Ursula had never met; people who, as far as they were aware, had never even been to one of the Swimming Days, had accosted them in the street, and asked anxiously whether the rumours were really true. The residents of the new development just outside the village had drawn up a petition. One young woman, who had only been living in Melbrook for a few months, had waited for Ursula outside church one Sunday, and proceeded to berate her soundly for eroding the character of the village.

In the end it hadn't been worth the struggle. Hugh and Ursula had capitulated and agreed to carry on; now it seemed as though the Swimming Days would go on for ever.

There was only one year in which they had not held a Swimming Day. Three years before, Simon, their

27

younger son, had died, suddenly, of a brain tumour, at the age of twenty-eight.

He died in February, on a cold grey day, and the coldness stayed inside Hugh and Ursula all year. After the funeral they stayed inside their house, avoiding the world, while outside the blossoms opened and the air grew warm and the sun played on the water of their swimming-pool. Then, when the leaves began to turn and the air grew cooler, they packed up and went to their little house in France. Hugh left his wine-importing business ticking over in the hands of his assistant. Ursula told people not to expect them back for Christmas.

They spoke to nobody. Matthew, their elder son, was in Hong Kong, working hard and coping with his grief as best he could on his own. Their own families, based respectively in Derbyshire and Scotland, were both too far away to have known Simon properly and too close to provide dispassionate comfort.

The only one who understood was Meredith. Their daughter-in-law; Simon's widow.

He had met her at a gallery opening; she was an artist from America, via most cities in Europe. She was slightly older and slightly cleverer than him, and quite a lot richer. Hugh found her fascinating; Ursula found her frightening. The wedding had been at a register office in London; Meredith had worn a black tailcoat and top hat and at the reception had decorated, in dark-red ink, the shirt-back of Simon's enchanted managing director.

After Simon's funeral, Hugh and Ursula looked at Meredith's blue-white face, her long lank hair and shaking hands, and pressed her warmly to stay with them for a while. Ursula filled her room with flowers and pot-pourri, and ran her hot baths; Hugh poured her deep glasses of whisky and offered her cigarettes. But after two days she disappeared. They received a postcard from the airport; Meredith had returned to her native San Francisco.

For months after that they heard nothing from her. They had not had the chance to get to know her very well; there were no grandchildren to be considered; now it seemed that Meredith, too, had left their lives for ever.

Until she turned up in France. 'I didn't realize you guys'd run away too,' were her first words. Her face was still white; she looked worse than she had done after the funeral. 'The States didn't work,' was all she would say.

They spent an uneasy first week all together in the cottage, skirting and hesitating and avoiding the subject of Simon. Then, one evening, as the windows of the little kitchen fogged up with condensation and Hugh built up the fire in the grate, Meredith began to talk. She talked about Simon, about herself, about herself and Simon, about herself and her family. Her hands shook. She smoked furiously. She made challenging assertions about Simon, then stared from Ursula's face to Hugh's face and back again, looking for a reaction. Around midnight, she began to cry. Ursula, strung up, confused and bewildered by most of what Meredith was saying, began to cry too. Hugh leaned across the table and clasped Meredith's hands tightly in his own. 'Please don't stop,' he said shakily. 'Don't stop. And please don't go away again.'

They stayed in France, all together, until the first anniversary of Simon's death had passed. Hugh began to communicate with his assistant in England, Meredith began to draw again, but it was Ursula who decided, with uncharacteristic firmness, as February turned into March and another spring began, that it was time for them to go home.

They arrived back in Melbrook on a bright, clear, sharp morning. While Hugh and Ursula unpacked, Meredith wandered around the house and garden as

29

though she'd never been there before. Eventually she came inside.

'You got two barns here,' she stated.

'That's right,' said Hugh, surprised. 'Although, actually, one's a stable.' Meredith waved her hands at him impatiently. 'What I want to know is', she said, 'which one can be my studio?'

A bubble of joy rose up inside Hugh. Meredith had always been vague about her plans. He and Ursula had felt sure she would soon announce her intention to move back to London – or further. After all, they had reasoned miserably to each other, what on earth was there to keep a young, independent, vibrant woman like Meredith in a village like Melbrook? Now he tried to catch Ursula's eye. She was looking confusedly at Meredith.

'Does that mean . . .' she began. Hugh broke her off.

'Whichever one you want,' he said, unable to keep the delight out of his voice. 'Have both. Have the whole house.'

Meredith had lived with them ever since. When Matthew got married in Hong Kong, she designed an outfit for Ursula and went to the wedding with them. When Hugh took Ursula on a wine-tasting trip around Burgundy, Meredith came too.

Every so often she would take off on her own – to London, or Amsterdam, or New York; once for a month to Sydney. During those times, while she was away, the atmosphere was taut, the shared unspoken fear hanging over the house like an exam result. But she always came back to her red-painted bedroom, and her gold-painted bathroom, and her muralled sitting-room. And relief would flood painfully through Hugh, and he would block from his mind the gnawing truth that, sooner or later, Meredith was going to find someone to share her life with, and was going to leave him and Ursula alone again, to live their lives as they did before, but no longer knowing quite how to go about it. It was Meredith who had masterminded the first Swimming Day after Simon's death. That year the weather was unremittingly gloomy throughout May; Hugh and Ursula expected that few people would turn up. But they were reckoning without the curiosity of the village. Everyone had heard about Meredith; few had met her. As family after family trooped in, their faces lit up as they saw the object of their visit sitting at the entrance, smiling rather ferociously as donations dropped into the plastic pot. It really was too cold to swim that year; only the hardiest children ventured into the pool. But it wasn't too cold to sit and stare at Meredith and tell each other what a striking girl she was, and what a tragedy the whole thing had been.

And now Meredith was as much part of the Delaneys' Swimming Day as Ursula's elderflower cordial. This year, expecting a large crowd, she had enlisted the help of the vicar's wife, Frances Mold, at the entrance table. After a shaky first meeting at Simon's funeral, at which Meredith pronounced herself 'Agnostic-stroke-Atheist-stroke (if anything) Buddhist, I guess', these two had developed an unlikely friendship, and could often be seen striding the fields together; a tweed skirt and brogues alongside a pair of velvet jodhpurs and riding boots.

Hugh and Ursula were having a cup of coffee in the conservatory when Meredith poked her head through the window.

'Lots of people are here already,' she said, gesturing behind her.

'So we can see,' said Hugh. 'Jolly good. We'll come out in a minute and help.'

'What I came for', said Meredith, 'was that list of people who have paid already.' She looked at Ursula. 'You know the one? You had it yesterday.'

'Ah yes,' said Ursula vaguely, 'the list.' She patted her

31

silvery blond hair, arranged becomingly in a French pleat, and took a sip of coffee.

'Do you know where the list is?' asked Meredith. 'Did you find it last night?'

'Not *last* night, no,' said Ursula, frowning slightly. 'Wasn't it on the dresser?' She looked at Meredith with large blue eyes, bright in the greenish gloom of the conservatory.

'No, Ursula,' said Meredith patiently. 'Don't you remember? We were talking about it last night. I couldn't find it, and you said you'd taken it off the dresser to add a couple of names, and you said you'd look for it.'

'Ah yes,' said Ursula, 'now I remember.'

'Did you look for it?' prompted Meredith.

'I may have had a little search,' said Ursula unconvincingly. Meredith exchanged glances with Hugh. This was the sort of behaviour that used to drive Simon mad with his mother, she thought. And before she could stop it, a familiar series of pictures flashed briefly through her mind: Simon, the wedding, Simon in hospital, the funeral. She felt a short pang of pain, but in a moment her mind was clear again; the memories packaged neatly away. All that was left behind was a strong feeling of fondness for Ursula.

'But you didn't find it,' she suggested.

'I don't think I did,' said Ursula eventually. 'But I'll go and have a look for it now, shall I?' She screwed up her face in thought. 'You know, dear, I'm sure it's on the dresser.'

'It's not on the dresser, Ursula,' said Meredith, grinning at her. 'That's the whole point. I already looked there.'

'Well, dear, you never know; you might have missed it,' said Ursula in gently obstinate tones. She put down her coffee cup on a bamboo table, and stood up. A white and green print crêpe de Chine dress rustled prettily in

32

soft folds around her. 'I'll go and look for it straight away,' she announced.

'OK then,' said Meredith, 'and maybe, Hugh, you could have a look too? Somewhere other than the dresser?' Hugh winked at her.

'I'll see what I can do,' he said.

By the time Louise and Amelia arrived at Devenish House, Hugh had found the list lurking behind an ormolu clock on the dining-room mantelpiece. Meredith had gone to change into her swimming things, and Ursula was presiding over the entrance table, together with Frances Mold.

Frances's husband, the Revd Alan Mold, was, that morning, taking family service in the neighbouring village of Tranton. He was in charge of both parishes – Melbrook and Tranton – and alternated between them every Sunday. This arrangement had been in existence for nearly ten years, and at first the general idea had been that the congregation from Melbrook would follow him to Tranton every other Sunday, and the congregation from Tranton would reciprocate. In practice, however, the arrangement was cheerfully regarded as a good excuse to attend church only once a fortnight.

The only person who regularly accompanied Alan to Tranton was Frances herself. However, this morning, even she had forgone the family service in favour of a quick eight o'clock communion, in order to be free to help the Delaneys. Now she sat, chatting cheerfully to Ursula at the entrance table, looking about her with a pleasant anticipation.

Although labelled 'The Entrance Table', there was, in fact, no obvious place of entrance to the swimming-pool of Devenish House. From the conservatory and French windows of the house, the garden sloped and stepped in a vague Italianate fashion, embellished with carved stone walls, urns and slabs, until the ground flattened

33

out a few hundred yards from the house. And here, framed by a decorative paving area and, beyond, endless smooth lawns, was the swimming-pool – cool, blue and shaped like a kidney bean. It had been installed by the people who lived in Devenish House before the Delaneys, at a time when the kidney-shaped swimming-pool was the ultimate in status symbols. Many times since moving in, Hugh had threatened to fill it in; to replace it with something oblong and functional and further away from the house, or even with nothing at all.

'That pool could be a putting-green, you know,' he would exclaim, on days when the tarpaulin cover flapped in the wind and the very idea of plunging into anything cooler than a hot bath brought on a shiver. 'It could be something useful. Or at least tasteful.'

'Count your lucky stars,' Meredith had retorted the first time she heard him. 'It could be painted black and in the shape of a penis.'

As Louise approached the entrance table, Ursula looked up.

'Louise, dear! How lovely to see you! And Amelia! No Katie?'

'Katie's gone fishing for the day with Barnaby,' said Louise shortly.

'Oh dear,' said Ursula, her face falling slightly. 'Hugh will be sad not to see Barnaby.' She paused. 'But I can quite see that it would be a little awkward . . .'

She broke off and looked from Louise to Amelia. Only recently had Meredith managed to persuade Ursula that it was really true about the Kembers splitting up, not just malicious village gossip, and when finally convinced, Ursula had been most upset. 'I find it terribly sad,' she said vaguely. 'I suppose . . .' She paused and adopted a delicate tone. 'I suppose you find it very *painful* to see Barnaby.'

'Not particularly,' said Louise tightly.

She glanced at Frances Mold, who smiled back sympathetically and said in a hurried, cheerful voice, 'Hello, Amelia! How nice to see you!' But Ursula was lost in her own hazy reflections.

'Poor dear Barnaby,' she said without thinking. Then, realizing what she had said, she gave a little start. 'Oh, Louise! My dear, I didn't mean . . .'

'It's quite all right,' said Louise shortly. She opened her purse and handed Frances Mold a note. 'Here; that's right, isn't it?'

'Yes, exactly right.' Frances gave Louise an apologetic glance. 'See you later.'

'Maybe,' said Louise, discouragingly, and stalked off. She was, she realized, being unfair to poor Frances, who was the most tactful creature in the village. But Ursula's foolish remarks had, today, for some reason touched Louise on the raw. She clenched her fists angrily by her sides as she strode towards the swimming-pool, and felt an angry frown crease her forehead.

'Stupid fool,' she muttered crossly. 'Stupid, stupid, stupid.'

Louise had never been quite as friendly with Ursula as Barnaby was with Hugh. The two men had become friends years before, when Amelia was a baby. Barnaby had overheard Hugh talking in The George about some hedging that needed doing on his land, and immediately offered to help; Hugh had reciprocated with a case of burgundy. After that, the two men had fallen into an easy, relaxed friendship, and Louise had made an honest attempt to forge the same kind of relationship with Ursula. But it had not been a great success. Louise found Ursula rather old, rather dull, and exceedingly stupid. When she started to fuss irritatingly over first Amelia and then Katie, Louise began to find more and more excuses not to accompany Barnaby to Devenish House.

And then everything had changed – with the dreadful death of the Delaneys' son, and the year they'd spent abroad, and the arrival of Meredith.

Louise had not taken to Meredith. At their very first meeting, Meredith had scowled at Louise's carefully composed expressions of sympathy and stalked off, black hair streaming behind her. She'd apologized later, but Louise already felt slighted. And ever since then, Louise had always sensed, perhaps unfairly, that Meredith looked down on her, laughed at her, even, for leading such a conventional unchallenging existence.

Since it was not safe to visit Devenish House without coming across Meredith, Louise had found herself seeing Ursula less and less frequently. Barnaby and Hugh were still good friends, but Barnaby often observed, ruefully, that Hugh was in less need of company these days. With Meredith there, the Delaney family had become far more self-sufficient than before.

Daisy Phillips arrived at Devenish House slightly after eleven, reached the middle of the drive, and then stopped, stricken with sudden nerves.

She had never been to the Delaneys' house before. Her parents had only bought the cottage in Melbrook a few months ago, and they hadn't really got to know anybody in the village. But Mrs Mold had told her to be sure to come to the Swimming Day, and said she would introduce her to everyone. Daisy liked Mrs Mold. She was a piano teacher, as well as the vicar's wife, and she had passed by the cottage one day as Daisy was practising. Immediately she had come down the path and knocked on the door.

'A pianist! In Melbrook!' she had exclaimed. 'What luck!'

Daisy was going to the Royal Academy of Music in the autumn. She had spent most of this academic year in Bologna, studying with Arturo Fosci, and picking up a little Italian. But then she'd come back to England, and all of a sudden there had arisen the problem of where Daisy should live. With her busy parents both working from their tranquil London flat, she couldn't really live there and practise. 'It was fine when it was just the school holidays,' her father had explained kindly, 'but if it's going to be for several months on end . . .' And then his mobile phone had rung, and he'd broken off to answer, and Daisy had stood waiting for him to finish, until he put his hand over the mouthpiece and said, 'We'll talk about it later, Daisy.'

One of her brothers lived in London, but in a tiny flat with room-mates and no space for a piano; the other was travelling round the world. In the autumn she would be able to practise at the Academy, but until then, she really needed somewhere of her own, where the noise didn't matter. For a while it had seemed as though she was going to have to find her own flat in London, or maybe rent a studio, and then suddenly, at supper one evening, her mother exclaimed, 'Of course, the cottage!'

'What cottage?' said Daisy.

'The cottage in Melbrook,' said her father. 'We bought it while you were in Italy. It's very pretty.'

'And tax efficient,' added her mother. She took a forkful of baby spinach. 'We don't actually go there very much.'

'We don't actually go there ever, you mean,' said her father.

'We went once,' retorted her mother. 'Don't you remember? It was bloody freezing.' She shuddered.

'Anyway,' said her father. 'What about it?'

'Daisy could live there and practise to her heart's content,' said her mother. Her eyes began to gleam. 'And if she was down on the employee roll . . .'

'She already is,' put in her father.

'. . . then all her expenses would be tax-deductible. What about it, Daisy?'

37

'You'll never fit Daisy's piano into that cottage,' her father had objected, before Daisy could reply.

'Yes you will!' her mother had retorted. 'Of course you will. That sitting-room's jolly big!'

'And so is a grand piano.'

'Not that big.'

'When was the last time you looked at one closely?'

And so they'd argued all through supper. Daisy's mother went and fetched the floor plan of the cottage and drew a grand piano into the sitting-room, fitting snugly next to the fireplace. Her father leaned back in his chair and roared with laughter.

'What's that supposed to be? A baby grand? Honestly, Diana, you're miles out. Now, *this* is where it could go, but it might be a tight squeeze . . .'

By the end of the evening the floor plan was criss-crossed with outlines of pianos, and the question of whether or not Daisy actually wanted to live in the cottage had been forgotten. And the next evening her mother announced that she'd spoken to the estate agent, who had confirmed that there had indeed once been a grand piano in the sitting-room.

'So there you are,' said her mother triumphantly to Daisy. 'All sorted. Now we just have to move you down there.'

Daisy had been down there now for three weeks and was starting to get used to it. Living on her own was all right – she'd done that in Bologna – and so was practising for most of the day, but not knowing anybody nearby was very strange. All her life she'd been used to having friends about, either at school, or in London; even in Bologna there had always been the other students to talk to. It wasn't as if she was a particularly sociable person. In fact, at school, she'd always been considered a loner. But being a loner when you were surrounded by 400 other girls was, she thought, a different matter from being a loner when you were surrounded by empty fields.

Her parents kept asking her if she'd started talking to the villagers.

'I'm sure they're very friendly,' her mother would say, her voice coming, crisp and familiar, down the phone line. 'Just ask them how the crops are growing, or how their cows are doing . . .'

'Lots of them live in bungalows,' Daisy objected, but her mother wasn't listening.

'And remember, you're *working* there for us, in case anyone asks.'

Daisy had remembered that when Mrs Mold had arrived.

'I'm doing some work for my parents,' she blurted out quickly, as Mrs Mold ran her hands lovingly over the curves of her piano. 'For their company. It's a management consultancy.' But Mrs Mold wasn't listening.

'A Bösendorfer. You lucky thing. Do you mind if I have a play?'

Mrs Mold wasn't actually terribly good at the piano, Daisy thought now, as she looked up at the windows of Devenish House, shiny and opaque in the sun. But she seemed very kind, and it would be nice to see her today.

She took a few steps back, until she was suddenly out of the shade of a huge rhododendron bush, and the sun was beating down on her face. She was sure today was the Swimming Day, but where was it all happening? Was she supposed to go round the side? What if she was somehow at the wrong house? She imagined herself bursting round the side of the house into a stranger's garden, startling some innocent family drinking coffee on the lawn.

She clutched her swimming things more tightly. Her mother's voice, firm and impatient, floated into her mind. 'For heaven's sake, Daisy. Just ring the bell and ask. They won't eat you.'

The dark-blue front door was set in a rather grand porch, with grey pillars and a curved stone pediment and a bell-pull made from wrought iron. While she waited for someone to come to the door, Daisy looked around for clues, but the only other thing in the porch with her was a boot scraper shaped like a hedgehog; nothing about swimming. This was probably the wrong house. There were probably two Devenish Houses, she thought. Or maybe an Old Devenish House and a New Devenish House . . .

'Hello?' It was a man, with grey hair and a brown face and a jolly expression.

'H-hello.' Daisy couldn't prevent her voice from trembling. 'I was told . . .' Suddenly she was lost for words. Was she really about to tell a strange man that she wanted to come and swim in his swimming-pool?

'Have you come for the swimming?' Hugh said, helpfully.

'Y-yes!' said Daisy thankfully. 'My name's Daisy Phillips. Mrs Mold told me . . .'

'Ah, of course! Frances!' said Hugh. 'Well, you're very welcome!'

Daisy looked helplessly at him. Suddenly Hugh's expression changed.

'The signs *are* up, aren't they?' he said.

'S-signs?' Hugh darted out into the drive.

'I might have known it! Ask her to do *anything* . . . Look, I'm sorry about this,' said Hugh. 'There should have been signs telling you where to go. The pool's through there.'

'Oh good,' said Daisy, with relief. 'And w-where should I get changed?'

Hugh looked again at Daisy Phillips. She was a tall girl, about eighteen, he guessed, with clouds of dark hair floating down to her waist, and a pale, pale complexion. Her dark eyes flew downwards at his gaze; her hands rubbed one another anxiously; one white-

40

espadrilled toe nervously circled the blue and green tiles of the porch. He tried to imagine this girl changing nonchalantly amongst the other ladies of the village in the sweaty, rubbery atmosphere of the changing tent and failed.

'Well,' he said slowly, 'quite a lot of people come already changed, so why don't you use one of our bedrooms?'

'Really? Are you sure that's all right?'

'Quite all right,' said Hugh heartily. He felt an unaccountable need to reassure her. 'Now,' he said, as though to a six-year-old, 'why don't you pop upstairs, and when you come down, you'll find the pool out there, through the conservatory. That way.' He pointed down a passage. Daisy nodded. 'And meanwhile, I'll go and sort out the signs for the drive,' added Hugh.

'Which room should I use?' asked Daisy, as he disappeared.

'Oh, just use any old room,' Hugh called over his shoulder. 'Any room at all.'

It was not Daisy's fault that the first room she should pick on was Meredith's. She cautiously pushed the door open, then gave a horrified, 'Oh!' She was looking at a large corner room, painted a deep red and dominated by a large mahogany bed. On one wall was a carved grey marble fireplace. Propped up against another was a huge gilt mirror. And in the middle was a thin, brown, sinewy woman, with long black hair, a forbidding expression and no clothes on.

'Don't you usually knock?' she said in a casual American accent, starting to pull on a black many-strapped swimming-costume.

'I'm so sorry,' Daisy said, bright red and trembling. 'I thought . . . I just . . .' Her words dried up. Why hadn't she knocked? 'I-I was looking for somewhere to change.'

'Well, how about the changing tent?' suggested

41

Meredith drily. 'That's where you're supposed to change.' Daisy gaped at her.

'He didn't say . . .' she began. 'He told me . . . to come upstairs.'

'Who?'

'Mr . . .' Daisy broke off. She didn't know his name; or did she? Had Mrs Mold told her? Was it Devenish, like the house?

'Look, never mind,' said Meredith abruptly. 'Since you're here, you can help me get into this thing. See these straps? I can't get them right.'

Cautiously, Daisy advanced towards Meredith. A web of interlaced black Lycra straps lay untidily across her back.

'Just yank them into place,' instructed Meredith. Daisy put up her hand awkwardly towards Meredith's back. She pulled one of the straps downwards and another upwards. 'I have a picture of it somewhere,' said Meredith. 'That might help.' She strode over to a small Victorian wash-stand in the corner of the room, piled with papers, magazines and books. 'Here!' She tossed a glossy magazine at Daisy, who, startled, dropped it on the floor.

'Butter-fingers,' said Meredith, coming over. She caught a glimpse of herself in the big gilt mirror as she passed. 'I guess it looks OK now.' She shook back her hair and looked at Daisy with glinting green eyes.

'So,' she said casually, 'what's your name? And what do you do? Nothing that needs co-ordination, I hope?'

'My name's Daisy Phillips,' said Daisy, blushing awkwardly. 'And I . . .' She stopped as a sound made Meredith's head rise suddenly. From outside came the purring and crackling of a car coming down the drive. Meredith quickly strode over to the window. Looking past her, Daisy could see a dark-green car and a slim man with dark eyes and greying temples getting out of the driver's seat. Meredith remained motionless for a moment. Then she turned around and gave Daisy a distracted look.

'Look, you can change in here if you like,' she said. 'Just take your stuff with you when you go, and pay at the entrance table. All right, Daisy Phillips?'

'Yes,' said Daisy. 'Thank you.' Meredith turned to her reflection in the gilt mirror and tossed back her hair. 'How does my suit look?' she demanded.

'Fantastic,' said Daisy honestly.

'It ought to,' said Meredith, 'it cost enough.' She picked up a deep-red towel, slipped her feet into a pair of black leather sandals and closed the door behind her.

Outside, on the landing, Meredith paused and allowed a small dart of delight in her chest to flower a little. Through the circular window above the stairs she could still just see the corner of Alexis Faraday's car. He was here; Alexis was here. Downstairs, maybe, or outside, already lying back and soaking up the sun. Meredith threw back her shoulders and began to walk down the stairs. Then she remembered: sunglasses. Abruptly she turned back and threw open the door to her room. Daisy looked round, startled. She was down to only a pair of knickers.

'Forgot my shades,' said Meredith. 'You don't mind, do you?' Daisy blushed; a delicate pink which spread down as far as her full white breasts. Meredith watched, interestedly, as the colour gradually faded. 'Got sun block?' she enquired, picking up a pair of opaque black sunglasses.

'Y-yes,' stumbled Daisy.

'Good,' said Meredith, 'you need it.' And without further comment she left the room, put on her dark glasses and made her way out to the swimming-pool, and to Alexis.

Ten miles away, in an unbearably hot, dusty and clogged line of traffic, Barnaby finally lost his temper.

43

'All right, Katie!' he shouted. There was sudden silence in the car. 'Stop whining! If you've really changed your mind; if you *really* want to go swimming, then we'll go swimming.'

With a suddenly heavy heart he brutally changed into reverse gear and, ignoring the irritation of the other drivers on the road, swung the car round. He changed gear again, put his foot down, and sped off down the clear side of the road, back towards Melbrook, the Delaneys' house, and the swimming-pool.

Chapter Three

Amelia and Katie were doing somersaults in the shallow end of the pool. Katie *loved* doing somersaults. She whirled round in the water, clutching her nose tight, feeling breathless and blue and shiny, then emerged into the warm sunny air with triumph.

'There!' She pushed her wet hair out of her eyes. 'I went round twice.'

'No you didn't,' said Amelia, who was bouncing up and down on the floor of the pool. 'I was watching.'

'I did! It felt like twice.'

'It was a very long once,' conceded Amelia, 'but it wasn't twice. Even I can't go round twice; I always run out of breath. Now,' she instructed, grabbing Katie before she could plunge into the water again, 'I'll do a handstand, and you see how long I stay up. Count like this, one thousand, two thousand.'

'OK,' agreed Katie. 'Then me.' She watched, swimming breathlessly on the spot, as Amelia disappeared under the blue water. A moment later a pair of wavering legs appeared.

'One thousand, two thousand, three thousand, four thousand, five thousand,' counted Katie rapidly. Then she stopped. Was she going too fast? 'Six thou–sand,' she enunciated carefully, 'sev–en thou–sand.' On the other hand, perhaps that was too slow. She trailed a finger in the bright iridescent surface of the swimming-pool. The water was just right; cold enough so that she'd squealed when she jumped in, but not so freezing that she had to keep moving. It was perfect.

Now that she was in the pool, she couldn't think why she'd *ever* wanted to go and do boring old fishing with Daddy. It had been horrible in the car; all boiling hot and smelly, and the car seat had burned her legs, and then when they got in the traffic jam, Daddy had started getting cross and shouting; not at her, at the other drivers, but still it wasn't very nice. And she'd started thinking about Amelia and Mummy, and started wishing she was with them, running and jumping with a huge refreshing splash into the pool. And the more she wished, the hotter she felt, and the longer the car journey seemed.

At first she hadn't said anything; she'd been very quiet and good. Then she'd just said a few things like, 'I'm hot,' and, 'Can we stop for a drink?' and, 'How much further is it?' But then, when Daddy started getting cross, she'd said in a half sob, half sigh, 'I wish we were going swimming.' She'd said it a few times, and at first she'd thought Daddy wasn't listening, so she'd said it with more and more feeling, until eventually he'd suddenly shouted very loudly and turned the car round. And when she'd started crying, he'd said that he wasn't really angry, and maybe, after all, a swimming-pool was the best place to be on such a hot day.

He was right, Katie now thought, leaning back and admiring her shiny starfish-decorated swimming-suit. She wanted to stay in here all day, and all night; for the rest of her life, maybe. She lay her head lazily against the surface of the water and felt cool blue wavelets lap into her ears.

Then, with a start, she realized she'd stopped counting Amelia's handstand. 'Eight thousand, nine thousand, ten thousand,' she said quickly, watching Amelia's legs. The legs faltered and fell back into the water.

'How many?' Amelia's wet face appeared in front of her.

'Ten thousand.' Amelia frowned.

'Is that all?'

'My go,' said Katie quickly. She plunged down, clutching her nose, feeling for the bottom of the pool with one outstretched hand. But balancing on a single palm wasn't easy, and after only a few seconds she collapsed back into the water.

'Only three thousand,' said Amelia. 'You should do it with two hands.' ⸙

'But it hurts my *nose*,' wailed Katie. 'All the water goes up it if I don't hold it.'

'Can you open your eyes underwater yet?'

'Of course I can.' Katie was scornful.

'OK then, let's dive for coins. We'll go and get them off Mummy.'

Louise was lying on her back, enjoying the sensation of the sun burning into her face. She had deliberately chosen a spot on the grass slightly apart from the group of chatting women which she would normally have joined. Now, above the sounds of splashes and shrieks from the pool, she could hear Sylvia Seddon-Wilson beginning on some long, no doubt exaggerated, and no doubt highly amusing anecdote. But Louise didn't feel like chatting, or even listening. She felt like being on her own and thinking.

If she lifted her head very slightly and swivelled her eyes to the right, she could see Barnaby, ensconced in a deck-chair next to Hugh Delaney. In spite of herself, she felt a pang of pity for him as she watched him. He should have known better than to expect Katie to last even a short car journey without vociferous complaint, Louise thought. If he'd just ignored her, and managed to get to wherever the fishing was, Katie would soon have forgotten her woes and they would probably have had a lovely day.

As it was, he'd arrived twenty minutes ago, a

disconsolate miserable sight, made even more so as Katie sprang free of his grasp, yelling, 'Mummy! We're here! We came swimming, after all!' Everyone had looked up; everyone had taken in the situation at a glance; eyes had swivelled from Barnaby to Louise and back to Barnaby.

Barnaby had come over and explained, in a few sentences, what had gone wrong. Louise had mustered a sympathetic word or two of reply. And then, as the surrounding eyes watched, Barnaby had made his way over to the other side of the swimming-pool where Hugh – stalwart Hugh – had already pulled over a chair in preparation for him. The entertainment for the village was almost complete, thought Louise bitterly. Now all that was needed for their delectation was an appearance by Cassian, village anti-Christ.

Louise knew the village's opinion of Cassian. She knew the village's version of events. No-one had asked; everyone had assumed. They had assumed that when Louise popped over to Cassian's cottage and ended up spending the evening there, something suspicious must be going on. They had assumed that when Barnaby arrived at The George, silent and angry and without Louise, he had found some sort of confirming evidence. No-one – and here Louise wriggled angrily on her towel – no-one had noticed that the problems between her and Barnaby stretched way back before Cassian had arrived in the village.

Louise and Barnaby had married soon after she left university. The wedding was a large glittering affair – only right for the only daughter of a man who, until recently, had been the local MP and, at one time, a cabinet minister. Louise Page – as she was then – had been a well-known figure on the local political campaign circuit. She had started to help out her father while she was at school and became even more involved after her mother died. When an election fell during her first year at university, she motored over from Bristol every weekend to put up posters and go from house to house with her clipboard, blue scarf and cheerful smile.

When she rang Barnaby's doorbell, she found a group of agricultural college chums watching the football, drinking beer, and unwilling to be disturbed.

'What does it matter?' said one of them, offering her a can. Louise stared.

'What does it *matter*?' she echoed in disbelief. 'It matters . . . it matters . . .' Her hands started to whirl helplessly in the air. 'It affects your whole life! If you don't vote for the right people . . .'

'I'm not going to vote,' said one of them. 'Bloody waste of time.'

'You must vote!' Louise's voice sounded through the house like a clarion. 'You must! My God! You're young, don't you care?'

'I'm going to vote.' Barnaby's voice came from the back of the room. Louise turned and looked at him. He's huge, was her first thought. He sat on a smallish wooden chair that looked as though it might break under his weight, and cupped a can of beer in a huge paw of a hand. But his voice was gentle and Louise smiled at him.

'Good,' she said.

'Not for your lot, though,' said Barnaby, gesturing to her rosette. 'I'm voting Green.' He took a swig of beer while his friends exchanged derisive glances.

'Green?'

'You're a bloody hippy, Barn.'

'Going to join the hunt sabs too?'

Louise ignored them and met his eye.

'Well, good for you,' she said. 'At least you care.'

And that would have been that had Barnaby not come to vote while Louise was on poll-monitoring duty. She smiled as he approached the polling station, and put her pen next to his name, ready to tick.

'Well,' she said, as he got near. 'I don't have to ask you who you're voting for, do I?'

'Not for you, if that's what you mean,' said Barnaby.

'I didn't expect you to,' said Louise. 'In fact, I would have been disappointed if you had.' Barnaby looked at her.

'How long do you have to stand there?'

'Another couple of hours.'

'And then?'

'Home, to wait for the results.' She flushed slightly. 'My father's the Conservative candidate.'

'John Page, I know.' Barnaby grinned at Louise's look of surprise. 'We're not all unaware yobs.' He looked at her clipboard. 'And is he going to win?'

'I should think so. It's closer run than last time, but still . . .'

'And then you celebrate madly?'

'Then we celebrate madly.'

'And tomorrow?'

Louise shrugged.

'Hang-over.' Barnaby grinned.

'You know, it just so happens, I've got a very good cure for hang-overs.'

His cure had been to take her to bed, with a directness that sent Louise, who was accustomed to sensitive thoughtful undergraduates, into slight shock. When they had finished, he went to make her a cup of tea, and she lay in his single bed, clutching the sheet up to her chin as though afraid of attack, shaking slightly, while thoughts, protests and attempts at indignation batted round her mind like butterflies. From his bedroom window was a view of some school playing-fields, and as she lay there, completely silent, a group of rugby players came running onto the field, dressed in bright-red kit. With their big burly legs, they reminded her of Barnaby, and suddenly she began to cry.

50

'I thought you'd gone away,' she wailed, as he came back into the room, and then stopped short, for this was not what she had meant to say at all. But it was too late. Barnaby, who, he later told her, had been pacing the kitchen anxiously, wondering if what he had just committed was an act of love or an act of violence, hastened to her side with a relieved solicitude. His tea was so strong it made Louise shudder, but she said it was lovely, and smiled at him with tears still dancing on her eyelashes, and Barnaby, feeling a sudden unfamiliar surge of tenderness, went straight away and carefully made her another cup, just the same.

Since then they had never really talked very much about politics. Louise's father stood down at the next election, which was a year before Louise and Barnaby married, and then, a couple of years later, was made a peer.

'If only we'd *known*,' Louise would say at regular intervals. 'We could have been married in the House of Lords.'

'But then we would have had to wait,' Barnaby would reply, 'and I would have had to move to Melbrook on my own.'

Barnaby had accepted a job running a medium-sized estate, ten minutes' drive from Melbrook, which he started two months after they married. He had been in the same job ever since. Louise had long ago given up suggesting he look for a more senior, more challenging, or more lucrative job.

'We're happy here,' he would say, 'that's all that matters.'

And for a long time they were happy. They moved into Larch Tree Cottage, and Louise commuted into Linningford for her job as marketing executive with a small publishing firm. Then she had Amelia and gave up her job, and then she had Katie. She was no longer involved in politics, her father wasn't an MP any more, and besides, Melbrook was in a different constituency. Besides which, she no longer felt quite as fervent about it all. For a few years, the minutiae of the children, the school run, village gossip and church fêtes kept her going. I'm lucky, she would tell herself at frequent intervals, I may not have a career, but I have a loving family and a happy life.

It never occurred to her to question why she needed to reaffirm these facts to herself quite so regularly. Nor did she understand why, as the tenth anniversary of her marriage to Barnaby approached, she began to get edgy and irritable; to attack Barnaby with unreasonable complaints and heap bitter criticisms on the village, her life, his job, Britain. It didn't help that her brother had recently moved with his family to a reportedly exciting new life in New York; nor did it help that Barnaby couldn't begin to understand or, it seemed, sympathize.

'But you grew up in the country!' he once shouted, when her impatience with Melbrook had spilled over into a suppertime diatribe.

'I know!' she retorted angrily. 'But it was different! It was exciting! We had important people to stay, and we had interesting discussions, and we had a flat in London, and we went to parties at the House of Commons, and . . .' she broke off, feeling foolish. 'You just don't understand,' she finished feebly.

'I do understand,' said Barnaby bitterly. 'You wish you'd married someone intelligent and important and glamorous. Not a country bumpkin like me.'

'No!' exclaimed Louise, a little too late. 'No, don't be silly.'

And then Cassian Brown had moved into the village. Smooth and sophisticated and intelligent and charming. Barnaby had distrusted him on first sight. But Louise had been enchanted when, at a welcoming drinks party at the vicarage, Cassian revealed, first that he was interested in politics, and then that Lord Page had always been a particular hero of his.

Cassian was a young lawyer with the biggest law firm in Linningford, a huge prestigious concern with offices in London and all over the world. He had been seconded to the Linningford office for two years to run the commercial litigation department, and had, he said charmingly to Frances Mold, decided to take the cottage in Melbrook as soon as he saw its exquisite view of the church. He smiled at Frances, revealing perfect white teeth against tanned, not quite English-looking skin. Frances said faintly, 'How nice,' and Barnaby nudged Louise. 'What a creep,' he whispered in her ear.

But Louise didn't think he was a creep. On the way home from the drinks party she'd been full of exhilarated chatter.

'He actually remembered that speech of Daddy's,' she said, striding ahead into the darkness. 'That one about housing.'

'It's a famous speech,' said Barnaby brusquely. But Louise wasn't listening; her thoughts had moved on.

'His grandparents were Italian,' she said. 'Did you know that?'

'Whose grandparents?' said Barnaby, feeling a deliberate angry need to misunderstand.

'Cassian's, of course,' said Louise. Her voice sounded, to Barnaby, light and happy. 'Bruni, they were called, but they changed it to Brown when they came to England. It's a shame, don't you think? He went to Oxford,' she added irrelevantly, 'like Daddy.'

Barnaby couldn't bear it any more.

'Do we have to keep talking about this chap?' His voice thundered through the dark street. Louise turned back, unsure how to react.

'Well . . .' she began, in hesitant mollifying tones. But as she marshalled her thoughts, her initial instinctive desire to pacify was taken over by indignation. 'Well!' she repeated. 'So now I'm not allowed to talk to anybody, is that it? One interesting person comes to live in Melbrook and we're not allowed to talk about him. Well, fine. What shall we talk about? Oh, I know, the lambing. We haven't talked about that for at least an hour.'

Her voice held an unfamiliar sarcasm, and Barnaby stared at her through the darkness for a few moments, unable to read her expression. Then he shrugged and walked on.

'What?' demanded Louise, grabbing him as he went past. 'What? Aren't you going to *say* anything? Talk to me!'

Barnaby paused and looked at her. Then he said, 'I haven't got anything to say,' and strode on ahead.

Maybe, thought Louise now, turning over onto her front and resting her sunbaked cheeks on her hands, maybe if Barnaby had talked to her a bit more, instead of listening to all those silly rumours; maybe if he'd trusted her a bit more, then they wouldn't have had all those awful rows. With a painful jolt, she remembered the last one they'd had. She'd been pink and outraged; he'd been obstinately determined. He'd actually told her, *commanded* her, to stop seeing Cassian. She'd shrieked back, in frustrated anger, that she was going to see whoever she wanted, whenever she wanted, and if he didn't like it he could bloody well move out.

She still wasn't sure where those last words had come from, but once they had burst out into the air, there was no taking them back. Barnaby had gazed at her, a look of disbelief on his face, and the air had seemed to resonate with shock. And Louise had slumped heavily into a chair, wanting to say, sorry, she didn't mean it, but, somehow, unable to.

'Mummy!' Drops of water pattered onto Louise's back, and a shadow fell over the sun. 'Can I have a two-penny piece to throw?'

54

'Can I have one, too? Can I have a pound coin?' Louise reluctantly looked up. There were Amelia and Katie, standing over her in breathless excitement, dripping water onto her bathing-suit and leaving wet footprints on her towel.

'Did you see me do a handstand?' asked Katie. 'Did you see when I did cycling in the air? Did you see when Amelia nearly did a backward somersault?' She hopped up and down, so that her hair flew out and sprayed Louise with water.

'Careful!' said Louise, sitting up. 'You'll get people all wet. Now, where's my purse?'

'Here,' said Amelia, promptly, holding it out. She watched carefully as Louise unzipped it. 'A two-penny piece,' she said. 'Or a penny.'

'And a pound coin for me,' said Katie, doing a quick bunny jump on the grass.

'Don't be *stupid*,' said Amelia. 'A pound coin will never show up. And what if you lost it?'

'I wouldn't lose it,' said Katie, giving Amelia a disdainful look.

'Here you are,' said Louise. 'A tuppenny piece each. Now go and play.'

'Watch me dive,' begged Amelia. 'I've got a really good dive.'

'Maybe later,' said Louise. 'After lunch I'll come and watch.'

Daisy stood at the edge of the grass and wondered where to sit. She had hastily changed into her swimming-suit as soon as Meredith had gone, then hurried down the stairs and out into the sunshine. Mrs Mold had been very welcoming at the entrance table, and had said, unfortunately, she was a bit tied up at the moment, but why didn't Daisy introduce herself to a few people; she'd soon find that everybody was *jolly* friendly.

And Daisy had smiled and nodded. Now she peered

anxiously around, trying to ignore the spasms of nerves in her stomach; trying to look confident, and wondering who she could approach. To the right was a group of women, all gaily laughing at something. But most of them seemed much older than Daisy. She wouldn't know what to talk to them about. Only one looked anywhere near Daisy's age, and she was busy with a baby.

Dotted round the pool were more little groups of families and friends, as well as a few loners, stretched out on chairs or on towels. None of them looked up at Daisy, or smiled, or waved her over. In desperation, Daisy looked around for the American woman whose bedroom she'd walked into, but she was nowhere to be seen, and neither was the friendly owner of the house.

Daisy took a hesitant step forward. She was going to have to sit down somewhere. People would start to stare at her if she stayed hovering on the edge of the lawn all afternoon. She would simply find her own spot now, she decided, and then perhaps talk to people a bit later on.

Slowly, self-consciously, she wended her way through the chattering groups, stepping over beach-mats and bags, apologizing whenever she came within six inches of someone's towel, until she reached a quiet patch of grass some way from the swimming-pool. Quickly she spread out her towel and lay down, trying to ignore the latent blush of embarrassment that was spreading over her cheeks.

From his steamer chair at the side of the pool, Alexis Faraday watched Daisy's progress with slow lazy amusement. His eyes followed her, swivelling under brown lizard lids, taking in her hair, her eyes, her pale skin and her gawky grace. She moved, with painful awkwardness, between the prone bodies on the grass, apologizing where there was no need, biting her soft pink underlip anxiously. When she reached her destination, she looked around, hesitated, then abruptly spread out her towel and lay down, as though avoiding gunfire.

Alexis stared at her for a few more seconds, and when it was obvious that she was not going to sit up again, he looked away. For Christ's sake, what was he doing, staring at a child like that? She couldn't be more than eighteen. Less than half his age, he realized, with a sobering thud, and he deliberately closed his eyes and leaned back in his chair.

A few moments later, he heard a cool attractive American voice beside him.

'So this is how the esteemed lawyer prepares his cases. Lying flat out in the sun.' Alexis opened one eye and grinned.

'So this is how the great artist composes her canvases,' he parried. Meredith shrugged, pulled up a deck-chair, and sat down.

'This is work,' she said. She smiled conspiratorially at him, and her eyes gave a tiny challenging glint. 'We all have to take inspiration from somewhere,' she elaborated.

'Aha! Yes.' Alexis shifted on his chair, and regarded Meredith quizzically. 'Inspiration. So should I expect to see *Man sleeping by swimming pool* in your next collection? And will I recognize myself?' Meredith grinned.

'I shouldn't think so. But you never know, you might get into one of Ursula's water-colours.'

'Of course.' They both involuntarily looked towards the terrace, where Ursula stood happily, an old paint-stained smock of Meredith's over her bathing-suit, gazing at the scene before her, with brush in hand. 'Tell me,' Alexis added casually, 'how is Ursula's painting going?' Meredith looked away.

'She paints a lot,' she said distantly.

'And, no doubt, she's improving as she goes,' suggested Alexis gravely. Meredith bit her lip.

'Something like that.' There was a short pause, then suddenly Meredith emitted a strange snuffle that sounded a bit like a laugh. Alexis looked at her in mock-surprise.

'Something wrong?' Meredith shook her head and clutched her mouth. Her shoulders shook.

'She's terrible!' she whispered suddenly, and gave a half-suppressed, half-hysterical giggle. She leaned closer to Alexis. 'I can't *tell* you how bad she is! I thought she'd get better; I even encouraged her, but . . .'

Alexis began to chuckle.

'And the thing is,' Meredith continued, wiping her mirth-filled eyes, 'everybody in Melbrook thinks she's a fucking genius! She's even had a show!' She began to shake again. 'And I bought the first picture!'

Suddenly she sat up. 'And where were you at the show?' she demanded. 'We sent you an invitation.'

'I know you did,' agreed Alexis. 'I was working, I'm afraid.'

'You work too hard,' said Meredith accusingly. 'We never see you.' She pushed back her long dark hair, and a pair of green eyes shone at him out of a tanned vibrant face. 'I thought country lawyers were supposed to take every afternoon off to play golf.'

'They do,' said Alexis. 'Unfortunately I don't play golf.' Then his expression changed and he sighed. 'You're right, I don't come over here enough. I should do, it's really not very far. But then, you know, these days I don't really seem to do anything enough.'

He seemed about to elaborate, and Meredith leaned forward interestedly. But suddenly Ursula's voice broke in from behind.

'Oh, Meredith dear,' she said. 'My painting's going so well today! You must come and have a look. And, look, it's Alexis! When did you get here? Hugh never said.'

'Ursula!' Alexis stood up, an elegant man with a slim figure which belied his greying temples and slightly hooded eyes. 'It's lovely to see you. Now let me come and look at this painting. Meredith, you can give us your expert opinion.'

He linked arms with each of the women, giving Meredith a little conspiratorial squeeze. And as he did so, and as they began walking together towards Ursula's easel, bare arm linked with bare arm, bare leg brushing against bare leg, Meredith felt her stomach leap, and her cheeks pinken and, in spite of herself, her heart begin to beat just a little more quickly.

Chapter Four

As morning turned into afternoon, the air became more still, the sun seemed to expand, and the heat intensified. Voices around the pool became lower, as though confiding secrets; many people fell asleep in a postpicnic torpor.

Barnaby and Hugh sat side by side on their deckchairs, in a companionable silence. By the diving-board, Louise was standing with her arms folded, watching Amelia and Katie diving, and sporadically offering help and encouragement. Their cries of, 'Watch me!' rang through the sleepy, subdued, heat-filled air, along with the squeals of some younger children splashing in the shallow end. Hugh glanced at Barnaby and gestured towards Louise.

'Hard for you,' he said succinctly. Barnaby shrugged.

'I'm all right. It could be worse . . .' He broke off.

Hugh nodded understandingly. There was another silence between them. Then Hugh said, 'If you ever feel like getting away . . .' Barnaby exhaled sharply.

'I do,' he said, 'frequently.' Hugh leaned back a little; shifted himself in his deck-chair.

'There's always our cottage in France. Use that; you can drive over.' He turned his head towards Barnaby. 'I mean it. If you feel you need some time on your own.' He paused. 'We went there, after Simon . . .' He broke off.

'Of course,' said Barnaby. 'I remember.' He turned his head towards Hugh.

'I'm very grateful,' he said simply. 'It's good of you to offer.' Hugh shrugged.

'It's extremely difficult to get things in perspective when you rub up against them every day. Difficult for both of you.' There was a pause, and Hugh looked over towards Louise. 'Can't be easy for Louise, either,' he said.

Barnaby felt a sudden spurt of indignation, as though Hugh had suddenly changed sides halfway through the match. But he managed to say, 'No, I'm sure it's very difficult for her, too.'

Hugh eyed Barnaby with amusement.

'I don't think you really mean that. And, fair enough, why should you? But I believe I'm right; that you're both suffering at the moment.' He leaned back and closed his eyes. 'At any rate, it's you I'm offering the cottage to. Take it any time, we haven't any particular plans this summer.'

'Thank you,' said Barnaby. He suddenly wanted to say more; to confide in Hugh; to ask his advice; to relate the story of his betrayal with the anger and pain which he had so far shown to nobody save Louise. But instead, he said again, 'Thank you,' in a voice that faltered slightly. Then he lay back, closed his eyes, and waited, miserably, for the onslaught of his own tangled, anguished, unavoidable thoughts.

Louise was unwillingly standing in the heat of the sun, watching Amelia and Katie cavorting in the water. Every time she attempted to leave, they called desperately to her again, requesting her to witness yet another obscure acrobatic feat. As she stood, she saw Barnaby and Hugh talking quietly and gesturing towards her, and felt a surge of hot embarrassed fury. She could guess what Hugh thought of her. The Delaneys had always been more Barnaby's friends than hers; no doubt

Barnaby was now pouring out some tale of woe to overly sympathetic ears.

'Hurry up,' she said sharply to Katie, who was dithering on the diving-board. She could feel Hugh's quizzical eyes on her, and determinedly ignored them. What was he thinking? Probably notching up even more black marks against her, for venting her frustrations on an innocent child. Katie looked up, surprised.

'I'm just making it bouncy,' she said.

'Yes, hurry up,' said Amelia, who was waiting behind to have her go. 'You always take ages.'

'I don't!'

'Yes you do! Slowcoach!'

'Mummy!' Katie's shrill voice appealed to Louise. 'She called me a slowcoach.'

'Well then, get on with it,' said Louise firmly.

'Yes, come on!'

Still Katie remained at the end of the board, and suddenly Amelia impatiently ran a few steps onto the diving-board, stamping hard. Katie gave a shriek and jumped off the end of the diving-board. When she surfaced, she was squealing angrily.

'That's not fair! Amelia, you . . .' But she didn't have time to finish before Amelia leaped off the diving-board, curled into a ball and dive-bombed her with an enormous splash.

Ursula, walking by the pool, looked at these goings-on with alarm. She quickly approached Louise.

'Dear, I think perhaps you should calm the children down a bit; they seem terribly excited.' Louise turned round at her voice. Bloody Ursula. Another censorious face, another voice of disapproval. So now, not only was she a heartless hussy for splitting up with Barnaby, she was also an inadequate mother.

'They're fine, Ursula,' she said tightly. She waited for Ursula to come out with another tactless comment about Barnaby. Perhaps, this time, she would say,

Oh, wasn't it a shame for the children.

But Ursula's eyes were on Katie.

'Hello, Katie!' she called.

'Hello, Mrs Delaney,' Katie called back. 'Do you want to watch Amelia swimming under my legs? It's really clever.' Ursula glanced hastily at Louise, who allowed herself the satisfaction of a small smile.

'Yes, why don't you watch the girls?' she said, with distant amusement. 'You'll find it's tremendous fun.' And quickly, before Ursula could protest, she stalked off.

Meredith had fallen asleep, lying on a chair next to Alexis. For a while, from behind his sunglasses, he affectionately watched her sleeping. His eyes ran idly over her face, and then over her tanned skin, and her long legs, and her strong narrow feet, and her determined hands. He paused, staring at Meredith's hands, and counted to ten. Then, holding his breath and without moving his head, he shifted his attention away from Meredith and towards the young girl with the pale skin and dark clouds of hair.

She was sitting up on her towel, now, pushing her heavy hair off her neck as though she were too hot, looking around cautiously. The patch of grass on which she was sitting was, by this hour of the afternoon, partially shaded by a tree, and as she moved, lacy, leafy shadows gently dappled her white skin. Slowly she rose to her feet, tugging awkwardly at her bathing-suit and pushing her hair back again. She glanced nervously at the family group sitting near her, then, as the father of the family rose his head questioningly, flushed and looked away again.

Alexis watched in fascination as she traced a halting solitary path towards the swimming-pool. She paused by the edge and looked at the water doubtfully, as though not entirely sure whether it was meant for her.

Then, slowly, she dipped in a toe. As she did so, her long milky-pale leg was reflected in the glimmering blue water, so that it briefly appeared to be one long swan-neck limb.

'Daisy!' A voice came from the other side of the pool, and at once the girl retrieved her toe, looking round in sudden apparent guilt. Alexis looked for the source of the voice. Waving from a garden chair, attired in a jolly scarlet bathing-suit, was a woman whom he recognized as the vicar's wife. She was now gesturing reassuringly at Daisy.

'It's absolutely lovely in the pool!' she was calling. 'Have a good swim, and then come over and have a chat with us!'

Alexis looked back towards the girl. Daisy. Suddenly, unexpectedly, she smiled at the vicar's wife; a shy, uncertain smile. Alexis felt a strange pang under his ribs. He watched her dive into the pool, dark hair streaming out behind her, white feet pointed. And as he did so, he suddenly wanted to see her smiling shyly again; this time, at him.

'So, Louise,' Sylvia Seddon-Wilson smiled charmingly, and drew on her cigarette, 'where's that sexy man of yours?' Louise shrugged hesitantly.

'Who do you mean?'

'Oh, Louise! You don't think I mean Barnaby!' Sylvia's playful voice rang out with a calculated resonance, and Louise shrank slightly into her chair. She had not meant to be drawn into Sylvia's coterie today, but after snubbing Ursula there had been nowhere else for her to go and sit. And Sylvia was, to be fair, a long-term acquaintance – if not exactly friend – of Louise's. Some years older than Louise, and with her teenage sons away at school, she lived a leisured life in the old vicarage, redecorating herself and the house at frequent intervals and observing the affairs of the village through sharp, if slightly jaundiced eyes.

As her voice rose provocatively over the sounds of the swimming-pool, Louise glanced hesitantly over towards Barnaby, but he was too far away to hear Sylvia's remarks.

'No, I mean your delicious toyboy,' said Sylvia. Louise blushed scarlet, but Sylvia appeared not to notice. 'Cassian. Gorgeous Cass. Is that what you call him? Cass?'

'No,' said Louise discouragingly. It had been, she acknowledged to herself, a mistake to sit down with Sylvia.

'Well, I must say', said Sylvia, leaning comfortably back in her chair, 'that I think he's divine. So sexy. That hair . . . He's Italian, is that right?'

'Half Italian,' mumbled Louise. She felt that she was being misrepresented; that she should somehow try to correct Sylvia's assumptions. But then, what would she say? What exactly *was* going on between her and Cassian? She wasn't, herself, entirely sure. And while she struggled in her mind to define, in simple terms, their relationship, she was also aware of a slight flowering pride at Sylvia's admiring comments; a desire for the alluring picture of herself and Cassian as a glamorous couple to continue.

She turned her head slightly, so that the reproaching sight of Barnaby vanished from the corner of her vision, and gave Sylvia a secretive smile.

'His grandparents were Italian,' she elaborated, casually laying claim to Cassian's family as well as him.

'Italian men!' exclaimed Sylvia, giving a theatrical shiver. 'To die for!'

'Oh no, you don't mean it! They're awful! Revolting!' Louise looked up. It was Mary Tracey, a cheerful young woman who lived not far from Louise and had often acted as baby-sitter for Amelia and Katie. She was dripping wet from the pool, and holding an equally wet, fat and happy baby. 'We went on holiday to Pisa once, and my bottom got sore from all the pinching! I wouldn't have minded if it had got any smaller,' she added, sitting down, 'but it didn't.' Louise giggled.

'I wasn't talking about peasants from Pisa,' Sylvia said airily. 'I was talking about gorgeous young lawyers.'

Mary glanced swiftly at Louise and her face closed up slightly. Louise looked away, with a small uncomfortable pang. Mary had been demonstrably upset when the Kembers had split up; it had happened just after she came home from the hospital with baby Luke, and Louise had always felt that she had let Mary down in some inexplicable way.

The baby began to grizzle and slither on Mary's lap, and she sighed.

'He's hungry again,' she said. 'He's always hungry.' She jogged him up and down a little, and he affectionately grabbed a strand of her hair.

'Ow!' she yelped. 'Get off!' Sylvia raised her eyebrows at Louise.

'Aren't you glad yours are past that stage?' she asked in mock-horror. Louise laughed, but she was mesmerized by Luke; by his determined, concentrated expression and his waving, grasping hands.

'Amelia and Katie were never like this great lump,' said Mary cheerfully. 'They were little sweethearts.' She sat Luke down on the grass. 'Why can't you be good, like they were?' she chided him. He gazed at her for a few seconds, then screwed up his face, and began to howl.

'I'll have to feed him, I suppose,' she sighed. 'See you later.'

As she retreated, Sylvia took another drag on her cigarette. She pulled out a gold compact and checked her reflection unhurriedly. Then she put it away, smiled, and regarded Louise lazily again from under azure-painted lids.

'Anyway,' she said, 'you must come over to dinner sometime, Louise . . . you and, of course, Cassian.'

'Yes, that would be nice,' said Louise hesitantly. She lay back in her chair, closed her eyes, and tried unsuccessfully to imagine herself actually attending a dinner party with Cassian as her acknowledged partner. The Law Society dinner, a fortnight ago, had been different. That was in London; no-one there knew or cared what their background story was. She'd gone as Cassian's guest, eaten four courses, listened intelligently to the speeches, joined in the discussion, even put one of Cassian's colleagues right on some political point. It had been a wonderful evening. But that had been in London, not here in Melbrook, in front of Barnaby, in front of all of them. Village events – even private dinner parties – were not the same thing at all. To go anywhere publicly with Cassian would be at best uncomfortable, at worst a fiasco. Sylvia should realize that, thought Louise. Then, looking sidelong at Sylvia's faint smirk, it occurred to her that Sylvia already did.

Meredith awoke to find the sun behind a cloud and an empty place beside her. Alexis must have gone for a stroll, she thought. She lifted herself up on her elbows and blinked sleepily. Cast in a sudden shade, the pool appeared chilly; the sleek wet heads of the swimmers bobbed darkly amid dull blue-grey waves, and the splashing and shrieks of the children seemed to have risen in volume.

She pushed her hair back, sat up cross-legged on her chair and stretched out languorously like a panther. Then, mid-stretch, she froze. There, in front of her, was Alexis, in the water. Alexis, who famously never swam. She stared at him. His hair was wet and he was inefficiently treading water, and he was smiling at someone.

Hating herself, Meredith casually lay back down on

her chair and reached for her sunglasses. The black-tinted lenses made everything around her seem even more gloomy, but at least with them on she could stare inconspicuously at Alexis and whoever it was he was talking to; still talking to – and still smiling at.

From the bathing-suit it appeared to be a woman, but her face was turned away from Meredith. Without really intending to, Meredith swiftly catalogued all the women of the village that it could be, dismissing each in turn with a snap judgement. *Too old. Too bossy. Too married.* Then, as the nameless woman began to turn in the water, a sudden realization hit her mind, flooding it with relief. It wasn't a woman, it was the dippy girl; the klutzy teenager. Daisy . . . Daisy Phillips.

Filled with a sudden lightness, she stood up, approached the pool and dived in.

'Hi, Alexis,' she said, surfacing near the pair of them.
'Hi, Daisy.' Alexis gave Daisy a surprised look.
'You know Meredith?'

'Yes,' said Daisy hesitantly. 'At least, I didn't know she was called Meredith; sorry,' she stumbled, turning to Meredith, 'I mean, I didn't know *you* were called Meredith. Thank you very much,' she added, 'for letting me use your room.'

As Daisy came to the end of this halting little speech, Meredith raised her eyebrows sardonically and tried to catch Alexis's eye. But he was still gazing at Daisy in apparent fascination.

'Oh, that's OK,' said Meredith, in friendly playing-along tones. 'Any time.' She registered, in slight disbelief, that Alexis was turning and smiling at her, as though thanking her. What the hell for? Who was this kid to him? A surrogate daughter?

'Feel free to use my room at the end of the day if you want to,' she offered, adding a cheery grin for good measure. The girl, Daisy, smiled gratefully at her. And then, like a fucking mirror image, so did Alexis. What's going on here? Meredith wanted to shout. Next I'll be asking this loopy girl if she wants to come bake cookies with me.

But instead she smiled at Alexis and Daisy, said, 'I'll catch you later,' and swam swiftly, confusedly, away.

The sun sat determinedly behind a cloud for the next half an hour, and eventually the prone sunbathers around the pool gradually began to stand up, stretch, look at their watches and start to gather their belongings together.

Meanwhile, Amelia and Katie, utterly oblivious of the weather, had commandeered the diving-board. Amelia was doing back dives and Katie was doing front dives.

'I'm going to be in the diving team when I go to senior school,' Amelia was announcing proudly, standing with her back to the water. She bounced up into the air, arched her back, and entered the water cleanly, hands in a neat point.

'So am I,' said Katie, as soon as Amelia's head popped up above the water again. 'Look at my star jump!' She leaped high into the air, with legs outstretched and toes pointed, then brought them together sharply before plunging into the water.

'That's not a dive,' said Amelia scornfully.

'Well, nor is a back dive,' said Katie, paddling breathlessly to the side of the pool.

'Yes it is,' retorted Amelia. 'Why do you think it's called a back *dive* if it's not a dive?'

'Dives are facing *forward*,' said Katie. 'Look!' She rushed recklessly past Amelia onto the diving-board, and essayed a cautious forward dive from the end, one hand clutching her nose.

'That was rubbish!' yelled Amelia, as soon as Katie's head was clear. 'I'm going to do another back dive. Get out of the way!'

'So am I!' retorted Katie desperately. 'So am I going to do a back dive! You just wait, Amelia.'

Louise was gathering up her things, preparing to leave, when Barnaby came striding over.

'I thought I'd take the girls out to supper,' he said, with no preamble. 'For a pizza, maybe. They'd like that.'

'They've got school tomorrow,' objected Louise, 'and it's already getting late. Maybe another time.'

'We won't be long,' insisted Barnaby. 'I've hardly seen them today.'

'Yes, you have,' retorted Louise. She paused. 'And anyway, they'll be too exhausted to go out after all this swimming.'

'No they won't,' said Barnaby obstinately. 'It's only five. We'll go straight from here, eat at six, be home by seven. Easy.'

'It's not easy,' said Louise, her voice rising. 'I then have to get them bathed and ready for bed, and check their homework, and make sure they're in a fit state for school tomorrow.'

'Oh, for God's sake!' exclaimed Barnaby. 'What does school matter?'

'Yes, well, I might have expected you to take that attitude,' said Louise. She folded up a towel with abrupt angry movements.

'What's that supposed to mean?' Barnaby glared at her.

'Mummy! Watch!' A piercing voice came from the diving-board.

'In a minute, Katie,' Louise called. She glared back at Barnaby. 'It means whatever you want it to mean.' There was a moment's silence. Then Amelia came bounding up, dripping wet and shivering.

'Where's my towel?' she demanded. Barnaby ignored Louise's gaze.

'Amelia!' he exclaimed. 'Feel like going out for pizza tonight?'

'Yeah! Pizza!' Amelia beamed up at Barnaby.

'Mummy! Amelia! Watch me!' Louise ignored Katie's cry. Her nostrils were white with anger.

'Barnaby!' she hissed. 'If you don't stop doing this, I'll . . .'

'You'll what?' Barnaby whipped round, and stared at her with a deep angry hurt in his eyes. 'What exactly will you do, Louise?'

'Am–ee–lia! Watch me do a back dive!' Katie's final appeal was so shrill that they all turned to watch.

Standing with her back to the water, Katie was bouncing on the end of the diving-board. She bounced and bounced until the board was vibrating vigorously, then, shooting a triumphant look at Amelia, hurled herself backwards into the air.

The last voice Louise heard was Amelia's, saying, 'Katie's never done a back dive before.'

And then there was just the sight of Katie's small body arching inexpertly in the air, looping round too far, until her head was directly above the corner of the diving-board. And then there was the sickening crack as the board smacked upwards, hitting her head with a terrible malevolent force. And then there was the silence, as her apparently lifeless little body slithered quietly down into the water.

Chapter Five

Cassian Brown was driving back to Melbrook from London, in self-congratulatory mood. He had spent most of the weekend in meetings with one of his law firm's most important Middle Eastern clients, striking a complicated out of court settlement worth, in the end, just short of £800,000. Which, he had to admit to himself, was of no great significance, financially, for the client. But still, it had been a triumph of negotiation. And even though he himself had played only a relatively small role in the dealings, his contribution would, he was sure, have been recognized by those that mattered.

Now he wondered to himself whether it would be worth telephoning Desmond Pickering, head of litigation at the London office. A casual friendly call, just to ensure that Desmond was aware of Cassian's part in the proceedings; just to make certain that no-one else was claiming too much of the credit. He could, Cassian thought, perhaps suggest an informal lunch meeting. Or even invite Desmond down to Melbrook for the weekend. Londoners, he'd noticed, were all too eager to come down to the country if it was only an hour or so away on the motorway.

They could drink white wine, sitting in Cassian's pretty little cottage garden, and talk business discreetly, and perhaps stroll around the village. And then he could introduce Desmond to Louise. Desmond would be impressed by Louise. The daughter of Lord Page, no less. The Honourable Louise Kember.

Kember. Cassian frowned. Such an ungainly name, like its owner. Why on earth had Louise taken on the surname of that oaf? And why, more to the point, had she married him in the first place?

Cassian liked to think that he had spotted the potential of Louise even before he'd been informed of her relationship to Lord Page. He'd noticed her immediately, he told himself; he'd seen at once that she was stifled, bored and suffering from a lack of stimulation. She was intelligent and educated, yet she was expected to have no interests above those of her children, the village, and that insufferable boor of a husband.

A picture of Barnaby's face swam into Cassian's mind: dim and brutish, with the suspicious stare of an ill-educated peasant. Those huge hulking shoulders, those clumsy hands, those boots, always caked in mud. And the inarticulateness of the man! Cassian recalled their very first meeting at a drinks party. He had attempted a number of pleasant conversational gambits, and Barnaby had seemed incapable of responding with anything more than a shrug or a grunt or a monosyllable.

Louise, on the other hand, had positively sparkled with wit and charm and important names. Cassian recalled, again, the *frisson* he'd received when she'd casually referred to current cabinet ministers by their Christian names; when she'd spoken, with the disparaging tone of an insider, of Commons food; then, later, after a few more drinks, when she'd related the story of the time the Prime Minister telephoned and she was the only one in, and she thought it was a hoaxer and didn't pass the message on.

Little idiot! Cassian gave a small grin. For all her knowledgeable veneer, Louise had, he'd soon discovered, less of a grip on the world of politics than she liked to think she had. Her mind revolved, he often observed, along the peculiarly feminine parochial grooves which he had noticed in female colleagues at work. They all had the same insistence on knowing irrelevant details; the same ability to take an episode of grave political or legal import and turn it into a trivial anecdote; the same fixation on names, faces and people, rather than issues, concepts and theories.

But no matter. What Louise did have was an effortless ease with the workings of British politics, a grounding in the party political system, an awareness of the lifestyle of a Member of Parliament, and, perhaps most importantly, experience of being involved in a successful political campaign. She had the background, the breeding. She would make an admirable politician's wife. Any selection committee in the country would love her.

At this thought, Cassian began to breathe slightly more quickly. He looked down and saw that his fingers were clenched tightly on the steering-wheel. Carefully, he loosened them and took a deep breath. He mustn't rush things; he mustn't ruin his chances. He knew what people were saying about him: that he was a home-breaker; that he'd lured Louise away from her honest husband. People must think he and Louise had been conducting some kind of torrid affair. At this, Cassian allowed himself a small smirk. As pretty as Louise was, it was a kind of girlish breathy prettiness that held no attraction for him. But that wasn't the point; she would make a lovely suitable bride.

As he began to imagine their smart London wedding, bristling with important people from both politics and law, perhaps with the two little girls as adorable photo-genic bridesmaids, the telephone in his car rang. He switched it on to speaker-phone. A young anxious voice filled the car.

'Cassian? It's Jamie.' Cassian frowned with annoy-ance. Jamie was one of the newest trainees at the Linningford office.

'How the fuck did you get this number?' he snapped.

74

'I-I phoned your secretary at home. I'm really sorry to bother you. It's just that . . .'

'What?'

'Well, I've been searching all weekend, and I still haven't tracked down that case for you. And I . . . well, I was just wondering, did you have any more information about it?'

'What case?' said Cassian impatiently.

'The one for the letter to Simmons Ltd. Y-you wanted me to check the details.'

'You haven't done it yet?'

'Well, n-no. I've been trying to find the case . . .'

'Jamie, I don't need this crap. That letter was urgent!'

'I know! I've been looking for the case. I'm in the library now, but you didn't give me very much to go on . . .'

'Well, that's just tough! You fucking well find that case, and you have the letter ready on my desk by tomorrow morning. All right?'

'All right.'

'And you don't ring me on this line again, OK?'

'Y-yes. I'm really sorry, Cassian . . .' But Cassian abruptly switched off the phone, cutting Jamie off mid-flow.

For a moment he couldn't remember what he had been thinking about. Then, gradually, a series of pleasant images began to filter back into his mind. A collage of blue eyes, feathery blond hair, a bright giggling laugh, a title, an important father and an easy entry into the world of high-flying politics.

As he neared Melbrook, Cassian decided he would go straight to see Louise, to relate to her the triumph of the weekend. Perhaps, he thought, taking the turning for her house, it was even time to move their relationship on to a new level. The rush of adrenalin from the weekend's deals had not completely faded; there lingered inside him still a faint frustrating arousal. He would get rid of it by taking Louise to bed, and simultaneously would get rid of the ambivalence still hanging over their relationship. It had surely been long enough by now. Barnaby had been out of the house for months. Louise must be ripe and ready; she wouldn't refuse him.

Filled with a faint anticipation, he sauntered up the path, rang the doorbell, and pushed a hand back through his glossy dark hair. When the door opened, he began a sexy half smile, and stepped forward to give Louise a kiss.

But it wasn't Louise who stood in front of him in the doorway, it was Mary Tracey, holding her baby. Automatically, Cassian frowned. Then, with sudden horror, he saw that her face was red and swollen, with bloodshot eyes and tear-stained skin. Immediately he thought of Louise.

'Has something happened?' he began in an alarmed voice. Mary's face crumpled up and she gave a little sob.

'It's Katie,' she managed, before dissolving into fresh, shuddering streams of tears. 'She's had an accident.'

Barnaby stood, clutching the door of the Accident and Emergency ward of Braybury Hospital, and shook with terror. Fifteen feet away, in a cleared space, lay Katie, unconscious, on a hospital bed. A plastic contraption was in her mouth; a battery of transparent tubes ran from her body to flashing green television screens; and now, looming over her immobile form, was a huge monster of a machine. Someone had explained to him in a clear careful voice, that this was the portable X-ray machine, and that he would, briefly, have to move away from the area of Katie's bed. Louise was allowed to put on a lead jacket and stay, together with one of the nurses, but everyone else moved out of the radiation zone, leaving the small form of Katie briefly marooned, like a leper or a corpse.

'OK.' The machine began to move away; the voice of

the X-ray operator resonated through the tense silence and immediately, as though on starting blocks, the team of doctors and nurses waiting on the sidelines rushed forward again, each sure of where to go, what to do and how to do it. Only Barnaby remained motionless. A paralysis of helplessness anchored him to the ground. He could not think what to do, or what to say, or what to feel. Pictures circled again and again in his mind, and with them billowed clouds of pain and disbelief.

He'd got to Katie first. Amid the screams and shouts and – from those who hadn't seen properly – giggles, he'd somehow got to the pool, dived in, and desperately groped in the water for her little body, and eventually managed to scoop her out and place her tenderly by the side of the pool. She hadn't drowned; she'd seemed to be breathing, and everyone had said, 'Thank God.'

Then the ambulance crew had arrived. And it was then, as Barnaby watched them wedging her head into a wooden frame, and placing her on a stiff board, and covering her face with an oxygen mask, and heard them radioing ahead to the hospital, saying, 'Please alert trauma team', that this feeling of unbearable, inarticulate panic had begun.

None of the ambulance crew had smiled at him, or said, Not to worry, or We'll soon have this little lady on her feet again. They'd worked quickly and efficiently, while the taut silence around the pool grew heavier and heavier. Louise had kept her head, to some degree, organizing Mary Tracey to look after Amelia, and talking soothingly to Katie. But Barnaby had stood mute, still dripping from the pool, unable to speak; unable to look, almost, as these calm professionals packaged up his daughter and swiftly took her away from him.

Only one parent in the ambulance, they'd said. And Barnaby had stared back at them, in numb, stupid incomprehension. But Louise had turned, pale-faced and hesitant, to Hugh, and even before she could ask, he was insisting on driving Barnaby to the hospital, behind the ambulance all the way. When they'd got here, the trauma team had been waiting for them at the door. And as the doctors leaped into their frantic work over his daughter's unconscious form, Barnaby had stood still and watched, while water dripped down his neck and a terrible, unspeakable fear seeped through his body.

Mary Tracey sat at the table in Louise Kember's kitchen, clutched baby Luke to her chest and surreptitiously watched Cassian. He had led her gently into the kitchen, sat her down on a chair, and was now making them both a cup of tea. As he waited for the kettle to boil, he leaned casually against a kitchen cupboard, an elegant figure, even in off-duty clothes. Slowly Mary took in his tanned muscular arms, his thick glossy hair, his curved lips and white teeth. He was, she admitted to herself at last, quite something to look at.

Mary had always been fond of both Barnaby and Louise. When the rumours had begun she had stoutly disbelieved them; when they had actually split up, she had felt devastated. If such a wonderfully happy couple could break up, she had thought to herself, what hope was there for the rest of them?

And at the bottom of her heart she had blamed Cassian Brown. If he hadn't moved into the village, she had decided, none of it would have happened. Never having met him properly, she had conjured up in her mind an image of him as an evil, lecherous character, preying on a happily married woman. Italian blood in him, she'd thought. No wonder. He was probably all mixed up with the Mafia. He was probably setting Louise up for some horrible life of crime.

Now she looked at him uncertainly, as he poured out a nice cup of tea for her and gave her a charming smile. He didn't seem such a bad person after all, she thought unwillingly. He was being very kind to her – he'd listened carefully as she told him all about the accident – and he was so good-looking. No wonder Louise . . .

'Do you like sugar?' Cassian's voice caught Mary by surprise.

'Oh, yes please,' she replied. She looked down at Luke, and hastily wiped away a dribble from his little chin. What must she look like herself? she suddenly found herself thinking. All blotchy and crumpled . . . Then, with a sudden emotional swoop, her thoughts returned to poor little Katie. Her heart gave an unpleasant thump and she began to shift uncomfortably in her chair. It didn't seem right to be sitting doing nothing.

'I'll take a drink up to Amelia in a minute,' she said quietly. 'Ask her what she wants for supper, poor little pet.'

'I suppose Louise might stay at the hospital all night', said Cassian, 'if things are really bad.'

Mary looked at him in alarm.

'H-how bad', she faltered, 'do you think they might be? Do you think . . .' She tailed off, unable to say the words. Cassian looked at her soberly.

'Head injuries are no joke,' he said. He put the tea down in front of her. 'Here,' he said, 'drink this.'

'Thank you,' mumbled Mary. She felt sudden respect for Cassian, a serious professional man. He was young, but he knew about things. He had the answers to her questions.

She sipped her tea and felt its sweet warming strength spread through her body. Cassian was still standing up, drinking his own tea. Suddenly he seemed to make a decision.

'I think I'll go along to the hospital,' he said. 'Unless you want me to help you here?'

He gave her a brief questioning smile, and Mary shook her head dumbly.

'No, of course not,' said Cassian smoothly. 'I'm sure you can manage. And I'd very much like to er . . . make myself useful to Louise.'

'Give them my love,' said Mary. 'And lots of love to Katie.' Her voice began to shake, and she felt her nose start to prickle again.

'Oh, sure,' said Cassian, picking up his jacket. 'Absolutely.'

Louise and Barnaby had been shepherded into a tiny room off the side of the ward, which was furnished with an oatmeal-coloured three-piece suite and a vase of plastic flowers. They sat in a white-faced silent blur, each battling with their own shocking, tormenting emotions.

Louise's thoughts skittered through her mind in a circular, repetitious cycle. Katie bouncing on the board, Katie shrieking, Katie falling; that scream. A knife-like pain in her heart, then, rushing tantalizingly into her head before she could stop them, the crowding unbearable what-might-have-beens. If she'd told Katie to get out of the pool earlier. If she'd told the girls not to go on the diving-board. If Katie had gone fishing after all. If they'd all gone fishing. A picture of them all happily eating pizza. A fleeting, deceiving sensation of relief, and then, with a flash, the icy stab of reality; of Katie's little body, unconscious, wired up. And immediately back to Katie bouncing on the board, Katie shrieking, Katie falling.

For the moment she could not wrench her mind from its repeating, circular pattern. Lurking in the shadows of her mind, waiting to pounce, towered emotions that were huge and frightening; that would consume and destroy her. For the moment they must be kept out. And so her mind raced around, lingering on no thought long enough for it to develop; allowing no conclusions to be drawn; no speculations to be made.

She avoided the very sight of Barnaby. One word; one look from him, and the vulture emotions would smash down the door and she would be no good to anybody. So she stared downwards, with an ashen face and a desperate inward absorption, and waited for the doctors to come, while her mind raced round and round, faster and faster and faster.

Mary was starting to trudge upstairs to Amelia's room when she heard a knock on the door. Startled, she went to open it. It was Cassian, back again already.

'Sorry to trouble you, Mary,' he said, and gave her a charming smile. Mary's heart gave a little flutter.

'Oh, no trouble,' she said breathlessly. 'Did you forget something?'

'Not exactly,' said Cassian casually. 'I just wanted to check something very unimportant. Something I was wondering about.' He smiled sympathetically at her. 'When the accident happened, there were still lots of people present, weren't there?' He spread his hands vaguely. 'Witnesses, if you like. People who saw what happened.'

'Oh,' said Mary in surprise. She hefted Luke up further on her chest and stroked his downy hair. 'Well, yes,' she said, 'I suppose there were. Heaps of people were there. All the village, really. Although, of course, not everybody was looking when it . . . when it actually happened.' Her face began to crumple.

'Yes, of course,' said Cassian quickly. 'Well, that's all I wanted to know. Thanks.' And he began to stride back towards his car, while Mary looked after him in slight puzzlement.

When the door of the little room opened, Louise jumped and looked up fearfully. A face peered round. It was a

81

young man, wearing round spectacles and a white coat.

'Mr and Mrs Kember? My name's Michael Taylor. I'm the consultant dealing with Katie.'

He came into the room, sat down, and looked earnestly at Louise and Barnaby.

'As you know,' he began rapidly, 'Katie has sustained an injury to the head. She was hit quite hard when she . . .' he consulted his notes . . . 'crashed down on the diving-board. Now,' he paused, 'we've just had back the results of Katie's scan. And we've found what we suspected might be the case, that a blood clot has formed, which is pressing on Katie's brain.' He looked from Barnaby to Louise. 'I don't want to appear to be rushing you,' he said, 'and I know it's difficult to take all this in, but we're going to have to remove the clot as soon as possible to maximize her chances of recovery.'

There was a silence. Barnaby looked away. Louise met the consultant's eyes.

'Brain surgery,' she faltered.

'I know it sounds frightening,' said the consultant earnestly. 'In actual fact, it's a fairly straightforward operation, and we need to give the brain as much chance as possible to heal.' He paused. 'We'd like to take her into theatre as soon as we can.'

There was another silence. Louise could hear her breaths coming quick and shallow. She felt as though she might be hallucinating. Suddenly Barnaby spoke, in a husky, almost inaudible voice.

'But she will be . . . all right.' The consultant's gaze did not flicker.

'There is a strong chance that once the pressure on her brain has been relieved, Katie will make a good recovery,' he said. He paused. 'But you must remember, she has received a considerable injury to the brain; not merely from the blow to the head, but also from lack of oxygen during the time spent underwater.' He looked at Barnaby. 'I gather she wasn't under for more than a few seconds?'

'I got to her . . .' Barnaby's voice was hoarse and cracked. 'I got to her as quickly as I could.'

'Well then,' said the consultant gently, 'you may well have saved her from serious brain damage.'

'But you don't know?' Louise's voice was high and brittle.

'I'm afraid we don't,' said the consultant. 'Not yet. After surgery, things may be clearer.' He flipped to another page of his notes. 'There are several encouraging factors. There seems to be no paralysis, and her spinal cord appears undamaged, and the swelling of her brain is less severe than we might have expected.' He looked at them. 'Until Katie regains consciousness, we won't know exactly what sort of damage has been done, if any.'

'And when will that be?' Louise tried to control her voice.

'I'm afraid that's something else that we don't know.' He looked at Louise. 'You're shivering, Mrs Kember. Would you like the nurse to bring you a cup of tea?'

Louise shook her head numbly.

'I'd like to see Katie, before she has her operation.'

'Of course. Do you have any more questions?'

Suddenly there was a knock on the door. A nurse poked her head into the room.

'Excuse me,' she said. 'A Mr Cassian Brown's here. He said he didn't want to disturb you, but he's brought a change of clothes for Mrs Kember and some bubble bath.' She looked at Louise. 'He thought, if you had to spend a long time here, you might want to have a bath.'

'That's a good idea,' said the consultant. 'When Katie's gone into theatre, one of the nurses will take you to a nice quiet bathroom. You'll want to be rested and refreshed for when she comes out.' He looked at the nurse. 'You can sort that out, can't you, Sandra?'

83

'Of course,' said the nurse sympathetically. 'Just tell me when you want it,' she said to Louise, 'and I'll run you a nice hot bath.'

Louise looked at the kindly face of the nurse, and to her horror, felt her shoulders heaving. She gave a single, involuntary, anguished cry; heavy hot tears began to splash onto her hands.

'You're very kind,' she struggled to say. Then, unable to stop herself, she gave way to pent-up juddering sobs. The nurse exchanged looks with the consultant.

'I've got to go, I'm afraid,' he said, 'but Sandra will look after you. Sandra,' he added, on his way out of the door, 'they'd like to see their daughter before she goes into theatre.'

'Of course,' said the nurse. She crossed the floor, sat down beside Louise, and brought out a tissue.

'Thank you,' managed Louise. For a moment she seemed to be calming down. She sat up and wiped her eyes. Then, suddenly, she began to weep again in a frenzy of gasping and shuddering.

'I know,' said the nurse soothingly. 'I know.' She put an arm round Louise, and Louise suddenly turned her sobbing face, burying it in the nurse's ample shoulder.

Barnaby stared blackly ahead, immobilized by grief, fear, and an impotent anger. Everybody seemed able to do something to help except him. Someone else was comforting Louise; someone else was operating on his daughter; someone else had even thought to bring bubble bath for Louise. A picture of Cassian's smug face passed briefly through Barnaby's mind, accompanied by a black, suspicious, envious resentment. Why had Cassian been the one to bring bubble bath for Louise? What was he doing at the hospital? What right did he have to interfere?

A cloud of despairing misery fell down upon Barnaby, and his head drooped lower until all he could see was the oatmeal fabric of the sofa. But even that was too much for him, so he shut his eyes and listened to the sound of Louise weeping, and found himself wishing, in a stark, hopeless way, that they could go back to the beginning of the day and start all over again.

Chapter Six

The next morning Meredith woke late, with a looming, menacing feeling in her head, and a painful dream about Simon slipping out of her mind before she could remember it. She got shakily out of bed, pulled back the curtains to reveal another shining bright day, and regarded herself in the mirror. Her face was pale and puffy, and down one side of it ran a deep red crease where she had slept, pressed up against the seam of her nightdress. Like a scar, she thought dully.

And then, in a flash, it all came back to her: the accident, the ambulance, the endless hours afterwards; hours of persuading people to go home, and fending off phone calls, and turning away visitors who had got hold of a garbled version of the story. They'd stayed up until midnight, until someone phoned to give them the news: Katie's operation had gone well, but she was in a coma.

Lightning visions of hospital wards, machines and nurses passed through Meredith's mind. Simon had only been in hospital for a day and a half before he had died, but that time had magnified in Meredith's mind until it seemed a lifetime; a lifetime of sitting by his bed, talking to him, holding his hand, battling with the dragons of fear and pessimism; trying always to keep her voice warm and positive, just in case he could hear. Now, she thought, she would never know if he really had heard any of the things she'd said; if he had taken in any of the love, the respect and the belief in him that she'd tried so desperately to convey.

They'd switched off his life-support machine early in

the morning, and for a few seconds afterwards she'd stared in desperation at his face, believing that if she willed hard enough, he would open his eyes and wake up. But of course, he hadn't, and he never would, and perhaps, Meredith thought, with a sudden stab of fearful pain, little Katie never would either.

She quickly dressed and opened her bedroom door. From downstairs she could hear the voices of Hugh and Ursula . . . and Frances . . . and a voice that sounded like Alexis. In spite of herself her spirits quickened slightly, and for a moment she battled with the desire to shut her bedroom door, choose a new outfit and check her appearance in the mirror. But a stern sense of priorities stopped her from doing so. Now was not the time for thinking of herself.

She came down to find Hugh and Ursula sitting in the kitchen. It was a large sunny room, with yellow-painted walls and a huge oak table. At one end of the table was the remains of breakfast; at the other end was Alexis, drinking a cup of coffee and looking concerned; and at the back door was Frances, wearing an unbecoming beige print frock and an anxious expression.

Meredith looked from face to face.

'Have you heard anything?' she said.

'She's still in a coma,' said Frances.

'Oh, God,' said Meredith. She sank onto a chair and poured herself some coffee.

'I just feel,' said Hugh miserably, 'so . . . so *helpless*.'

'I can't bear to think about it,' said Ursula. 'Poor Louise. Poor Barnaby.'

'Poor Katie,' said Meredith soberly. She looked at Frances. 'And they don't know what the prognosis is?' Frances shook her head.

'I don't think they do. I think they're just waiting for her to wake up.'

'Waiting,' said Meredith. 'That's the worst part. Just sitting there, with that feeling that there's nothing you can do.' There was a short silent pause. From the hall came the sound of the grandfather clock ticking quietly and steadily along.

'Well, actually,' said Frances eventually, 'there is something that you can do, if you wouldn't mind. Alan's holding a service for Katie tonight at six o'clock. We expect that quite a lot of people will come, so we're going to need extra chairs from the church hall, and I was wondering if you could help me move them.' She looked around. 'If we all move a few it won't take long.'

'Of course we'll help,' said Hugh. He sighed. 'It's the least we can do.' He looked at Frances. 'Do you think Louise and Barnaby will come to the service?'

'I don't know,' said Frances. 'It all depends, I suppose, on what happens . . .' There was a brief sobering silence.

'OK,' said Meredith. She put down her coffee-cup. 'Let's go.'

'I don't want to rush you,' protested Frances. 'Have some breakfast first.'

'No, I'm not having breakfast,' said Meredith. Alexis looked at her.

'Your not eating breakfast', he said seriously, 'is not going to help young Katie.'

'I know,' said Meredith impatiently. 'I know it won't help, but still . . . it seems like an insult – to be *eating*, when she's . . .' She tailed off.

'Meredith!' interjected Ursula in alarm. 'You mustn't starve yourself.'

'I'm not going to starve myself,' said Meredith, 'but you know what I mean.' She looked at Alexis. There was a pause, then he nodded.

'Yes,' he said slowly, 'I know exactly what you mean.'

When the others had gone off to the church, Ursula began to clear the breakfast things away, picking up plates and cups, and stacking them haphazardly by the sink. Despite what Meredith repeatedly told her, Ursula could never quite believe that the three of them ever used enough china to make it worthwhile using the dishwasher. And so the usual pattern was that, after every meal, she would put on a pair of rubber gloves and attempt to begin washing-up by hand, while Meredith furiously grabbed the plates from the sink and thrust them into the machine. But today there was no Meredith to stop her. And so, for a while, Ursula stood, diligently scrubbing each plate by hand, rinsing it free of foam and checking its shiny surface in the sunlight. It was a slow process, but she had done all the plates and nearly all the cups and saucers before she was interrupted by the sound of footsteps on the gravel.

At first she thought it was the others returning from the church, but there only seemed to be one pair of feet. And instead of making confidently for the back door, they were hesitating, swivelling around on the gravel, stopping altogether, then starting again. Ursula put down the cup she was holding, took off her apron, patted her hair, and went out of the back door. It was probably somebody from the village, wanting news of Katie.

But when she reached the drive, she stopped in surprise. There, standing with his head tilted back, surveying the house with a full and frank stare, was the young man with the dark hair whom everybody said had broken up the Kembers' marriage. What was his name, now? The only name that came to her mind was Dawn Treader, and that couldn't be it, surely?

'Hello,' said Ursula hesitantly. The young man started, then regained his composure, gave Ursula an unctuous smile and held out his hand.

'Good morning, Mrs Delaney,' he said smoothly. 'I don't know if you remember me. Cassian Brown.'

'Of course!' exclaimed Ursula. 'Prince Caspian!' Cassian stared at her.

'No,' he said, 'not Caspian, Cassian. And I'm afraid I'm not quite a prince.' Ursula blushed.

'No,' she said, 'I mean in the book. *The Voyage of the Dawn Treader.* C.S. Lewis, you know,' she added feebly. 'Prince Caspian. That's where I remembered you from. Although of course the name isn't *quite* the same . . .' She tailed off foolishly as she saw Cassian's blank face. He waited for her to finish, then smiled again, a very brief smile, before adopting a solemn expression.

'I was wondering whether you would allow me to have a look at the swimming-pool where Katie was hurt yesterday,' he said, in grave tones. 'Since I wasn't actually there, I'd just like to see it for myself . . .' Ursula's face crumpled slightly.

'Yes, of course,' she said. 'Poor Katie. Do you know how . . .?'

'She's still unconscious, I'm afraid,' said Cassian. He began to lead the way round the house, and Ursula followed him timidly, feeling that this seemed a little wrong, but not quite sure why.

When they got to the pool, Cassian made his way straight to the diving-board. He looked at Ursula.

'This is where she slipped?'

'Yes,' said Ursula, in a distressed voice. 'I can hardly bear to look.' There was a pause. 'Actually,' she amended, 'I'm not sure whether she actually slipped . . .' But Cassian didn't seem to be listening. He was bending down and running a finger along the surface of the board.

'How old is the pool?' he said.

'Well, I don't really know,' said Ursula. She looked around vaguely. 'It was here when we moved in, and that was over twenty years ago.'

'The diving-board too?'

'Well, yes,' said Ursula. She looked at the diving-board and shivered. 'I'd like to get rid of the horrid dangerous thing.' Cassian looked up sharply.

'Why dangerous?' Ursula looked at him in puzzlement.

90

'Well, dear,' she said gently. 'Katie had her accident trying to dive off it, you know, and I believe professional divers quite often have accidents too.'

'Yes, but you said *this* board was dangerous,' persisted Cassian. 'Why would this particular board be dangerous?' Ursula looked at him confusedly.

'Is it?' she said. 'I don't think it is, really.' Cassian gave up. He stood up and looked around.

'Do you remember how many people were here yesterday?' he asked conversationally. Ursula screwed up her face.

'I suppose . . . about a hundred,' she said. 'I could tell you if we'd counted the donations, but we haven't yet. It didn't seem, somehow . . .' She broke off and clasped her hand to her mouth, her eyes shining slightly. 'Of course,' she said. 'The money must go to Katie. And we must start an appeal. We can begin at the church tonight.' She looked at Cassian expectantly, but he didn't seem to be listening.

'And who was supervising the children?' he said.

'Well,' said Ursula slowly, 'no-one was actually *supervising* them. But they were all here with their parents, you know, and there was always someone watching them. Louise was watching Amelia and Katie for quite a long time, I remember, and then I watched them for a bit . . .' She broke off and looked at him, tears bright in her eyes.

'You know, I find this rather distressing,' she said. 'Would you mind if we went inside?' She paused. 'Perhaps you would like a cup of coffee. The others should be back soon and you can chat to them.' She regarded him sympathetically. 'You must be terribly upset.'

Meredith and Alexis arrived back at the house to find the kitchen empty and the back door open.

'I wonder where . . .' began Meredith.

Then they heard Ursula's voice from outside, saying, 'Ah, that sounds like them!'

She appeared at the back door, looking a little flustered. Meredith opened her mouth to speak, then stopped in surprise as she saw, hovering behind Ursula, the unlikely figure of Cassian Brown, wearing an immaculate suit and carrying a dark heavy-looking briefcase. Her initial temptation was to ask what the fuck he was doing there, but instead she took a step forward and smiled at Cassian. He beamed charmingly back, and nodded his head politely towards Alexis with a smooth deferential courtesy which Meredith, in her mind, labelled creepy.

'Hello,' she said. 'We have met before. I'm Meredith.'

'I remember very well,' said Cassian. 'The artist.' His eyes briefly met Meredith's, and to her astonishment she felt herself staring back at him, unwillingly mesmerized by his deep dark gaze. Briskly, she tore her attention away. 'And this is our friend Alexis Faraday . . .' Suddenly she interrupted herself. 'Is there some news about Katie? Is that why you came?' Cassian shook his head gravely.

'Cassian wanted to have a look at the swimming-pool,' put in Ursula.

'But I'm afraid I've got to go now,' said Cassian smoothly. 'Thank you very much for your kindness.'

He held out one hand to Ursula. She hesitated, then took it, smiling falteringly back at him with the foolish gaze of a fascinated rabbit. Meredith watched Cassian distrustfully, and felt a sudden obscure need to protect Ursula. But against what? A young man with mesmerizing eyes?

They all watched as Cassian made his exit out of the kitchen door, and listened in silence as his feet crunched away on the gravel of the drive. When the sound had faded to nothing, Ursula looked at Meredith with an animated expression on her face.

'I've had an idea,' she said. 'We should give all the donations from yesterday to Katie, and we should start an appeal.'

'Good idea, Ursula,' said Meredith vaguely, but her face was still wary. 'What exactly did that guy Cassian want?' she asked.

'To look at where poor Katie had her accident,' said Ursula. She frowned. 'Something like that.'

'Who is he?' said Alexis. He screwed up his face in thought. 'I'm sure I know him from somewhere.'

'Louise Kember's lover,' said Meredith succinctly.

'Now, Meredith,' chided Ursula, 'we don't know that.'

'But why do I recognize him?' said Alexis. 'Have I met him?'

'Well,' said Meredith, 'he's a lawyer. Maybe he hangs out in the same joints you do.'

'A lawyer?' said Alexis. He looked at Ursula's innocent expression and his face darkened slightly. 'Did he tell you why he wanted to look at the pool?'

'Well,' began Ursula, 'no, not really. He just said that it was because he hadn't been here yesterday. I thought he was probably very upset.'

'He didn't look very upset to me,' observed Meredith. 'He looked . . .'

'You didn't say anything to him,' interrupted Alexis, 'did you, Ursula? Anything about the accident?'

'Well, no,' said Ursula. 'I mean, yes.' She looked from Alexis to Meredith with puzzled eyes. 'What do you mean? Is anything wrong?'

'No, nothing,' said Alexis, quickly. 'I hope not.'

Later on, as Meredith came up the stairs, she heard a voice from Hugh's study. It was a subdued voice, and it was saying, 'Shit.' She gently pushed the door open. There was Alexis, standing at Hugh's open desk, holding some sort of brochure open in front of him.

'What's wrong?' said Meredith lightly. 'Hugh owe you

money?' Alexis whipped round and gave Meredith a rather hesitant smile.

'No, nothing's wrong,' he said, in a voice that wasn't quite cheerful. He quickly put the brochure back in a drawer and shut it. Meredith stared at him sternly.

'Something's wrong, isn't it? What? Is Hugh's business in trouble?'

'No, honestly, Meredith,' said Alexis. 'I was just . . . just checking something.' He began to move towards the door. 'Now,' he said, giving her a charming crinkled smile, 'how about some Meredith-strength coffee to set me up for the rest of the day?'

He took her arm, and as he did so, she felt a sudden foolish tingle of pleasure. But even as she allowed Alexis to lead her down the stairs; even as she glimpsed, with a pang of delight, the reflection of the two of them together in the landing mirror, she could feel a faint web of anxiety anchoring itself throughout her body, tugging gently at her thoughts and causing her face to wrinkle with an unspecified alarm.

Cassian arrived at the hospital at four o'clock. He had spent much of the day loitering in the village grocery store, the post office, outside the church and in The George. And by the time he arrived at the hospital, he had talked to over twenty people in the village about the accident, carefully taking notes and writing down names after each conversation.

As he entered the ward where Katie lay, he adopted a sober expression and looked around gingerly. It was a very small, very quiet ward, with only four beds, all shrouded, to some extent, by floral curtains. One bed was completely shrouded, and from it came the sound of murmurings, then a small cry of pain. A nurse in a blue uniform appeared from behind the curtains, carrying a bowl of something. Cassian averted his eyes.

'Cassian!' A faltering voice attracted his attention. It

94

was Louise, looking up from where she was seated beside Katie's bed.

'Louise,' said Cassian, in smooth sympathetic tones. She looked, he thought, absolutely terrible; her face was pale and suddenly seemed much older than before; her eyes were bloodshot; her hands were wringing anxiously together.

Then he glanced down at Katie, and his stomach flipped over unpleasantly. Katie's head had been partially shaved; her tiny white face was obscured by a tube; every bit of her seemed connected to one of several television monitors, along which green lines were merrily flickering. On the wall beside her high clanking metal bed was a laminated chart, labelled Glasgow Coma Scale.

'How is she?' he asked. Louise swallowed.

'She's still in a coma, but it isn't as deep as it was, apparently.' She ran a hand distractedly through her hair. 'The blood clot's gone, and they scanned her this afternoon and, so far, no more clots have formed. They were pleased about that.' She looked at Cassian beseechingly. 'It could be a lot worse,' she said, as though to reassure herself.

Cassian stared at Katie, unconvinced, and gave a little shiver.

'Perhaps', he said, 'we could go and have a cup of coffee? Is there a canteen or something?'

The hospital corridors were warm and pastel-coloured, and reminded Cassian of the inside of a smart motorway service station. An impression which was borne out further when they reached the hospital's Four-Grain Eaterie and were given, along with their cups of coffee, a questionnaire to fill in on aspects of the menu, service and decor.

Louise took a sip of coffee and winced.

'I've drunk so much coffee today,' she said. 'That's all I've done. Sit with Katie and drink coffee.' She took another sip. 'I keep talking to her, and singing to her, and rubbing her feet, and none of it does any good.' She looked at Cassian. 'She could be in a coma for weeks!' Her voice was trembling. 'Or months! I mean, she could, couldn't she? What if she never wakes up?'

Cassian looked at Louise silently for a moment. Then he reached out, put her coffee cup down, and took her hands in his.

'You mustn't think like that,' he said. 'You must think positively. She might wake up any moment.'

'I know,' faltered Louise, 'but . . .' Cassian interrupted her.

'On the other hand,' he said solemnly, 'there's no point in denying the facts. Katie has been badly hurt. We don't know when or how well she's going to recover.' Cassian clasped Louise's hands a little more tightly and looked deeply into her eyes. 'And I believe', he continued, in a low sincere voice, 'that it's up to you and Barnaby – and even me –' he dropped his eyes modestly downwards, 'it's up to all of us to do as much for Katie as we can. Whatever that means.'

Louise gazed back at him with a worried, uncomprehending expression.

'We're . . . we're doing everything we can,' she faltered. 'Barnaby's coming along as soon as he's finished work, and then we're going to the special service they're holding at the church. And the doctors have said all they can do now is wait. One of the nurses said . . .' she swallowed '. . . that Katie's body has put itself into a coma just because she needs a good rest, and that everything will be healing while she sleeps.' A tear glistened at the corner of Louise's eye.

'Of course, of course,' soothed Cassian. 'I'm sure that's right, but, you know, there's more you could be doing than that.' He pulled his briefcase onto the table and opened it discreetly. 'I've been doing a bit of research into this accident,' he said. 'I don't want to upset you, but it seems that someone, somewhere, was negligent.'

At those words Louise froze, and her already white face became whiter. Into her tired mind, before she could stop them, flowed the memories that she'd been trying to stave off until now. The vision of Ursula, warning her that the children were overexcited. The picture of herself, ignoring Katie's shrieks; of her and Barnaby, thoughtlessly arguing while their daughter hurled herself into injury; into what might have been death.

It was all her fault; her fault. A violent putrefying guilt exploded inside her, making her shudder with nausea. She clutched at her stomach and looked despairingly at Cassian.

'It was an accident,' she said weakly, pleadingly. She could feel her insides wrenching painfully, and feel a self-loathing rising swiftly through her body.

'Of course it was an accident,' said Cassian briskly, still head-down in his briefcase. 'But even so, there may well have been negligence. In fact, I'm almost sure there was. And so . . .' He broke off suddenly and looked up at Louise. 'You'll have to think about it,' he said, 'and, of course, talk to Barnaby.' He paused, as though for effect. 'But what I recommend, Louise, is that you go to court.'

Louise looked at him through a blur. 'Go to court?' Black shadows were dancing in front of her eyes. 'Be pro-prosecuted?' She took a deep gasp of air. 'I didn't mean . . . I didn't think . . . I'm sorry, I'm sorry . . .'

'Louise, what are you talking about?' Cassian's voice pierced her consciousness. 'I'm not talking about prosecution. I'm talking about a civil case. From what I've discovered, I think you've got very good grounds for suing Hugh and Ursula Delaney.'

Barnaby arrived at the hospital at five o'clock and went straight to the ward, clutching the piles of cards and toys which had arrived at Larch Tree Cottage that day. The chair by Katie's bed was empty and he couldn't see Louise anywhere on the ward. As he gazed around uncomprehendingly, a nurse whom he didn't recognize saw him looking, and said, 'I think Mrs Kember went to the cafeteria. With . . . her husband, is it?'

Barnaby stared, speechless for a moment. Only when he had recovered his composure could he ask where the cafeteria was. He bent down, stroked Katie's hair and whispered, 'I'll be back in a minute, Katkin.' Then he strode off down the corridor with a burning face and a thumping heart.

When he reached the cafeteria, he saw them instantly, sitting back, relaxed, as though nothing was wrong. He was immediately filled with a bleak fury.

'Louise!' he called.

'Barnaby!' She looked up and smiled; she actually smiled. Barnaby strode over.

'Katie's all alone,' he said, aware that his voice sounded accusing, yet unable to stop himself. 'She's been all alone for half an hour.'

'She's not all alone,' protested Louise. 'She's being looked after by a team of trained medical experts.' She took a sip of coffee and Barnaby, suddenly enraged, thumped his huge fist on the table with a bang.

'That's neither here nor there!' he exclaimed. 'The doctors said that *our* voices would help to bring her round! My God, if you can't even sit and talk to her . . .'

Louise stood up, her face pink with anger.

'I've been with her all day. I've been talking to her and massaging her feet and doing everything I can for her. I came here for one cup of coffee! One cup of coffee, Barnaby!' Her distressed voice rose through the room, and various members of the cafeteria staff began to look in their direction. 'And anyway,' added Louise, calming down slightly, 'Cassian and I have been talking about the accident. You should listen to what Cassian's got to say.' She sat back down on her chair and, with slightly trembling lips, took another sip of coffee.

'What?' Barnaby looked at Cassian with black suspicion.

'Perhaps later,' murmured Cassian to Louise.

'No, now!' thundered Barnaby. 'Tell me what he's said, that's so important it's kept you from being with Katie.'

'All right,' said Louise. She took a breath. 'He says we should sue Hugh and Ursula. On Katie's behalf,' she added.

'What?'

'I'm not really sure this is the time or place for this discussion,' said Cassian smoothly. 'Perhaps the two of you could talk, and . . .' He stood up, then flinched as Barnaby roughly pushed him back into his seat. Louise looked anxiously at Barnaby; his face was bright red and his whole body was trembling.

'Talk?' he roared. 'Talk about what? Are you serious?'

'Apparently we could prove they were negligent,' began Louise. Barnaby gazed at her, aghast.

'Hugh and Ursula? Are you saying Hugh and Ursula are to *blame*? My God . . .'

'It's not a matter of blame,' put in Cassian swiftly. 'It's a matter of . . . compensation.'

'Compensation?' echoed Barnaby. 'You mean money! You're just talking about money, aren't you?' Louise looked down awkwardly at the table. 'Katie's been in hospital for less than a day,' Barnaby shouted, 'and already all you can think about is *money*!'

He looked from Louise to Cassian, with an incredulous pent-up expression. All the misery, worry and despair of the last twenty-four hours seemed to be building up inside him like a furnace.

'You're sick,' he suddenly shouted. 'You're both sick!' And with an abrupt savage movement, he kicked over a chair. It hit the table noisily as it fell, and the cups and saucers clattered. From the other side of the cafeteria began some interested murmurings. Cassian smiled apologetically in the direction of the staff, keeping one eye on Barnaby.

'Barnaby, don't be like this,' said Louise. She looked anxiously around the cafeteria. 'This isn't helping Katie either.'

For a few seconds Barnaby stared back at her. Then he sighed, bent down, and righted the chair. Louise and Cassian watched in a nervous silence.

'I'm going, now,' said Barnaby at last, 'to see my daughter, and then I'm going to church to pray for her.' He looked at Louise. 'You can do what the hell you like.'

'Barnaby . . .'

'Leave it, Lou,' Barnaby said in a shaky voice.

And before Louise could say anything more, he left; picking his way clumsily between the tables and chairs and customers; barging out of the door without looking back, with his shoulders hunched up and a stray glittery get-well card for Katie sticking out of the back pocket of his jeans.

The little church was packed when Barnaby arrived. People were milling around, talking and whispering, pulling chairs into line, depositing gifts of toys and flowers on a side-table that seemed to have been set aside for the purpose. The air was tight with uncertain anticipation, and as he surveyed the scene from the porch, Barnaby found himself hesitating like a nervous bride. When he heard his name being called, he gave a startled jump.

'Barnaby!' It was Frances Mold, coming through into the porch and pulling the door behind her. She didn't smile, but took his arm and squeezed it. 'I'm glad you could come,' she said simply.

'There are so many people here,' said Barnaby uncertainly. He gazed down at Frances. 'I don't know half of them.'

'Lots of them seem to know Katie,' said Frances. 'Friends from school, I think.'

'I suppose Louise knows them,' said Barnaby, scowling in spite of himself. The mere thought of Louise still sent a thudding anger through his body. 'Is she here yet?'

Frances looked up at him.

'Louise isn't coming to the service,' she said. 'She phoned from the hospital. She feels she should stay with Katie, just in case she wakes up.'

'Oh,' said Barnaby dully, 'I see.' And suddenly he felt a sense of abandonment. He was going to have to do this on his own.

Frances looked at her watch and reached for the porch door. 'We should really be going in. I've saved you a seat next to me.'

'Wait,' said Barnaby suddenly. 'I'm not . . .' He swallowed and looked away. 'Just give me a second.' Frances waited silently, watching him compose himself, take a few deep breaths and push his fingers through his dark springy hair.

'Right,' he said at last. 'I'm ready.'

As they walked in there was a rippling effect along the pews, as people gradually realized that Barnaby had arrived, and turned to see. Many immediately turned back, but some remained, staring at him with expressions of sympathy ranging from mild compassion to deep distress. Somebody somewhere was quietly crying, and as Barnaby made his way to the front of the church, a baby began to wail.

Alan Mold was already standing at the front of the church, and he gave a kindly nod to Barnaby as he took his seat.

'Let us pray,' he said.

There was a moment's silence. Then, from behind

Barnaby, came a rustling sound, as, wordlessly, the congregation sank together to their knees. And as Barnaby himself slowly knelt down, he felt, through the stillness, the silent support of a hundred people flowing towards him in a single strengthening wave.

It was a short simple service. Alan Mold addressed the congregation in warm tones, read prayers full of love and hope, and led the singing of 'All Things Bright and Beautiful'. When the service had ended, Barnaby stood up to leave, but Frances tugged at his sleeve.

'If I were you,' she said, 'I'd stay here for a bit. Unless you want to have to talk to everybody.'

Barnaby looked down at her. Throughout the service he had felt unable to open his mouth; unable to join in the prayers; unable to sing the hymns. Talking to people was unthinkable. So he nodded gratefully and sank back down next to Frances.

Behind him he could hear the chatterings and murmurings of people leaving; there were many voices that he recognized or half recognized. Several times he heard his name, but he didn't turn round.

'Barnaby?' Suddenly somebody was right beside him. 'Barnaby?'

He looked up. It was Ursula, peering at him in mild concern.

'Hello, Ursula,' he managed. Ursula smiled hesitantly at him.

'I don't know what your plans are,' she said, 'but we wondered whether you'd like to come back to our house for some supper.' She paused, then added anxiously, 'You really must eat properly.'

Barnaby tried to give a jovial smile and failed.

'Don't worry,' he said. 'I'm eating fine.'

'Just for the company, then?'

'To be honest, Ursula,' said Barnaby, 'I'm not much good in company at the moment. It's very kind of you, but I think I'll head back to the hospital.'

'Of course,' said Ursula in slightly crestfallen tones. 'I understand.' Barnaby took her hand.

'I'm very grateful for the offer,' he said, 'but I've got to be with Katie. She might . . .' He swallowed. 'She might wake up any minute.'

'We'll pray that she does,' said Ursula fervently.

'Yes, I know you will,' said Barnaby, and he squeezed her hand. 'I know you will.'

Chapter Seven

Three days later, Barnaby woke early, with a start. He immediately sat up with a beating heart, hoping that he had been woken up by the sound of the telephone ringing. But the phone beside his bed was silent. Another night had passed with no summons to the hospital; no joyful announcement that Katie had woken up. His excitement subsiding, Barnaby got out of bed, padded into his little kitchen and put the kettle on to boil.

Since moving out of Larch Tree Cottage, Barnaby had been renting a tiny ground-floor flat in the new development on the other side of Melbrook. There was only one bedroom and no space for the girls to play when they came to visit, but it was all he could afford, on top of supporting Louise and the girls.

Now he looked around morosely. He suddenly felt weary and depressed. Every night, since the accident, he had fallen into bed hoping, like a child on Christmas Eve, that by the time he woke up, something would have happened. Katie would have woken, smiled, perhaps even asked for him . . .

And every morning he awoke to find no news. No change. She was still stable, the nurses would tell him. No, they couldn't say when she might wake up. No, they couldn't say what damage her injuries might have done. It was early days, they kept saying. All they could do was wait and see.

Until now, Barnaby had quietly obeyed the nurses; had agreed with them that there was no point in thinking the worst; had avoided probing them for the alarming thoughts he could see behind their eyes. Like a coward, what they didn't want to tell him he hadn't wanted to know. But today he did want to know, he suddenly thought, pouring boiling water onto a tea-bag. Today, at the meeting with the consultant, he would demand some answers. He would write out a list of questions and ask them, and would keep asking them until he found out what he wanted to know.

He sat down with his cup of tea and shuffled through the pile of letters he had opened the night before. Many were cards for Katie; letters of concern and sympathy – as though she were dead, he thought savagely to himself. Why was everyone being so bloody gloomy about it? She was going to get better. She was.

At the bottom of the pile were all the other letters. Day-to-day correspondence, mostly bills. Since moving out of Larch Tree Cottage, the bills had been coming thick and fast, like angry rain. There seemed no end to them; no controlling them. Every time Barnaby thought he'd managed to work out a monthly budget, something else came along to surprise him. This week it had been the bill for servicing Louise's car – £300, out of the blue. He was going to have to dip into his savings again.

Why was life suddenly so much more expensive? Living together with Louise in Larch Tree Cottage, his salary had seemed ample for all their needs; now it seemed stretched beyond endurance. None of his sums seemed to add up; however careful he was, at the end of every month he found himself with an overdraft. Despite the fact that he was living in the cheapest accommodation he had been able to find; despite the fact that he'd cut back on practically everything that wasn't essential.

Of course it was his duty to support Louise and the girls, he thought dejectedly to himself, taking a sip of tea and pushing the bill from the garage underneath the pile of cards. They were dependent on him. It was only right. But did that mean he was never going to be able to afford a life of his own?

At ten to eleven, a nurse came over to Katie's bed and tapped Louise on the shoulder.

'Yes?' She turned, startled.

'Sorry,' said the nurse. 'Didn't mean to alarm you. I just thought I'd remind you that you've got a meeting with the consultant at eleven. Just in case . . .' she paused tactfully, '. . . in case you wanted to comb your hair or pop to the loo or anything.'

'Oh, yes,' said Louise dully. 'Yes, thank you. I expect I look dreadful.' She paused. 'Not that it matters what I look like,' she added, slowly getting to her feet. 'I mean, the doctor won't care what I look like, and I shouldn't think Barnaby will, either.'

Since Monday, Louise had barely talked to Barnaby. She had barely talked to anyone, except the nurses and the odd doctor and, of course, all day long, Katie. She spent hours at a time wearily staring at Katie's little face; uttering encouraging words; peering in exhausted desperation for some kind of response. And when there was none she found herself irrationally beginning to doubt her own powers of communication. Sometimes she felt as though she were retreating into a detached light-headed world of her own, in which only she and her own whirling thoughts existed; in which she had been sitting by the same bed for an eternity, staring at Katie's face, willing her to wake up.

On the locker beside Katie's bed was a notebook, which one of the nurses had given to Louise, suggesting she keep a journal of Katie's progress, and of her own thoughts and emotions. So far it was empty. Louise's thoughts were too wild and random to be written down. When she slept, her head filled with dark menacing dreams, which lingered on, like looming

106

shadows, after she woke. Her mind felt stretched; wrung out like an old cloth. Sometimes she thought she might open her mouth and find she had forgotten how to speak.

She hadn't been able to bring herself to attend the church service on Monday evening. The official reason was that Katie might wake up while she wasn't there, but the real reason was that she wasn't sure she could face it. She shuddered as she imagined sitting there, under the glare of all those curious eyes – benevolent and sympathetic, maybe, but curious too, without a doubt. Somehow forcing herself to tell people again and again how Katie was doing; somehow managing to express a suitable gratitude for everyone's interest. Hearing, out loud, the prayers for Katie; trying not to crumble; trying not to cry; trying not to break down completely.

And then there had been the matter of Hugh and Ursula. They had helped to organize the service; if she'd gone to it, she would have seen them; she would have had to talk to them. Louise closed her eyes briefly. She didn't know what to think about Hugh and Ursula; she couldn't think about them rationally; couldn't dissociate them from the accident; from the malevolent nightmares still looming in her mind. Sometimes, as she sat, endlessly replaying the accident in her mind, she would begin to shake with a black nauseous hatred for them; a hatred for their stupid swimming-pool and evil dangerous diving-board. And she would feel a desperate need for them – someone – to be punished for what had happened to Katie. But then something would click in her mind and she would suddenly have an image of a benign smiling Ursula; a kindly Hugh. Old friends of the family, who loved Katie; who would never want to harm her. Tears would well up in her eyes, and suddenly the idea of taking them to court would seem ridiculous, unthinkable.

107

To Cassian, however, it didn't seem unthinkable at all. As Louise walked along the corridor to the Ladies, swaying slightly with tiredness, she thought about Cassian's proposal. He really seemed to think they had a case. He'd explained it all carefully to her, the night after Barnaby's outburst, and then had sat back, and in a smooth voice, said, 'It's your decision. I won't say another word about it if you don't want me to.'

'No,' Louise faltered. 'It's all very interesting. I'll speak to Barnaby, I don't think he understands properly.'

'You're right,' Cassian had replied. 'I'm sure he doesn't understand.' He looked at her hard. 'I won't say this again,' he said, 'but I think that you and Barnaby should see it as your duty to Katie to take the Delaneys to court.' Then he looked away. 'You owe it to your little girl,' he said in a softer voice. And Louise, strung up and weary, had felt tears trickling down her face, and a sudden conviction that Cassian was right; that he was Katie's saviour; that he was prepared to go into battle on her behalf.

Barnaby arrived at the hospital a few minutes early for the meeting, and went straight to Katie's ward. Louise wasn't sitting beside her bed, and Barnaby felt an immediate, unreasonable wave of anger, and a faint sense of relief. He would have a few moments alone with Katie; would be able to talk to her naturally without Louise standing by and watching, making him feel stupid. He had hardly spoken to Louise since the row in the cafeteria. On the few occasions that they had met beside Katie's bed, they had exchanged a few meaningless pleasantries, just in case she could hear them; otherwise Louise seemed almost to be avoiding him.

'Katie,' he said in a low voice, taking her pale little hand carefully, without dislodging the plastic tube taped to it. 'Katie, it's Daddy. Katie, you're going to be fine. Soon you'll wake up and you'll be able to come home . . .' He broke off. She would be going home to Louise, of course, to Larch Tree Cottage; not home to him.

'Barnaby!' A voice from behind made him jump. He turned to see Louise standing by Katie's curtain rail. She looked pale and exhausted.

'Hello, Louise,' said Barnaby. He suddenly felt stilted and unnatural. 'Has anything . . .' He glanced at Katie. 'Have there been any developments?'

'No,' said Louise shortly. 'Nothing.' She looked at her watch. 'We'd better go.'

The meeting was with the same consultant with round spectacles who had spoken to them in the waiting-room, plus Janine, the nurse who had special responsibility for Katie. Barnaby watched as Louise greeted the consultant with a tremulous smile, then sat down next to Janine and began to talk to her in a familiar undertone, as though they were old friends; as though they were keeping some sort of secret together. Without meaning to, he suddenly said, 'What are you talking about?'

'It doesn't matter,' said Louise.

'Was it about Katie? Is there something I should know?' persisted Barnaby. He tried to smile pleasantly at Janine, but he could feel his face turning red, his breath coming more quickly.

'I was asking Janine for some painkillers, actually,' said Louise curtly. 'I've got a splitting headache.'

'Oh,' said Barnaby. 'I'm sorry to hear that,' he added, but Louise had looked away.

The consultant cleared his throat, shuffled the papers in front of him and then looked up.

'I'm glad you could both come in today,' he said. 'We feel it's very useful to have regular meetings with the parents of children in our wards, to update you on any progress, explain what's happening and give you a

109

chance to ask any questions.' He looked down at his notes. 'In Katie's case, it's still very early days, and as I'm sure you're both aware, there's little we can do other than monitor her very carefully and wait until she begins to regain consciousness. We are keeping a very close eye on her, and if there's any change in her condition, we'll let you know immediately.'

'When do you think . . .' began Barnaby. Everyone looked at him and he gave an awkward cough. 'When do you think she'll wake up?'

'I'm afraid it's very difficult to tell,' said the consultant.

'You must have some idea,' said Barnaby. 'In a week? In a month? In a year?' The consultant sighed.

'I don't want to appear difficult,' he said, 'but we really don't think it's a good idea to try and get into predictions.' He smiled kindly at Barnaby. 'Katie will wake up when she's ready.'

'But you must at least . . .' began Barnaby. Louise interrupted him.

'Barnaby, leave it!' she said. 'They don't know, OK? We just have to wait.'

'It may seem to you as though we're hiding something,' said the consultant earnestly, 'but I can assure you, we're not. When it comes to a head injury, very little is certain.' He looked at Barnaby. 'It really is best to try to keep an open mind. Don't build up any kind of expectations at the moment, just take each day as it comes. And when Katie does regain consciousness, a lot of things should become clearer.'

There was a short silence, during which an unarticulated panic began to grow inside Barnaby. What was going to become clearer? What weren't they telling him?

'She will be OK, though,' he said suddenly, in a voice made belligerent through alarm. 'I mean, you said she wasn't paralysed. She will be able to walk and everything? And talk properly? She won't be a vegetable?'

110

'Barnaby!' exclaimed Louise.

'Well, what's going to become clearer? What are you talking about?'

'Mr Kember,' said the consultant soothingly, 'obviously you're very concerned for your daughter.'

'Yes,' said Barnaby roughly, 'I am. And I want to know what she's going to be like when she wakes up.'

'Of course you do,' said the consultant. 'We all do. However, at the moment, there's very little we can tell you.'

'But you've done tests, haven't you?' cried Barnaby. 'You've done scans and things.'

'Yes, we have,' said the consultant patiently, 'but a scan can't tell us everything.'

'What can't it tell you? What might be wrong with her?'

'Barnaby,' cried Louise suddenly, in a taut voice, 'why can't you just leave it alone? Why can't you just wait and see, like everyone else?'

'I just want to know!' said Barnaby. 'I want to know what might be wrong with Katie! You must have some idea,' he insisted to the consultant. 'I mean, other people must have had injuries like Katie's. Can't you tell us what happened to them?' The consultant sighed. He picked up his silver ball-point pen and began to trace inkless circles on the top of his folder.

'Damage to the brain can have many different consequences,' he said. 'Many victims will, for example, suffer a certain confusion when they wake up; what we call post-traumatic amnesia.'

'Is that all?' said Barnaby. 'A bit of confusion?'

'Well, no, not always,' said the consultant. 'There may perhaps be problems with . . . well, with speech, for instance. Or there may be some form of post-traumatic epilepsy, or changes in personality. But until Katie wakes up . . .'

'What about walking?' said Barnaby. There was a

pause. The consultant began to examine the cap of his pen.

'There may initially be problems with balance and co-ordination, yes,' he said eventually. 'Some patients have to learn how to walk again. But only some,' he added firmly. 'And in most cases rehabilitation is a tremendous help.'

'I see,' said Barnaby, trying to stay calm. He felt as though all his worst fears had been confirmed, as though he was finally being let into a secret which everyone else had known about for days.

'If Katie did need rehabilitation,' said Louise in a shaky voice, 'would that happen here?'

'No, probably at Forest Lodge. It's a rehab centre near here.'

'Does it . . .' began Louise.

'Forest Lodge?' interrupted Barnaby. He felt a cold trickle run down his spine. 'That place on the hill? With all the children in wheelchairs?'

'I don't think they're all in wheelchairs,' said the consultant gently. He looked at Louise. 'It's quite a famous centre, you know. You're lucky to be living so close to it.'

'Lucky,' echoed Barnaby bleakly.

'But it's very early days to be thinking of anything like that,' said the consultant briskly. 'At the moment we must concentrate on bringing Katie round.' He smiled at Louise. 'I gather her classmates made a tape for her; that kind of thing always helps.'

'Oh, good.' Louise flushed slightly. 'There was just one other thing,' she said, not looking at Barnaby. 'If we needed medical reports for a . . . for a court case, would you be able to give them to us?'

'Absolutely,' said the consultant. 'We're quite used to that, aren't we, Janine?' He looked at the nurse, who nodded.

'Oh, sure,' she said. 'Will you be going to court, then?'

'No,' said Barnaby, scowling at Louise. 'We won't.'
Louise ignored him.

'We might,' she said.

The consultant looked from one to another.

'It's none of my business,' he said, 'but I've seen quite a lot of parents in your situation, and I'd say that if you do decide to go to court, you should really try to agree to do it together.' He frowned. 'The whole thing can get pretty stressful, as it is, not to mention expensive.'

'Well, that wouldn't actually be a problem,' said Louise, flushing slightly. 'My . . . my father's very generously agreed to help us out with the legal fees. And, of course, if we win costs, it won't actually . . .' She was interrupted by Barnaby.

'Are you telling me that your father thinks we should sue?' His voice was outraged. 'I don't believe it! I just don't believe it!'

Louise's eyes flashed angrily at him.

'You don't believe he would put his granddaughter before anything else,' she hissed. 'His own flesh and blood. Is that so strange to you? Because if it is, Barnaby, it says more about you . . .'

'Ahem.' The consultant politely cleared his throat, and Louise stopped abruptly, mid-flow.

'Sorry,' she muttered. 'Do carry on.'

'Perhaps we should agree', said the consultant, 'to bring this meeting to an end. Just remember, whatever you decide to do, we'll try and help.' He smiled at Louise and got up. 'We'll have another meeting soon. Meanwhile, do ask Janine if there's anything you'd like to know.'

'Wait!' said Barnaby hurriedly. 'Just one more thing. Do people ever . . . do they ever just wake up out of a coma and they're fine? Back to normal straight away?'

There was a pause. Louise muttered something under her breath.

'To be honest, not very often,' said the consultant kindly. 'Not very often at all.'

'But it's possible,' persisted Barnaby. The consultant sighed.

'Yes, it's just about possible,' he began. 'But . . .'

'Don't worry,' interrupted Barnaby. 'It's possible. That's all I wanted to know.'

Cassian was waiting for Louise when they came out of the meeting.

'So,' he said. 'Do they know any more?'

'No,' said Louise, rubbing her eyes wearily. 'They don't know anything. They don't know when she's going to wake up, or whether she'll be epileptic, or whether she'll be able to walk, or whether she'll have the same personality as she did before . . .'

'They said all that? They said she might not be able to walk?'

'Barnaby wouldn't stop badgering them,' said Louise curtly. 'They had to shut him up somehow.' Barnaby scowled.

'They also said she might just wake up and be fine,' he said roughly.

'Oh, Barnaby!' exclaimed Louise. 'Get real! That's not going to happen and you know it.' Cassian nodded seriously.

'That sounds most unlikely to me,' he said in a grave professional voice. 'Head injuries can have all sorts of consequences. Katie's life will probably never be the same again. Even if she recovers, rehabilitation might take months. Years.' He paused. 'She's going to have to be your main priority. You're going to have to put her above everything else.'

'Of course,' snapped Barnaby. Cassian raised his eyebrows.

'You say that,' he said coolly, examining his fingernails. 'But if you're not even willing to go to court on her behalf . . .'

'That's different,' said Barnaby fiercely.

'I can't see how,' said Cassian smoothly. 'You have the opportunity to set her up financially, to relieve the burden on your family, to recompense Katie and yourselves for all this trouble and suffering. The chances are, any award would be made by the Delaneys' insurance company, but you're refusing to go ahead simply because the Delaneys are your . . . friends.' His voice was suddenly scathing. There was a pause.

'It's not just that,' said Barnaby eventually, in an uncertain voice. He looked at Louise. 'How can we go into court and say it's Hugh's and Ursula's fault that Katie's in hospital? How can we blame them? It was an accident. An *accident*,' he repeated, with emphasis.

'An accident which could have been avoided,' said Cassian swiftly. 'I went to inspect that diving-board, and, frankly, I was shocked. The surface is all slippery; the tread has worn down . . .'

'It's not that bad,' said Louise uncomfortably.

'Bad enough,' said Cassian. 'Especially where excitable children are involved. By law, a householder has a special duty of care towards visiting children. Hugh and Ursula should have prevented children from using the board, or else issued a warning, or at least hired a supervisor.' His voice was suddenly hard and censorious. 'Who in their right mind allows children to play on a slippery, unsafe diving-board? It's outrageously negligent!'

'Katie didn't hit her head because the board was slippery,' said Barnaby robustly. 'She just didn't know how to do a back dive properly.'

'How do you know that?' countered Cassian. 'How do you know her foot didn't skid as she took off?'

There was silence. Barnaby looked down,

discomfited. With an unpleasant pang, Louise again remembered Ursula saying something to her about the children; warning her that they seemed overexcited. A sickening sensation of guilt began to rise up inside her, but she firmly quelled it.

'I think Cassian's right,' she said quickly to Barnaby. 'We owe it to Katie to go to court.'

'You don't know how long she'll be in treatment,' said Cassian. 'She might need special care for years. Nurses don't come cheap, you know. And then, what if she can't look after herself when she's older? You'll want to set her up with some money.'

'She's going to be fine,' said Barnaby shakily. 'You'll see.'

'Barnaby!' exclaimed Louise in frustration. 'Weren't you listening in there? You can't just close your ears and pretend nothing's wrong.'

'You're letting Katie down, Barnaby,' stated Cassian. 'She needs help and support and money, not a parent who won't face up to the facts.'

'Leave me alone!' Barnaby suddenly lashed out. 'I'm going in to see her.' And he disappeared down the corridor.

Cassian raised his eyebrows at Louise, who looked away uncomfortably. She felt torn between Cassian's cool reasoning and Barnaby's honest emotional re-action. Again, the vision of Ursula's anxious face rose up in her mind, and Hugh, stalwart Hugh, who had been the first to offer to take Barnaby to the hospital. Were they really thinking of taking those decent people to court? No, it couldn't be. But then . . . shouldn't they be doing everything they could for their own daughter, no matter whom it hurt? Didn't they owe more to Katie than to Hugh and Ursula?

For a minute or two, Louise stared down at the pastel corridor floor, while the arguments swung backwards and forwards in her mind. The more she thought, the

116

less clear the answer seemed. Eventually she looked up at Cassian, and hesitantly opened her mouth to speak, but Barnaby's voice was suddenly behind her. He sounded gruff and upset.

'I couldn't stay. Some people are in there, moving Katie's arms and legs around, as if she was a doll.'

'Who are?' Louise turned round. Barnaby looked weary and defeated. He shrugged.

'Doctors, or something.'

'Physiotherapists,' said Louise, suddenly remembering. 'They're exercising her limbs to keep some tone in the muscles, and to make sure she doesn't get sore.' She looked at Barnaby. 'It's quite normal, apparently.'

'She looked like a doll,' repeated Barnaby. He looked at Louise, and suddenly there were tears in his eyes. 'She's in a bad way, Lou.'

'I know,' said Louise. She put her hand gently on Barnaby's. But he shrugged it off, blinked hard several times, then abruptly turned and walked off down the corridor.

Chapter Eight

With every day that passed, Barnaby's hopes diminished, and his secret conviction – that Katie would soon wake up and be back to her bright normal self – seemed a little less likely. But if she wasn't going to be back to her normal self, what was she going to be? His mind could not drag itself away from the darkest, most frightening conclusions; he could not stop himself conjuring up pictures of his daughter, a battered, damaged cripple. Confined to a wheelchair, maybe; unable to talk; unable to lead any kind of normal life. How would she cope? How would any of them cope?

He couldn't persuade his thoughts into any kind of middle ground; couldn't seem to attain the sort of positive but realistic outlook that Louise had adopted. He constantly swung from foolish desperate optimism to bleak pessimism and back again to foolish optimism. And underneath it all burned an angry, mortifying, unspecified guilt, which did not abate with time but got stronger.

And so he threw himself into hard outdoor work with no room for thought – tackling all the physical tasks which needed doing on the estate; leaving the paperwork on his desk to mount up.

On the following Tuesday, the ninth day of Katie's coma, he spent the morning checking walls on the estate, and then popped into a nearby pub for lunch. Eileen, the owner's wife, was behind the bar, and clucked sympathetically when she saw Barnaby.

'How's your little girl?' she said, handing him a pint. 'Has she woken up yet?'

Barnaby shook his head and looked around for somewhere to go and sit. He didn't feel like talking about Katie. But the pub was filling up, and all the tables were taken.

'How long is it now?' asked Eileen.

'Nine days,' said Barnaby. He felt a deep gloom falling over him. Eileen clucked again.

'I was watching a programme about people in comas the other night,' she said, leaning forward on the bar and talking straight into Barnaby's left ear. 'This one poor chap was out for two whole years. Can you believe it? Then he woke up, right as rain.'

'Really?' muttered Barnaby.

'Another one was only in a coma for three hours, but when he woke up he'd lost all his memory. Didn't recognize his own wife!'

Eileen looked at Barnaby for a reaction, and he hurriedly took another slug of beer. He would drink up and then go. Forget about lunch.

'But they cured him at the institute,' continued Eileen, opening a packet of crisps and offering it to Barnaby. 'It was marvellous, really.' Barnaby looked up.

'Institute?' he said. 'What institute?'

'The institute in the documentary,' said Eileen patiently. 'The one in America. It was ever so interesting.' She examined her long magenta nails. 'I love that kind of thing,' she added. 'Medical programmes. I'm not squeamish or anything. Graham thinks I'm crazy.'

'Can you remember what it was called?' said Barnaby, trying not to sound too urgent. 'The institute?' Eileen screwed up her face.

'I don't think I can,' she said. 'It was a really famous place, though. I mean, apparently people go there from all over the world. There was this poor lad from Saudi Arabia, couldn't understand a word anyone said to him. I mean, it doesn't really help, does it?' She broke off into peals of laughter.

Barnaby stared at her. Thoughts were buzzing round his head. But before he could say anything, the mobile phone in his pocket rang.

'Barnaby? It's Louise.' He could hardly hear her over the pub noise.

'Hang on a moment,' he said, 'I'll go outside.'

In the car park he blinked a few times in the bright light.

'Hi,' he said. 'What is it?'

'It's Katie.' Louise's voice was trembling slightly and Barnaby felt his heart give a terrified swoop. He had been waiting so long to hear some news; had thought he was desperate for something to happen, but now he felt suddenly frightened; unwilling to leave his haven of ignorance.

'What . . .' He could hardly speak.

'She woke up this morning.'

A flash of relief exploded in Barnaby's mind.

'That's fantastic!' he shouted. 'That's wonderful news! I'll come straight away. Is she OK? Has she said anything?'

'No, she hasn't,' said Louise curtly. 'She only regained consciousness for about thirty seconds.'

'What?'

'Apparently that's normal. It could be ages before she wakes up properly.'

'Oh,' said Barnaby. He felt suddenly deflated. 'Well, I suppose that's good.'

'Of course it's good!' Louise's voice came furiously down the line. 'For God's sake, Barnaby, what did you expect? That she would just sit up and smile and say, "Where's Daddy"?'

'No,' said Barnaby at once, 'of course not.'

'You've got to be realistic.'

'I am realistic,' said Barnaby indignantly.

'You're not! You're completely unrealistic! You constantly go from one stupid extreme to the other, and it doesn't help, Barnaby. It really doesn't help.' Louise sounded rattled, almost tearful.

'OK, then,' said Barnaby hurriedly. 'Well, here's something that might help. I was just talking to Eileen at The Fox and Hounds, and she said there was an institute in America which cures people who have been in comas. She said people go there from all over the world.'

'And?' Barnaby ignored the ominous tone in Louise's voice.

'And we could send Katie there,' he said.

'Oh, for Christ's sake, Barnaby!' shrieked Louise. 'You're in another world, aren't you?'

'I'm not!' Barnaby shouted. 'It sounded really good!' A couple of people walking through the car park looked curiously at him, and he turned away with a scowl.

'Yes, and I suppose you'd pay for it, would you?' snapped Louise. 'I suppose you'd fork out the half a million, or whatever it takes?' Then she sighed. 'Barnaby, we don't even know what's wrong with Katie yet; if anything. She hasn't even woken up properly yet. So now is really not the time to start talking about institutes in America, is it?'

Barnaby stared miserably at the ground. He couldn't think of anything to say.

'I'll see you this evening at the hospital,' said Louise.

'OK,' said Barnaby. 'Thanks for calling.'

'Yes, well, I had to, didn't I?' said Louise. She sounded suddenly bitter, and Barnaby winced.

When he had put his phone away, he went over to a bench at the edge of the car park and sat down shakily. He felt heavy with guilt, with despair, with indignation. Something was going wrong. He was obviously failing

Louise. Maybe he was failing Katie, too. Maybe he was making everything worse for everybody.

He buried his head in his hands and allowed a little of his buried resentment to surface. What else was he supposed to do? Hide his worries? Not speak to anyone? He'd thought the institute in America sounded like a good idea. He wouldn't have mentioned it otherwise.

Again he winced as he remembered Louise's voice. She sounded hard, full of tension and exhausted. And she made him feel completely useless. 'I suppose you'd pay for it, would you?' Her words ran round his brain like busy mice. What if Katie needed money and he couldn't give it to her? How could he let her down? A picture came into his mind of his helpless little daughter, waking up for a confused, bewildering thirty seconds, wondering where she was, perhaps even wondering who she was; perhaps unable to move; perhaps in dreadful pain. And here he was, sitting uselessly in the sun. He couldn't stand it any longer. He had to do something to help. Take some positive action. He had to do *something* . . .

A sudden surprising thought entered his mind like a slippery fish. Before he could focus on it, it had darted away. Then it returned and lingered for a bit longer, wriggling away when he tried to fix his attention on it, only to dance intriguingly at the corners of his mind.

Was he serious? Could he really be contemplating such a thing? What had happened to him? Where were all his objections? His morals? He tried as hard as he could to conjure up the sensation of indignant outrage which had consumed him only days before, but he couldn't. Somehow everything had vanished from his mind but Katie. Katie governed his thoughts, his feelings, his convictions. He had to put her first, he simply had to. Whatever it took; whatever it meant for other people.

For a long time he sat completely still, allowing his

fermenting thoughts to settle down into hard serious intention. Then he took a few deep breaths, reached for his mobile phone, and felt in his pocket for the little white card which had been sitting there for several days. He shut his eyes, counted to ten, and dialled the number.

'Cassian?' As he spoke the name he felt suddenly self-conscious, and glanced around. Could anyone hear him? And if they could, would they realize what he was doing? For a moment he felt a slight faltering.

'Barnaby? Is that you?'

'Yes. Yes, it is.' Barnaby took a deep breath. For Katie's sake. 'I've been thinking hard,' he said, 'about what you said. About suing Hugh and Ursula. And . . .' He swallowed hard. 'And I think, if there's any chance it would help Katie, then we should go ahead.'

There was a short silence. Barnaby realized he was clenching the mobile phone so hard, it was digging into his flesh. What was the bastard going to say? Was he going to make him feel stupid? Had he done the wrong thing yet again?

'Barnaby, I'm so glad!' The warm congratulatory tone in Cassian's voice took Barnaby by surprise. 'I realize what a tough decision it was to make, but I really think you've done the right thing for little Katie. And you know, Barnaby, I'd like to say that on a personal level I have a lot of respect for your thoughtful approach to this whole matter.' He paused, and Barnaby felt a slight flush come to his cheeks. 'You didn't allow yourself to be rushed,' continued Cassian, 'you took your time, and in the end you came to a decision which I'm sure you'll find is the right one. Barnaby, I'm very glad to be working with you.'

'I just did what I thought was right,' said Barnaby gruffly.

'Of course you did,' said Cassian reassuringly, 'and I know these things are never easy. But you really are doing the best thing you possibly can for your daughter.'

There was a pause. Barnaby leaned back and felt a warm sensation of relief pass through him. At last, maybe, he'd got something right.

'So what happens now?' he said eventually.

'If you and Louise just pop into the office this afternoon,' said Cassian smoothly, 'then I can introduce you to our personal injury experts, and we can get the whole thing going at once. Say, three o'clock?'

'This afternoon?'

'The quicker the better,' said Cassian. 'And after that, you won't have to worry about a thing.'

It was teatime the next day, and everyone was outside, when the doorbell rang at Devenish House. Hugh put his cup down and said, 'I'll go.' Meredith looked severely at Ursula.

'Have you asked someone to tea without telling us?' She turned to Alexis. 'She meets people in the street and asks them to tea, and then forgets all about it! I expect right now the whole village is on the doorstep.'

Ursula began an unconvincing protestation. Alexis simply smiled and bit into a crumbly, buttery biscuit. Meredith looked surreptitiously at him; at the way he leaned back elegantly in his chair; at the way his skin creased up when he smiled, and as she watched, a faint yearning pulled at the pit of her stomach. Alexis had been spending a lot of time with them that week. At first, of course, he had been helping out and generally being supportive in the aftermath of the accident. But now . . . In spite of herself, she felt a fluttering of hope.

As if he were reading her mind, he turned and smiled at her.

'Doing anything this weekend?'

'Oh!' Taken by surprise, Meredith gave a sharp intake of breath. Then, tossing her hair back in a determinedly casual fashion, she said, lightly, 'Nothing much.' She took a sip of tea. Jeez, this was ridiculous. She was behaving like some kooky kid angling for a date. 'I thought I'd check out that new movie,' she added, keeping her voice natural. 'That one, *The Grandfather's Tale*. It's supposed to be a bit weird, but . . .'

'I saw it a couple of weeks ago,' said Alexis. Meredith's heart dropped slightly and she smiled at Alexis to cover it. 'It was excellent,' Alexis added warmly. 'You'll love it.'

'Don't say that!' Meredith forced a light-hearted animation into her voice. 'If anyone tells me I'll love a film, I find myself deliberately hating it.' Alexis laughed. 'It's true,' insisted Meredith, 'I'm very protective about what I like and don't like. If people start dictating I rebel.' She sighed. 'The number of perfectly good films which have been ruined for me . . .'

Ursula was listening, a look of puzzlement on her face.

'But Meredith, dear,' she said, 'what about that charming film I took you to see last Christmas? I told you I was sure you'd love it, and when we'd seen it, you agreed. You said you'd enjoyed it very much.' She screwed up her face in thought. 'What was it called, now? It was a *lovely* film. You must remember. Those beautiful period costumes.'

'Uh, yes, Ursula,' said Meredith. 'I remember. I guess that was an exception.' She caught Alexis's eye, and he gave the barest acknowledging flicker of a smile. And suddenly, inexplicably, Meredith felt her heart pounding violently and her face beginning to flush. We would go so well together, she found herself thinking, the thoughts piling over one another in foolish desperation. We enjoy talking to one another, and we have the same sense of humour, and I certainly find him attractive and . . . She pulled up short, hit by a sudden uncharacteristic loss of self-confidence; and looked away quickly. Perhaps that was it; she'd mistaken the signs: Alexis didn't find *her* attractive, after all.

Surreptitiously, she glanced down at her body, lean and tanned and clad today in a clinging black dress made from an expensive stretchy fabric. If he didn't like the way she looked, there wasn't a lot she could do . . . except perhaps blimp out, she found herself thinking. In case he liked larger women. Eat cheeseburgers every day and put on twenty pounds. Would that do the trick? She gave a stifled giggle, in spite of herself.

Alexis looked up and Meredith's grin died away. Ask him out! she told herself fiercely. Just ask. It isn't such a big deal; he can only say no . . . But for some reason her mouth stayed closed.

Ursula was frowning at the newspaper.

'It says here', she said, 'that women live longer than men.' She put down the paper and gave Meredith a puzzled look. 'That can't be right.'

'Sure,' said Meredith, taking a bite of biscuit. 'They do.' Ursula's eyes flickered doubtfully to Alexis.

'It's true, Ursula,' he said pleasantly. 'Women live longer.'

'But surely that's impossible,' said Ursula in gently obstinate tones. She put down the newspaper and appeared to be thinking. Meredith watched her affectionately, realizing, with a slight shock, that the few remaining blond streaks in Ursula's hair had, without her noticing, vanished into a sea of silver. 'Surely,' added Ursula, 'if it were true, it would mean that there were far more women than men on the earth.'

'Maybe there are,' said Meredith lazily. 'Long may it last.'

'And if that imbalance continued, year after year . . . then eventually there wouldn't be any men left at all,' said Ursula. She gave Meredith an impressive look. 'So I don't think you can be right, dear.'

'Ursula!' exclaimed Meredith, clutching her head in mock-despair. 'Where do you get your logic from?'

'It seems very clear to me,' protested Ursula.

'I'm sure it does,' said Meredith, beginning to laugh. 'Alexis, help me out here.'

'Let's have a look at the article,' said Alexis. He leaned over Meredith to take the paper from Ursula, and Meredith felt a stab of yearning desire.

'Let me see,' she said, without thinking. 'Let me look over your shoulder.'

'OK,' said Alexis easily. He shuffled up so that his chair was next to hers, and shook the paper open on her knee. She could smell his scent; could feel his leg lying against hers; could sense him breathing in and out. For a few seconds she felt pinned down; transfixed by wanting.

'Alexis,' she said softly. He turned and looked at her. 'Yes?'

Meredith took a breath, ignoring the knife-like nerves in her chest. She paused to select exactly the right words; the most noncommittal, yet unambiguous phrase possible. 'Do you think,' she began quietly, shaking back her hair and staring at her hands. 'Do you think—'

She was interrupted by a gasp from Alexis. He was looking over her shoulder.

'Hugh!' Ursula was exclaiming. 'What's wrong?'

Hugh looked back at them. His face looked drained; his eyes had lost their good cheer, and he was holding a letter in his hand. Meredith was suddenly, fearfully reminded of Simon's death.

'This is a registered letter', Hugh began, 'from that chap, Cassian Brown. Louise Kember's friend.'

'Katie . . .' began Ursula in a choked voice. Hugh raised a hand.

'I've just tried to phone Louise,' he said. 'She wasn't there, but the babysitter told me that Katie is making reasonable progress. Apparently she woke up briefly from her coma yesterday morning.'

127

A sensation of relief flooded through Meredith, and in a tiny corner of her soul, a tinge of envy. Her loved one had never woken up. They were lucky . . .

'Nevertheless,' Hugh was saying, in halting, disbelieving tones, 'it seems that Louise and Barnaby have made a . . . a rather strange decision.' He looked at Alexis and took a deep breath. 'They're going to sue us. For negligence.'

'They're going to *what*?' Meredith's voice rose, outraged, into the afternoon air.

'Sue us, apparently.' Hugh ran a hand through his greying locks. He was still looking at Alexis. 'Can they, Alexis?' Ursula tugged at Meredith's sleeve.

'What exactly do they want to do?' she whispered.

'Take you to court, Ursula,' said Meredith. 'To get some damages out of you. Money,' she added. 'Lots of it.'

'But, Meredith, dear,' said Ursula, 'I don't think that can be right. It was an *accident*, you know. It wasn't our fault.' She looked at Hugh. 'Are you sure he wasn't talking about the appeal? We've raised quite a lot of money, you know . . .'

'Ursula,' said Alexis gently, 'I really don't think the appeal's got anything to do with it. Hugh's obviously right. The Kembers are intending to take you to court.'

'But it was an accident,' insisted Ursula, bewildered.

There was a taut silence. Everyone looked at Alexis.

'I'm afraid that won't make any difference,' he said, and exhaled sharply. 'You'll be sued for negligence, under the Occupiers' Liability Act.' He sounded suddenly resigned, and Meredith gave him a hard look.

'But they're our friends,' said Hugh in bleak tones. 'Why do they have to take us to court? Why couldn't they just come and talk to us about it?' He looked at Alexis with a hurt, betrayed expression. 'Wouldn't that be simpler? I mean, don't they realize we want to help in whatever way we can? We'll give them money, if that's what they need . . .'

'It's that smarmy lawyer,' broke in Meredith suddenly. 'He's talked them into it.'

Hugh picked up a teacup, took a sip of tea, then grimaced as he discovered it was cold.

'I'll go and talk to Barnaby,' he said, putting the cup down. 'I'm sure that if we all got together . . .'

'No,' said Alexis firmly. Hugh looked up in surprise. 'It'll be easier all round', said Alexis more gently, 'if you keep away from the Kembers for the moment, just to be on the safe side.'

'Oh, Jesus,' said Meredith. 'Isn't that going a bit far?'

'Wait till you see the claim that the Kembers will make,' said Alexis drily, 'and then talk to me about going too far.'

There was a short frightened silence. Alexis looked around at the worried faces and relented slightly.

'You may find,' he said, 'that when everyone's calmed down a bit, all this talk of legal action comes to nothing. The best thing is not to rush into doing anything that you may regret. Just sit tight and wait to see what happens.'

Meredith gave him a sharp look.

'You don't really think it'll come to nothing, do you?' she said. 'You're just trying to make us feel better.' Alexis shrugged.

'It all depends. If they're determined to sue, then they'll sue.'

'But we didn't do anything wrong!' said Ursula suddenly. She looked at Alexis with an expression of panic, as though realizing for the first time what was going on. 'We didn't do anything wrong!' she repeated, and looked helplessly at Meredith and Hugh, as though for confirmation.

Meredith took Ursula's hand and gave it a comforting squeeze.

'Of course we didn't,' she said. 'And let's hope that's the way the court sees it, too.'

When Hugh and Ursula had taken the tea things inside, Meredith turned to Alexis.

'You knew, didn't you?' she said in a low trembling voice. 'You knew this was going to happen.'

'I didn't know,' said Alexis wearily, 'but I did have my suspicions. When I saw that young lawyer coming to poke around the swimming-pool for no good reason.' Meredith thought for a moment.

'What were you looking at in Hugh's study?' she abruptly demanded. 'That piece of paper?' Alexis looked at her, a grim unsmiling look. Meredith felt her heart begin to pound nervously.

'I was looking at Hugh's insurance policy,' he said quietly. 'I was checking to see whether the swimming-pool was covered – and whether they were covered for negligence.'

'And are they?' Alexis gave a sigh and looked away.

'They are, and they aren't. They're covered for negligence, but only in the context of domestic use.' He paused. 'Would you call a hundred people, all paying at the door, a domestic use?'

'But it was for charity!' protested Meredith. 'They weren't making any money!'

'I know,' said Alexis. 'but I also know what insurance companies are like. If they can get out of paying, they will . . .' He broke off. 'I'm just afraid that this will prove a good enough excuse.'

'So . . .'

'So if Louise and Barnaby win any damages, Hugh and Ursula will have to pay out of their own pocket. And it could be a serious amount.'

'How much?' Meredith's voice was sharp. Alexis sighed.

'I wish I knew. It really depends on the little girl's

130

condition, but it could be anything from a few thousand pounds to – I don't know – a hundred thousand pounds, two hundred thousand. Maybe more.' Alexis looked at Meredith, his face clouded with worry. 'Perhaps I should have said something earlier,' he said. 'Warned Hugh. But I really didn't think it would come to this . . .'

Meredith stared back at him, feeling a white anger creeping up inside her.

'How can they do this?' she expostulated at last, keeping her voice low and one wary eye on the house. 'How can they stand up in court and say that Hugh and Ursula were to blame? It was an accident, for Christ's sake. An accident! No-one was to blame. Hugh and Ursula weren't *negligent*. That kid just didn't know how to dive properly.' Alexis shrugged.

'Can you prove that?'

'Well, of course I can't *prove* it, but . . .' Meredith broke off, frustratedly. Alexis gave her a half grin.

'You should be used to this,' he said. 'America's just about the most litigious country in the world.'

'I know,' said Meredith bitterly, 'but somehow I thought it was different here. I thought people valued friendship above money. I thought . . .' She broke off, suddenly pushed back her chair and got to her feet, full of angry energy. Alexis watched as she paced a few aimless steps, then abruptly turned around. 'Well, they're not getting Hugh and Ursula's money,' she said defiantly. 'I mean, I'm very sorry for them and everything, and I know what they're going through.' She paused. 'I mean, believe me, I really know.'

'Yes,' said Alexis quietly, 'I know you do.'

'But I'm not going to let them walk all over Hugh and Ursula. They're innocent. They don't deserve this.' She looked determinedly at Alexis. 'We're going to fight this, and you'll help us.'

'I'll do my best,' said Alexis, 'but it'll be hard. I've been asking around and I gather this Cassian Brown is

131

a very sharp customer.' He looked at her and lowered his voice. 'This isn't going to be pretty, Meredith.'

'None of it's pretty,' said Meredith. 'Life isn't pretty.'

She looked away, her expression suddenly bleak. Alexis stood up and began to put on his jacket.

'I'll come round tomorrow evening,' he said, 'to talk about it properly.' He caught Meredith's expression. 'It's OK,' he added, 'there's no rush. Quite the contrary.' He pulled a face. 'Most lawsuits go on for several years, and this one hasn't even started yet. In fact, in my opinion, the Kembers are being very premature, if Katie's condition hasn't even stabilized . . .' He looked at Meredith. 'As Katie's a minor, you see, there's absolutely no rush. They could leave it until she was eighteen before they even think about suing.' But Meredith wasn't listening.

'Aren't you going to stay for dinner?' she asked abruptly, sitting down beside Alexis. 'I know Hugh and Ursula would really appreciate it.'

'I'm sure they would,' said Alexis regretfully, 'and normally, of course, I would. But tonight, I've . . . I've got another arrangement.'

He looked away hastily. And ignoring the crestfallen pang in her chest, Meredith smiled at him, nodded, and said, 'Sure thing,' in a casual, friendly kind of way, and didn't ask him what he was doing. There was a momentary pause, then Alexis leaned over and kissed her quickly, once on each cheek.

'Don't worry,' he said, 'we'll pull through this.'

'I hope so,' said Meredith sombrely.

As he left, she sat completely still, as though in a trance. She hugged herself tightly against the late afternoon breeze, and felt her unwilling disappointment mingle with a sudden vengeful hatred for Louise and Barnaby Kember.

After a while a gust of wind caught her bare arm, giving her goose bumps and making her shiver. And as she pulled her jacket around her and got up to go inside, she suddenly found herself wishing, bleakly, that she could somehow confide in Simon; that she could feel his arms around her once again, and hear his voice, and ask him for some advice and some help and some love.

Chapter Nine

Daisy lay in the bath, watching the green crab-apple leaves fluttering outside the bathroom window, and wondered what sort of an evening it was going to be. Her mother had phoned earlier that afternoon, just to check up on things, and Daisy had foolishly let slip that she had been asked out to dinner.

'How nice!' her mother had said, in the distracted voice that probably meant she was typing something onto the computer at the same time. 'I didn't know there were any boys your age in Melbrook.'

And stupidly, instead of saying nothing, Daisy said, 'Actually, he's not really my age.'

There was an ominous pause. Daisy imagined her mother stopping typing in mid-sentence, then automatically pressing the Save button while deciding exactly what to say.

'Oh?' came her mother's voice at last; a single meaningful syllable, encapsulating both a note of enquiry and a hint that she already knew the answer. 'How old is he, then?'

'Older than me,' said Daisy, cursing herself for having said anything.

'How *much* older, exactly?' Daisy was momentarily silent. She wasn't actually sure how old he was. But thinking about it now, she decided he must be at least forty-something. Nearly as old as her father, she thought, with a little jump.

Her mother sounded as though she was standing up; Daisy imagined her striding to the door of the study, beckoning to her father, mouthing to him to come and listen to this conversation, Daisy was in another pickle.

'He's quite a lot older,' said Daisy at last. 'But it's not . . .'

'Not what?' Daisy blushed.

'You know . . .'

'Are you just going to a dinner party or something?' said her mother, as though suddenly understanding the situation. 'Well, that's quite different.'

'No, I don't think so,' said Daisy. 'I think it's just the two of us. But I'm not quite sure why . . .' She broke off. She couldn't possibly say the truth: that she wasn't at all sure why he had asked her.

'Daisy.' Her mother's voice came crisply down the line in her efficient crisis-management manner. 'Daisy, you're very young and very naïve. Are you sure you really want to go out to dinner with this man?' Daisy flinched. Somehow her mother was making it sound all horrible and sordid.

'It's not like that!' she cried. 'It's . . .'

'What?'

'I don't know,' said Daisy feebly. Her mother was breathing impatiently down the phone.

'Daisy, darling, get a grip. You don't just go out to dinner with people for no reason at all. You have to be careful.' From the background came a sound of electronic bleeping. 'Oh, damn. Look, darling, I've got to go. If you're sensible, you'll cancel this fellow. But if you do decide to go, make sure you ring us when you get back. We worry about you, all alone down there. I don't know what your father will say when I tell him about this . . .' The bleeping sounded again. 'Right, now I really have got to go. Bye, sweetheart.'

'Bye, Mummy,' Daisy had said. And she had put down the receiver and stared into space rather disconsolately for a few minutes.

But now she felt cheered up. She lay luxuriously back

135

in her bath and listened to the sound of a Beethoven piano concerto thundering through the cottage, feeling a pleasant anticipation steal over her. It would, she thought, be nice to go out to a restaurant and look down a menu and have some wine. What they would talk about, she wasn't sure. But he was such a friendly man, it was bound to be OK. He'd been terribly nice to her at the swimming-pool. And then he'd dropped by one day, while she was practising, and had stayed for coffee, and they'd chatted about the village and her time in Italy and the awful accident. Then he'd phoned up and asked her out to dinner, and she'd said yes.

She turned on the hot tap with her toe, leaned back and felt warm water creeping slowly around her body. That was all very well, she thought reluctantly. But what did it all mean? Her mother's voice echoed in her mind: 'You don't just go out to dinner with people for no reason at all.'

At first, at the swimming-pool, she'd thought he was just being amiable, like Frances Mold, or one of her father's friends. And she had still thought that when he dropped round for coffee. But now – out to dinner? Didn't that mean . . . a date? Was he serious? Would he expect to . . . to come back? To have sex with her? A pang of agitation shot through Daisy and she wriggled nervously in her bath water. But even as she pictured it, pictured him putting his arm round her, or kissing her – let alone anything further – it seemed such a ridiculous idea that she was sure that she must have got it all wrong; that she'd completely misconstrued him. And that would be the worst thing to do, she thought suddenly: to give him the wrong impression; to offend him by making the wrong assumption. If only she could be certain, she thought, reaching for a towel; if only she could be certain *which* was the wrong assumption. It didn't really matter which of them it was, just as long as she didn't pick the wrong one.

Alexis was feeling ridiculously nervous about dinner with Daisy. All day he had been half expecting her to cancel; when he got home to find no winking message on his answer-machine he felt almost caught out. He hurriedly showered, avoiding the sight of his leathery skin in the bathroom mirror; he decided not to shave again, but splashed on a discreet amount of aftershave. He dressed carefully in pale trousers, a pale blue shirt. No tie. A fashionable jacket made from crumpled beige linen.

He put everything on and looked at himself. A middle-aged man stared back at him. A memory of Daisy's young, unblemished, eighteen-year-old skin flickered through his mind and, again, he felt the shock he'd experienced when it had occurred to him just hcw old he was when she was born. When she was *born*, for Christ's sake. And here he was, dressed up in a young man's clothes, actually contemplating taking her out to dinner. He must be crazy.

When he arrived at her cottage, piano music was coming from within. He rang the bell and stood back on the path, admiring the pretty orchard garden, listening as the sound of a thrush mingled with the sounds of the piano. After a while he rang again. The music continued. Eventually he lifted a cautious hand and pushed at the front door. As he did so, the music increased in volume. It was powerful stirring music that sounded familiar to Alexis, yet which he couldn't identify. For a moment he just stood there in the tiny hall, listening, and looking at his ridiculous reflection in the glass of a carved walnut hall-stand, feeling his heart beat faster and faster. Then, forcing himself to move, he pushed at the sitting-room door.

Daisy looked up from her seat at the grand piano and abruptly stopped playing.

'Oh!' she gasped. 'Sorry, I wasn't listening out for the door.'

'Don't worry,' said Alexis. He looked at the piano. 'That sounded powerful stuff.'

'Oh, yes,' Daisy blushed. 'It was Chopin,' she said. There was a pause. 'One of the Etudes,' she added, biting her lip. She blushed again, looked at the book of music in front of her and closed it. Then she looked at Alexis expectantly.

Alexis looked back at her. She was dressed smartly, as though for a school function, in a sleeveless white T-shirt, dark-red flowing skirt and pale tights. Her hair flowed from a velvet band down to her waist in shining dark waves, and she smelt faintly of roses.

Daisy noticed Alexis looking at her and flushed.

'I didn't know how smart . . .' she began hesitantly. 'Do I look all right?'

Alexis stared back at her and nodded. He wanted to say she looked beautiful, but suddenly he felt unable to speak.

'I haven't really gone out much,' said Daisy. 'Since I've been living down here, I mean.'

She got up, awkwardly pushing the piano-stool back, and knocking a pile of music onto the floor. Alexis made a move to pick it up.

'Don't worry,' said Daisy quickly, 'I'll pick it up later.' There was a tiny pause. 'My-my jacket's in the hall,' she added.

'Right,' said Alexis, attempting a cheery tone, holding the door open for her. But his voice sounded strange to his own ears. What the hell was wrong with him? What kind of evening were they going to have, if he couldn't string two words together?

In the dusky hall, Daisy turned suddenly and reached for a jacket hanging on the hall-stand. Alexis, taken by surprise, found himself stepping forward and colliding with her soft warm skin.

138

'Sorry!' he exclaimed.

'Oh, that's all right,' said Daisy shyly. 'I mean, I got in your way.' Her voice fluttered gently through the air, and Alexis felt a dangerous feeling of desire begin to creep inexorably through him.

'Let me help you with that,' he said. He took the jacket from her and held it up, watching as her pale milky arms slid inside the sleeves. Then, suddenly, Daisy turned and looked at him with questioning eyes.

'I wasn't going to ask,' she said, 'but . . . are we . . .' She broke off. 'Is this . . .' She coloured slightly. 'It's just, this is all a bit new to me, and I was just wondering . . .' She tailed away, her cheeks suffused with an embarrassed colour.

Alexis gazed at her, almost paralysed with longing.

'Well, you know . . . this is all a bit new to me, too,' he managed to say. He relaxed a little. 'This is all a bit new to me, too,' he repeated, 'so, let's just play it by ear, shall we?' He looked down at her and smiled. 'It's not really one thing or the other. I just thought it would be nice for us to have dinner together, that's all.'

'Oh,' said Daisy doubtfully. 'OK, then.' And she allowed him to lead her gently out of the cottage into the scented evening air.

The restaurant Alexis had chosen was relatively new in Linningford. It was bright and bustly, with a pale polished wooden floor, mirrors on the walls, huge ferny plants between the tables and splashy water-colours on the walls. Daisy looked around with a delighted smile.

'I like this place!' she exclaimed, as they sat down. 'It's so pretty!'

A waiter came over and presented two enormous menus with a flourish.

'Mademoiselle; monsieur,' he murmured in deferential tones. Daisy beamed at Alexis, who gave the waiter a sharp look. Was the fellow insinuating anything? But the waiter looked blandly back at Alexis and murmured something about an aperitif. Alexis looked at Daisy's glowing face.

'Two glasses of champagne,' he said quietly to the waiter. Then, 'No, make that a bottle.'

When he had gone, they looked at each other. Daisy carefully unfolded her napkin and lay it across her lap. Alexis glanced around the restaurant, as though in search of a topic of conversation, but it was Daisy who spoke first.

'I saw Mrs Kember yesterday,' she said, 'driving along. She didn't see me,' she added humbly. 'I mean, I just saw her through her car window. But I thought . . . poor them.' Her hands fluttered sympathetically.

'Yes, poor old them,' said Alexis, unable to keep a hostile note out of his voice. Daisy stared at him.

'What . . . why . . .'

'Oh . . . I'm sorry,' said Alexis, 'I do feel for them. But it's just—' Daisy stared at him, eyes wide. He sighed. 'I don't suppose it's any great secret.' He looked at her. 'The Kembers are planning to sue Hugh and Ursula on behalf of Katie.'

'Sue them?' Daisy looked at him, aghast. 'What, because it was their swimming-pool?'

'Yes,' said Alexis, 'and because Louise's lawyer friend has convinced them, no doubt, that they can get lots of money out of Hugh and Ursula.'

'And can . . . can they?' Alexis shrugged.

'Good question. Possibly, yes.'

'But . . .' Daisy hesitated. 'I expect I'm very ignorant,' she said cautiously. Alexis grinned encouragingly.

'I shouldn't think you are,' he said.

'But . . . don't you have to do something wrong to be sued? I mean, they didn't do anything wrong, did they?' Alexis shrugged.

'Define "wrong". Is it wrong to invite people to swim

140

in your pool without providing a life guard?' Daisy stared at him.

'But that's silly,' she said. 'If it's someone's *house* . . .' Alexis shrugged again.

'If you invite people to your house, you have a duty towards them.' He sighed. 'That's the law.'

There was a pause. Daisy gazed at Alexis, a bewildered look on her face.

'It's really difficult,' she said. 'It was so awful, the accident, and I feel really sorry for the little girl, and it . . . it would be really good if she could get some money.' She stopped. 'But going to court seems so horrible. And I thought they were friends.'

'They were,' said Alexis, almost to himself. 'Not for much longer.' He glanced at Daisy. She was staring sombrely down at the tablecloth. 'What are we talking about!' he exclaimed. 'Let's not think about such depressing things.' He looked up and his expression changed. 'Look, just in time!'

The waiter had arrived with the champagne. As he popped it open, a cautious smile reappeared on Daisy's face. She looked at Alexis and blushed.

'Champagne,' she said, looking at her bubbling glass. 'Gosh—'

'You don't have to have it if you don't want it,' said Alexis seriously. 'I should have asked you first. But don't worry, we can order something else. Waiter . . .'

Daisy gasped.

'No, I didn't mean . . . honestly . . .' She broke off as she saw Alexis's face.

'You're teasing me,' she said in surprise.

'Yes,' said Alexis. 'Do you mind?'

'No,' said Daisy slowly. She looked at Alexis, at his brown face and his clever eyes and his crinkly smile, and she smiled back. 'No, I don't . . . I don't mind at all.'

*   *   *

141

Later on, when they had finished eating, Alexis slid his palm across the table and picked up Daisy's hand.

'Look at those pianist's fingers,' he said admiringly. 'I bet you've got more muscle in those than I've got in . . .'

'Your little finger,' suggested Daisy, whose cheeks had become rather pink from the champagne. 'Oh no. That doesn't work.' She looked disparagingly at the hand still on the table. 'The trouble with playing the piano', she said, 'is you never get to have long nails. Mine are horrible, *and* I bite them.'

'They're beautiful,' said Alexis. He looked at her. 'You're beautiful.' Daisy blushed.

'It's been a lovely dinner,' she said in a rather flustered voice. 'I've really enjoyed it.'

'Good,' said Alexis.

He looked at her carefully for a second, then casually relaxed his grip on her hand. An infinitesimal beat of silence passed. Daisy didn't move her hand away. Alexis stared downwards and counted to five. An unspeakable excitement was growing inside him. Slowly he raised his head and looked straight at her. A fiery red had covered her cheeks; her eyes were lowered; her thick dark lashes were casting shadows on her face. Gradually, scarcely daring to breathe, he closed his hand over hers again.

While Alexis ordered the bill and paid it, neither of them spoke very much. Outside in the street it was dark; a warm indigo-blue summer darkness, punctuated by glowing shop signs, and snatches of low laughter, and glimpses of brightly coloured dresses under yellow street lamps. They walked silently to the car. Daisy found that she had begun to shiver. The leather seats of Alexis's car seemed cold and unforgiving as she got in; her legs were trembling and she could think of nothing to say.

'I must hear you play properly some time,' said Alexis

conversationally, as he switched on the engine.

'Oh, yes,' said Daisy. 'Well . . . I'm doing a concert in Linningford at the beginning of September.'

'Splendid!' said Alexis. 'What is it?'

'A piano concerto,' said Daisy shyly, 'with the Linningford Symphony Orchestra.'

'Really?' said Alexis. 'I am impressed.' He glanced sideways at Daisy. 'That must be very exciting,' he said.

'Yes, it is,' said Daisy. She could feel her voice trembling and clasped her hands nervously. What was going to happen when they got out of the car? she thought frantically. Was Alexis going to want to come in? Was he going to kiss her? Was he going to want to . . .

'Which piano concerto?' Alexis asked, suddenly breaking the silence. Daisy gave a little jump.

'Oh!' she gasped. 'Er . . . Brahms. The second.'

'I don't know it, I'm afraid,' said Alexis easily. 'I'm not very well up on Brahms.'

'Oh, it's really beautiful,' said Daisy earnestly. There was a pause. Then the car stopped and she looked up, startled, at Alexis. 'Why are we stopping?' she said faintly.

'Because we're here.' Alexis turned and smiled at her. 'Look, there's your cottage.'

'Oh, yes.' Daisy's voice was no more than a husky whisper and she was quivering with nerves. Alexis gazed at her. Her lips were trembling; her dark eyes darted about. He felt as though he had trapped a baby deer inside his car.

Abruptly, he opened his door. Before Daisy could think to move, he was round the other side of the car and gallantly opening the passenger door for her, bowing in a flowery manner that made her giggle, in spite of herself.

'Well, good night,' he said in friendly tones. 'Thank you very much for coming.'

'Well, thank *you*,' said Daisy, feeling her heart

pounding painfully in her chest. She looked at Alexis, just visible in the darkness. He took a step forward and she began to breathe a little more quickly.

'It was . . . good fun,' he said.

'Yes, it was,' managed Daisy.

There was a silence. Then, slowly, gradually, Alexis bent his head towards her. He kissed her softly once on the cheek. Then, before she could say anything, before she could even breathe, he was tilting his head slightly, moving a hand up to support the back of her head, and bringing his lips down onto hers. Daisy closed her eyes, and felt his warm lips, and his mouth gently opening hers, and a cool breeze blowing through her hair, and couldn't think of anything else. When he lifted his head, she stared back, slightly dazed, and numb to the nerves leaping in her stomach. I would, she suddenly found herself thinking, if he wanted to . . . I would say yes. A quivering anticipation began to build inside her, but already he was moving away, towards the car.

'I've got to go, I'm afraid,' he said regretfully. He gave her a little smile. 'Have you got your key?'

'Y-yes,' said Daisy confusedly.

'I'll wait until you're safely in,' Alexis said. He opened his door. 'How about', he added casually, 'meeting up again sometime?'

'Yes,' said Daisy. Her words seemed to be struggling to come out. 'Th-that would be nice.'

'I could come round for coffee tomorrow,' said Alexis. 'Unless you're busy practising?' Daisy swallowed.

'No,' she said slowly, 'I'm not busy.'

'Good,' said Alexis. 'See you tomorrow.'

'See you then,' said Daisy.

She crossed the road, walked down the path, waved shyly at Alexis, then opened the door of the cottage and disappeared. Alexis sat quite still for a few seconds, then started the engine of his car, put his foot down, and drove off into the darkness.

Chapter Ten

The news that the Kembers were going to sue the
Delaneys over Katie's accident spread quickly through
the village amidst a welter of contrary reports and
confused opinion. No-one seemed to be quite sure what
the details were, or to have more than a vague third-
hand account. Eventually, frustrated by hearing a
number of conflicting accounts of the story, Sylvia
Seddon-Wilson decided to organize a fund-raising
coffee-morning in aid of Katie's appeal. She invited all
the ladies of the village, including Louise, Ursula and
Meredith.

'They won't come, of course,' she said confidently, as
she sat at breakfast, licking envelopes. James, her
husband, looked politely up from *The Financial Times*.

'Who won't?'

'Well, Louise won't, for a start. She'll be far too busy.'
James's brow wrinkled.

'Which one's Louise?' Sylvia sighed impatiently.

'You *know*, James. I told you. The mother of the little
girl who had the accident.'

'Oh, yes.' James frowned. 'Bloody awful business.
How's she doing?' he added. 'The little girl?' Sylvia
paused, mid-lick.

'Apparently, she's woken up from her coma. But . . .'
she fixed James with an impressive look '. . . she's been
brain damaged. And the latest is that they're taking the
Delaneys to court. Suing them. Can you believe it?'

'Jesus Christ.' James shuddered and took a sip of
coffee. He looked at Sylvia as though expecting more,

but she was licking envelopes again, so he turned his gaze back to the paper. But his attention wandered, and after a few seconds he put the paper down.

'So – how bad is it?'

'What?' Sylvia's eyebrows rose enquiringly.

'How badly has the little girl been brain damaged?'

'Oh,' Sylvia shrugged, 'I don't know.'

'Have you been to visit her?' Sylvia flushed slightly.

'No,' she said shortly. 'And don't look at me like that! You know I'm no good in hospitals.' She finished licking the envelope she was holding and put it down on the pile by her plate. 'I'm holding this coffee-morning instead,' she added, 'as a gesture of support.'

'Support!' James guffawed with laughter.

'It'll be a fund-raising occasion,' said Sylvia angrily, 'so you can stop laughing, James.'

'Oh, a fund-raising occasion.' James grinned derisively. 'I know your fund-raising methods. A sponsored gossip, is it? Fifty pence for every piece of information provided, whether true or not.'

'Oh, shut up,' cried Sylvia. She picked up a piece of toast and bit into it crossly. 'Anyway,' she added irrelevantly, 'I thought you were supposed to be in Antwerp this week.'

'I'm not going till Thursday.'

'Good,' said Sylvia, 'you'll be out of the way for my coffee-morning. How long are you there?'

'Three days. Then I'm flying straight to Oslo.'

'Even better,' said Sylvia. She leaned back in her chair and stretched her arms lazily. 'Well, you needn't hurry back.'

'Don't worry, my darling,' said James, grinning at her, 'I won't.'

By eleven o'clock on the day of the coffee-morning, fourteen ladies had assembled in Sylvia's drawing-room, and all were looking expectantly at the door.

146

From the hall could be heard the rather flustered tones of Mary Tracey, who had just arrived. Mary, it was tacitly acknowledged by all, must know more about the whole affair than any of them. After all, she seemed to be Louise's closest friend in the village.

And so, in deference to her, nobody began speaking on the subject of the swimming-pool accident until she had been persuaded to entrust baby Luke to the tender care of Mrs Greenly in the kitchen, had been led into the room, and then ensconced on a large Knole sofa in the centre of the room. Sylvia smiled warmly at her and held out a cup of coffee.

'There you are,' she said sweetly. 'I hope it's not too strong.'

'Oh, er, no,' said Mary, turning rather pink. 'I'm sure it's fine. Lovely.'

Mary didn't usually attend Sylvia's coffee-mornings, considering them a bit fancy for her, especially now she had Luke to consider. But Sylvia had been so charming on the telephone that she had felt unable to refuse. Now she looked around in slight alarm; she was probably the youngest woman in the room, and definitely the shabbiest.

There was a pause, as Sylvia returned to her own chair and took a sip of coffee. Then she drew breath. Everybody looked up.

'And so, Mary,' she said in sympathetic tones. 'How is poor little Katie?' Mary swallowed. Every eye seemed to be on her.

'Well,' she began hesitatingly, 'she's woken up from the coma.'

There was a general sigh of relief.

'Thank goodness for that,' said Mrs Prendergast, a large lady who lived across the road from Sylvia.

'That's marvellous news!' said someone else, rather too gaily for Mary's liking.

'Yes,' added Mary quickly, 'but that doesn't mean

she's better. She's still very woozy, and they say . . .' she swallowed and took a sip of coffee, '. . . they say she'll probably be brain damaged.' Her eyes suddenly filled with tears. What was wrong with her? she thought furiously. She'd known all about Katie for days. She should be able to speak more matter-of-factly about it, but somehow, telling all these women brought the horror of it back to her all over again. She felt a tear trickle down her cheek.

'Oh, Mary!' Suddenly Sylvia was by her side, stroking her hand. 'Don't talk about it if you don't want to.'

'No, it's all right.' Mary struggled to control herself.

'It's just that we're all so concerned about the poor little thing,' continued Sylvia.

'Brain damage!' murmured one of the ladies sitting by the window. 'How frightful.'

'She won't be a . . . you know, a total . . .' Mary searched for an acceptable word, and gave up. 'You know. And there is a small chance she might recover completely.' She looked around the room hopefully, but none of the other ladies looked convinced by this show of optimism. They exchanged determinedly sombre glances.

'How shattering it must be for them,' exclaimed Mrs Prendergast, giving a little shudder. 'I don't know how I'd cope.'

'Awful!'

'Dreadful!' There was a short respectful pause, then Sylvia turned to Mary.

'But I gather', she said in vague tones, 'that there's some talk of compensation? Damages? A court case?' She cocked her head enquiringly. There was a tiny rustling sound as all the ladies moved forward on their seats.

'Well,' began Mary. She looked around. 'Yes, that's right. Louise and Barnaby are taking the Delaneys to court. Apparently . . .' She paused and wiped her nose.

'Apparently the Delaneys were negligent. The diving-board was dangerous.'

Mrs Prendergast gasped.

'How horrendous!' she cried. 'I mean, my own children used to swim in that pool! They used to dive off that board all the time!'

'So did mine!' chimed in another lady. 'To think it was dangerous all that time! It's criminal!' She looked around agitatedly.

'Terrible!' came another voice.

'They haven't actually proved anything yet,' put in Mrs Quint, a quietly spoken woman who had so far contributed nothing to the conversation. 'I don't think it's quite fair to assume it definitely was dangerous. And I have to say, it didn't look particularly dangerous to me.' The general air of excitement subsided slightly, and Mrs Prendergast looked rather aggrievedly at Mrs Quint.

'Well, they wouldn't be taking them to court if they didn't have a case, would they?' she said in triumphant tones.

There was a pause. No-one seemed able to contradict that assertion.

'Well, I think those Kembers should go for everything they can get,' said Janice Sharp, who had a weekend cottage in Melbrook and had come down especially for Sylvia's coffee-morning. 'Good luck to them! I mean, the Delaneys certainly look as though they can afford it.' Mrs Prendergast nodded.

'Did you know they've got houses all over Europe?' she said, brushing crumbs vigorously off her lap.

'Are you sure?' said Mrs Quint.

'Oh, yes,' said Mrs Prendergast confidently. 'One in France, certainly, and then I think there's one in Italy and one somewhere else . . . They've got all that, but they're too mean to keep their pool safe for our children to swim in! It's outrageous!'

'I don't know,' said Mrs Quint dubiously. 'I'm not sure they're as rich as that, and I assume the Kembers will be suing for a very large amount?'

All eyes turned to Mary, who blushed. She herself had been astounded when she'd heard the sort of sums that were being bandied about by Cassian and Louise. Staggered. But Cassian had been quick to show her exactly why Katie needed so much money and why it would be letting her down to claim any less. Mary blushed even harder as she remembered Cassian sitting next to her at Louise's kitchen table, touching her bare arm with the soft cotton of his shirt; as she remembered the faint expensive scent of his aftershave and the way he smiled at her . . . Then, as she realized everyone was waiting for an answer, she shook her head impatiently to clear her thoughts, took a breath and said abruptly, 'About half a million pounds. Or thereabouts.' There was a sharp intake of breath around her.

'What?'

'You must be joking!'

Even Sylvia was surprised.

'Is that true, Mary?' she said. 'Are they really going to ask for that much?'

'So they say.' Suddenly Mary became aware of the goggle eyes around her, and wondered whether she ought not to have kept some pieces of information to herself. But it was too late, exclamations of astonishment were breaking out all around the room. Mrs Prendergast was nodding at her neighbour and saying repeatedly, 'I'm not at all surprised,' in a defiant voice, as though daring someone to contradict her.

'Imagine,' said Janice Sharp. 'Half a million pounds!'

'That's a lot of money,' said Mrs Quint soberly. 'Let's hope the Delaneys are insured.'

Mary began to feel slightly defensive.

'Well, Katie's been very badly hurt!' she exclaimed.

'She may need special care for years. She deserves the money.'

'Oh, I'm not saying . . .' began Mrs Quint. She was interrupted by the sound of the doorbell. Sylvia stood up.

'Do excuse me,' she said, bestowing a gracious smile around the room, 'and help yourselves to more coffee.'

There was animated chatter while she was gone. Mrs Quint tried to introduce a subject of more general interest into the conversation, but no-one appeared interested in the plight of her garden, nor willing to divulge their holiday plans.

'I just think', Mrs Prendergast was saying as the door opened, 'that if people are actually charging you to use their pool, then they jolly well have a responsibility . . .'

Suddenly she was interrupted by Sylvia speaking from outside the room. Her voice was deliberately raised in a mixture of delight and malice, and she was saying, 'Have you got time for a quick cup of coffee, Ursula?'

A couple of the ladies gasped. Mrs Prendergast's head shot round. There, in the doorway, stood Ursula Delaney, with a benign expression on her face and a cake, sprinkled with almonds, balanced on her upturned hands.

'Hello, everyone,' she said simply. 'I can't stay, I'm afraid, but I wanted to contribute a little something.'

'Not to worry, Ursula,' said Sylvia, giving an amused little grin round the room. 'I'd say it's enough that you've come at all. You know most people here, don't you?' she added.

'I think so,' said Ursula, smiling vaguely around. She walked over to the table and deposited her cake. As she looked up again, there was an embarrassed shuffling. Nobody spoke.

'Dear me!' she exclaimed. 'Please don't stop the

151

conversation just because of me. What were you talking about?'

There was a dreadful little silence. Mary Tracey felt her cheeks growing hotter and hotter. Then Mrs Quint cleared her throat.

'I was talking', she said firmly, 'about the dreadful state of my garden.' She looked severely at Mrs Prendergast. 'Wasn't I?'

'Oh yes,' said Mrs Prendergast hastily. 'Yes, you were. And . . . and so was I,' she added. 'Mine's in a terrible state, too.'

'So is mine,' chimed in several voices. Ursula looked around, a puzzled expression on her face.

'Oh dear,' she said, 'what bad luck! Our garden seems to be doing quite well.' She gazed out of the window with a thoughtful expression on her face. 'We do have very good mulch,' she said eventually. 'Perhaps that's the answer.'

She looked around with raised questioning eyebrows. But no-one seemed to have a reply.

Chapter Eleven

Two weeks later a letter arrived for Hugh from his insurance company. He opened it at breakfast, read it, then silently put it back into the envelope.

'What?' said Meredith, whose eyes had homed in sharply on the logo on the front of the envelope. 'What did they say?'

Ever since the announcement that Hugh and Ursula were going to be sued, Meredith had found herself waking every morning with an urgent fighting energy which she longed to put to good use. But Alexis had informed her candidly that there was little she could do in such early days, and he'd added again that the case was likely to last a very long time – maybe years.

Years of this tension? Meredith couldn't stand the thought, and she knew she wasn't the only one who was feeling the strain. While she'd been striding around the house with an impotent adrenalin; unable to work; unable to relax, Hugh had retreated silently into himself. His face was subdued and haggard; he'd admitted he wasn't sleeping well.

'What did they say?' Meredith repeated, trying not to sound impatient.

Hugh looked up. He glanced at Ursula, who was peacefully eating a boiled egg and reading the *Daily Mail*, then attempted to smile optimistically at Meredith, but his eyes had a blank devastated look.

'They think it's most unlikely that they would be able to meet any claim for damages arising from a non-domestic use of the pool. They say . . .' he gazed down at the letter, 'they say that if we'd informed them that we were using it for a public function, they could have arranged additional cover. But we didn't.' Hugh put down the letter and looked bleakly at Meredith. 'Basically, they say they're not going to pay.'

'Bastards!' exclaimed Meredith. 'They're just using any excuse to weasel out of it!'

'Maybe,' said Hugh. He rubbed his face miserably. 'But maybe they're right. Maybe I should have given them a call; arranged extra insurance. It just never occurred to me . . .' He broke off.

'Let me see the letter,' demanded Meredith. She grabbed the sheet from Hugh's plate and scanned it. 'It doesn't say they definitely won't pay,' she said, after a few minutes. 'It just says probably.'

'I know,' said Hugh, 'but frankly, I don't hold out much hope that they'll change their minds.'

Meredith looked at the letter again.

'I guess you're right,' she said. She leaned backwards in her chair and looked distantly out of the window. She couldn't quite bear to meet Hugh's gaze; to feel the unspoken implications of this letter flickering fearfully from his eyes to hers – bypassing Ursula, as did so many of their tacit communications. What if Hugh and Ursula somehow lost the case? she found herself thinking. What if they had to pay out huge damages? Hundreds of thousands of pounds? What would they do?

A bubbling fury rose up in Meredith and abruptly she pushed her chair back.

'I'm going out,' she said, and left the room before either Hugh or Ursula could comment.

She stalked out of the drive of Devenish House, and without really knowing what her intention was, strode briskly and deliberately towards Larch Tree Cottage, at the other end of the village. A vision of Hugh's defeated eyes burned in her brain, making her stride more and more quickly, and she reached her destination panting slightly and wondering what she was about to do, exactly. But as she neared Larch Tree Cottage, she saw Louise coming out of the front door, and all hesitation disappeared.

'I just thought you might like to know', she said in a harsh abrasive voice, ignoring Louise's gasp of surprise, 'that it looks like our insurers are pulling out. So if you do win your God-awful case, Hugh and Ursula will have to pay you out of their own pocket and they'll probably be ruined. Just so you know.' She stopped halfway down the path, and looked at Louise for a reaction.

'I'm afraid,' began Louise in a shaky, but rather formal voice, 'I really don't think . . .'

'No, you don't, do you?' broke in Meredith angrily. 'You don't think at all. If you did, you wouldn't be bringing this fucking case to court. You wouldn't be ruining the lives of two perfectly innocent people!'

'I'm not . . .'

'Do you know what this is going to do to them?'

'Well, do you know what this accident has done to us?' interrupted Louise, with sudden indignation. 'Do you know what we've been going through? My God, you haven't even visited Katie in hospital! None of you! You haven't seen what state she's in! So don't start talking about ruining lives. You've no idea what this is like for us!' Louise's eyes blazed, blue and angry, at Meredith.

'The reason we haven't been to the hospital is because you're suing us!' Meredith's voice rose, furious, through the air. 'Did that ever occur to you? We've been advised not to go near you. If you'd only drop the stupid case, we could help! We want to help!'

A smooth voice interrupted her.

'If you want to help, you can leave the premises of my client at once.'

Both women's heads whipped round. It was Cassian,

155

coming out of the front door. Meredith scowled at him.

'Yes,' said Louise, emboldened by his arrival. 'Just leave me alone, Meredith.'

'Oh, for Christ's sake,' said Meredith scornfully, 'I'll go, then. But just for the record, I do have some idea what you're going through, you know . . .'

'Will you please stop harassing my client,' interrupted Cassian impatiently. Meredith ignored him and looked directly at Louise.

'In case you'd forgotten, my husband went into a coma a few years ago, like your daughter. The difference is, he died.' She broke off suddenly and Louise flushed faintly.

'I can tell you now,' Cassian said, 'this outburst isn't helping your case at all.' He took out a notebook and began to write in it.

'And the other difference is,' said Meredith curtly, 'I just accepted it. I didn't look around for someone to blame, or try to make money out of it.'

'I must request . . .' began Cassian again.

'Oh, fuck off, you little toad,' interrupted Meredith. Louise broke in, without looking at Cassian.

'Well, OK, so your husband died,' she said, in a jerky voice, 'but maybe what's happened to Katie is worse; she could be brain damaged for life!'

'Louise,' snapped Cassian, 'this conversation has got to stop. Go and get in the car.' Louise glanced at him hesitantly, then obeyed.

'Right,' said Cassian. He brought out a mobile phone. 'Now,' he said to Meredith. 'I can call the police – or you can go now.'

Without answering, Meredith began to walk back down the path. She stopped as she passed the car and tried to catch Louise's eye, but Louise frowned and looked away. Meredith shrugged, and carried on walking back to Devenish House.

*   *   *

Hugh had spent the rest of breakfast patiently explaining to Ursula the meaning of the letter from the insurers, trying to make the situation quite clear, without frightening her. When he'd finished, she looked at him with a face only mildly wrinkled with anxiety, and said, 'Oh dear.'

And Hugh had stared back at her, feeling an uncharacteristic frustration rising through him. Is that all you can say? he wanted to shout. Don't you see what this means for us? But instead of shouting, he clenched his fists under the table and gazed out of the window, and tried to calm his pounding, angry, terrified heart.

Ursula, meanwhile, sat in silence, consumed by difficult and rather perplexing thoughts. She leaned back in her chair and screwed up her face, and when Hugh got up to leave the table, she nodded absently at him as though he were a stranger on a train. She sat for another ten minutes or so after he had gone, then abruptly came to a conclusion. Leaving the dishes for Mrs Viney, who came in twice a week to clean the house, Ursula quickly went upstairs to the pretty satinwood dressing-table which she used as a desk. She sat down, took out a piece of rough paper and, with a missionary zeal, began to compose a letter.

The next day, when everybody had gone out, Ursula left Devenish House clutching a large basket and a pale mauve envelope. She walked briskly through the village, deserted at that hour of the morning, until she reached Larch Tree Cottage.

She was well aware that she was repeating the path which Meredith had taken just the day before; that Alexis would be furious if he discovered what she was doing; that she shouldn't be there at all, but a firm belief in what she was doing kept her step from faltering. Her mission, she thought, was very different from poor Meredith's outburst.

157

Ursula had been astonished when Meredith confessed to her confrontation with Louise. Yelling in the street! What were they all coming to? It just showed, she thought, that nobody was quite themselves at the moment. Indeed, this was one of the very points she had put in her letter to Louise.

Ursula had great hopes of her letter. She had toiled over it for almost three hours the previous day, then had written it out neatly before hurrying into Linningford to buy a selection of toys. Now she looked at the envelope, addressed to Mrs Barnaby Kember, and felt her heart give a flutter of hope. Alexis might insist, she thought, that they should avoid contact with the Kembers, but what harm could an honest letter do? Surely Louise would melt when she read Ursula's heartfelt appeal – from one mother to another? Surely she would drop this silly case?

She had intended simply to leave the basket in the porch and then go, but outside the cottage, playing on the grassy verge in a rather desultory way, was Amelia. She looked up as Ursula approached.

'Hello, Mrs Delaney,' she said.

'Hello, Amelia,' said Ursula, in surprise. 'Shouldn't you be at school?'

'I've got an earache,' said Amelia, 'so I'm at home.'

'And is Mummy at home, looking after you?' said Ursula, looking, with sudden alarm, towards the cottage. She certainly didn't want to bump into Louise.

'No, she isn't at home,' said Amelia. Ursula relaxed slightly. 'She's at the hospital,' added Amelia grumpily, giving the verge a little kick. 'She's *always* at the hospital.'

'Well, dear, I expect she's worried about Katie,' said Ursula mildly.

'I had an earache,' continued Amelia doggedly, 'and I told her, and all she said was, "Oh, buck up, Amelia." And then it hurt so much I cried in the night, and she took me to the doctor, and all he said was "How's Katie?" And now', she added, with stony emphasis, 'I'm ill too, but I'm being looked after by Mary, and Mummy's gone to see Katie, like she always does.'

Ursula gazed at Amelia in a sudden discomfiture. Poor child. Of course she must be feeling rather left out.

'I hate Katie,' said Amelia, and darted a quick defiant glance at Ursula. Ursula essayed a hesitant smile.

'I'm sure you don't really,' she said. Amelia stared rigidly at Ursula for a few seconds, then flushed and looked away.

'But look,' said Ursula hurriedly. 'Look what I've brought you.' She put a hand into the basket and pulled out the first toy that her hand touched. It was a Barbie doll, dressed in a pink leotard and encased in a shiny wrapper. Amelia stared at it.

'For me?' she said suspiciously. 'You brought this for me?'

'Yes,' said Ursula, hoping she sounded convincing. 'Some of these toys are for Katie, and . . . some of them are for you.' Amelia turned the doll round in her hands for a silent minute. Then, suddenly, she gave a sob.

'I don't want it,' she wailed. 'I want Katie to have it.'

With that she began to cry properly, with splashy tears and a runny nose, and without stopping to think, Ursula sat down on the verge and took Amelia into her arms. Amelia buried her head in Ursula's soft lavender-scented blouse.

'Don't worry,' soothed Ursula, 'everything will be all right.'

Amelia looked up at Ursula, her face red and her eyes wet.

'Katie's all bald on her head, and she's got a horrible tube in her arm,' she said jerkily. Ursula felt an unpleasant twinge in her stomach, but she ignored it and continued stroking Amelia's hair. 'And she can't speak properly,' carried on Amelia, 'and she didn't

159

know who I was.' She gave a small shudder. 'I said, "Hello, Katie, it's me, Amelia," but she just looked at me, as if she didn't even *recognize* me, and then she went back to sleep. She didn't even look at the cards we made for her in Art. Everybody made a card,' she added, 'even Mrs Jacob. And we made a tape.'

Ursula clasped Amelia more tightly. Painful memories of Simon, which she thought she had firmly buried, were beginning to jump to the surface of her mind. To distract herself, she said to Amelia, trying to adopt a reassuring voice, 'Well, now, I wouldn't worry about any of that. Katie's still half asleep, you know.'

'That's what Mummy said,' said Amelia, looking suspiciously at Ursula. 'But Sarah Wyatt, in my form, said she saw a film where the girl had a coma and she died. She said Katie was going to *die*.' She broke into fresh sobs.

'Nonsense,' said Ursula briskly. 'Katie will get much better. You'll see. You'll see.'

There was a short pause. Ursula began to look around anxiously. It occurred to her that Mary must be wondering where Amelia had got to. She shifted slightly, as though to get up, but Amelia still clung to her. Suddenly she said, in a gasping voice, 'It was all my fault.' Ursula jumped, genuinely startled.

'No!' she exclaimed. 'Amelia! You mustn't think that! Whatever gave you that idea?'

'It was my fault,' repeated Amelia hopelessly. 'Katie only tried to do a backward dive because I was doing them. She always copies me.' She looked up at Ursula, entreatingly.

'It was me that wanted to go swimming!' she wailed, and gave a sudden desperate sob. 'Daddy wanted to go f-fishing, but I wanted to go swimming instead, an-and Katie copied me. And then she copied me doing a back dive, too. If I hadn't . . .' She stopped and wiped her nose with her hand. 'If I hadn't done one, then Katie wouldn't have either . . .'

Ursula stared back at Amelia. For a panicked second she could think of nothing to say; her mind was blank and empty. But that wasn't good enough, she told herself frantically. Here was a troubled child, relying on her for comfort and reassurance; she must say something. She *must*.

'That's utter nonsense,' she said at last, trying to adopt an authoritative tone. 'I've never heard anything so silly.' Amelia gazed at her, silent but unconvinced. 'Katie only copies you sometimes,' continued Ursula, cautiously feeling her way, 'but mostly she does exactly what she wants, whether you've been doing it or not. She only came swimming because she wanted to – and she was only doing a back dive because she felt like it.' Ursula scanned Amelia's face for a reaction. 'It was nothing to do with you,' she added for good measure.

Amelia's face was unmoved. Ursula cast round anxiously in her mind for something more persuasive to say.

'I mean,' she added suddenly, 'I'm sure you've both seen professional divers on the television doing splendid back dives, but you're not saying it's their fault, are you?' Slowly, reluctantly, Amelia shook her head. 'Well, then,' said Ursula, with an air of confidence she was far from feeling, 'that proves my point.' She gave Amelia a cheerful distracting smile. 'Now, let's have no more of these silly thoughts.'

She glanced at the doll still in Amelia's hand.

'What are you going to call her? She really is yours to keep, you know.' Amelia slowly looked down at the Barbie doll.

'I'm going to call her Katie,' she said in a low voice. She rubbed her face, took a breath, and began to tear off the packaging.

'Good,' said Ursula. 'Now, why don't you take in the

161

rest of these toys and show Mary? And perhaps Mummy will let you take them to the hospital.'

She picked up the pale mauve envelope sitting on top of the basket.

'And, Amelia,' she said, 'be sure to give this envelope straight to Mary, or Mummy. Don't drop it or forget about it.' Amelia took the envelope and looked at it.

'What is it?' she said.

'Well . . .' said Ursula hesitantly. 'It's . . . it's some money. For Katie. For all of you really. Just a little present from me, and a letter for Mummy.' She got to her feet. 'Now, in you go,' she said.

She watched as Amelia carried the basket in through the gate. Then, hurriedly, she began to walk away, back home, before anyone saw her.

Later on that day, Alexis sat down with Hugh, Ursula and Meredith in the kitchen of Devenish House.

'Until we actually see a writ and see what claims are being made,' he said, 'we can't begin to prepare a defence.' He looked at Hugh. 'But the earlier we start thinking about it, the better. So I'm working on a few assumptions which I think are safe to make.' He glanced down at a sheet of paper.

'They'll be suing you under the Occupier's Liability Act.' He read aloud. '"An occupier owes to a visitor a duty to take such care as in all the circumstances of the case is reasonable to see that the visitor will be reasonably safe in using the premises for the purposes for which he is invited or permitted by the occupier to be there, except insofar as the occupier has validly extended, restricted, modified or excluded that duty by agreement or otherwise."'

Alexis finished and looked up at his audience. Hugh's face was downcast; Ursula's was bewildered. Only Meredith looked back at him with animation in her face.

'You mean', she said, 'that what we should have had

162

is a notice up, saying, "We do not accept responsibility for your children's safety".'

'Perhaps that would have helped,' said Alexis slowly. 'Although there are some duties you can't simply opt out of by putting up a notice, especially if you've charged at the door.' He sighed. 'This business of taking money for charity confuses the matter.'

'Or else we could have put up a notice saying, "Please do not use the swimming-pool",' said Meredith, in a voice suddenly scorched with sarcasm. 'We could have charged people just to come in and *look* at the pool.'

'Meredith,' began Alexis. She ignored him.

'Or perhaps even that's too dangerous,' she exclaimed. 'Of course! We could have sent everybody a Polaroid of the pool and told them to stay at home. That would have been nice and safe, wouldn't it?' She looked at Alexis with scornful eyes. He sighed.

'You know, you're not being entirely helpful.'

'Well, for Christ's sake!' she exclaimed. 'It's just so . . .' She broke off, as the kettle came to a screeching boil behind her. 'OK, OK,' she said, and gave Alexis a quick grin. 'I'll be helpful. Who wants some coffee?'

As she spooned coffee into the coffee-maker, Alexis turned back to his notes.

'The Act states that an occupier must be prepared for children to be less careful than adults,' he read. Hugh looked up.

'Meaning what, exactly?' Alexis sighed.

'There's nothing exact about it,' he said. 'You're supposed to take into account that children find certain things alluring, and that they haven't got the sense to see that they're dangerous.'

'Oh, come on,' said Meredith impatiently, bringing a cup of coffee over and putting it in front of Alexis. 'A diving-board isn't *alluring*. It's not some kind of gingerbread house. It's a diving-board, period. Everyone knows what a diving-board is, for Christ's sake.' Alexis looked up at her.

'I'm not giving you my own opinion,' he said patiently. 'I'm just trying to explain the law to you.' Meredith paused and ran an exasperated hand through her hair.

'I know,' she said, exhaling slowly. 'I'm sorry. I'm not mad at you. It just all seems such a load of bullshit.'

'I know,' said Alexis. He gave her a sudden smile. 'Haven't I always warned you, keep well away from lawyers?'

To his surprise, Meredith didn't smile back. She flushed slightly and turned away. But before Alexis could react to this, his attention was distracted by Ursula.

'I did say to Louise, at the time, that the children really should calm down a bit,' she was saying, thoughtfully. Her face crumpled slightly. 'Next time, I don't think we should allow children to go on the diving-board.'

'Next time?' Meredith's voice rang harshly through the air. Ursula looked back at her benignly. 'Ursula,' Meredith said more gently, 'I don't honestly think there'll be a next time. I don't think we'll be having any more Swimming Days. Not for a while.'

'Oh!' Ursula raised a distressed hand to her mouth. 'I hadn't even thought . . .' But before she could finish, Alexis broke in thoughtfully.

'Are you saying you actually gave Louise a warning, Ursula?' Ursula looked at him, surprised.

'Well,' she said hesitantly, 'I wouldn't say it was exactly a warning, but I did say something to her. It was the children, you see,' she explained. 'They were getting rather overexcited. And I said . . .' She stopped and looked at Alexis. He had picked up a pen and was staring at her, waiting for her to continue. 'Is this important?' she faltered.

'It could be,' said Alexis. 'It could be crucial. If you actually *warned* Louise and she took no notice . . .' He looked at Ursula. 'Listen, Ursula,' he said. 'I want you to try to remember exactly what you said to Louise. Your exact words.' Ursula stared back at him uncertainly.

'Well,' she said eventually, her voice quavering slightly. 'I went up to Louise, and . . .' She broke off. 'Or did Louise come up to me?' She looked at Alexis anxiously. Alexis put down his pen.

'I tell you what,' he said kindly, 'you try to remember later on, when it's a bit quieter, and write it all down. And try to remember exactly how you said it. For example, Louise couldn't possibly have thought you were joking, could she?'

'Oh,' said Ursula. 'No, I don't *think* so. Although,' she added doubtfully, 'you never know. Sometimes I make a joke and nobody realizes . . . so it could well have been the other way around, couldn't it?' Alexis looked blank.

'Yes,' he said eventually. 'I suppose so.'

Meredith was looking at him. 'So what are you getting at?' she said slowly. 'That Louise is some kind of irresponsible mother? That *she* was negligent? Is that what we're going to say?' Alexis met her eyes unflinchingly.

'If we need to, then yes,' he said steadily. 'We're going to need all the ammunition we can get. If we can somehow show that Louise was at fault . . .'

'At fault?' Ursula looked up, perturbed. 'Louise wasn't to blame, surely?' She looked anxiously at Hugh, who was still staring downwards. 'Hugh, are you listening to what they're saying? That poor Louise was to blame for Katie's accident.'

'We don't really think she was to blame, Ursula,' said Meredith patiently. 'But Alexis is right. We've got to use every defence we've got. I mean, look at Louise; she's blaming us, isn't she? We can't just stand back and say nothing.'

'Yes, well . . . you know, I think poor Louise is a little upset at the moment,' said Ursula. 'And Barnaby. They probably don't quite know what they're saying, but that doesn't mean we have to sink to the same level.'

She looked at Meredith with suddenly severe blue eyes.

'I think, dear, that it would be very wrong of us to tell anyone that we thought it was *Louise's* fault that poor Katie got injured.' She paused and added informatively, as though clinching the matter, 'It was just an accident, you know.'

'Of course it was an accident!' cried Meredith impatiently. 'And of course it's wrong to blame Louise, but what else can we do? Ursula, you don't seem to understand. These people are taking you to court. To court! They're going to stand up and say the accident was all your fault, and unless you come up with some sort of defence, they'll end up screwing you for every penny.'

There was a short silence. For a moment Ursula stared at Meredith in distress. Then her brow cleared and a complacent expression appeared on her face.

'You know, dear,' she said, 'I don't believe Louise and Barnaby will go to court.'

'What?' Meredith gazed at Ursula, red with incredulous frustration. 'But they're doing it! This isn't some hypothetical case we're constructing here.' She paused, took a breath, and added, in the clearest, plainest tones she could muster, 'The Kembers have informed you, through their lawyer, that they're taking you to court!'

'I know they have,' said Ursula mildly, 'but I'm sure they'll change their minds when they've calmed down a bit.' She nodded at Meredith. 'You'll see, dear, this will all blow over. I've got a feeling about it.' And she gave Meredith a comfortable, almost secretive smile.

Meredith stared at Ursula as though she couldn't believe her ears. Alexis tactfully intervened.

'Let's hope you're right, Ursula,' he said heartily. He

smiled at her. 'And I agree, it is a bit upsetting having to muster evidence against friends. But I'm afraid you can be quite sure that Louise and Barnaby and all their lawyer chums will be putting together as strong a case against you as they possibly can, so the sensible thing is for us to start thinking about a defence.' He saw Ursula opening her mouth again and added quickly, 'Just in case.' Ursula gave a little shrug.

'Well, Alexis dear – you know best,' she said in agreeable, unconvinced tones.

'Yes, he does,' put in Hugh, surprisingly.

Everyone looked at him. Hugh raised his head, and Meredith noticed, with a pang of shock, the weary pockets of flesh drooping under his eyes. This court case was going to be too much for him, she thought with sudden panic. It was going to drive him down into the ground. Simon's death had hit him hard; he was only just beginning to recover from that; this case might go on for years. He was no longer a young man. How was he going to cope? Fucking Barnaby and Louise, she suddenly thought, with a bitterness that threatened to turn into tears. How *dare* they ruin the lives of the most decent people in the world?

Almost immediately, inevitably, her thoughts switched self-reproachfully to little Katie, lying in hospital, and a noisy, fuzzy guilt began to fill her mind. But over the guilt, above its relentless castigating clamour, her thoughts rang out, loud and defiant. So what? So what if they've suffered. Being a victim doesn't give you the right to trample over everybody else. If Katie's life has been ruined, why should Hugh's automatically be ruined too? Why look for blame? Why . . .

Her thoughts were interrupted by Hugh speaking again.

'The best thing we can all do is to listen to what Alexis has to say and help him as much as we can,' he said.

'And, Ursula, if that means you writing down the comment you made to Louise, then I suggest you do it.' Hugh looked hard at Ursula and she nodded meekly. Then he turned to Alexis with worried eyes. 'I spoke to Barnaby myself that day,' he said heavily, 'we were sitting together. But I honestly can't think of anything that either of us said which might be relevant to our defence.' He shrugged hopelessly. 'Sorry not to be more help.'

Alexis smiled warmly at him.

'Don't worry, Hugh. You'll be a help, all right. This case is only just beginning. There's a long way to go yet. You'll see.'

Cassian stared at Louise. He looked at the pale mauve-coloured letter fluttering in his hand, and again scanned a couple of sentences. Then he looked down at the basket of toys sitting on the table. His expression was incredulous.

'Are these people *trying* to lose, or what?'

Louise shrugged uncomfortably.

'First the girl comes and threatens you, and now this!' Cassian picked up the pale mauve matching envelope, pulled out the wad of notes and began to count them.

'The woman's a moron,' he said cheerfully. 'She's a complete fucking moron!' He looked up at Louise and grinned. 'You know, if I were her lawyer, and I saw what's in this letter, I'd be throwing in the towel right now.'

Chapter Twelve

Louise had not told Barnaby about Meredith's visit. Her instinct had been to telephone him straight away, but Cassian had forcefully persuaded her to keep quiet.

'There's really no point in stirring things up,' he said. 'You know what Barnaby's like, he'll completely over-react.'

But news of the scene had already travelled round the village, and when Barnaby arrived at Larch Tree Cottage the following night to discuss the case, he was full of alarmed rage.

'What did she say to you?' he said, as soon as Louise opened the door. 'That girl, Meredith. Did she threaten you? Someone told me she attacked you in the street!'

Louise stared up at his huge angry face, outraged on her behalf, and felt suddenly touched.

'Yes, well, it was quite frightening,' she said in the gently teasing tones which she hadn't used for months. 'She came at me with . . . with five hand grenades and a machete!' Barnaby gave a small astonished start, then his expression changed to an unwilling grin. Louise giggled.

'I was worried!' he said accusingly.

'Of course you were.' Cassian's smooth tones travelled from the back of the hall. Barnaby looked up and scowled. 'But there's no need for alarm,' continued Cassian, gliding swiftly towards the front door and taking Louise's hand, 'I was present when the girl made her attack.' He smiled complacently at Barnaby. 'I was able to get rid of her and note down some of the wilder comments she made. Really,' he added, leading the way to the kitchen, 'these people seem determined to hinder their chances of success.'

Barnaby looked at Louise.

'Why does he say that?'

'Oh.' Louise sighed. 'Ursula wrote me a letter which apparently we'll be able to use in the case. It was a very sweet letter, but she practically admitted liability in it. And she enclosed some money, too.'

'Money? How much?'

'A thousand quid. For a holiday, she said.' Louise looked away uncomfortably. 'Ursula's so stupid. Cassian says her lawyer couldn't possibly have known what she was doing.'

They had reached the kitchen and Louise sat down. In the middle of the table, like an exhibit, sat the mauve letter. Louise glanced down at Ursula's careful loopy writing. Somehow the sight of it made her feel both unbearably touched and horribly guilty at the same time.

She rubbed a hand wearily over her eyes and felt her face droop with fatigue. The past few weeks seemed, in her mind, to have consisted of nothing but the hospital. Driving to and from the hospital, walking up and down the corridors, drinking coffee in the cafeteria, and the endless hours seated by Katie's bed.

She knew every inch of that ward by now; every square of linoleum and every crack in the paintwork. She could have described, from memory, each of the cheery childish paintings which decorated the corridor; could even have listed the names of their creators – Ben, Sam, Lucy M., Lucy B. – written on the paintings in a rounded teacher's handwriting. If she closed her eyes she could hear, over and over in her head, the distinctive tinkling laugh of one of the nurses and the sound of the squeaking trolley which came round every morning. And all the time she could smell that antiseptic hospital smell which lingered on her hands and in her clothes and hair.

Louise's mind felt blurred; her hair felt lank; her face felt robbed of resilience. Her muscles seemed to have forgotten how to smile, and yet there were things to smile about. Katie was improving, everybody said so, and, of course, Louise could see herself that it was true. Katie was opening her eyes now, for quite long periods of time. And each time she seemed to know, just about, who she was and what her name was. But every time she woke, she seemed to have forgotten about the accident and why she was in hospital, and had to be told all over again. Louise's explanations were beginning to sound stale to her own ears; sometimes she could feel a note of unforgivable impatience creeping into her voice. She would break off, abruptly, staring into Katie's confused face, willing her to remember. And then she would silently, uselessly berate herself, as Katie's eyes dulled and she fell back into her heavy unnatural sleep. And Louise would sit back in her chair and begin her waiting again. Waiting either for Katie to wake up, or for it to be time to leave the hospital, drive home, pick up Amelia from whoever was baby-sitting, put Amelia to bed, microwave a quick supper and fall, exhausted, into bed.

Barnaby had offered, a couple of weeks ago, to move back in and give her a hand; since changing his mind on the court case, he'd become enthusiastically, irritatingly helpful. Louise had immediately refused his offer, but now she felt so fatigued that she wouldn't have minded who helped her. And yet, what on earth was she doing all day that made her so tired? Sitting still, pacing about, talking to the nurses, reading magazines. Hardly strenuous stuff. It didn't make any sense, she thought blearily.

Barnaby watched Louise covertly from the other side of the table, and miserably thought how pale and drawn she looked. She needed him, he thought fiercely. She said she didn't, but she did. And a familiar pain began to gnaw at his chest.

'Don't worry,' he said impulsively. Louise looked up and gave him a weak smile. 'I've been doing a lot of thinking,' he continued earnestly. 'I'm sure we're doing the right thing, and I'm sure we're going to win this case. And then we'll be able to give Katie the best treatment there is.'

Louise met Barnaby's honest gaze and wished she could feel so certain. Meredith's furious tirade in the street had affected her more than she had admitted, and Ursula's foolish letter only made her feel more guilty. How on earth would the Delaneys find half a million pounds if they weren't insured? she found herself thinking all the time. What would they do? How would they manage?

The initial thrill she'd had at the thought of going to court had subsided, and hardened into a grim resignation. The more she understood about the case, the less she liked it. And somehow it seemed irrelevant to the real, everyday consequences of the accident. She couldn't make the connection between an abstract half a million pounds' worth of damages, floating uncertainly somewhere in the future, and Katie.

Cassian had uncorked a bottle of wine and now poured out three glasses. Louise relaxed slightly at the reassuring glug-glug sound. She knew she was drinking more now than she had before the accident, but still, she told herself, only a reasonable amount. And if she was always desperate for a drink when she got home from the hospital, well, that was only the same as lots of people with stressful jobs, she reasoned. Nothing to worry about.

'Lu-Lu,' Cassian said caressingly, as he put a glass in front of her. He sat down, then casually took Louise's hand and began to play with her fingers.

Barnaby looked away and clenched his fists. A rising anger started to burn inside his chest. Bastard. For a frightening moment, he thought his temper might take over. Desperately, he conjured up in his mind a vision of Katie; of the way she had smiled at him vaguely that afternoon; of her eyes, dulled by the accident but still his Katkin, underneath all the confusion and pain and drugs. I'm doing all this for Katie, he said to himself. For Katie.

'I've been reading up a bit,' he said abruptly, 'in the papers. There was a case just recently about a brain-damaged child who was given six hundred and thirty thousand pounds. Did you see that?' Cassian looked at Barnaby in mild surprise.

'Yes,' he said, 'I believe I did, but that was a rather different case. It was a medical negligence case, rather than occupiers' liability.'

'Oh,' said Barnaby in a chastened voice.

'But there were certainly some relevant similarities there,' added Cassian, kindly. 'And I must say, Barnaby, it's good that you're becoming up to date with recent developments.' Barnaby flushed a dark red.

'I want to do everything I can,' he said in a hoarse voice.

'Of course you do,' said Cassian smoothly. He opened his briefcase and took out a folder.

'Now,' he said, 'I'm about to start putting together draft witness statements. We need as many as possible, and to get them as quickly as possible, before people start to forget what happened.' He passed a list to Louise. 'These are the people who are being contacted by my assistant. Can you think of any others?'

Louise glanced down the list. Suddenly her gaze stopped.

'Amelia?' she exclaimed. 'She can't possibly be a witness!'

'What do you mean?' said Cassian, frowning. 'She'll

173

be one of the most important witnesses we've got.' He took a sip of wine. 'Don't worry,' he said, 'the courts are very understanding to child witnesses, and she won't have to do very much.'

'But she'll have to remember the whole thing!' Louise's voice was loud and shrill. 'That's bad enough! She'll have to go through it all over again! It'll be terrible for her.'

'Oh, really, Louise!' Cassian was smoothly dismissive. 'She'll be absolutely fine.'

'How do you know?' retorted Louise. 'Barnaby, we can't let Amelia go through all that, can we?'

There was silence. Barnaby said nothing.

'Barnaby!' said Louise sharply. 'You do agree with me, don't you?'

Barnaby slowly raised his head.

'Well,' he said heavily. He took a slug of wine. 'Actually, no. I don't think I do.'

'What?' Louise's voice rang, outraged, round the kitchen.

'I think Cassian's right,' said Barnaby. 'Amelia should give evidence. I mean, she was playing with Katie just before it happened.'

'But think what it'll do to her!'

'She'll be all right,' said Barnaby stolidly. 'She's a sensible girl. And if it helps Katie . . .'

'Well, what if it doesn't!' shrieked Louise angrily. 'What if we put Amelia through all that misery and then lose the case! Or what if we win the money and Katie still doesn't get better? What then?'

'Lu-Lu,' began Cassian smoothly, but Barnaby interrupted him.

'What are you saying, Lou?' he said loudly. 'That you don't want to go to court, after all?' There was a short tense silence.

'No!' exclaimed Louise. 'Oh, I don't know! It's just . . .' Suddenly tears sprang into her eyes and she gave a sob.

'I'm just so tired,' she cried, her voice rising sharply in distress, 'and Katie just doesn't get better, and sometimes I think . . .' she sniffed and wiped her nose with the back of her hand, '. . . I think, well, what good would all that money be to us, anyway?'

Her voice echoed round the kitchen; Cassian and Barnaby said nothing.

'And it'll all take for ever,' continued Louise tearfully, 'and we might not win, and even if we do, the Delaneys aren't insured, so they'll have to sell their house or something, and we all used to be such good f-friends . . .' She gave another heaving sob and buried her head in her hands.

Barnaby looked at Cassian. His expression was sombre.

'I didn't know that,' he said, 'about the insurance.'

Cassian took a sip of wine. He didn't look pleased.

'What you must understand,' he said curtly, 'is that the issue of insurance has no bearing on the merits of this case. If you are due damages, then you are due damages. This is justice we're talking about here. Justice! You can't just ignore it!'

'Even if you ruin your friends?' cried Louise.

'Yes!' snapped Cassian, suddenly losing his patience. 'Look, Louise, these people might be your friends, but you owe more to your daughter than you do to them. Don't you?'

Louise didn't answer.

'You can't have it both ways!' continued Cassian. 'Either you sacrifice your friendship – a rather dubious friendship, I might add – or you sacrifice Katie. Which is it to be?' He turned and looked at Barnaby. 'Which is it to be, Barnaby? Which is more important?' There was a pause, then Barnaby exhaled sharply.

'Katie,' he said. 'It's got to be Katie.'

'Exactly,' said Cassian, closing his folder, 'and let me tell you both . . .'

175

He paused, until Louise unwillingly looked up at him.

'Let me tell you,' repeated Cassian, 'that the worst thing you can do for your little girl is prepare this case half-heartedly. If we're going to win some money for her, we need to give it one hundred per cent. Which means using all the evidence and all the witnesses we can muster, whether or not we like it. And if you're not prepared to do that, Louise, then I'm afraid we might as well forget the whole thing.'

'He's right,' said Barnaby suddenly, then flushed a deep red as the two of them turned to look at him. 'He's right, Lou. I mean, if we went through all this and then lost just because we didn't have the right piece of evidence . . .'

'Exactly,' said Cassian, 'Barnaby's got it exactly.'

'Don't you see what I mean, Lou?' said Barnaby in gruff pleading tones. He tried to catch her eye, but she looked away. 'It's not that I'm not fond of Hugh and Ursula, especially Hugh, but now we've decided to go to court, it's all got to be different. It's got to be.'

'But what about the fact that they aren't insured?' said Louise, suddenly, with a note of desperation in her voice. 'Doesn't that affect you? Doesn't that change your mind?'

Barnaby looked at her steadily, with pain in his eyes.

'I never wanted to sue,' he said eventually. 'It was you that wanted to sue. I thought it was wrong.' He paused and took a slug of wine. 'But I thought and thought about it, and eventually I decided that you were right; that we owed it to Katie. That's what I decided, and that stays the same.' He looked down at his huge hands resting on the table, 'that stays the same, whether or not Hugh and Ursula are insured. We still owe it to Katie. We should still sue.'

Louise stared at him for a moment. She picked up her glass and drained it. Then she looked up.

'Well, I never,' she said in slow bitter tones. Her cheeks were burning pink and her eyes flickered from Barnaby's face to Cassian's, and back to Barnaby's. 'I never thought I'd see the two of you ganging up together against me. Men know best. Is that it?'

'Of course not,' said Barnaby uncomfortably. 'But you must see . . .'

'I see nothing. Nothing!' Louise stood up, scraping her chair loudly against the floorboards. She pushed her hands shakily through her hair. 'Why don't you just go, Barnaby!' she said, glaring at him. 'We'll have this meeting another day. Or perhaps you don't even need me to come to it, since I'm so obviously in the wrong.'

'Louise,' pleaded Barnaby. 'Why don't you just relax . . .'

'Relax!' Louise's eyes glittered furiously at Barnaby. 'I spend all day at the hospital, I come home, you start lecturing me, and then you tell me to relax!'

'I didn't mean . . .' began Barnaby helplessly.

'I've had enough of all this. Just go, Barnaby! Go!'

Cassian met Barnaby's eyes.

'Perhaps it might be better', he said softly, 'if we all met another day.'

Barnaby nodded numbly.

'Look, Lou, I'm sorry,' he said hoarsely. 'I didn't realize . . .'

'Just go,' said Louise wearily. Barnaby nodded bleakly. He turned slowly away, then looked back, but Louise was staring blankly down at the floor.

'Bye,' he whispered dolefully.

'Bye, Barnaby,' said Cassian. Louise said nothing.

'Bye,' whispered Barnaby again. And with a heavy heart, he tiptoed out of the cottage and made his way back to his lonely empty home.

Much later on Cassian came and sat beside Louise on the sofa, where she was blankly watching the television, turned down low so that it wouldn't wake Amelia. He began to massage her shoulders with a deft expertise.

'I know it's difficult,' he murmured softly into her neck, 'but it'll all be worth it in the end.'

Louise didn't move.

'The important thing is to secure Katie's future,' he added. There was a little pause. 'And our future,' he whispered seductively. 'Together.'

Slowly he pushed aside her hair and kissed her on the back of her neck.

Louise's shoulders froze in uncertain anticipation. There had been so many moments like this since she'd known Cassian; so many times when she'd expected him to make a move, to turn a light kiss into something more intense, to take a casual caress forward into the beginnings of love-making. And, so far, it had never happened. At first she'd felt slightly relieved; let off the hook. After some time, relief had turned into frustrated disappointment. And then, when she heard the rumours going round of her steamy affair, she had begun to feel an ironic amusement. She'd felt a private self-vindication at the knowledge that, whatever everyone thought, she hadn't been unfaithful to Barnaby.

She still hadn't. At least, not yet.

Cassian was still nuzzling the back of her neck. Louise could scarcely breathe. Was it finally going to happen? Now? When she was feeling so tired and groggy?

'I really hate to see you upset,' Cassian said, huskily, against her skin. 'I just want to make you feel better. Darling,' he added.

He felt Louise beginning to unbend slightly, and quickly moved a hand up inside her T-shirt, cupping a breast. With the other hand, he adeptly undid her bra. As it loosened, his fingers slipped underneath it, and he began to caress her soft flesh.

'Cassian,' said Louise weakly. She felt bruised by the

178

evening's arguments, vulnerable and unsure of herself; unsure of Cassian, even . . . But as she turned to face him, she felt her heart give a little leap. His eyes were gleaming; his expression intense, as though full of ardent fervour.

'Darling,' said Cassian. He looked straight at her with his dark-brown eyes. 'The reason I'm taking this case so seriously', he said huskily, 'is that . . . I love you.'

Louise's battered heart gave a little flutter.

'You must have known how I felt,' said Cassian. 'All this time.' He gave a small self-deprecating smile.

'Well,' said Louise falteringly.

'I've been waiting for the right moment to tell you,' said Cassian. He looked at her, his face suddenly serious. 'Is this the right moment, Louise?'

For a few moments Louise silently stared at him, her lips trembling and her face pale. Then, still silent, she nodded.

Cassian traced a finger down her face, then gently pulled her towards him. As their lips met, a fleeting image of Barnaby's face went through Louise's mind, accompanied by a hazy resentful guilt. But as Cassian's hands began to move with skilful care over her body, the image of Barnaby grew dim and vanished, and her mind and body surrendered, in sudden weary relief, to a blank unthinking pleasure.

Chapter Thirteen

Ten days later the weather broke. Sitting in the children's play-room at the hospital, Louise heard a clap of thunder and saw the first huge splashy drops of rain fall on the window-pane.

She shivered, even though the room itself was warm and bright, and looked at Katie, who was sitting on a play-mat, dispiritedly holding a shoe-lace threaded with wooden beads in primary colours. The play leader had started Katie off, threading the beads onto the shoe-lace herself, and had then surrounded her with more beads to carry on with and make a necklace. But although that was twenty minutes ago, Katie had not managed to add a single bead. She stared dully at the shoe-lace as though she couldn't understand what it was for, and resisted Louise's attempts to encourage her.

Louise sighed and looked at her watch. Still only eleven-forty. At twelve o'clock Barnaby was due to arrive at the hospital to collect them both and take them to Forest Lodge. Katie was now at the rehabilitation stage, it had been explained to them. She was physically independent, although her reactions were still slow; she was able to speak and eat and wash herself, and her memory had, to some degree, returned.

A noise made Louise look up. Katie had scattered the spare beads angrily on the floor.

'I don't like them,' she said, in her new thick heavy voice. Louise smiled encouragingly at Katie.

'Don't you like the pretty beads?' she said. Katie

scowled and looked away. Louise smiled again. Sometimes it was only by smiling that she could stop herself from screaming.

Mrs Innes from Forest Lodge had been very encouraging when she had assessed Katie. She had explained the rehabilitation centre to Louise, outlined the individually planned intensive programmes, spoken of multi-disciplinary teams, of reintegration into the education system, of parental involvement.

She had then said, somewhat to Louise's surprise, that she thought Katie should begin at Forest Lodge as a residential patient, to benefit from the twenty-four-hour care. Louise, who for some time had been imagining Katie back at home and everything back to normal, had felt tears come to her eyes and an inexplicable rage, directed primarily against the blameless Mrs Innes.

But now, watching Katie's uncertain progress across the room towards the Wendy house, she could see that everything was not back to normal. Katie was not the little girl she had been. Her speech was blurred; she often seemed to be at a loss for the right word; she grew angry easily, and tired even more easily; and her attention span, which had never been great at the best of times, now seemed non-existent.

They all found it difficult to relate to this new Katie; they all reacted to her in different ways. Barnaby had recently adopted a determined optimism. Every time he visited he relentlessly pointed out improvements in Katie's behaviour, until Louise, who spent more time with Katie than any of them, found herself snapping back – countering each of his optimistic observations with her own pessimistic ones.

She herself found it difficult to gain any perspective. For every achievement there seemed to be a set-back; Katie's progress appeared unbearably slow to her. Buried deep inside her was a foolish wish – belief, almost – that one day she was going to arrive at the hospital to find Katie running down the corridor, cracking the silly jokes she'd loved before the accident, talking in the same voice, back to her old self. The leaden truth – that any progress Katie made would be, at best, gradual – hit her with a depressing thud every day, as she arrived to find Katie only minimally improved from the day before, or not improved at all, or even slightly worse.

Meanwhile poor Amelia, who had pestered and pestered to be allowed to come to the hospital and play with Katie, now often stayed at home instead. Katie wasn't much good at playing with Amelia any more, Louise had soberly come to realize.

A week or so ago, Amelia had insisted on bringing the Noah's ark set to the hospital. She had set out the animals in their twos, then, in a conciliatory voice, said, 'You can have the elephants this time, Katie, because you're ill.' She looked at Katie for some recognition of this generous gesture, but Katie simply grabbed for the elephants. Amelia glanced uncertainly at Louise, then turned back to Katie and said, in a challenging voice that usually presaged an argument, 'Well, I'll have the monkeys then.' The monkeys had always been Katie's favourites, but today there was no shrill reaction from Katie, no cry of 'Am–ee–lia, that's *so* unfair.' Katie didn't seem to care about the monkeys any more. She didn't seem to care about anything any more.

The door opened and Barnaby appeared. He gave Louise a quick smile, then looked around for Katie.

'She's in the Wendy house,' said Louise.

'Kat-kin!' called Barnaby. 'I'm coming to find you!' He glanced down and suddenly spotted the wooden bead necklace, abandoned on the play-mat. 'Did Katie do this?' he asked, his voice suddenly full of pleasure. 'Look at that!'

'Actually,' said Louise gently, 'the play leader did it.

Katie was supposed to carry on, but she wasn't very keen.'

Barnaby's face fell. He turned away from Louise and began to approach the Wendy house, overshadowing it with his hulking frame. Suddenly Katie's head poked out of the window. She was grinning.

'Katie! You clever joker!' cried Barnaby joyfully. He looked over to Louise, as though to say *You see . . .* Louise smiled tightly back.

Had she always felt as irritated as this by Barnaby? she wondered. Or was it just since Cassian had given her a new yardstick to measure him by? Cassian, who was astute and professional, who cared about her and her children. Cassian, who understood that Katie's recovery would take time, who didn't grin at her with that stupid pointless optimism, but talked soberly about Katie and made helpful serious suggestions. Cassian, who came to her tenderly in bed, making her shiver and shudder with delight. Cassian, who . . .

Katie's new raucous laugh rang through the air, breaking her thoughts, and she looked up. Barnaby was standing in front of her, with Katie in his arms and an eager expression on his face. Louise sighed.

'All right,' she said, 'let's go.'

It was some time before they had said goodbye to all the nurses and medical staff on the ward and distributed the presents labelled, 'Thank you, love from Katie.' As she walked with Barnaby, out of the main entrance of the hospital, dodging the rain and watching Katie getting into the car just like any other child, Louise suddenly felt a sense of lifting; a relief. Perhaps things were almost getting back to normal.

Her spirits lifted still further as they entered the gates of Forest Lodge. The centre had been established in a large beautiful country house, surrounded by gardens. Louise turned and smiled at Katie.

'Look, Katie,' she said, 'look at the trees.' She raised

her voice over the sound of rain drumming on the roof of the car. 'Look at the lovely house you're going to stay in.' As she spoke, she looked hard at Katie's face for signs of distress. Mrs Innes had emphasized that if, at any time, Katie became upset at the idea of staying full time at Forest Lodge, they would think again, but to Louise's secret hurt and surprise, Katie had taken the news calmly. Or perhaps, thought Louise, she didn't really understand what was happening.

The entrance hall was large and wood panelled; Mrs Innes was waiting for them as they entered.

'Lovely!' she exclaimed, beaming as though genuinely pleased to see them. 'Well, Katie, you do look better already. I'm sure you're going to make wonderful progress here.' She turned to Louise and Barnaby. 'It's getting on for lunchtime,' she said, 'if you'd like to stay and meet some of the other residents here, and then you can meet the team which will be working with Katie.'

'I've got to go,' said Barnaby regretfully, 'but Louise, you'll stay, won't you?'

'Of course I'll stay,' said Louise. 'Come on, Katie,' she said cheerfully, 'let's meet your new friends.'

The news that Katie Kember was now at Forest Lodge spread swiftly through the village. Mrs Potter, who ran the village shop, heard it from Mary Tracey, and the two of them were discussing it when Sylvia Seddon-Wilson popped in out of the rain for some cigarettes.

'Forest Lodge?' she said, raising her eyebrows. 'The place for disabled children? I didn't realize she was that bad.'

'She's not,' said Mary robustly. 'Not really. She's getting much better. She's talking, and reading a bit, and . . .'

'Well, anyway,' said Sylvia, interrupting her. 'I've got some news! I've been asked to be a witness in the case for the Kembers!' She looked around triumphantly. 'I

184

got a letter yesterday, asking for a statement. Isn't it exciting? I'm going to be a witness! I'll have to buy a new outfit!'

'Actually,' said Mary, 'lots of people have got letters. They wrote to me, too.'

'Oh,' said Sylvia disappointedly.

'They've drawn up a big list of people who were there,' explained Mary, adopting an air of nonchalant self-importance. Rarely had she been in the position of explaining things to Sylvia Seddon-Wilson. 'Cassian says . . .'

'Gorgeous Cass!' broke in Sylvia. 'Isn't he a honey? Perhaps he could come over some time and help me with my statement!' She grinned lasciviously at Mary, who stared sternly back. 'Sorry, Mary, i interrupted you. What does Cassian say?' Mary cleared her throat awkwardly.

'He says, in a case like this, you need as much evidence as possible, as quickly as possible.' Her voice unconsciously imitated Cassian's smooth tones. 'He says they want to know as much as they can before they put together the writ.' She hefted Luke up on her chest. 'But that doesn't mean everybody who gets a letter will be called as a witness in court. They'll only appear if they've got something of crucial importance to say.'

'Something of crucial importance!' exclaimed Sylvia. 'My God, I don't think I've ever said anything of crucial importance in my life.' She gave a sudden guffaw of laughter, and ripped open the packet of cigarettes on the counter in front of her.

'You haven't paid for those yet,' reminded Mrs Potter.

'I know,' said Sylvia impatiently, 'you can put them on James's account if you like. Are you going to be a witness?' she added airily, as Mrs Potter reached down behind the counter for the account book.

'No, I'm certainly not,' said Mrs Potter, emerging red-faced and flustered-looking, 'and I wouldn't, even if I was asked.' She scribbled in the account book and closed it. 'I think it's shocking, the whole thing,' she said with stern emphasis. 'Taking those poor Delaneys to court! What did they ever do wrong? They was only doing their bit for charity and look where it's got 'em.'

'Yes, well, look where it's got Katie,' retorted Mary, feeling a need to defend Louise. 'In hospital.'

'I know that,' said Mrs Potter, folding her arms and leaning against the counter. 'And I'm very sorry. But if you ask me, those parents have got their priorities all wrong. The child's not injured for two minutes, and her parents are already working out how much money they can make out of her! And from friends, too!'

'That's not fair!' said Mary hotly. 'They had to act quickly, otherwise all the witnesses would have forgotten what happened. And she deserves the money! She needs it! If you could see her . . . She could have been killed in that accident.'

'Hmm, yes,' said Sylvia thoughtfully, taking a puff on her cigarette, 'but Mrs Potter's got a point. If it really was just an accident, why should anyone have to pay compensation? Why should Hugh and Ursula be ruined?' Mary looked at her, discomfited.

'Exactly,' said Mrs Potter. 'That's just it. Why . . .'

'On the other hand,' interrupted Sylvia carelessly, 'why *shouldn't* the Kembers do everything they can for their daughter?' She picked up a glossy magazine and began to flip through it. 'I mean, if the diving-board really was dangerous – that's what they're saying, isn't it? And Hugh and Ursula may well have enough money to cover it . . .' Mrs Potter looked at Sylvia, puzzled.

'But you just said . . .' she began.

'Oh, don't listen to me,' said Sylvia cheerfully, 'I never know what I'm talking about.' She brandished the magazine at Mrs Potter. 'Can you add this to the account? I must run. Cheerio.'

She put the magazine over her head and darted out

186

into the rain. Mary and Mrs Potter watched her getting into her car, a large Jaguar, with a sticker in the back window saying, 'Go First Class – Your Heirs Will.'

'Oh, I don't know,' said Mrs Potter, sighing. 'It seems all wrong to me.'

'Well, I think they're doing the right thing, suing,' said Mary stoutly. 'I really do. I mean,' she said, searching for a comparison, 'if you ate one of my . . . my home-made fish cakes, and it made you ill, you'd want some compensation, wouldn't you? You'd take me to court.' Mrs Potter looked at her in surprise.

'Well, now,' she said consideringly. 'Would I? I'm not sure I would. I think I'd just say, "Oh, that was bad luck," and leave it at that. Or, no, you're right, maybe I would like a little something.' She paused, and appeared to be thinking. 'A Marks & Spencer token, perhaps,' she suggested, 'that would be a nice gesture. But I wouldn't take you to court, not for a fish cake.'

'Well, what if it killed you,' said Mary, unwilling to concede her point. 'Then you'd want something, wouldn't you? You'd want some compensation? Some money?'

Mrs Potter began to laugh; a hoarse bubbling chuckle.

'I'd be dead, Mary, love,' she said. 'If your fish cake killed me, I'd be dead! Money wouldn't be much use to me in my coffin, would it? Nor a Marks & Spencer token, come to that.' Her chuckles increased, and after a while, Mary couldn't help giggling, too.

'Oh, I don't know,' said Mrs Potter at last, wiping her eyes. 'It seems wrong to be laughing. Poor little girl; she didn't deserve this to happen. And I do feel sorry for those Delaneys, too. I'd say they've had enough trouble these past few years, without all of this to-do.' Mary's face fell.

'Yes, I suppose they have,' she said eventually. She looked out into the teeming rain. 'It's a shame. It's a shame for all of them.'

187

Meredith had risen early and spent the morning peering at law books – some newly bought, some borrowed from the library at Linningford. Half a foolscap pad was filled with dense notes before she stopped, stretched and looked out of the window. The rain was still pouring down unremittingly, and her sitting-room was filled with a soft grey light. She reached over, switched on a lamp, then winced as a harsh pool of yellow fell on the sheet in front of her. Better to be in the dark. She switched off the light, leaned back, and tried to make some sense of the facts whirling around in her mind.

Were Hugh and Ursula liable for letting a child dive, unguarded, off their diving-board? Or was it the child's own fault? No-one's fault? The mother's fault? Should Hugh and Ursula put in a claim against Louise for contributory negligence? Should they trump up some kind of counter-suit?

Meredith shut her eyes and pulled a face. All the legal jargon was making her brain ache. She seemed to have read hundreds of accounts of cases of negligence in the British law courts. People who left spilt yoghurt on the floor of their store for people to slip up. People who allowed children to play with dangerous bits of wire. People who didn't fix the bannisters on their stairs.

None of these cases quite appeared to resemble their own situation, and it now seemed to Meredith even more obvious that Hugh and Ursula *hadn't* been negligent, not like some people were negligent. But at the same time, in her heart of hearts, she was beginning to see how Cassian Brown might put together some kind of phoney case against them; how he might even be able to convince a very stupid jury that Katie was a victim of the Delaneys' negligence, and that she was owed damages. And if that happened, how much might Hugh and Ursula have to pay out? Meredith's eyes glanced, unwillingly, down the list of examples of damages claims which she'd compiled. Huge sums stared back at her, and she gave a little shiver. She'd heard the rumour about half a million pounds, which was going round the village, and dismissed it. Now she wasn't so sure. A recent well-publicized case – in which a head-injured child had received nearly £700,000 from a negligent local council – jumped out at her particularly blackly.

Half a million pounds? Hugh simply didn't have that kind of money. Not money sitting around, just waiting for an emergency. His business had dwindled considerably since Simon's death; Meredith knew for a fact that it was bringing in only a small income. Of course, they could sell the little house in France – but that wouldn't fetch much. Not these days. So . . . what? Would they have to sell Devenish House? Sell what little there was of the business? Take out some sort of loan? Declare themselves bankrupt? How on earth would Hugh and Ursula cope with that? Hadn't they had enough?

Meredith stared into the pouring rain and felt an impotent frustrated anger rising through her. Abruptly, she got to her feet. She'd had enough of law books. Enough of the law altogether.

Hugh looked out of the window of his study and saw Meredith walking through the garden, in the rain, wearing her black strappy swimming-costume. She was heading towards the swimming-pool. He waited a few moments, then put down his pen and went outside after her.

The swimming-pool was heated to its normal temperature, and clouds of steam were pouring off it into the rainy atmosphere. Huge raindrops pounded fiercely down onto the surface of the water, which seemed, in this weather, grey and uninviting. But through the misty clouds, Hugh could see Meredith swimming determinedly up and down the length of the pool, efficiently cleaving the water with her strong muscular arms, turning at each end in a seamless movement, purging something out of her system, he guessed. He stood by the side of the pool for a few minutes, sheltering from the loud battering rain under a bright-yellow umbrella. Eventually Meredith noticed him. She stopped swimming and began to tread water, holding her face up to the rain, closing her eyes.

'I fucking hate them all,' she said, above the pounding noise of the rain. Her eyes were still closed. Hugh gave a small grin, and squatted down by the side of the pool.

'I had a letter from the Kembers' lawyers today,' he said, 'requesting permission for some sort of safety expert to come and examine the diving-board.'

They both turned and stared at the diving-board, glistening wet in the rain.

'The diving-board's fine,' said Meredith in a tight voice. 'It's just a diving-board. What's he expect to find? Oil smeared all over it?'

'I really don't know,' said Hugh wearily. 'As far as I'm concerned, it's perfectly safe, but . . .' He tailed off.

'Perhaps we should rip it out,' said Meredith, 'and when this safety expert comes along, we'll say, "Diving-board? What diving-board?"'

She gave Hugh a grin and he smiled reluctantly back. He looked old and defeated. Meredith could hardly bear to look at him. She took a deep breath and plunged under the surface, feeling cold water pour into her ears; hearing the sound of the rain on water suddenly muffled. When she surfaced, Hugh was still there, staring at the diving-board.

'They won't be able to prove anything,' said Meredith, trying to sound confident.

'And what if they do?' said Hugh. He looked at Meredith, a haggard expression on his face. 'What if it's proved in a court of law that it was our negligence that put an innocent child in hospital? That our diving-board was unsafe? How will we live with ourselves?'

'It won't be,' said Meredith uncertainly. 'No way.'
There was a doubtful pause.

'It's not the money,' said Hugh suddenly. 'I mean, of
course the money is worrying, yes.' He looked at
Meredith. 'You know what sort of sums we might be
talking about, don't you?' She nodded. 'But even if we
had to sell everything . . .' Hugh waved one hand in the
rainy air, 'it wouldn't be the end of the world. We'd be
able to live with ourselves.' He looked at Meredith.
'What I couldn't live with is the thought that the accident was our fault.' He looked bleakly at Meredith and
transferred the dripping umbrella handle from one
hand to the other.

'No-one's saying it was your *fault*,' said Meredith,
fiercely. 'For Christ's sake, what were you supposed to
do? Guard the diving-board against stupid kids? When
it's perfectly plain that diving can, yes, can be risky?
And when the kid's mother was actually there?'

'Maybe,' said Hugh wearily. 'Maybe that's just what
we were supposed to do.'

'What, so nothing's obvious any more?' said Meredith
angrily, slapping her hand down on the surface of the
water with a sharp splash. 'We have to protect everybody against everything? Whatever happened to
common sense? Someone should have told that kid, if
you leap high into the air you might hurt yourself.
That's a fact of life. It's not anyone's *fault*.' Hugh
shrugged.

'But what if the board was dangerous?' he said in a
quiet voice.

'It wasn't dangerous,' said Meredith angrily. 'No more
dangerous than any other diving-board.'

'Maybe that's enough,' said Hugh. 'Maybe the very
fact that a diving-board is dangerous at all will be
enough for them to win the case. I just don't know.'

Meredith felt a stab of uncharacteristic fearful panic.

191

She and Hugh looked at each other for a moment, silent, except for the rain.

'Well, God help the world, then,' said Meredith at last, looking away from Hugh's weary face. 'And God save us from the fucking lawyers.'

A pair of sudden hot tears fell from her eyes, mingling with the drips on her face. Quickly, before Hugh could see, Meredith plunged back into the blue-grey depths of the pool, her legs thrusting furiously through the yielding water, her hair streaming out behind her, and the raindrops falling in splashy circles on the surface above her. She swam silently and desperately, holding her breath, until she felt able to surface and talk to Hugh again. But when, eventually, she surfaced, breathless, he had gone. And she was left alone, cocooned from the pounding rain in the warmth of the water, surrounded by steamy clouds, with no-one to talk to.

Chapter Fourteen

By the time the end of term arrived it was baking hot once more, and Amelia was asking, every day, if they could please, *please* go swimming.

They hadn't been swimming at all since the accident; the vision of Amelia plunging again into the forbidding blue water of a swimming-pool made Louise shudder and feel sick. But she couldn't say that to the child, and give her a complex for the rest of her life, so instead she said again, sharply, that they didn't have time. Not at the moment.

Amelia stared resentfully at her mother, then stamped back up the stairs to get her school hat. She hated her mother, and she hated Katie, and she hated everybody. Today was the last day of term, and everybody was taking a present to school for their form teacher. But although she'd kept promising they would go and find something nice at the shops, Louise had forgotten, until Amelia reminded her last night, when it was too late.

'We'll buy something on the way to school,' she'd said hastily. 'Something nice.' But the only shop on the way to school was the garage, and Amelia knew they wouldn't find anything nice there, only jars of coffee and pints of milk and Mars bars.

And it was all because her mother spent the whole time at Forest Lodge. Amelia *hated* Forest Lodge. It was really creepy and it smelt horrible, and all the people in it were weird. Some of them couldn't speak properly and some of them had strange jerky arms, and last time she went there for lunch she'd sat opposite a boy who was much older than her, but dribbled his food. It was *disgusting*. And then he'd smiled at her and tried to take hold of her hand. She'd stared at him in panic, feeling her face turn red and her heart thumping, until a nurse noticed what was happening and hurried over, and said, 'Martin, leave Amelia alone.' And then she'd turned to Amelia and smiled, and said, 'Don't worry! He won't bite!' And Amelia had smiled back, but inside she felt all shaky and frightened.

She didn't see why Katie had to stay there. Katie wasn't a bit like those people. She could walk and talk properly now, and sort of read, and last time Amelia had visited, they'd even played French skipping. Katie had forgotten all about French skipping after the accident, but Amelia had taught her how to do it again, and she'd been quite good – at least, at the very easy jumps.

Everyone kept going on about how well Katie was doing, so much better than they'd expected, and Amelia always said, 'Well, why doesn't she come home, then?' And her mother would say, 'She will, darling, very soon.' But she never did, so they kept having to go to horrible revolting Forest Lodge.

Amelia picked up her satchel and put on her hat, and scowled at herself in the mirror. Nothing was fun any more. She didn't have anyone to play with, and they weren't going on holiday, and everyone seemed cross all the time.

By the end of the morning, however, Amelia's spirits had risen. After they'd had a story, and before they went down for final prayers, Mrs Jacob had taken the star chart off the wall to announce the winner. And it was Amelia!

She was so surprised she just sat still, while Clara, who sat next to her, tugged at her school dress and hissed, 'Go up! Go up and get your prize!'

Mrs Jacob smiled at Amelia and said, 'I've been

194

awarding stars for good behaviour, as well as the stars I've put in your exercise books, and Amelia has done very well this term! Well done!' And Amelia struggled to her feet and Mrs Jacob gave her a huge tube of Smarties, and everybody clapped.

Then everyone crowded round Amelia's desk for a Smartie, and Amelia handed them out, keeping back the orange ones for herself. And Anna Russet, whom she didn't know very well, said shyly, 'I think you deserved to win the star chart, Amelia.' And Clara, sitting next to her, said at once, 'Yes, so do I. I think you *deserved* to win it.'

Amelia had glowed, pink with pleasure, as she doled out Smarties into thrusting hands, and thought how impressed Katie and Mummy would be when she told them. Then they'd gone down to the hall for final prayers, and Amelia's name was read out, along with all the other star-chart winners, and all the teachers smiled at her. Then they sang Amelia's favourite hymn, and did three cheers for the teachers, and then it really was the end of term.

All the parents were waiting outside, mostly mothers, but a few fathers too, and the playground was filled with children, carrying satchels and pencil-cases and rolled-up paintings and recorders and shoe bags. Amelia looked for Louise in the throng, but she couldn't see her anywhere, so she sat down comfortably on the low wall at the front of the playground and waited for her to arrive.

Half an hour later she still hadn't come. The playground was now nearly empty, with just a few parents and children and a couple of teachers, and a book dropped face-down on the ground. Amelia sidled over and picked up the book. It was a very junior reading book that she remembered from Form Two, and she began to leaf through it, recalling the bright pictures and the story, and all the big words that she'd found so difficult then, but now seemed really easy.

'Amelia!' Amelia looked up, startled. Mrs Jacob was in front of her.

'Hasn't Mummy come yet?'

'No,' admitted Amelia. 'She's often late,' she added quickly.

'I know,' said Mrs Jacob, 'but not normally this late.' She looked hard at Amelia. 'She does know it's a half day today?' Amelia thought.

'Well, she knows it's the end of term,' she said eventually. 'She must know it's a half day.'

'Did you tell her?' persisted Mrs Jacob.

'No,' said Amelia in surprise, 'but she must know! It's always a half day on the last day of term.'

Mrs Jacob sighed.

'Perhaps', she said, 'she's forgotten. Just this once.'

Amelia stared at Mrs Jacob and felt a sudden angry hurt. Mrs Jacob must be right, her mother had forgotten to come and pick her up. She'd *forgotten* about her. No-one else's mother forgot about them.

A voice interrupted them both. It was Mrs Russet, Anna's mother, coming over from the other side of the playground.

'Is there a problem?' she said. She addressed Amelia in a sugary voice. 'Has Mummy forgotten all about you?' Amelia shrugged and went pink. Mrs Russet came closer. She was a very large lady, with curly hair; Amelia had sometimes seen her in church, doing readings in a loud voice with lots of flapping arms.

'I'll go and phone her,' said Mrs Jacob. She looked at Amelia and smiled reassuringly. 'Will she be at home, do you think?'

'She's probably at Forest Lodge,' said Amelia. 'She's always at Forest Lodge,' she added, gloomily, as Mrs Jacob hurried off.

'Is she?' Mrs Russet's eyes bored beadily into Amelia's face. 'Does she leave you all alone?'

'Well,' began Amelia, meaning to explain how Mary always came and looked after her. But a sudden resentment at her mother took over.

'Yes, she does,' she said sorrowfully. 'She leaves me all alone. All she cares about is Katie.'

Mrs Russet's mouth tightened and she folded her arms.

'Well, Amelia,' she said. 'What about coming home with us? If Mummy's too busy to remember about you?'

'Yes, go on,' said Anna. 'You can see my guinea-pig.'

'And then we can have some nice lunch,' said Mrs Russet cosily, 'and you can tell me *all* about it.'

Louise had spent much of the day in Linningford, trying to catch up with the minutiae of daily life. Since the accident, she realized, she hadn't paid a single household bill. Food shopping had been reduced to buying a few tins whenever she had a spare moment; most basic household items had run out or broken and not been replaced. And tomorrow was the start of Amelia's school holidays. She wanted the house to be in some kind of order before then. So the night before, she had sat down with a pencil and begun a list, starting modestly with light-bulbs; pay gas bill; first-class stamps. By the time the catalogue was finished, it was running onto a fourth sheet, and she was staring at it in amazed despair. But she had decided that, if it were at all possible, she would get everything done before she picked up Amelia from school.

Somewhere in her mind she had once been aware that on the last day of term, school finished at lunchtime. But this fact was submerged as she battled with a pair of heavy carrier bags through the morning throng, and found herself thinking, I'm never going to get everything done by three-thirty. As the day progressed she began to move more quickly; imbuing each transaction with a sense of urgency; pitting herself against crowds of people, overheated lifts and surly shop assistants. She abandoned all thought of taking the toaster for repair, in favour of finding a special present for Amelia. She decided, hastily crossing it off the list, that plant food could wait for another day – but they really did need new tooth-brushes.

She arrived at the school on the dot of quarter to four, with a red face and a full car and a colouring book for Amelia waiting on the front seat. And then, as she opened the door and got out to an uncharacteristic silence, the truth hit her, and she leaned weakly against the car, her heart thudding and a light-headed amazement pervading her body. How could she have been so stupid? How could she have forgotten that school finished at lunchtime today?

For a moment or two she couldn't move, so astonished was she at her lapse of memory. It almost seemed a feat of achievement to have forgotten something so important. Then, as her astonishment began to abate, she felt a sudden guilty pang, all the stronger for being delayed. Where was Amelia? What had happened to her, if nobody had arrived to collect her?

Stupidly, Louise began to run towards the playground. Of course she wouldn't be there. The teachers wouldn't have left her. Louise imagined kind steady Mrs Jacob, Amelia's teacher, and her heart began to quail. What on earth would Mrs Jacob think of her? And all the other teachers? Would they put a black mark against her name?

And where, thought Louise again, arriving in the deserted playground, looking hopelessly around; where the hell was Amelia?

'If we win in the court,' said Amelia, sitting back comfortably on Mrs Russet's cushioned garden swing and accepting another chocolate biscuit, 'we're going to get half a million pounds.' She looked at Mrs Russet for a reaction and bit into the biscuit. Mrs Russet gave a satisfactory gasp.

'Half a million pounds,' repeated Amelia. 'We'll be half-millionaires.'

Anna, crouched down in front of the guinea-pig pen on the other side of the garden, called, 'Come *on*, Amelia. Come and see Nutmeg.'

But Amelia ignored her and looked at Mrs Russet. Mrs Russet was being very kind to her, Amelia thought. She'd given her a lovely lunch, full of treats, and now it was teatime already, and more treats. And all Amelia had to do was keep talking about the accident. Mrs Russet seemed very interested in it.

Now she looked at Amelia with huge brown eyes, and said, 'That seems an awful lot of money for a little girl like you to be talking about.'

'I know,' said Amelia simply.

'Did Mummy tell you about it?' Amelia flushed slightly.

'No,' she said, 'I just sort of heard it. Mummy and Cassian were talking about it one time.' She bit into her biscuit again. It was delicious, all chocolatey and filled with sweetened cream. The sort of biscuit they never had at home.

'The accident was all Mr and Mrs Delaney's fault,' Amelia added, with her mouth full. 'Cassian told me.' She licked her chocolatey fingers and looked at Mrs Russet. 'I'm not allowed to speak to Mrs Delaney any more,' she continued indistinctly, 'even though she gave me a Barbie doll. I like Mrs Delaney,' she added, 'but Cassian says she's neg-lent.' She said the word cautiously and looked up for approval, but Mrs Russet was gazing at her silently, waiting for her to continue. Amelia gave an inward sigh. She was running out of things to say.

'I hate the boring old court case,' she said eventually. 'That's all they talk about: Katie and the court case.' She eyed Mrs Russet surreptitiously and added pitifully, 'No-one cares abut me any more.'

She was hoping that Mrs Russet would offer her another biscuit, but instead Mrs Russet grabbed her hand.

'I've never heard anything so terrible,' she said. 'That you should feel so abandoned!' She looked at Amelia and blinked a few times. 'Does Mummy know you feel like this?'

'Well,' began Amelia, 'not . . .'

'Doesn't have time to listen, I expect,' said Mrs Russet, nodding vigorously. 'Or doesn't want to listen. Too busy with her million-pound court case to bother about her children. It's immoral, that's what it is. She wasn't even at Forest Lodge today. Who *knows* what she's been doing . . .' She broke off and leaned closer to Amelia.

'That Cassian,' she said. 'Does he . . . visit the house very much?' Amelia took another biscuit without asking and tried to think. What counted as very much?

'Well . . . quite a lot,' she said at last. Mrs Russet nodded vigorously again. The collection of bead necklaces strung about her neck jangled, and a red glow began to spread over her face.

'And what about poor Daddy?' she said. Amelia stared back at Mrs Russet. How did Mrs Russet know so much about them?

'We see him every weekend,' she said, her voice starting to tremble.

'And is he in favour of this court case?' said Mrs Russet in a suddenly fierce voice. 'Or does he think, as I do, that God moves in mysterious ways?' She looked at Amelia sternly. 'Everything happens for a reason,' she said, 'and every sinner receives his punishment.' She brought her face suddenly close to Amelia's. 'Would your sister's accident have happened if your mother hadn't been so distracted, thinking about her lover? Would it have happened if she'd been a decent responsible mother?' She spat the words out and Amelia shrank back in her seat. She didn't know what to say.

'Look,' called Anna, from the other side of the garden. 'Amelia's mummy's car is here.'

Amelia had never seen her mother so angry. She barely waited until they'd got into the car before she screamed, in a voice which made Amelia give a terrified jump, 'What did you say to that woman?'

Amelia stared back at her mother with a white face.

'Nothing,' she said in a shaking voice. 'Nothing really. Just things she asked me.'

'And what did she ask you?' said Louise bitterly. 'I know,' she added, before Amelia could reply. 'Is your mother a good Christian or an irresponsible harlot who brought this accident on herself?'

Amelia peered at Louise in terror.

'I don't know,' she muttered.

'She said she's going to testify against us!' shouted Louise. 'She's going to offer herself as a character witness, and give evidence in court that I don't look after my children properly!' Louise turned briefly towards Amelia.

'How do you think that makes me feel?'

Amelia gazed back in silence. She didn't really understand what had happened. One minute Mrs Russet had been all friendly, then she'd suddenly changed and started saying horrible things. And she'd had a huge row with Mummy, and now Mummy was furious, and it all seemed to be Amelia's fault. Suddenly Amelia gave a little sob. Louise turned to look at her, and the angry lines in her forehead softened.

'Oh, Amelia, darling,' she said. 'I'm sorry. It's not your fault.' She gave a small strange laugh, and changed gear roughly. 'It's my fault, just like she said. If I'd remembered to pick you up, this would never have happened.'

'It's not your fault,' said Amelia fiercely. 'I hate Mrs Russet,' she added. 'I wish she'd just go away.' Louise sighed.

'So do I,' she said, 'but somehow I think that's a bit unlikely.'

When they got home, Frances Mold was waiting on the doorstep. She looked worried and stepped forward as soon as the car stopped. Louise looked at her with a curious, not particularly friendly expression. She knew Frances was a close friend of Meredith Delaney. No doubt she was firmly in the Delaneys' camp.

'I've just had Gillian Russet on the phone,' said Frances, as Louise got out of the car. 'I'm afraid she was . . . a little worked up.' Her eyes moved briefly to Amelia and back to Louise.

'Amelia,' said Louise, handing her the door key, 'let yourself in, and then go and play in the garden.' As Amelia clattered off, Louise turned towards Frances with frank bitterness in her face.

'Don't tell me,' she said, 'you think she's right. You think I brought Katie's accident on myself as a punishment.' Frances's face didn't flicker.

'Of course not,' she said steadily. 'I'm afraid Gillian tends to get things out of proportion,' she added. 'Alan's had to speak to her before about this sort of thing.'

'Really?' said Louise sharply. 'And is he going to speak to her this time?'

'Of course,' said Frances simply. She sighed. 'Actually, I think he'll get quite angry with her.' She ran a weary hand over her face. 'Gillian has a lot to learn about compassion, but she's actually very well-meaning in many respects.' Frances looked at Louise earnestly. 'I hope you can manage to forgive her.'

Louise leaned back against the car. She felt suddenly very weak.

'That woman has no idea,' she said unsteadily, 'no idea what this has been like for us.'

'I know she hasn't,' agreed Frances. 'None of us has.' She came over and leaned back next to Louise.

'I feel I haven't been as supportive as I should.' She looked at Louise. 'I was wondering, when Katie comes home, whether I could help you with her. Perhaps I could come and read with her? Would that be helpful?'

Louise looked at Frances's earnest ugly face and felt almost tearful.

'I'm sure that would be a great help,' she said. 'Thank you.' Then, before she could stop it, her old defensive anger flooded to the front of her mind, and she added in a sharp voice, 'What will Meredith think? I thought you were a great friend of hers?'

'I am,' agreed Frances, 'but Meredith will, I'm sure, simply be glad that I can help.' She looked steadily at Louise. 'We all want to help, really. Unfortunately the Delaneys have been legally advised . . .'

'To stay away from us?'

Frances nodded slightly.

'I suppose you think', said Louise, her voice harsh and defensive, 'that we're evil people, taking Hugh and Ursula to court.'

'Not at all,' said Frances mildly. 'I have every faith in British justice. If you do have a case, then I'm sure the system will work.'

Louise stared at Frances, unaccountably dissatisfied by this answer. Then she shrugged. 'Well, Katie's coming home in a week or so,' she said.

'That's marvellous!' said Frances. 'I'll look out some easy reading books.' She looked anxiously at Louise. 'She is reading, isn't she?'

'Oh, yes,' said Louise, suddenly breaking into a smile. 'She's done so well! The programme at Forest Lodge is just wonderful. You'd almost never know . . .'

She broke off suddenly, as though struck by something, and frowned.

'Well, I'll be in touch,' said Frances. She looked seriously at Louise. 'And I'm sorry about Gillian Russet. I hope very much that Alan will be able to persuade her that testifying against you is not, as she seems to think, her duty. But I'm afraid she's not constrained to do what he advises; she's her own person.' She spread her hands helplessly.

'Well, thanks for trying, anyway,' said Louise. 'Thank you . . .' She swallowed. 'Thank you for everything.'

Meredith was not as glad as Frances had predicted. She glared at Frances as she handed her a glass of sherry, and said, reproachfully, 'You're supposed to be on our side.'

'Meredith,' remonstrated Frances. 'I'll pretend you didn't really say that.'

'Well, for Pete's sake, Frances,' said Meredith, 'this is taking good behaviour a bit far, isn't it? You'll be testifying against us in court, next.'

'Meredith!' said Frances, suddenly angry, 'I can't believe you're so obsessed by this case that you can't feel compassion for an injured child.'

Meredith stared at Frances, chastened.

'I know,' she muttered eventually, 'I'm sorry. I think it's really good of you to help out like that.' She took a sip of vodka. 'And I even think you're right about this nut-case woman,' she added. 'If she offers to besmirch Louise's character in court for us, we'll say, no thanks.'

'I think that would be wise,' said Frances.

'Even though', Meredith's eyes began to gleam, 'it would be great to have her up there on the stand. Wouldn't it? I mean, she's practically saying Louise threw Katie off the diving-board herself!'

'She's completely overreacted to the situation,' said Frances. 'I'm sure she'll calm down eventually.'

'That's what I keep saying,' put in Ursula, surprisingly, from her corner chair. 'I'm sure everyone will calm down eventually and this silly case will all blow over.'

Frances glanced at Meredith, who raised her eyebrows and shrugged her shoulders.

'I hope you're right, Ursula,' said Frances pleasantly, 'but, you know, I'd say there's a fair chance it might not blow over. You really should be prepared for that.'

Ursula, who was bent once more over her tapestry, looked up. She opened her mouth to speak, then closed it again. She had to admit, in her own mind, that her conciliatory letter to Louise had not been as effective as she had hoped. Louise had returned the bundle of banknotes almost immediately, accompanied by a short note which thanked Ursula politely for her kind wishes and added that she couldn't possibly accept so much money.

But Ursula had not given up. The bundle of money still sat, untouched, in her dressing-table, together with another, unfinished letter. She was absolutely sure that if only she could express herself properly; if only she could find exactly the right words, then all this unpleasantness could be overcome . . .

Ursula's thoughts were interrupted by Meredith.

'You know,' she was saying to Frances, 'what gets me is walking through the village and seeing everyone's faces, and knowing they've been talking about it.' She gestured dramatically with her arm. 'Seeing their gleaming eyes, and their hands rubbing together, waiting for our downfall. They just can't wait.'

'Rubbish,' said Frances. She grinned at Meredith. 'You're just getting paranoid.'

'It's true,' insisted Meredith. 'All the sympathy's on Katie's side. They think we must be child murderers or something. And what they really want is for the courts to make a huge award to the Kembers. A kind of lottery award. A couple of million pounds would do the trick. So they can all gasp to each other, and wonder what they would do if *they* won two million. Then, of course, when they realize it's us who's got to pay it, a few will start feeling sorry for us, but it'll be too late by then. Far, far too late.' She tossed her hair melodramatically.

'Meredith!' Frances was laughing. 'I'm sure no-one thinks like that.'

'Don't be too sure,' said Meredith darkly. 'You don't know how low people sink when the vicar's wife isn't around to keep them in line.'

She grinned wickedly at Frances, who blushed very slightly and said, 'Nonsense!'

Ursula, whose attention had drifted away during Meredith's little speech, put down her tapestry and stood up.

'I'm going to pick some raspberries for supper,' she said.

'I'll come out in a minute,' said Meredith. 'Have another drink, Frances.'

Frances hesitated, then she held out her glass.

'I think I need it,' she said cheerfully. 'After listening to nonsensical tirades from you *and* Gillian Russet in one evening . . .' She looked at Meredith and gave a little giggle.

'Actually,' she said, as Ursula closed the door, 'I was thinking, as I listened to Gillian shouting down the phone, that if any court heard such a dreadful diatribe against Louise, they would probably immediately find in Louise's favour. Just out of sympathy.'

Meredith grinned.

'I guess no witness is better than a lousy witness.' She lowered her voice. 'Mind you, what about poor old Ursula? If she has to testify as a witness, we're done for. Witless, more like.' She began to shake with giggles. 'She'll say something like . . . she always thought the swimming-pool was dangerous for children.'

'Don't!' said Frances, trying not to laugh. Suddenly Meredith stopped giggling.

'Oh Jeez. Why am I laughing about it?' She leaned back and closed her eyes. 'The worst thing is how long everything is taking. I mean, they haven't even filed their claim against us yet. This whole case could take years, and meanwhile we can't make any plans. Oh, no, better not do that; we might go bankrupt next year. What kind of life is that?' She took a swig of vodka, emptying her glass, and roughly put it down on a side-table, with a little crash.

Frances took a sip of sherry and looked seriously at Meredith.

'Why is it taking so long?'

Meredith shrugged. 'Alexis says there's been some delay on the other side. Apparently these things always take ages; lawyers are never in a hurry.' She ran a hand through her hair and winced as it was caught up in a tangle. 'It's fine for them,' she said in a bitter voice. 'They're not even paying their own fucking legal fees. Nothing to lose.'

'And you . . .'

'Alexis is being very generous,' said Meredith in a carefully flat voice, 'but he has to eat. He can't do it all for nothing.' She picked up her glass and got up to pour another drink, ignoring Frances's quizzical look.

When she sat down again, she seemed to be pondering whether to say something. Frances waited. Eventually Meredith said, in a low casual voice, 'What is it with Alexis, Frances? I really like him, you know.' She swallowed. 'I always thought he and I might . . . you know, get together.' She fingered the soft fabric of the sofa. 'And he's round here often enough – I'm sure he wants to make a move on me, but nothing ever happens.'

Meredith paused. She could feel Frances drawing breath, and hurriedly carried on, 'So I was wondering,' she said in a rush, 'do you think it would be a good idea to make a pass? Or do you think that would frighten him off?'

Meredith looked up. The expression on Frances's face scared her.

'What?' she said. 'What is it?'

'Don't you know?' said Frances. She exhaled sharply. 'I can't believe you don't know.'

'Know? Know what?' Meredith's heart began to thud. 'What should I know?'

'Oh, Meredith,' said Frances sadly. She took hold of Meredith's hand. 'Alexis is having an affair.' She paused and squeezed Meredith's cold hand tighter. 'He's having an affair . . . with little Daisy Phillips.'

Chapter Fifteen

Alexis lay entwined with Daisy on the floor of her sitting-room, while around them pounded and swirled a Sibelius symphony. He had just brought Daisy to a shuddering orgasm, and was now watching her face with almost unbearable tenderness, as her contorted features softened, her eyes slowly opened, and she gave him a shy embarrassed smile.

He stared at her silently, running his eyes over her flushed face; breathing in her scent; feeling the haunting, pulsating, powerful music coursing through the air and into his body. He felt as though each sense and every emotion was being tested to breaking-point. Daisy gave a little sigh and snuggled closer, so that her body fitted neatly into his. She smiled up at Alexis and he looked back; unable to express himself; unable to do anything except put out a trembling finger and gently push back a strand of her hair.

'I always . . .' began Daisy in a soft voice against his chest. She stopped. Alexis ran an encouraging hand down her back, around her waist, and began to tickle her tummy. She giggled.

'What do you always?' he said tenderly.

'I always think . . .' Daisy blushed. 'I think . . . will it really happen again? You know . . . will I . . .' She broke off and blushed even harder. 'Each time, it's so lovely, I can't believe it'll ever happen again.'

Alexis stopped tickling Daisy's tummy and kissed her neck. Daisy gave a little gasp.

'I don't mean', she added hurriedly, 'that I don't think

you . . . I mean, I know you're really . . .' She broke off and looked at him with worried eyes, as though afraid she might have given offence. Alexis threw back his head and laughed.

'Daisy, my darling, it's all right. You're allowed to doubt my technique if you like.' Daisy gave a little jump.

'But I don't,' she said anxiously. 'I didn't mean . . .'

'It's all right,' said Alexis. 'I know what you meant.' Daisy stared at him doubtfully for a moment, then smiled and closed her eyes.

Alexis stared at the roughly plastered, oak-beamed ceiling. The symphony had reached its inexorable climax; triumphant horns and strings pounded loudly around him. And inside, Alexis felt a soaring triumph to match. But it was a triumph dulled by a strange, chastening humility. He had felt humble ever since, a few weeks ago, they had made love for the first time – and for Daisy, it had transpired, the first time ever.

He still remembered the shock – of panic, guilt, and a sneaking relief – as he'd discovered that he was the first. He'd been sliding a cautious hand up between her legs, hastily shaking off his own trousers at the same time, trying desperately to judge her expression, ready at any moment to retreat if necessary. And, to pave the way slightly, he had murmured against her neck, 'It must seem strange for you – doing this with someone so much older.'

And she'd looked at him with dark aroused eyes, and said in a soft husky voice, 'It's strange anyway . . . the first time. It wouldn't really matter who it was with.'

Somehow the possibility that Daisy was a virgin had never before occurred to Alexis. He had always thought of her simply as . . . very young, unthinkably young. But a virgin, too? Wasn't that taking things too far? For a few moments he froze, and it came to him that he must immediately call a halt to the whole affair; that the idea of seducing a young, vulnerable, teenage virgin

210

was disgusting, risky and morally unforgivable.

But a glimpse of Daisy's unsheathed breasts in front of him, of her quivering lips and her warm pink cheeks, distracted him from his principles. Furiously he reminded himself that she was eighteen; that she could make her own decisions; that he had not, by any means, forced himself on her. And when she gently put up one hand to caress his chest, Alexis's resolve had crumbled, his desire took over, and there was no turning back.

That first time had been painful, funny, unbearably moving. Painful for Daisy, funny for both of them, unbearably moving for Alexis. He'd left her in the early hours of the morning and driven home, staggered into the bathroom, and stared at himself in the mirror, in a kind of silent, elated, horrified amazement.

Since then the amazement had never quite gone away. Alexis sometimes found himself staring at Daisy, as though he were a stranger – taking in, as he had that day at the swimming-pool, her pale beautiful face, her hesitant manner, and her doubtful smile – and felt as though he had no right to be so close to her; as though he'd somehow tricked his way into a position of intimacy and would, any day now, be discovered, exposed, rejected.

And then he would begin, rather bleakly, to consider once again the huge chasm between their ages. Deliberately torturing himself, he would look first at her smooth face, and then at his own lined forehead; at her luxuriant locks and then at his own thinning greying hair. Her eyes were large and bright; his were small, hooded and weary-looking. He was old and jaded; she was fresh and new. A walnut and a peach.

Daisy shifted slightly and Alexis found his arms closing protectively around her.

'What,' she began softly, still with her eyes closed. 'What are we going to have for supper?'

*   *   *

211

Alexis had been staggered to discover Daisy's lack of culinary knowledge. He was used to women his own age, experienced cooks, who would tease him about his limited bachelor's kitchen, allow him to chop an onion or two, but basically take over the cooking for the duration of their relationship. This, despite the fact that he was not at all a bad cook. He generally favoured straightforward food that didn't take long to prepare: fillet steaks – charred on the outside, pink in the middle; grilled fish, basted with olive oil and lime juice; lamb chops, sprinkled with garlic and rosemary; roasted vegetables; interesting salads.

Daisy's repertoire, as far as he could make out, extended only as far as dried pasta combined with bottled pesto sauce – and maybe a can of tuna thrown in. She seemed to live on this diet, together with bowls of Shreddies, chocolate digestives, and the occasional pink grapefruit. The first time he'd cooked supper for her, she had astounded him by saying, in a casual way, 'Oh, *that's* what garlic looks like.' Alexis stared at her, almost lost for words.

'You're not serious? You've never seen garlic before?'

'Oh, yes, of course I have,' said Daisy quickly. 'Strings of garlic. But I've never seen what they look like inside.' She took in Alexis's expression and added earnestly, 'But I do love it. I love garlic bread.' She thought. 'Actually, there might be some garlic bread in the freezer.'

'Daisy,' Alexis had said, beginning to laugh, 'there's a little bit more to garlic than pre-packed frozen garlic bread.'

Now, watching Daisy as she inexpertly sliced a red pepper, Alexis said, 'Haven't you ever done any cooking?' Daisy looked up and pushed back the sleeves of her pale cotton kimono.

'Well, not really,' she said. 'At school . . . well, you don't really cook at school. And then on holiday we

212

didn't really cook either, and at home . . .' She screwed up her face. 'I suppose we must cook a bit at home,' she said eventually, 'but not very much. My parents often go out for supper, and when my brothers were at home they just used to phone up for pizzas and things like that. And if Mummy has a dinner party she gets in caterers . . .' She tailed off and looked down at the chopping board. 'I've done the pepper,' she said. 'What shall I do now?'

Alexis stared at her, feeling a sudden anger at these parents who blithely left Daisy alone in the dubious care of two brothers and a pizza delivery firm. A thought struck him.

'Didn't you have cookery lessons at school?'

'Oh, yes,' said Daisy. 'I made a swiss roll, but it broke when I tried to roll it up. And then I was given extra piano lessons instead, and I didn't have cookery any more.' She looked at Alexis anxiously. 'And I can't remember how to make the swiss roll.'

Alexis laughed.

'Well, that's a relief,' he said. 'Swiss roll is one of my least favourite things.' He opened the fridge, took out a bottle of Chardonnay, and briskly uncorked it. 'Anyway,' he said, 'school isn't where you should learn how to cook.'

'Where should you learn?' said Daisy.

'In your own kitchen, of course. You should learn to cook by cooking for people you really like,' said Alexis. 'Family, friends, lovers. That's how I learned. Not by making swiss roll in a classroom.'

He handed a glass of wine to Daisy, who stared into the bottom of it for a minute or two. When she looked up, her cheeks were burning red.

'Who did you . . .' she began hesitantly. 'Did you ever . . . have you been . . .' She broke off and looked away. For a few moments Alexis stared at her in puzzlement. Then his expression changed.

'Are you trying to ask me if I've ever been married?' he said gently. Daisy's head didn't move.

'The answer's no, I've never been married,' said Alexis carefully. He sat down on a kitchen chair. 'I had a long-term relationship with a woman I met through the law,' he said slowly. 'She was the same age as me and very ambitious. I asked her to marry me, but she didn't want to; she wanted to concentrate on her career.'

He stopped and took a slug of wine.

'Wh-what happened?' asked Daisy timidly.

'She left me after twelve years and married another man,' said Alexis. A sudden bleak expression came over his face. 'They've just had their second baby,' he said quietly.

Daisy stared at him in horror. She didn't know what to say.

'That's awful,' she whispered.

'It was pretty bad at the time,' said Alexis, 'but that's a while ago now; years, in fact. I've completely recovered.' He grinned at Daisy and took another huge gulp of wine.

Daisy gazed at him silently, unconvinced.

'Oh, Daisy,' said Alexis, 'don't look so upset.'

'I'm not,' protested Daisy. 'I'm just . . .' She broke off and looked at the floor.

'Talking about the past is never a good idea,' said Alexis easily. 'Now, why don't you go and play the piano? You said you needed to practise,' he reminded her.

'Oh, yes,' said Daisy. 'I do.' She looked at Alexis. 'But what about the supper?'

'I'll manage,' said Alexis, glancing at the ragged slices of red pepper on Daisy's chopping board and trying not to smile. 'I'll finish off and then come and listen.'

When she had gone, he worked quickly, assembling a fragrant chicken casserole, popping it into the oven and putting on a pan of rice. Then, refilling his glass, he went through into the sitting-room.

Daisy was practising the Brahms concerto which she was due to perform soon with the Linningford Symphony Orchestra. She was playing through the second movement, and had reached a passage of thundering chords which Alexis recognized. In the weeks that he'd heard her practising them, the chords had become louder, faster and more assured. Now she was hitting the keys of the piano with a confident power which staggered him.

As he watched, her hands pounded furiously up and down the keyboard, filling the room with blazing sound, until suddenly her fingers tripped up on the sleeve of her kimono. Impatiently, she pushed the sleeve up and began again. The music got louder and more impassioned. All of a sudden her fingers tripped on the kimono sleeve again; this time, without pausing, she shrugged off the kimono altogether. The two empty cotton sleeves dropped down to the floor behind her, and seemingly without missing a beat, Daisy kept playing. Her bare arms moved with even more vitality; her fingers thundered out the tune of the concerto; and her clouds of dark hair rose and fell around her naked shoulders. And Alexis watched her playing, oblivious of him; oblivious of anything else, and thought that in his whole life, he had never felt such overwhelming happiness as he did now.

Chapter Sixteen

Cassian was feeling very pleased at the way things were progressing. Louise's case seemed more promising every day; evidence was mounting up nicely, and the senior partner at the Linningford office had personally praised him, in a large meeting, for having spotted the litigious possibilities of the situation so quickly. This had been followed by some light-hearted joshing about Louise and her father, Lord Page, which Cassian had taken in good spirit. The chaps were obviously impressed, both by his work and by his connections.

And on the strength of all this, he'd persuaded some of the London boys to come down and get involved with the case. Just to make sure he wasn't forgotten about, back in the London office. That very day, Desmond Pickering and Karl Foster, both personal injury experts, were in Linningford for a meeting, and Cassian had persuaded them to come along afterwards to Melbrook and meet up with himself, Louise and – unfortunately but unavoidably – Barnaby. They were going to discuss the case for an hour or two, then Barnaby was going to leave, and Louise would cook the rest of them dinner. The conversation would turn to politics. Louise would impress Desmond and Karl with inside stories of the former Cabinet. Cassian would glow in reflected glory. And the result would surely be that next time a partnership was on offer, his name would be remembered.

So far so good. Cassian's one slight lingering annoyance was that he hadn't yet managed to meet Lord Page. Meeting Lord Page, and becoming friendly with him, was crucial to Cassian's political game plan. To grind up to Parliament through a series of dreary local government posts was one thing, but if he had the patronage of a senior statesman, Cassian reasoned, he would naturally find himself on a quicker and more successful route into politics. What easier way to impress a selection committee and inveigle himself into the right crowd, than by appearing as Lord Page's heir apparent?

And now that he was fully-fledged as Louise's lover; now that he was spending whole nights in her bed; now that he was actually involved in a case which Lord Page was funding, he felt entitled to a meeting with the great man. But she had not suggested it and, until now, he had felt that it would be too crude to mention it himself. Now he was not so sure.

A thrill ran through him as he imagined developing a friendship with Lord Page; with a peer of the realm. In spite of himself, he had a sudden brief memory of his grandmother, attired in lurid pink, drinking sweet tea from a silver jubilee mug. Despite the Italian accent still lingering under her whining Macclesfield vowels, she had always been devoted to the British royal family, and, by extension, all members of the titled classes. She would have been overwhelmed if he had told her about Lord Page.

But Cassian didn't communicate with his grandmother any more, nor with his parents, nor with his two stupid sisters. He had not been back to Macclesfield once since leaving for his first term at Oxford; and over the years since then, he had reinvented his background to such an extent that he now almost genuinely believed he came from some kind of Italian aristocratic stock.

He looked at Louise. The Honourable Louise.

'Darling,' he began pleasantly. Louise looked up from the paper banner she was making and flushed. She was still unused to sharing a breakfast table with Cassian, let alone hearing endearments over the toast.

'Yes?'

'I was just wondering how your father was.' Cassian looked earnestly at Louise. 'You mentioned a while ago that he wasn't well.'

'Oh,' said Louise vaguely. 'Well, he's much better now. He's got a private nurse who looks after him, so there's nothing to worry about.'

'You can't have seen him for a bit,' said Cassian lightly.

'No,' said Louise. She put down her marker pen and sighed. 'I did mean to go over when he wasn't well, but I just couldn't bear to take the time out from seeing Katie. But maybe now we can all go over there together.' She grinned at Cassian. 'Isn't it exciting!'

'What?' For a split second, Cassian looked blank. 'Oh, yes,' he added hastily. 'Tremendously exciting!' He glanced down at the banner which Louise was now decorating with flowers. 'WELCOME HOME KATIE,' it said, in bold multi-coloured letters.

'And are you keeping your father informed about the case?' persisted Cassian. 'Does he know how hard we're fighting?' That ought to earn him a few Brownie points in the old man's books, he thought complacently to himself.

'Oh, erm, yes. I told him all about it.' Louise flushed slightly and looked down. She could not tell Cassian that her father refused to take any interest in the details of the litigation, despite the fact that he was paying for it.

'Bloody lawyers!' he'd yelled, as soon as she'd begun to explain it. 'Can't stand the chaps. Just send along the bills and I'll settle them, but don't expect me to listen to their bloody claptrap! And don't start trusting the fellows, whatever you do!' Then, before she could gather her wits enough to interrupt, he'd told her at great length about his old chum, Dick Foxton, who was a marvellous lawyer, full of good sense, and why on earth hadn't Louise gone to old Dickie instead of these dreadful city chaps?

'The thing is,' Cassian was saying, 'it would be great to meet him.'

'Oh. Yes, I suppose it would,' said Louise. She smiled. 'Yes, that would be nice. Well, maybe in a couple of weeks' time. When Katie's got used to being at home.' As she said the words, a wide smile stretched involuntarily across her face. Cassian looked at her glowing expression, and realized that now was not the time to pursue a meeting with Lord Page.

Katie had improved so much over the last couple of weeks that her home-coming had been brought forward substantially. Today she was leaving Forest Lodge for good. She was due to arrive home at lunchtime, and Louise had spent some time creating a special celebration lunch. Bunches of blown-up balloons were bouncing around the kitchen, waiting to be put up, and Amelia was in her bedroom, busily making a welcome-home card. The air in the house was one of festive anticipation.

Cassian found it all rather irritating. He had long ago earmarked today as the date for the meeting with Desmond and Karl. They were important busy men; it was a huge honour, a momentous occasion. Louise should have been spending the day preparing a sophisticated dinner and witty anecdotes, not blowing up balloons and making banners.

And when he'd gently reminded her about the meeting, she'd been insultingly cavalier. First she'd casually suggested postponing it. Postponing it! As if Desmond and Karl didn't have bursting, fully booked diaries! As if this meeting hadn't been nearly impossible to arrange in the first place! Gently but firmly, feeling a frustrated impatience, Cassian had impressed upon her the important nature of this event; the prestige of working with Desmond and Karl; the absolute

necessity of meeting them that evening. Whereupon
Louise had shrugged and said, 'Oh, OK then.' No thanks
for Cassian's efforts; no humble acknowledgement of
the honour being bestowed upon her. It was almost
degrading.

Now he looked firmly at Louise and took a sip of
coffee.

'We'll have to make sure that Amelia and Katie are in
bed before the meeting starts,' he said. 'We don't want
them getting in the way.'

'Amelia won't go to bed at six o'clock!' objected
Louise, giving a little laugh. 'I'll make sure she plays
quietly in her room, and then she can go to bed at eight
as usual. But I expect Katie will have an early night.'

'Well, we don't want any disturbances,' said Cassian.
'Perhaps Barnaby could go and supervise Amelia while
we're having the meeting.'

'But he needs to be at the meeting!'

'Well, then maybe you could ask Mary Tracey to come
and sit with Amelia.'

'What, and bring little Luke? He makes more noise
than either of them!' Louise put down the pink marker
she was using to draw flowers, and smiled at Cassian.
'Don't worry,' she said, 'I'm sure the girls will have had
such an exciting day they'll go straight to sleep.'

Cassian looked sternly at Louise and wondered
whether it was worth trying once again to convince her
of the importance of this meeting. But as he was formulating the right phrases in his mind; as he was trying to
adopt a severe, meaningful expression, the doorbell
rang. Louise threw down the banner and hurried to the
door; a moment later the unmistakable heavy tread of
Barnaby could be heard in the hall.

As he entered the kitchen, Barnaby was saying gruffly
to Louise, 'I got a bit upset by it. Hi, Cassian,' he added.

'Hello, Barnaby,' said Cassian politely. 'What upset
you?' Some tedious agricultural catastrophe, no doubt.

'I just passed Hugh in the street,' said Barnaby uncomfortably. 'He looked absolutely awful. Really haggard and miserable.'

'Did you speak to him?' said Cassian sharply.

'No,' said Barnaby, looking downwards miserably. 'When he saw me coming, he . . . he crossed over onto the other side of the street.'

'Oh, well then,' said Cassian. 'It doesn't matter then.'

'It does matter!' exclaimed Barnaby. 'He looked appalling! I had no idea . . .'

'Oh, Barnaby, honestly,' said Louise. 'He was probably just having a bad day. Come on.' Her voice softened slightly. 'You're the one who's always saying that Katie should be our number one priority and nobody else matters. Don't get all worried about Hugh! Think about Katie!'

'I know,' said Barnaby slowly. 'You're right.' He looked at Louise's cheerful face and smiled cautiously. 'Tell you what,' he said, glancing around, 'I'll get going on the balloons.'

They arrived back from Forest Lodge just after one o'clock. The first thing Katie saw as the car pulled up was the old brown wooden gate. She peered at it through the car window, and felt, vaguely, that she'd seen it before.

'Welcome home!' said her mother, turning round and smiling brightly at her. 'You're home again!' Katie smiled because her mother was smiling, but inside she felt confused. She'd heard lots about home in the last few days, but she wasn't sure she remembered properly what it was.

Since the accident, there were lots of things that she didn't remember properly, and there were some things that she thought she remembered but weren't true. A couple of weeks ago, she'd been convinced that she had lived at Forest Lodge when she was a tiny baby; she could remember her father living there, and her mother, and Amelia, too. But Mummy had said that it wasn't true and she must have dreamed it.

'Come on, then,' said her father. 'Let's get you out of the car.' He leaned over and unbuckled Katie's seat-belt, then got out of the car and opened her door. Slowly, cautiously, Katie got out.

In front of her was a familiar house. Katie peered at it, then looked uncertainly at her father.

'Do you remember?' he was saying. He was smiling at her with his big wide smile. Everybody was smiling. Katie looked at the house again and felt a strange tweaking in her head. As she stared, she had a fleeting dreamlike memory of being inside the house, once, long ago. But the vision evaporated almost immediately, and suddenly she wasn't sure whether she'd ever seen the house before in her life. She felt cold and rather scared, and looked up at her father.

'When are we going back to Forest Lodge?' she said carefully. Sometimes, if she spoke too quickly, no-one could understand her. But Debbie, who came to see her every morning, had practised speaking slowly and steadily with her, and now she hardly ever rushed her words.

'We're not going back to Forest Lodge, Katkin,' her father said happily. 'You're coming back here for good!'

Katie felt a cold nervous fear creeping through her. She didn't want to stay at this strange-familiar house. She wanted her own bed and all her friends, and Mummy and Daddy to come and see her every day. She looked down at her shoes; smart new shoes that had been bought especially for today. Her face grew hot and for a moment she thought she might start to cry.

Then, suddenly, the front door opened. Amelia came running out, shouting, 'Welcome home!' Katie looked past her and saw the wooden floor and pale blue walls of the hall. As she did so, she felt more tweakings in her head. Gradually a cosy feeling began to spread through her; memories and pictures began to fill her head, and above all, a comforting weighty certainty. She knew this house; it was home.

'Let's play French skipping!' said Amelia, running up to Katie and giving her a hug. 'I missed you!'

Katie stood silently for a minute, her face blank and her mind painfully working. Then suddenly her face lit up and she gave a roar of delight. She ran down the path and into the house. Amelia followed right behind her and Louise and Barnaby hastened after them. They found Katie joyfully running from one room to another, stroking the sofa and the curtains and the kitchen stools. Amelia tried to stop her, but Katie shrugged her off with another roar.

'Leave her,' said Louise quietly. 'She's just so pleased to be home.'

By twenty to six the house had quietened down slightly, Barnaby had gone home to get changed for the meeting, and Katie had been persuaded into bed.

'Thank God for routine,' said Louise, descending the stairs and grinning at Cassian. 'That was the great thing about Forest Lodge. Bedtime was exactly the same, every day.'

'Yes, I'm sure,' said Cassian, who wasn't listening. He was peering out of the hall window, watching for Desmond and Karl.

'I hope they aren't lost,' he muttered.

'I'm sure they're fine,' said Louise cheerfully. 'Let's have a drink.'

As they went into the kitchen Louise felt her spirits lifting and a strange joyful lightness pervading her body. She felt as though she might float away with happiness. Katie was home, back in her old bed. Life was getting back to normal, and normal life had never looked so attractive.

'It's the relief which is so wonderful,' she said slowly, opening the fridge and getting out a bottle of wine. 'It's this amazing sensation of relief. I feel as though I've had a terrible headache for the last few months and it's finally going. My whole body feels happy.'

She poured out two glasses, watching the light reflected in the pale amber liquid, anticipating the taste, feeling an unbearable pleasure in being a simple unconcerned mother, able to drink a glass of wine while her children slept peacefully upstairs. Just like any other mother.

Then the doorbell rang, and Louise felt a predictable spasm of panic tear through her. Ever since Katie had started to improve; ever since things had started to look up, Louise had found herself experiencing flurries of nervous panic several times every day; almost as though her mind wasn't going to let her get away with it that easily. Every wave of panic was accompanied by a sensation of guilt and followed, like a stern reminder, by a painful recollection of the deep dragging despair of those first few weeks.

'I wonder who that is,' she said in an almost shaky voice, but Cassian had already leaped up to answer the door.

'Hello, Barnaby,' Louise heard him say in undisguised disappointment. 'Oh!' His voice was suddenly alert. 'Is that Karl and Desmond parking over there? Excellent. Why don't you go on through, Barnaby, and I'll wait for them.'

Louise had opened a beer for Barnaby by the time he reached the kitchen. He grinned shyly at her.

'Katie in bed?'

'Yes,' said Louise. She smiled back at Barnaby. 'That was a wonderful home-coming. I'm so glad you took the afternoon off.' Barnaby flushed slightly.

'It was good fun,' he said gruffly.

'Here we are!' They both looked up at Cassian's voice.

'Louise, this is Desmond Pickering and Karl Foster, from our London office. Desmond, Karl, allow me to introduce Louise Kember.'

Louise stood up. Behind Cassian in the hall were standing two extremely smart men. Both wore expensive-looking suits with button-down shirts and silk ties. Desmond's tie was covered in a repeating pattern of horseshoes, while Karl's was wittily decorated with little winged pigs. The two men smiled at Louise with identical smiles, and she had a sudden terrible desire to giggle.

'And this is Barnaby,' added Cassian, in kind but patronizing tones, as though Barnaby were the dog or the budgie.

'Hello!' said Barnaby, giving the two men his wide smile. Louise saw the younger man, Karl, running his eyes over Barnaby's suit, in what looked like mirthful amazement, and she felt a brief flicker of indignation. But there was no time for her to say anything because Cassian was ushering them all into the sitting-room, where he had laid out pads of paper and pencils and glasses of wine.

'So,' said the older man, Desmond, when they had all sat down. He looked at Louise. 'The facts of this case, as I understand them, are that your daughter was injured in a swimming-pool accident, and you would like to sue the owners of the swimming-pool. Is that it?'

Louise glanced at Cassian, and then, hesitantly, nodded. Desmond smiled kindly at her. Now that the two London lawyers were closer, Louise could see that they weren't quite the identical twins she had first perceived. Karl had fresh boyish looks, plumped out with a serene gloss of confidence. Desmond, meanwhile, had a long, intelligent, strangely ugly face. He looked older and wearier than Karl, but wore his confidence more easily, as though it were deeply and permanently ingrained in him.

'The first thing I always say to potential litigants', he was saying now, 'is that the law is a strange, rather unpredictable beast. However strong a case you have, you must be prepared for the chance of failure. You must also be prepared for a long hard fight.' He took a sip of wine. 'But I'm sure Cassian has said all this to you already,' he added, smiling at Cassian.

'Oh, yes,' began Louise. But Barnaby's voice cut across hers.

'Not to me, he hasn't,' he said. He gazed at Desmond with huge brown eyes. 'Are you trying to say we're going to lose?' Desmond exchanged the briefest of glances with Karl.

'Of course not,' he said warmly to Barnaby. 'I say these things to everybody. It's just a general warning.' He gave Barnaby his kind smile. 'You must realize that in a case such as this, nothing can be certain.'

'I thought you said . . .' began Barnaby, in a voice that was too loud for the little sitting-room. He coughed and started again, lowering his voice. 'I thought you said it was definite?' He looked at Cassian. 'I thought the letter from Ursula clinched it?'

Cassian looked at Barnaby in annoyance.

'Well, of course it's not definite!' he snapped. 'If the thing were completely and utterly definite, we wouldn't have to bother to go to court, would we? It'd just be "Advance to Go. Collect two hundred pounds". Or half a million, in our case.'

Karl gave a little snigger, but Desmond was looking concernedly at Barnaby.

'You seem to have been given the wrong impression,' he said. 'Nothing is certain until the judgment is given. That applies to all cases.'

'Or until you settle,' put in Karl, who had taken out a tiny calculator and was squinting at it.

'Yes indeed,' said Desmond irritably. 'But we won't get on to the issue of settling just yet. Do you

226

understand . . .' He frowned. 'Sorry, it's . . .'

'Barnaby,' said Barnaby. He took a slug of beer and frowned. 'Yes, I understand. Sorry, I just got a bit rattled.' He shrugged. 'Going on about how we might fail. It just . . . I don't know. It worried me.'

'Of course it did,' said Desmond kindly.

'Of course it did,' echoed Karl, looking up from his calculator. They smiled in smooth unison at Barnaby.

'Shall we get on?' said Cassian, with ill-disguised impatience. He handed Karl and Desmond each a pile of photocopied sheets of paper. 'This is the case as it stands. Have a look.'

As the two men studied the papers in front of them, Cassian tried to impart his irritated impatience to Louise, but she was giving Barnaby a sympathetic smile. There was silence in the room, apart from the rustling of the sheets of paper.

'Where's the evidence from the diving-board expert?' said Desmond suddenly.

'Still waiting for it,' said Cassian. Desmond gave a grunt and turned the sheet.

Louise began to feel inexplicably nervous, as though she were on trial herself.

'Hmm,' said Desmond, when he had got to the bottom of the pile. 'There's a lot to work with here. Well done, Cassian.' Louise turned and beamed at Cassian, who tried to prevent a smile from spreading across his face. 'You've got some nice eye-witness evidence. I take it the diving-board expert will come up with the goods?' Cassian's face clouded.

'I don't know,' he admitted. 'He wouldn't say anything on the spot.'

'Well, I'm sure there are more where he came from,' said Desmond. 'If we need them.' He put the papers down and leaned easily back in his chair. 'A couple of things worry me, though,' he said. 'The first I think we can deal with quite easily.'

'What is it?' said Cassian quickly.

'The piece of evidence from the woman who said the children were running around and shouting before the accident.' Desmond shook his head at Cassian. 'I don't like that. Implies carelessness on the child's part.'

'But she's the same one who emphasized the fact that there wasn't a supervisor present,' Cassian said hurriedly. 'It's a useful bit of evidence, and I'm sure she'll be fine in court.'

Desmond frowned.

'Not good enough, Cassian,' he said. Cassian flushed. 'We need to anticipate the fact that the other side will claim contributory negligence.'

'Contributory negligence?' said Barnaby. 'What the hell's that?'

'That's when the plaintiff is found to have contributed to the accident, through his or her own carelessness or negligence,' reeled off Karl, who had begun tapping at his calculator again.

'But surely a child . . .' began Louise.

'Doesn't matter,' said Karl, without looking up. 'I'm thinking of cases like Davis v Leemings. And Brakespear v Smith.'

Louise and Barnaby exchanged glances.

'What happened in Brakespear v Smith?' Louise asked meekly.

'A ten-year-old girl was found seventy-five per cent to blame for being run over,' said Karl smoothly. 'Ran out into the road without looking.'

'Oh my God!' exclaimed Louise. 'That's awful! But Katie wouldn't . . .'

'In Davis v Leemings,' continued Karl inexorably, 'a twelve-year-old boy's damages were reduced by two-thirds because he ignored a warning sign. In Phillips v Fanshawe County Council . . .'

'Thank you, Karl,' interrupted Desmond testily. 'I think we get the picture.'

Louise was looking horrified.

'Surely no-one would try to say that Katie was to blame for her own accident,' she said in a rather shaky voice.

'I'm afraid they will,' said Desmond. 'If they've got anything about them, they'll certainly try. So we'll have to defuse their attack.' He looked at Louise. 'Does your daughter have a swimming teacher?'

'Yes,' said Louise, falteringly. 'But I just can't believe . . .' Desmond's smooth voice rode over hers.

'Right. Then we get the teacher to testify that Katie was a careful responsible pupil.'

'What if she wasn't?' said Karl impassively. Louise gave an indignant gasp.

'What do you mean?' shouted Barnaby. 'Are you saying . . .' Desmond ignored both of them.

'Doesn't matter. The teacher will testify that she was.' He paused. 'Think about it. You're the teacher. Are you going to admit that one of your pupils wasn't taught how to behave at a swimming-pool? No chance.'

Karl grinned admiringly down at his calculator.

'Good one,' he said and resumed tapping.

'But Katie was always careful!' exclaimed Louise. 'I mean, high-spirited, yes, but . . .'

'Yes, I'm sure she was,' said Desmond smoothly. 'Absolutely.' He smiled briefly at Louise, then looked down at his papers. 'Anyway, that's the first problem dealt with; the second is not so easy.' He looked at Cassian. 'These medical reports seem to imply a remarkably good recovery.'

'I know,' said Barnaby joyfully. 'Isn't it marvellous? She suddenly made great strides; she even came home early!' He stopped and looked helplessly at Louise. No-one was listening to him; Desmond's attention was still with Cassian.

'I thought this was a case of severe brain injury,' he said.

229

'It is!' said Cassian defensively. 'It was!' He looked down at his papers. 'Coma, brain clot, the works.'

'So what happened?' Cassian shrugged slightly.

'I don't know,' he said flatly, 'she just got better.' Suddenly he felt Louise's eyes burning into him. 'Which, of course, is wonderful news,' he added quickly.

'Wonderful for the child,' said Desmond; 'not so wonderful for the case. I'm not at all sure about five hundred thousand.' He glanced at Karl. 'You're the expert, Karl. What do you think?'

'I agree,' said Karl, finally looking up. 'We need a lot more than this to get anything like five hundred grand. We need – I don't know – psychiatric problems, maybe put in a bigger loss of earnings factor . . .' He broke off and looked at Louise. 'Was she particularly talented at anything?' Louise looked helplessly at Barnaby.

'She was talented at everything,' he said stoutly.

'Anything in particular?' pressed Karl. He looked at the others. 'You know Norrie Forbes? He had a great little case the other day. Young chap's hands crushed in a train door. Turns out he's a budding javelin thrower. Norrie had an Olympic selector in to rave about his chances. Won the case, of course. Fucking huge award.' He grinned. 'Anyway, the punch-line is, it turns out the chap was bored with javelin throwing. Apparently wants to go into computers, which he can do anyway.'

Cassian laughed and Desmond gave a wry grin. Louise caught Barnaby's eye. He had the same astounded look on his face that she could feel on hers.

'Don't you think . . .' she began, but she was interrupted by the door opening. It was Katie, clad in pyjamas and wearing a sleepy expression.

'Hello, Katie!' said Louise cheerfully. 'We've just been talking about you. Now, let's go back to bed.' Katie looked silently around the room, at the men in suits and the pieces of paper and glasses of wine. Then, suddenly she gave a huge grin.

'I'll play too!' she said in a loud clumsy voice.

'Not now,' said Louise and got up. Katie darted past her and ran into the centre of the room.

'Come on, Katkin,' said Barnaby. 'I'll read you a story.'

'No!' shouted Katie. She suddenly smiled again and, without pausing, began to take off her pyjama top.

'Katie!' exclaimed Louise. She glanced around apologetically. 'Sorry about this,' she said. 'It's one of the side-effects of the injury. They call it a loss of inhibition. We call it showing off.' Katie threw the pyjama top on the floor, and before she could start on her pyjama bottoms, both Louise and Barnaby hastily rushed forward. Barnaby got to her first.

'Now then!' he said, scooping Katie into his arms. 'Let's count the steps to the door!' He took a step. 'One!'

'One!' repeated Katie obediently. Clearly this was an old game. Louise picked up the pyjama top and handed it to Barnaby.

'I think you might want this,' she said, grinning ruefully at him.

'Thanks!' said Barnaby, grinning back. 'Two!' he added, and took another step.

'Two!' echoed Katie.

'Good girl!' said Louise. She looked at Barnaby. 'Do you want me to take over?'

'No, it's OK,' said Barnaby. 'I won't be too long. Three!'

'Three!'

'Well done!' As Barnaby shut the sitting-room door behind him, the sound of Katie's guffaw could be heard from the hall. Cassian sighed and leaned back in his chair.

'Well, she seems a lovely child,' said Desmond politely.

'She's wonderful,' said Louise, with shining eyes. 'She's still got a real sense of humour and she never gives up, however hard things seem.'

'She seems perfectly normal to me,' said Karl flatly.
'Is she really brain damaged?'

'Well,' said Louise steadily, 'part of her brain was
damaged in the accident, yes; so some of her brain functions were impaired. But the point of rehab is that it tries
to help other parts of the brain take over those functions.
It's amazing, really, just how adaptable the human brain
can be.' She flushed with pleasure. 'And Katie's
responded very well to treatment so far. I mean, there's
still a long road ahead, but it's been an absolute
miracle . . .'

'She's still very disturbed, though,' said Cassian
hastily. 'I mean, you saw her. She's lost all sense of how
to behave; she laughs at things which aren't funny; she
takes her clothes off at the wrong time . . . I mean, as far
as her personality goes, the accident was a catastrophe.'

'Personality disorders,' said Karl interestedly. 'I love
'em. We had a great case, couple of years ago, where a
woman was hit on the head and became a complete
nympho. But the husband didn't want a nympho, he
wanted his old frigid wife back. It was classic!' He
looked at Desmond. 'You must remember that one.
Brooks v Murkoff.' He began to tap again.

'Well, I think we can go a long way with personality
disorder here,' said Cassian confidently. 'Since her accident, Katie's noisy, uncontrollable, impossible to live
with . . . basically a complete walking disaster.'

'No she's not!' Louise's voice rose indignantly. 'She's
fine! She's lovely!' Cassian sighed impatiently.

'Louise, she's not fine and she's not lovely,' he
snapped. 'She's brain damaged! I mean, why the hell do
you think we're suing?' Louise looked from one lawyer
to another.

'Because of Katie's accident,' she said, in a voice
which trembled slightly. 'Because of all the pain and
suffering she went through. Because . . .'

'Pain and suffering!' Cassian's voice was dismissive.

232

'That's peanuts! We need long-term effects; we need psychiatric problems; we need loss of amenities of life; and we need you to testify.'

'What, and say my daughter's a complete walking disaster?'

'Yes!'

'Well, I won't! She isn't!' Louise's voice rose in distress through the house. There was a pause, then the sound of Barnaby running down the stairs. Desmond and Karl exchanged glances. Then the sitting-room door burst open and Barnaby appeared.

'What's wrong?' he demanded. Louise drew an indignant breath to speak, but before she could answer, from outside came the sudden loud wailing sound of an ambulance siren. Louise visibly jumped, and went pale. She clutched the arm of her chair and shut her eyes.

'Louise!' cried Cassian theatrically. 'Are you all right?' He leaped up and rushed to Louise, who put a trembling hand to her head.

'I'm fine,' she said in a faltering voice. 'Sirens still make me feel jumpy. It's stupid, really.' She grimaced. 'I wonder which poor person that was for.'

'Don't worry about that now,' soothed Cassian. 'Just lean back and take it easy.'

'Try to relax,' suggested Desmond.

'Absolutely,' said Karl cheerfully. 'How about some hot sweet tea? Or brandy? Or . . .'

Barnaby's hoarse voice interrupted him.

'What was all the fuss about?' he asked bluntly. 'I came down because I heard some shouting.'

'Nothing for you to worry about,' said Cassian at once. 'Just a small misunderstanding. I suggest, Barnaby, that we talk about it later. Now, I'm going to get Louise a glass of water.'

He got up and pushed past Barnaby, who opened his mouth, then closed it again. There was no point trying to argue with these fellows, he thought gloomily.

'In the circumstances,' said Desmond, 'perhaps we might leave it there for the moment.' He shuffled his papers and snapped shut his briefcase.

'Right,' said Barnaby reluctantly. 'Well, I'll be off, I suppose.'

'Good idea,' said Cassian, returning with a glass full of water.

'Bye, Barnaby,' said Louise. She smiled at him shakily. 'Thanks for coming.'

Barnaby said nothing. He felt irrationally angry, with Cassian, with himself, with Louise, with everyone. As he opened the front door, he heard the voice of that smarmy git, Desmond, saying in low engaging tones, 'You know, Louise, I've always been a terrific fan of your father.'

Barnaby closed the front door with a savage bang, feeling unsettled by the evening. As he stepped into the fragrant evening air, he said to himself, as he always did, 'I'm doing this for Katie. It'll be worth it for Katie.' But suddenly even that didn't seem certain any more; nothing seemed certain. Filled with doubts and fears and misgivings, Barnaby made his lonely way home.

Alexis and Daisy were curled up together in Alexis's generous double bed when the telephone rang.

'Damn,' said Alexis. 'Who the hell can that be?'

'Go on,' said Daisy, nudging him with her toes. 'It might be important.'

'Wrong number, more likely,' said Alexis, snuggling back down.

'Go on,' persisted Daisy, 'or I'll really embarrass you by answering it myself.'

Alexis gave her a strange unsmiling look.

'That wouldn't embarrass me at all,' he said. 'If you knew . . .'

'Go on!' said Daisy, pushing him hard with her toes

and giving a little giggle. 'Serves you right for not having a phone in your bedroom.'

'All right.' Alexis haphazardly wrapped his dressing-gown around him and pattered, barefoot, down the stairs. Daisy heard him cursing as he stubbed his toe and giggled. She couldn't hear him speaking because he was too far away, so she leaned back and looked at the ceiling and thought about the fingering in the third movement of the Brahms.

When Alexis reappeared at the door of the bedroom, she turned to him with a bright smile, saying, 'I think I've worked it . . .' But when she saw his expression, she tailed off. She had never seen Alexis look so shaken.

'Wh-what's happened?' she stammered. She felt an old familiar nervousness run through her body. Could it be anything she'd done? Had she upset him, somehow?

'What's wrong?' she tried again. Alexis blinked at her, and tried to smile.

'That was Meredith,' he began.

'Meredith Delaney? Is she OK?' Daisy peered at Alexis worriedly.

'She's fine,' said Alexis shakily. 'Fine.'

'Then what . . .'

'It's Hugh. He's had a heart attack.'

Chapter Seventeen

Hugh had been put in a private room on the cardiology ward. When Alexis arrived he was lying quite still in bed, his head resting on three plump pillows, his arm attached to some kind of drip. His eyes were closed and his face was pale and he was dressed in a white hospital gown which made him look disarmed and vulnerable. By the window stood Meredith, her shoulders hunched, her face downcast, and by Hugh's bed sat Ursula, looking small and frail and confused, like a little grey child.

Meredith was the first to look up.

'Hi there,' she said. Her voice sounded scorched and cracked. 'Thanks for coming.' Alexis met her eyes and then glanced at Hugh.

'Is he asleep?' he said gently. Meredith nodded.

'I think so.' She looked at Ursula.

'I'll take Alexis to get some coffee,' she said. 'You want some?' Ursula looked at her with blank frightened eyes.

'No thank you, dear,' she whispered eventually. 'Not just at the moment.'

As Meredith picked up her bag and shrugged on a jacket, Alexis looked around the silent cocooned room. He surveyed the low ceiling and smooth pale walls; he took in the plastic pitcher of water and blank television screen. The air was heavy and overwarm, and the whole atmosphere was one of oppression. And in the middle of all of it lay Hugh, still and pale and defenceless. Alexis could hardly bear to look at him.

Outside the room, Meredith gasped and sank down on a bench.

'You don't really want coffee, do you?' she asked, wrinkling her brow. Alexis shook his head. 'It's just so hard to talk about it with Ursula there,' continued Meredith, rubbing a hand over her face. 'I don't want to frighten her.' She paused and added in a low voice, 'I'm real grateful that you came. It was . . . it was good of you.'

Alexis looked carefully at her.

'What . . . What's the situation? Have they told you anything?' Meredith glanced down. For a few moments she was silent, then she looked up at Alexis with hot searing eyes.

'Basically, Hugh had a heart attack', she said slowly, in a voice which was tense with emotion, 'because he was stressed out. Because all day, all night, he does nothing except worry.' She paused and ran a thin hand through her hair. 'Because all he can think about is this *fucking* court case.'

She exhaled slowly and reached in her pocket for a cigarette. Alexis stared at her for a moment, then realized he was also holding his breath. He emptied his lungs in a gusty sigh, and watched, almost mesmerized, as Meredith flicked on the flame of her lighter.

'They're killing him,' she said suddenly, dragging deeply on her cigarette. 'They're fucking *killing* him!'

Alexis snapped back to attention.

'Are you sure . . .' he began cautiously, then broke off, as Meredith gave him a suspicious glare. He took a breath and tried again. 'Have the doctors actually *said* it was stress?'

'More or less,' said Meredith. She took a puff on her cigarette and hunched her shoulders miserably.

'Did they mention any other factors?' said Alexis in reasonable tones. Meredith scowled at him.

'Well, of course they did.'

'What, exactly? Too much alcohol?'

'Oh, Jesus! Why are you trying to shift the blame?' Meredith stood up angrily and her green eyes glittered at Alexis. 'You know why Hugh had this heart attack. It wasn't alcohol. It wasn't too many rare steaks. It was Louise and Barnaby fucking Kember and their stupid fucking court case.'

'Meredith, you don't know that . . .'

'Are you saying the case has got nothing to do with it?' Alexis stared at Meredith silently for a moment, then he sighed.

'Well . . . no,' he said slowly, 'I suppose not.' There was a short pause. Meredith stubbed out her cigarette, pulled out her cigarette packet, then changed her mind and put it away again.

'But I don't think', said Alexis suddenly, 'that the court case can be the only factor.' Meredith opened her mouth to protest and Alexis raised a hand. 'Think about it, Meredith,' he said firmly. 'Think about Hugh's lifestyle. He runs his own business; he drinks a lot – well, I mean, he's a wine-importer, for God's sake. And then . . . he's had a lot of strain in recent years. You all have.' Alexis broke off and looked at Meredith, to see how she was reacting. Her face was blank. 'I don't think', he continued, 'that blaming Louise and Barnaby for this is really going to help Hugh – and I don't think it's completely fair, either.'

'For Christ's sake!' shouted Meredith suddenly. 'Stop being so fucking British!' Her voice bounced off the walls of the little corridor and Alexis's head jerked up in surprise. 'I know what you're saying,' continued Meredith in shaky tones, taking out another cigarette and lighting it with trembling fingers. 'I know it's un-reasonable to blame the Kembers for this. I know there are other factors. I know that blaming them won't help Hugh get better.' She took a deep drag on her cigarette. 'But I don't fucking care, all right?' Her voice rose higher, and Alexis stared back at her, transfixed. 'I *want* to blame them,' she cried, 'and I *do* blame them. I don't give a shit about seeing both sides of the story. I love Hugh, and he's had a heart attack, and it's all their fault! I'll never forgive them. And if you weren't so fucking uptight and reasonable, you'd never forgive them either.'

Alexis stared at Meredith. His heart was pounding with astonishment and, despite himself, a kind of awed admiration. His thoughts flickered between Hugh – blameless honest Hugh, lying in his silent hospital room – and Meredith. Impassioned, unreasonable, warm-hearted, red-blooded Meredith, battling on Hugh's behalf. In comparison, Alexis suddenly felt old and rather colourless.

'You're right,' he said abruptly.

'What?' Meredith gave an exaggerated double take, and the glimmer of a smile appeared on her face. 'I'm right? Don't I get a ticking off? Don't I get a lecture on "forgive and forget"?'

Alexis shrugged. His face felt dry and his reactions slow.

'I don't know,' he said. 'Maybe I am too reasonable, too uptight. Maybe we need more . . . more warriors, like you.' Meredith laughed.

'Hardly a warrior. I picketed against the Gulf War.'

'Exactly.' Alexis looked at her with serious eyes. 'I've never picketed against anything. You make me feel as though I've been sitting on the fence all my life. I wish . . .' He spread his hands helplessly. 'I wish I had a bit of your fire.'

'But I'm sure you have,' said Meredith quietly. 'Underneath it all . . .' She broke off and, for a moment, Alexis simply stared at her. His eyes ran over her strong intelligent face; her green eyes, still bright with excitement; her high forehead, tanned and faintly lined; her sensitive witty mouth. Her eyes met his, and Alexis found himself caught in her gaze.

Suddenly he realized he was holding his breath.

But then, breaking the spell, Meredith stood up. Alexis felt a slight surprising shock of disappointment.

'I ought to go back,' she said matter-of-factly. 'Hugh might wake up any moment.'

'Of course,' said Alexis. 'I'll come too.' He gave a heavy sigh and stood up. 'God, this is a bloody awful affair.' Meredith glanced at him.

'I know it is,' she said. 'That's what I've been saying all along.'

The next morning was dull and sunless, with a flat white sky and the feel of autumn in the air. Barnaby was walking slowly towards the village shop, when Sylvia Seddon-Wilson stopped her car and called him over.

'Barnaby!' she exclaimed. 'It's terrible news, isn't it?' Her eyes scanned his face greedily for a reaction, and when his expression turned only to puzzlement, a faint fleeting look of glee passed over her face. 'Oh dear,' she said, in tones that didn't quite hide her triumph at being the first to impart the news. 'I take it that you haven't heard?'

'Heard what?'

'About Hugh Delaney having a heart attack!' She paused dramatically, but immediately her attention was distracted as a car noisily overtook her, hooting as it did so. 'Shut up!' she yelled angrily after it. 'Bloody nerve, these people have got! Anyway,' she resumed chattily. 'Isn't it awful?'

She looked sidelong at Barnaby through the car window.

'Barnaby!' she exclaimed. 'Barnaby, are you all right?'

Cassian was saying goodbye to Desmond on the steps of the Linningford office. While Karl had taken the first train back to London, Desmond had spent the morning in further meetings and discussions with the

Linningford partners. The whole office had been made aware that a big shot from London was visiting, and the atmosphere that morning had been one of slight suppressed tension. Cassian, meanwhile, had sat smugly at his desk, glowing in the knowledge that everyone was well aware that Desmond had stayed with him the night before, and that they were working together on what everyone was now calling the Lord Page case.

Now he shook hands warmly with Desmond, wondering how many people could see the pair of them from their windows.

'It was very good of you and Karl to meet with the Kembers,' he said smoothly. 'And I think we're really well on course now with the case.'

'I hope so, Cassian,' said Desmond. He gave Cassian a quizzical look. 'I was talking about it with Karl this morning, and we both had to agree, it's not the strongest case in the world. You'll be doing very well to get half a million in damages. Very well indeed.' He smiled kindly at Cassian, who felt a slight splinter of alarm in the base of his spine.

'I'm quite confident,' he said firmly. 'I've taken on board the points you made, and they'll be dealt with.'

'And you're quite sure the parents will go through with it?' Desmond put down his briefcase and felt in his pocket for his car keys. 'Both Karl and I felt that they were . . . a little unprepared; that they might be reluctant to testify fully and convincingly on the damage done to their daughter . . .' He raised his eyebrows.

'They'll be fine,' replied Cassian quickly. 'They just need a bit of time to get into it.'

'Yes,' said Desmond. 'Time.' He narrowed his eyes slightly. 'Things seem to have moved extraordinarily rapidly in this case, Cassian. You didn't put any pressure on the Kembers, did you? You didn't hurry them at all?'

'No!' exclaimed Cassian at once. 'Of course not. They were just anxious to get things going. For their daughter's sake,' he added.

'Hmm,' said Desmond, 'I'm glad to hear it. Well, I'll be following events with interest, and I'll be very impressed if we succeed.' He walked towards his car, then turned back. 'As I'm sure you're aware,' he said, 'this case could provide some good publicity for us. Acting successfully for the granddaughter of Lord Page can't do us any harm.' He opened his car door. 'Some time,' he added, 'when you're in London, perhaps we could have dinner together at my club. Perhaps we could even ask Lord Page to come along.' He smiled at Cassian. 'So long, Cassian.'

As Cassian watched Desmond driving off smoothly, he felt a confusing mixture of emotions. His initial sensation of triumphant exhilaration slowly dwindled into a curious down-hearted feeling. Did Desmond and Karl really think his case was weak? A sudden unwelcome vision popped into Cassian's mind, of Desmond and Karl, gently laughing together at him. He scowled. He'd show them. He'd fucking well win this case; that would wipe the patronizing smile off Desmond's face.

Suddenly there was a noise behind him, and Cassian's secretary, Elaine, appeared at the top of the steps, carrying her handbag.

'I thought I'd go for lunch,' she said. 'If that's OK.'

'Fine,' said Cassian absently.

'Has he gone, then?' said Elaine. 'That guy from London?'

'Yes, he has,' said Cassian. Elaine looked around and lowered her voice.

'Has he offered you a flashy job in London?' she said. 'That's what everyone's saying.' She lowered her voice further. 'They're all dead impressed.'

At her words, Cassian felt an expanding sensation of

pride. The heavy feeling around his heart released itself and vanished. It was paranoid, he told himself, to imagine that Desmond's final smile had been anything but encouraging.

'Well . . . you never know,' he said impressively. 'I'm afraid I can't really talk about it.'

'Gosh,' said Elaine. She shifted her handbag strap on her shoulder and looked hopefully at Cassian for further scraps of information. When it was clear he wasn't going to say anything more, she sighed. 'Oh well,' she said. 'Shall I get you a sandwich while I'm out?'

'No thanks,' said Cassian. He wondered briefly whether to say, Lunch is for wimps, then decided against it. 'I think today I'll have lunch with Louise,' he said instead.

Barnaby didn't know what to do with himself. When Sylvia Seddon-Wilson had driven off, he stood quite still in the middle of the road, oblivious of passing cars, incapable of moving. His face was blank and his mouth was dry and a heavy pain had anchored itself in his stomach. An old woman passed by with her little dog, and he flinched, unable to meet her eye, or even move out of the way. He felt numb with shock; numb to the tiny flames of panic darting round the edges of his frozen mind; numb even to the incipient stirrings of a heavy looming guilt.

He had to find out more, he suddenly said to himself. He had to find out what had happened. He had to find out how Hugh was. His friend, Hugh, his old friend. The thought made him want to sit down on the pavement and bury his face in his hands, but instead, Barnaby took a deep desperate breath, and found himself beginning to walk. Without thinking, his steps began to take him in the direction of the Delaneys' house. He had to find out how Hugh was, he thought desperately. He had to find out . . .

243

And then, like a slap, he remembered. He stopped still again. What was he thinking of, going to the Delaneys' house? What was he thinking of? With a shudder he imagined Meredith shrieking at him, as she had at Louise. He imagined Ursula's distraught face. Maybe even Hugh himself, discharged from hospital. He would look up, with an ill grey face . . . Maybe the sight of Barnaby would bring on another attack . . .

'Oh God,' said Barnaby aloud, in a hoarse desperate voice. He looked around him at the empty street, then took a few uncertain steps back towards the shop. But as he thought of the eager curious face of Mrs Potter; the gossip; the voices dying down as he entered, his steps slowed down and once more he stopped still. He felt marooned and alone and suddenly desperate to see a friendly face.

And then, suddenly, it came to him. Without pausing, he retraced his steps and walked towards the village shop. He passed it without going in, took the next turning on the right, and went down the hill, towards the church.

Frances Mold and Daisy had just finished their usual morning cup of tea when the figure of Barnaby appeared on the vicarage path. Frances waved at him cheerily through the drawing-room window and mouthed, 'The door's open!' Then she turned back to Daisy.

'You know Barnaby, don't you, Daisy?'

'Sort of,' said Daisy shyly. 'I mean, I know who he is, but I've never spoken to him. I've never bumped into him or anything.'

'No,' said Frances thoughtfully, 'I don't suppose you have. None of us have seen much of the Kembers this summer. Understandably.'

There was a sound from the door and Barnaby appeared, pale-faced and breathing heavily. When he saw Daisy he gave a visible start.

'Oh,' he said in a gruff voice. 'Hello.' Daisy's eyes slid anxiously towards Frances, and she put her teacup down with a hand which trembled slightly.

'Hello,' she said breathlessly, 'I'm Daisy.' She smiled nervously at Barnaby, who made a visible unsuccessful attempt to smile back.

'Well,' said Daisy hurriedly, 'I think I'll go now, shall I?' She scrabbled under her chair for her bag, knocking against a little side-table with her foot as she did so.

'Daisy,' said Frances, 'there's no hurry. Why don't you have another cup of tea?'

Daisy looked up, her face red from exertion. She eyed Barnaby's distraught face and swallowed.

'Actually,' she said, 'I've really got to go. Thank you for the lovely tea and everything.' She paused by the door. 'And you'll come round and listen to the Brahms, before I perform it?'

'Of course I will,' said Frances warmly. 'Bye, Daisy. It was lovely to see you.'

When Daisy had disappeared up the path, Frances turned to Barnaby.

'You frightened her away,' she said in gently reproachful tones. Barnaby's gaze didn't move.

'I've just heard about Hugh,' he said. Frances's expression changed.

'Oh, yes,' she said soberly. 'Meredith phoned me this morning.' She looked up in sudden alarm. 'Nothing's happened since then, has it?'

'He had a heart attack,' said Barnaby hoarsely. 'He could have died.' Frances sighed.

'Sit down, Barnaby,' she said, 'let me pour you some tea.' She swirled the pot round and winced as she poured out a dark-brown stream of liquid. 'It's very strong,' she said, 'but then, perhaps that's just what you need.' She waited until he had begun to drink before she spoke again.

'As I understand it,' she said, 'Hugh's attack was

245

only very small. Of course it was frightening for them all, but I think he's on the mend now. Meredith was actually sounding quite cheerful this morning.' She looked at Barnaby. 'I think he was very lucky,' she said gently.

'I saw him a few days ago,' said Barnaby abruptly. 'In the street. He looked terrible, but I had no idea.'

'I don't think anyone had,' said Frances.

'He looked grey and old and sort of crushed,' said Barnaby. 'And . . . and he wouldn't meet my eye. He moved away across the street . . .' He broke off.

'Well now,' said Frances comfortingly. 'I wouldn't . . .'

'We used to be friends,' interrupted Barnaby bleakly. 'We used to go drinking together. We used to do each other favours.' He took a sip of the dark-brown tea. 'What sort of favour have I done for him now?' Barnaby's huge dark eyes looked up at Frances. 'What have I done to him?' he whispered. There was a pause. Frances looked at Barnaby with gentle compassion.

'Don't torture yourself, Barnaby,' she said. 'Remember, you've only been doing what you thought was right.'

'Right?' said Barnaby fiercely. 'Is it right to put your friend in hospital? To nearly kill him?' Frances looked at Barnaby carefully.

'Is that what you think you've done?' she said.

'Yes! Oh, I don't know.' Barnaby pushed a hand through his rumpled hair. 'I suppose it could have been anything, couldn't it? I mean, lots of people Hugh's age have heart attacks.'

'Certainly they do,' agreed Frances. Barnaby stared at her, unconvinced.

'We used to be such good friends,' he said heavily.

'I know,' said Frances. 'Perhaps you will be again.' Barnaby shook his head.

'It's too late for that,' he said.

'Maybe,' said Frances, 'maybe not.'

There was a pause. Frances took a sip of tea and waited.

'All summer', said Barnaby suddenly, 'my whole life has been Katie, and her treatment, and the case. That's all I've thought about. As though nothing else matters.'

'And now?'

'Now,' said Barnaby slowly, 'now I'm starting to remember that other people exist, too.'

Louise and Katie had spent an enjoyable morning in Katie's old classroom, with her old teacher, Mrs Tully, and a woman called Jennifer Douglas, who was in charge of reintroducing Forest Lodge children back into normal school life.

'I think', she had said at the end of the session, 'that Katie can start back straight away, if she likes. Mornings only, to begin with, and lots of rest when she needs it, but we want her to feel part of normal school life from the word go.' She looked at Mrs Tully. 'Staying down a year,' she said, 'being in a class with younger children; that won't make her feel stigmatized?' Mrs Tully frowned.

'I think it's unlikely,' she said. 'I'll be on the lookout for any kind of teasing, of course, but, you know, she won't be the first child to stay down a year, and on the whole the children here are very kind and accepting. They know Katie had an accident; they know she may need some extra help.' She smiled at Louise. 'They're all very fond of Katie. We all are.'

A sound from outside attracted their attention. Katie, who had been sent out to play, was joyfully screaming, as she careered around the playground on a plastic tricycle from the kindergarten. Louise gave a small grimace and looked at Mrs Tully.

'She isn't the same Katie,' she said bluntly. 'You don't quite realize . . . She may cause havoc to begin with.'

'Well, we're used to havoc,' said Mrs Tully cheerfully.

She looked at Jennifer Douglas. 'As long as she gets lots of rest . . .'

'Yes,' said Jennifer Douglas. 'The more tired she gets, the more attention-seeking she'll be. I like your idea of a little bed permanently set up for her.' She sighed. 'Not all schools are quite so accommodating.' She had looked at Louise. 'You know, you're very lucky.'

Now, eating lunch in the kitchen with Cassian and the girls, watching Katie carefully slicing her half apple into smaller pieces, watching Cassian clowning with Amelia and making her giggle, those words returned to Louise. She leaned back in her chair and felt a warm glowing sensation of relaxation spread through her body, until she wanted to wriggle with pleasure. Happiness, she supposed it was.

Cassian looked up at her and smiled.

'Desmond was very pleased with the case,' he said.

'Oh, good,' said Louise.

She smiled brightly back at Cassian, but underneath she could feel a shadow falling gently over her glow. Somewhere, somehow, she had lost enthusiasm for the case; for talking about it, or thinking about it, or even reminding herself of its existence. After Barnaby had left the night before, she had sat for a while, listening to the chat of the three lawyers over her head, telling herself firmly that she had overreacted, that she was irrational, that it would all be worth it in the end. But whatever she told herself, she could not get rid of a dismaying vision in her mind – a vision of herself having to declare in court, in public, that Katie was . . . what was the phrase? A walking disaster. Her darling little daughter a disaster. A trial to live with. A nightmare. How could she do it? How would she explain herself? – to Katie, to Amelia, to all their friends, to Mrs Tully? No point in thinking they wouldn't find out. No point thinking Katie wouldn't catch on to what was happening. No point thinking it wouldn't affect her morale; perhaps even her recovery. But there was nothing she could do about it now. It was too late to back out; she was powerless. Teams of important people were working on the case; everyone but her was committed to it. Everyone but her seemed to think that to go to court was an obvious rational course of events. And, of course, there was always the money at the end . . .

'I think we're really on course for victory,' continued Cassian. 'And I have to tell you, the boys at the office are pretty impressed. If we're successful, it could really help my career.'

'Oh, good,' said Louise again. She pictured Cassian's career in her mind: a long, abstract, glittering thing, disappearing into the distance – and now, it seemed, dependent on the case succeeding. The case was no longer, she realized wearily, just a court case; somehow it had become the foundation for Cassian's career, for their own relationship, for their future together. Her entire life seemed to be tied up in it; there was no way of escape.

'If things go well, it could mean a move to London,' said Cassian. He grinned at Katie. 'How would you like to live in London?'

'I've been to London,' said Amelia self-importantly. 'I saw Big Ben.'

'London?' said Louise. She gave a short little laugh. 'Why London? I thought you were based in Linningford.' Cassian grinned.

'Everyone has at least one stint in the provinces; to test their loyalty. But, I mean, I'm hardly going to stay here for ever, am I?'

'Oh,' said Louise. 'No. I suppose not.' Cassian's eyes met hers.

'London,' he said seductively. 'Shops and galleries and theatres and interesting people all around . . .'

'Maybe,' said Louise. She briskly began to gather the

plates together, as though to change the subject. Cassian regarded her for a few seconds, then looked at his watch.

'I've got to go,' he said regretfully. He looked at Katie. 'Although I hate to leave my favourite client.'

'See you this evening?' said Louise.

'Of course,' said Cassian. 'We can talk some more then.' He gave her a kiss, then blew kisses to each of the girls. They giggled and blew kisses back, more and more, until Katie blew one so energetically that she knocked over her glass of water, and Cassian raised his eyebrows comically and left.

When he had gone Louise sent the children out into the garden and started to clear up. But after dispiritedly mopping up the water on the floor, her energy seemed to evaporate, and for a while she simply stood still, staring out of the window, allowing her thoughts to patter lightly in and out of her head.

What she really wanted, she suddenly thought, was a holiday. She wanted a holiday. She wanted to lie down on a hot sandy beach and close her eyes, and listen to the sounds of people laughing and talking . . . and even swimming.

She paused in her thoughts. Swimming. Could she really consider going swimming? To test herself, she deliberately imagined Katie and Amelia paddling in the shallows, splashing each other, even swimming further out to sea. She conjured up image after image, waiting for the wave of terrible panic to overwhelm her, but it didn't come; she was safe.

'Swimming,' she said out loud. 'We could go swimming. We could all go swimming.'

'Mummy!' A shrill voice from outside interrupted her thoughts. It was Amelia. 'Can we have a chair for French skipping?'

'No,' Louise called back cheerfully. She put down the mop and walked straight past the pile of washing-up waiting to be done. 'You can't have a chair, but you can have me instead.'

As Barnaby came out of the vicarage he bumped into Sylvia Seddon-Wilson.

'Barnaby!' she exclaimed. 'I knew there was something I'd meant to ask you. It's my charity barbecue next week. In aid of Save the Children. Will you come?'

'Oh,' said Barnaby discouragingly, 'I'm not sure.'

'Oh, go on,' wheedled Sylvia. 'You need a nice evening out. It's only five pounds each, and that includes all the food, plus entertainment.'

'What's the entertainment?' asked Barnaby, in spite of himself. Sylvia's brow wrinkled.

'I'm not sure yet,' she said, 'but it'll be jolly good, whatever it is.' She paused. 'I don't expect any of the Delaneys to come,' she added brightly. 'What with Hugh in hospital and everything, so there's no need to worry about that.'

'I wasn't worried about that,' retorted Barnaby gruffly. He looked down, avoiding Sylvia's piercing gaze.

'No?' she said in disbelieving tones. 'Oh, good.' There was a slight pause. 'Then you'll come?' said Sylvia. 'It's next Friday.'

'Oh, OK,' said Barnaby, 'I'll come.'

'Marvellous,' said Sylvia, moving off down the path towards the vicarage. 'You can have some fun and forget all about that gruesome court case.'

When Barnaby arrived at Larch Tree Cottage, Sylvia's words were still in his mind. He knocked on the door, and when there was no answer, went round to the garden. Katie and Amelia were sitting on the grass, listening to Louise tell them a story. They all looked up when they saw Barnaby.

'Daddy!' squealed Katie, and leaped up to greet him.

'I've got some news,' said Barnaby, looking at Louise.

'I don't know if you've heard it. It's about Hugh. Perhaps', he glanced at the girls, 'we should go inside.'

After he'd told her, Louise sat completely still for a while, staring blankly out of the window, allowing her thoughts to settle.

'It could have been anything that caused it,' she said suddenly. 'Couldn't it?' She met Barnaby's gaze, urging him to convince her.

'Oh, yes,' he said, a little too late. 'It could have been anything, I'm sure.'

'I mean,' said Louise energetically, 'loads of people have heart attacks, don't they? I mean . . .' She broke off and looked at Barnaby. 'I feel awful,' she said more soberly. 'I had no idea . . .'

'I don't think anybody had,' said Barnaby.

'This bloody case . . .' said Louise, then she stopped. There was no point having another row with Barnaby about the court case. He would never understand her misgivings. He would just start telling her again how important it was to put Katie first, and how she had to stop being so irrational . . . 'I mean,' she continued weakly, 'it's completely taken over our lives.'

Barnaby looked at Louise. He supposed she was talking about her life and Cassian's life, not his life. He didn't count any more. A dull familiar pain began to gnaw at his chest. Somehow, while Katie had been in hospital and Forest Lodge, it had almost seemed as though he and Louise were, in some sense, back together again. They had been united as Katie's parents, like a proper family. But now, suddenly, he could see that as Katie got better and better, and as Louise and Cassian built up a life together, he would once again find himself being pushed onto the sidelines. He would be marginalized. Forgotten about.

He looked at Louise; she was waiting for him to reply. What were they talking about? Oh yes, the case; the gruesome court case. Barnaby suddenly felt sick of the case, sick of the whole thing. It was the court case which had turned Louise and Cassian into a couple. It was the court case which had given Hugh a heart attack. What else would happen before it was over? Was it really worth it? Was it really worth . . .

'Barnaby?'

Barnaby stared miserably at Louise and thought how scathing she would be if she knew what he was thinking.

'Well,' he said automatically, 'once they've issued the writ, things ought to start moving. And . . . and it'll be worth it in the end. For Katie.' Louise looked at him silently for a minute.

'Yes,' she repeated. 'It'll be worth it for Katie.'

And they looked blankly at each other, in a dull dissatisfying silence.

Chapter Eighteen

Alexis stood in Daisy's sitting-room, waiting for her to come downstairs. In less than two hours she was due to perform Brahms's second Piano Concerto in Linningford Abbey, and Alexis had never felt quite so nervous about anything in his whole life.

He stood staring out of the window, clenching his fists inside his pockets, imagining the gradual assembling of people that was to take place that night; that perhaps was already starting to take place. The orchestra gathering together; the audience filing slowly into the abbey; the expectant faces; the anticipation; the tension.

And then he imagined Daisy walking out, alone, into the middle of all that, into the bright lights and the attention. Daisy, who blushed if she caught the eye of a stranger in the street, who apologized as she let others through doors first, who shrank from public scrutiny like a shy deer. His quiet timid Daisy. He couldn't begin to imagine her surviving such an ordeal, yet that was what she was about to go through, and that was what was making him clench his fists, and disguise his nerves with a heavy frown.

There was a sound from the stairs and Alexis looked round. Coming into the room was Daisy. She was wearing a long navy-blue taffeta dress, with a narrow waist and a full rustling skirt. Her skin looked pale and milky against the deep blue and her dark hair fell like an inky cloud down her back.

'Hi,' she said shyly. 'Do I . . . do I look all right?'

Alexis stared back at her in foolish silence. He had never seen Daisy looking so beautiful, or so sophisticated.

'You look . . .' he began. He stopped. His eyes had landed on her hands, clad in a pair of red woollen fingerless gloves. Daisy followed his gaze.

'Oh yes,' she said, and giggled, 'I mustn't forget to take them off, must I?' She frowned and wriggled her fingers.

'I'll just do a bit more warming up,' she said, and abruptly sat down at the piano. A series of exercises, by now familiar to Alexis, immediately filled the little room. Alexis sat down and waited. He had something to give her, something which he should have whipped out of his pocket as soon as she entered the room, but her appearance had taken him by surprise. She looked suddenly poised as well as graceful; elegant as well as beautiful. She looked, he supposed, grown-up.

Eventually Daisy came to a stop. She paused, played a few random passages from the concerto, then got up and closed the piano lid firmly.

'That's enough,' she said. She rubbed her hands together briskly, and looked at Alexis. 'Shall we go?'

'In a minute,' said Alexis. He felt in his pocket. 'I've got something for you.' Daisy watched with huge eyes as he took a leather box out and handed it to her.

She opened it awkwardly and pulled out a gold necklace; a thin sinuous chain which trailed over her fingers and gleamed in the early evening light.

'It's beautiful,' said Daisy softly. 'I can wear it tonight, can't I?' She gave a sudden childish smile of delight. 'I can wear it tonight and it'll bring me luck! Oh, thank you!' She came close to Alexis and stood, beaming at him, rustling slightly in her taffeta dress. 'Thank you,' she said again, and kissed him gently. 'I love it.'

'And I love you,' Alexis found himself saying. Something which he'd never said to her before. 'I love you, Daisy.'

There was a short beating silence. Daisy's cheeks filled with a dark pink colour and she looked down. Alexis stood perfectly still and waited. Eventually, slowly, Daisy's eyes rose to meet his.

'And I . . .' Her old stammer had returned, and Alexis cursed himself. What kind of pressure was he putting her under? Tonight, of all nights. Bloody thoughtless idiot.

'And I l-love you, too.' She gave a little surprised gasp, and Alexis suddenly pulled her close to him, feeling the shiny fabric of her dress slipping against his shirt, smelling her rosy scent.

'You're going to be wonderful tonight,' he said fiercely. 'You're going to be just wonderful. And I'm going to be so proud of you . . .' He broke off. Daisy was panting slightly. He released her and looked at his watch.

'OK then,' he said more normally. 'Enough talk. Let's go.'

Louise was getting ready for Sylvia Seddon-Wilson's barbecue. It had taken a lot of persuading to make her agree to go to it, particularly when she discovered that Cassian was going to be away in London that night, discussing the final draft of the writ and statement of claims with Karl and Desmond. To her surprise, however, it had been Cassian who was most keen that she should go.

'You mustn't turn into a recluse!' he'd said, when she told him about it. 'I don't think you've been out since the accident, have you?'

'Of course I have,' retorted Louise.

'When?'

Louise stared at him and cast her mind back over the summer. What had she done in all those long summer evenings? All she could remember was sitting in hospital with Katie, or driving back from Forest Lodge, or slumping with exhaustion onto the sofa.

'Well, OK,' she said, 'maybe I haven't been much of a socialite. But to be honest, I don't really feel like seeing people at the moment.'

'Exactly,' exclaimed Cassian. 'That's what you've got to fight against. You've got to get back to your old sparkly self.' He grinned at her. 'Think of it as a dry run for next week.'

Louise grimaced. Cassian had arranged for them all to spend next week – the week before the girls' school term began – in London. A friend's nanny was going to look after the girls, while Louise and Cassian were going to spend the time doing nothing, as far as she could make out, but having lunch with people, or drinks, or dinner and the theatre. The busier their schedule became, the more pleased Cassian seemed and the lower Louise's heart sank.

'Why don't you buy a new dress?' Cassian was now saying.

'Oh, I don't know,' said Louise irritably. 'Anyway,' she suddenly added, 'I can't go. What about the girls?'

'Barnaby can have them.'

'He's going to the barbecue.'

'Oh.' Cassian frowned. 'OK then, get them to spend the night with a friend. Children still do that, don't they? They'd probably love it.'

And so it had all been fixed up. Katie and Amelia had been dispatched, with squeals of delight and plans of midnight feasts, to the house of Emily Fairly, a friend of Amelia's with a sensible mother. Cassian had driven off to London, promising to return the next morning with the writ, and Louise had been left alone to put on her party dress and brush her hair and try to pretend that she was looking forward to the evening.

She looked in the mirror and pulled a face. She looked, she thought, terrible. Her blond hair appeared lifeless; her skin was dull; and the turquoise cotton dress that had fitted so well last summer now hung, sack-like, off her frame.

Quickly she brushed a glowing bronze powder onto her cheeks, sprayed her hair with tiny shiny droplets, and painted her lips coral pink. She stared at herself. Now the surface was a little glossier, a little brighter, but underneath, she was still the same. She screwed up her face, then grinned energetically at herself, but above the grin, two dull defeated eyes peered back at her. Something's all wrong, she thought suddenly. Something's all wrong with me, but I don't know what it is.

By seven-thirty the abbey was nicely full of people and the orchestra was assembled. Alexis, who had chosen a seat as near the front as he dared, stared round at all the people who had gathered together to hear this concert – to hear Daisy – and felt a strange awed amazement, punctuated only by terrible pounding nerves. Daisy wasn't on until the second half; somehow he would have to sit calmly through some dreary piece of Mozart, clap and smile at the end, stretch his legs in the interval, all the while feeling this unbearable petrifying tension.

'Alexis!' At the sound of his name he jumped, as though expecting bad news, but it was Frances Mold, standing in the aisle at the end of his row and smiling cheerfully. 'I got here a bit late,' she continued, 'so I'm at the back. I just thought I'd come and say hello. It's exciting, isn't it?'

'I'm absolutely terrified,' admitted Alexis. Frances laughed merrily.

'She'll be fine!' she exclaimed. 'Look, I'd better go. See you in the interval?'

'Can't you sit up here, near the front?' said Alexis. 'What about those seats in the front row?'

'They're reserved,' said Frances. 'Never mind! The sound will be just as good at the back.' And she hurried off. Alexis looked crossly at the empty row of reserved seats. Who was it, he thought angrily, that hadn't even bothered to take advantage of their privileged position; hadn't even bothered to turn up?

During the first half he found out. The first piece – a nondescript little overture about which he hadn't even bothered to consult his programme – was over, and the applause from the audience had begun, when suddenly there was the sound of footsteps from the back of the abbey. Looking round, Alexis saw a smartly dressed couple hurrying up the aisle. Behind them, moving more slowly, was a twenty-something young man, dressed in ripped jeans and a crumpled T-shirt.

'Come *on*, Alistair,' Alexis heard the woman exclaim as she passed his row. 'We're late enough as it is!'

A jolt of recognition went through Alexis. Alistair – he knew that name. Of course – this must be Daisy's brother; the one who seemed to spend all his time travelling round the world, and those two must be her parents. This was Daisy's family.

He stared at them in surreptitious fascination as they sat down; these people about whom he knew so much, but had never met. He watched as Daisy's father sat down, stretched out his legs, and opened his programme with a shaking-out movement as though it were the *Daily Telegraph*. He watched as Daisy's mother began to take off her smart cream jacket, realized there was nowhere to put it, and shrugged it back on again. He watched as Daisy's brother sank easily into his chair and began to drum aimlessly on his denim-clad thigh.

As he watched, he began to feel an uncomfortable guilt at observing these strange-familiar people while they sat, completely unaware of him. At the same time, he felt a warm, overflowing friendliness towards them. Here was the most important part of Daisy's life to date, sitting a few feet away from him. Here were her roots;

her background; her formative influences. He stared at each of them in turn, looking for Daisy's features, searching for her expressions and mannerisms.

Suddenly the young man, Alistair, became aware he was being watched. He turned round, caught Alexis's eye, gave a puzzled frown, then turned back again. Alexis quickly looked away. Ridiculously, his heart began to beat more quickly, and for the first time, he began to wonder what he must look like to them.

Louise arrived at Sylvia Seddon-Wilson's house to find the garden full of people, music playing, and the smell of barbecuing meat filling the air. She paused at the gate, tossed back her hair, and tried to summon a feeling of cheery self-confidence, but the sight of the party in front of her filled her with an unaccountable sensation of sick anxiety.

She took a deep breath and swallowed, and tried to force herself to move forward, but her legs were tense and pinioned to the ground. She bit her lips, and looked around desperately for a friendly face to focus on, a kindred spirit whom she could quietly approach; but the bright faces in front of her all seemed to be those of threatening strangers.

'Come on,' she said aloud, 'stop being so stupid.' With a huge effort, she took a couple of steps forward and put her hand on the gate. Then suddenly, through a chance separation of the throng, she saw Barnaby. He was sitting on a low wall munching a chicken leg, talking animatedly to some woman she didn't recognize. And the sight of him – smarter than usual in a creamy pale shirt, but still instantly, almost joltingly familiar – filled her with a warm feeling of confidence. The crowd suddenly seemed benevolent. As she looked again, some of the apparent strangers metamorphosed into people she recognized; friends, even.

Without waiting for her fears to return, Louise strode

forward into the garden, struggling through the crowd towards the low wall. When she got there Barnaby had vanished, and for a moment she felt a resurging panic, but suddenly she heard his voice from behind.

'Louise!' He was holding a plastic cup in one hand and the remains of his chicken leg in the other. 'Haven't you got a drink?' he said. 'Let me get you one.' And to Louise's dismay, he began to move off.

'Barnaby!' she said. 'Can I come too?' she added more softly. 'I don't . . .' She shrugged. 'I'm a bit nervous about standing here all on my own.' For a moment Barnaby stared at her in puzzlement. Then, gradually, his face softened in understanding.

'Sure,' he said, 'we'll go together.'

As they walked, Louise cast around for something to say. She had spoken to Barnaby about nothing over the last few months except Katie and the case. It would have been easy to slip into the same well-worn grooves of conversation; begin with some comment on Katie's progress or what Cassian had said about the writ, but she didn't want to. She wanted to talk about something else; something different; something new. Surreptitiously she eyed Barnaby. What she would really have liked to ask was how come he'd bought himself a new shirt, but something made her hesitate. Did she still have the right to ask that kind of thing?

'Do you like my shirt?' said Barnaby suddenly. 'It's new.'

'I know,' said Louise. 'It's very nice.'

'I suddenly felt like wearing something new tonight,' he said. 'I don't know why. So I bought a new shirt.' He spoke proudly. 'It was easy.' Louise grinned.

'You look very good in it.'

'Really? Do I?' Barnaby turned to face her and she felt herself blushing slightly.

'Yes,' she said firmly, 'you do.' She sighed. 'I wish I'd bought something new. I feel so grotty.'

'You don't look it.' Louise gave a short laugh.

'Oh, come on,' she said. 'Yes, I do. I look dreadful.' Barnaby looked carefully at her.

'You look a bit tired,' he said.

'Exactly,' said Louise. 'I look tired and washed out and about forty-five years old.'

There was a pause, then Barnaby said, 'Rubbish.' Louise grinned.

'Nice try, Barnaby.'

They had reached the drinks table, and Louise watched as Barnaby poured her a plastic cup full of white wine.

'Cassian's taking us all to London next week,' she said, and noticed with a slight obscure satisfaction that Barnaby's hand wavered.

'London? Why?'

'To have some fun; to meet people and see things and go shopping . . .'

'Oh.' Barnaby handed her drink to her. 'Just your kind of thing.'

'Yes,' said Louise, 'I suppose so.' She took a sip of wine. Then she looked up and met Barnaby's face. He looked so gloomy that she said, without thinking, 'Actually, I'm dreading it.'

'Dreading it?' Louise gave a huge sigh.

'I don't know what's wrong with me. I just don't really feel like seeing people. I feel like hiding at home for the rest of my life.'

'Maybe it's just a reaction,' said Barnaby uncertainly.

'Maybe,' said Louise. She took another sip of wine. 'I just feel so tense all the time,' she continued suddenly, 'and depressed. As though I've got a big black cloud hanging over me. I just can't be all happy and lively and sparkly, like . . .' She broke off and shrugged. 'I suppose it's partly the case.'

'Yes,' said Barnaby slowly. 'The case.'

They looked at each other. Louise waited for Barnaby

to say, 'It'll all be worth it for Katie.' But he said nothing and took a sip of wine.

'Sometimes I think . . .' he began slowly. Louise stared at him.

'What?'

'I think . . .' But before he could continue they were interrupted by the unmistakable, penetrating voice of Sylvia Seddon-Wilson.

'Louise!' she cried gaily. 'I didn't see you arrive. So thrilled you could make it!'

They both looked up to see Sylvia bearing down on them. She was dressed in bright fuchsia pink and waving a book of tickets at them. 'Have you gone in for the raffle?'

'Not yet,' said Barnaby, feeling in his pocket for some change.

Sylvia looked at Louise.

'No Cassian?'

'No,' said Louise, 'he's in London. Working on the writ.' As she finished speaking, she was unable to prevent herself from glancing at Barnaby. He looked up and met her eyes.

'Oh dear,' said Sylvia, 'what a shame. Still, Barnaby's looking after you, is he?'

'Yes,' said Louise. 'Barnaby's looking after me.'

As the audience assembled back in its seats for the second half of the concert, Alexis sat perfectly still, trying to breathe normally and relax the muscles of his legs. But every time it occurred to him that, within minutes, Daisy would walk out to the grand piano gleaming darkly in front of him and begin her performance, his knees shot up again and his stomach flipped over and he felt an urge to swivel his chair round so that he was facing the other way.

To calm himself, he looked once again at the biography of Daisy in the programme, at the glamorous studio photograph and the long list of her awards and achievements. It was an impressive catalogue. She had won this prize and that prize; she had studied with this famous teacher and at that prestigious summer school. Alexis frowned. He could relate none of this to Daisy – a giggling girl who had never even seen the inside of a garlic clove.

Suddenly there was the rippling sound of applause breaking out. Alexis looked up, his stomach clenched. There in front of him was Daisy, walking to the front of the orchestra with the conductor, smiling, bowing, taking her seat at the piano. The conductor went to his stand, ponderously opened his score, and looked around at the faces of the orchestra. He looked down at Daisy, who smiled back. She placed her hands on the keyboard, and Alexis closed his eyes; he couldn't bear it.

Dimly he heard the first haunting notes of the concerto, played by a solo horn. He clenched his fists and felt his whole body tremble with tension. And then, as though from a great distance, he heard the first rising chords of the piano. Chords which he had heard on Daisy's piano, in isolation, many times, but until now, had never really made sense. Chords which Daisy had played to him in jeans, in her dressing-gown, in the morning and in the afternoon, and late at night. She'd mocked herself, telling him what a dreadful temptation it was to always start practising right at the beginning of a piece, assuring him he must know the start of the concerto off by heart by now.

What she'd forgotten was that while she could see and hear in her mind the part of the orchestra: the strings, the brass, the woodwind, Alexis – who had no musical training; who had, he now told himself, no imagination at all – had always been unable to flesh out Daisy's simple chords into the rich round orchestral sound that was now creeping through the abbey. He had never even begun to imagine this achingly beautiful, rising, flying music.

The orchestra made way for a solo virtuosic passage, and Alexis opened his eyes; this was familiar to him. The sound of the solo piano rang out into the air of the abbey as Daisy's fingers moved swiftly, expertly over the keys. Everybody was watching as she played: the audience, the orchestra, the conductor. Then, suddenly, the conductor turned back to his stand, brought down his arms, and with a pounding exuberance, brought the orchestra in. Alexis caught his breath. This music was half battle, half love affair, and Daisy was playing her part in each with a confident ease that he could never have imagined she possessed.

As the concerto thundered along, he watched her face, mesmerized. She was almost playing a game with the orchestra, smiling as their themes coincided, frowning as the music became more urgent and impassioned. His gaze ran slowly over the rest of her. Everything was elegantly in its place: her blue dress flowed faultlessly down to the ground; her hair shone glossily in the lights; her milky white arms looked suddenly strong and sure and invulnerable. This Daisy was someone he hardly recognized.

He sat still, gazing ahead, as the first movement gave way to the second; as the music grew urgent and desperate, as the crashing chords of Daisy's part echoed triumphantly around the abbey. Between the movements no-one moved. Everyone was, like him, staring agog at Daisy.

And then, as the third movement began, and the slow pearly piano melody began to rise slowly into the air, Alexis leaned back and closed his eyes. Into his mind came a memory of Daisy as he'd first seen her: tall, slender and gawky, tiptoeing her way through the Delaneys' garden, dipping her toe into the water, starting and blushing and biting her lip. He could barely reconcile that shy creature with the girl – the woman – performing in front of him now.

He frowned and shook his head slightly, as though to work it out. Then, as the music rose higher and higher, he suddenly realized that this was the first time he'd ever seen Daisy in a context apart from his own; in an environment other than that of the two of them, together in his house, or her house, or the village. They had spent the summer wrapped in one another's arms, ignoring everyone else, creating their own world. And in that world, he had built up a picture of Daisy in which she was isolated from the rest of her life – her parents, her friends, her life as a musician, all the other things which mattered to her.

Now, slowly, it came to him that his isolated summer-image of Daisy was as incomplete without the rest of her life as were the rising piano chords without the accompanying orchestra. She was not simply his beautiful, shy, stuttering girl. She was a pianist, a performer, a shining glittering talent.

She was, he suddenly thought, beyond him.

He leaned back in his seat and let the music soar over his head, and told himself several times how proud and amazed and happy he was; how thrilled he was to see Daisy looking so strong and confident; how pleased he was that finally he was hearing her perform. But underneath all the happy phrases, lurking in a distant corner of his heart which he rarely looked at, Alexis could feel, in spite of himself, the beginnings of a strange sad foreboding.

When Sylvia had finally left them, Louise looked at Barnaby.

'Perhaps,' she began, then stopped awkwardly.

'What?' Barnaby's eyes met hers.

'Perhaps, some time, we could have a talk. About things. Just the two of us.' Louise bit her lip. 'You know,

266

about Katie and everything. Without anyone else there . . .' She tailed off, feeling foolish. But Barnaby nodded.

'I'd like that,' he said, and put his drink down on a stone bird-bath. 'What about now?'

'Now?' said Louise. 'But what about the barbecue?' Barnaby shrugged.

'I'm stuffed,' he said, 'I've already eaten about six chicken drumsticks.' Louise laughed.

'That wasn't what I meant,' she said. 'I meant, you know, talking to people and everything. It seems a shame leaving so early . . .' A thought suddenly struck her. 'What about your lovely new shirt?'

'It'll be just as lovely', said Barnaby, 'sitting over a glass of wine with you.' He took her drink out of her hand and put it down, next to his. 'C'mon, Lou, let's go.'

Chapter Nineteen

As the concerto galloped towards its conclusion and Daisy's final chords thundered into the air, Alexis sank back into his seat, feeling suddenly drained. There was an infinitesimal pause as the sound echoed round the abbey, then, all around him, the applause began; loud, steady, serious applause, that erupted into a roar as Daisy rose, beaming, to her feet.

Alexis gazed at her, at her glowing cheeks, and sparkling eyes, and at the gleam of gold around her neck. She bowed, once, twice, then allowed the conductor to lead her off. The applause continued as loud as ever.

Alexis noticed Daisy's mother, in between claps, consulting her watch. She said something to her husband, who nodded and said something back. And then both their heads turned to the front once more, as Daisy reappeared in front of the orchestra. A lady in a black dress appeared from nowhere and presented Daisy with a huge bouquet of flowers, and the man sitting next to Alexis gave a throaty cheer. When she heard the sound, Daisy's head swivelled towards Alexis and she gave him an embarrassed smile.

Immediately Daisy's mother turned and scanned the crowd suspiciously. Alexis looked down and studiously gazed at his hands; his old, wrinkled, untalented hands. The sight of them filled him with a sudden depression.

Eventually the applause died away. Daisy walked off for the last time and the orchestra began to stand up and leave. Around Alexis, people began gathering their things together, waving to friends, suggesting a quick drink. Alexis sat perfectly still. He could see Daisy's parents heading towards the side of the abbey, obviously in search of Daisy. The natural thing would have been to get up, introduce himself, and join them, but the thought of greeting Daisy's parents, explaining who he was, watching their concealed expressions of shock and dismay . . . Alexis shuddered.

It seemed to him now that he and Daisy had spent the summer living in a bubble. A sheltered guarded world, cut off from public scrutiny, cut off from the rest of their lives, in which the only things which had mattered had been themselves. And now the bubble was about to burst.

'Alexis!' He looked up. It was Frances Mold again. She was flushed, and there was a huge smile on her face. 'Oh, Alexis! Wasn't she fantastic!'

'Wonderful!' said Alexis warmly. 'It was a brilliant performance.'

'Terribly moving, I thought,' said Frances, wrinkling her brow expressively. 'That slow movement. And such assured playing for someone so young. I mean, she's still just a child, really! She's amazing!'

'Amazing,' said Alexis quietly. His face felt numb.

'The thing is,' said Frances sorrowfully, 'I've got to dash, I'm afraid. I promised Sylvia I'd go to her silly barbecue. Tell Daisy I thought it was wonderful and I'll phone her in the morning, will you?'

'Of course,' said Alexis. 'She'll be thrilled that you came.'

'The whole village should have come,' retorted Frances. 'They're such Philistines, preferring a barbecue to this! I think we're the only ones here, aren't we?'

'I think so,' said Alexis. 'The Delaneys were going to come, but what with Hugh coming out of hospital today . . .'

'Yes,' said Frances, 'I suppose so. Anyway, I must go. Tell Daisy well done, won't you? Bye.' And she strode off back down the aisle, clopping in her sensible sandals on the ancient worn-down stones.

Alexis watched her go, and told himself firmly that now he *had* to go and see Daisy; he had a message to give her; it would be unforgivable not to deliver it. Slowly, creakily, he rose from his seat and shuffled past the row of empty chairs into the aisle. And then, even more slowly, he began to make his way, like a condemned man, towards the side of the abbey, towards Daisy and her family.

As he neared the vestry, he heard the sound of animated voices. He paused outside the door.

'I've no idea where she gets it from,' a woman's voice was saying. 'Not me, certainly.' She laughed gaily.

'Well, it was really quite a staggering performance,' said a man's voice. 'I bet the Academy can't wait to get its hands on you.'

'Well, I don't really know about that.' Daisy's gentle voice floated hesitantly through the door of the vestry, and Alexis felt a gnawing yearning pain in his chest. That was his Daisy.

He put his eye to the crack of the vestry door. In front of him, standing in an admiring circle round Daisy, were her parents, the conductor, the lady who had given her flowers, and another woman whom Alexis didn't recognize. Over in the corner, leafing abstractly through an old copy of *Church Times*, was Daisy's brother.

'Anyway,' Daisy's mother was saying, 'unfortunately we have to go back to London tonight.' Daisy looked up.

'I thought we were all going out to supper?' she said. 'With Alexis.' She frowned. 'I must find Alexis.'

'Yes,' said her father, 'where is this famous Alexis? We'd like to meet him.'

'I don't know,' said Daisy. 'I expect he's waiting somewhere.' The conductor grinned.

'Boyfriend?' he asked in perky tones.

'Sort of,' said Daisy shyly.

'You should have told us,' said the conductor, winking at her. 'We would have got him to present the flowers to you, wouldn't we, Maureen?'

'Oh, yes,' exclaimed the lady in the black dress. 'That would have been really romantic! To have a handsome young man, instead of an old crone like me!'

'Nonsense!' said the conductor gallantly. 'You did the job beautifully.'

Alexis moved away from the vestry door, leaned weakly back against the stone wall and closed his eyes. The gnawing pain in his chest grew stronger. What he wanted to do was rush into the vestry, take Daisy in his arms, cover her with kisses, and ignoring everyone else, tell her how proud he was of her, how beautiful she was and how much he loved her. But when he imagined pushing the vestry door open and seeing all those faces turning enquiringly towards him, a paralysing dread came upon him. He took a deep breath and stared up into the lofty roof of the abbey, willing himself courage, trying to summon up some confidence.

And then, suddenly, he heard Daisy's voice, raised in distress.

'But you can't go yet,' she was saying. 'You haven't met Alexis.'

'Well, darling, that's hardly our fault, is it? If he's gone home . . .' Daisy's mother's voice was crisp and efficient, and made Alexis wince just to hear it.

'He hasn't! He wouldn't just go home like that.'

'Well, then, where is he?'

'I don't know where he is.'

Daisy sounded desolate, and Alexis had a sudden vision of her standing, like a forgotten child, with a drooping lip and her flowers dragging sadly on the floor. He simply couldn't bear it. With a sudden burst of passion, he strode forward and pushed open the vestry door.

'Hello,' he said in a slightly trembling voice. 'I'm sorry I took so long, my darling.' He smiled tenderly at Daisy, then held out his hand to her mother. 'How do you do,' he said, forcing himself to meet her gaze. 'You may have heard about me. I'm Alexis Faraday.'

Louise and Barnaby were sitting in the garden of Larch Tree Cottage. Louise had poured out two glasses of wine and Barnaby had unfolded a couple of garden chairs. He now sat on one of them, cradling his drink in his huge hand, leaning forward and frowning. Louise clenched her own glass and said nothing. They had walked back here from Sylvia's party almost in silence, and all the while there had grown inside her a strange, almost heady tension.

Now the tension was even stronger. She didn't dare to speak; inside her was an unarticulated obscure conviction that this moment was an important one; that to speak might ruin it – and her chances – for ever. Her chances of what? She didn't know. Neither did she know why this moment should be so important, nor why her heart started beating painfully every time Barnaby raised his head as though to speak. She felt as though she didn't know anything any more.

'I've been thinking,' said Barnaby abruptly, in a gruff earnest voice.

Louise jumped and stared down at her drink. Please, she found herself thinking. *Please.* And suddenly she realized what was wrong with her. I know what I want him to say, she thought, trying to keep her breathing steady. And I'm terrified that he won't say it, and if he doesn't say it, then neither can I.

'About the case,' continued Barnaby. 'You'll probably think I'm crazy,' he added. Louise's heart gave another little leap, and she gazed at him, holding her breath, half

272

willing him to continue, half dreading what his words might be.

'But you know,' he said, 'sometimes I start to have my doubts.' He paused. Louise exhaled slowly. 'Serious doubts,' he added, gazing at her intently, trying to judge her reaction. Louise stared back at him, not daring to move a muscle of her face, not daring to risk throwing him off course before he'd even begun. 'I know I've always said it'll be worth it in the end,' he said in a defensive apologetic voice. 'But now . . . I'm not sure.' He frowned deeply. 'Hugh's heart attack really put things into perspective for me.'

'Wh-what are you saying, exactly?' said Louise. Her voice was trembling, and she took a deep shuddering breath. Barnaby leaned back in his chair.

'Last night', he said slowly, 'I was getting really depressed. I sat there, thinking about Hugh, who's in hospital, and Katie, who's out of hospital and doing fine, and the case, and all that money, and everything seemed all wrong, but there didn't seem to be any way out. I was going round and round in circles and feeling more and more miserable.' He paused and took a slug of wine. 'And then', he said, 'it suddenly occurred to me. We're *choosing* to go to court, we don't have to. No-one's forcing us. And . . .' He paused and looked uncertainly at Louise.

'What?' prompted Louise, falteringly.

'And, if we wanted to, we could . . .' He stopped, then continued in a rush. 'We could just call the whole thing off.'

There was a long shocked silence. Louise stared at Barnaby. She could feel her face turning pink and her breaths coming in short sharp gasps.

'I know,' exclaimed Barnaby, 'I'm crazy. You don't have to agree with me.'

'But I do!' cried Louise suddenly, her voice ringing through the garden. 'I do agree with you!'

To her astonishment a tear began to roll down her cheeks, and she gave a sudden involuntary sob. Barnaby stared at her in alarm.

'I'm the same as you! I don't want to go to court any more!' she wailed. 'I just want to get back to normal life. I just can't stand it hanging over us all the time . . .' She tailed off and broke down into shuddering sobs.

'Lou!' said Barnaby. He sounded shaken. 'Lou, are you all right?'

'Don't worry,' she spluttered, 'I'm fine. It's just . . .' She looked up at him through teary blue eyes. 'It's just . . . I don't know . . . the relief . . .' And she broke down again.

For a few minutes she sat with her head buried in her hands, rocking slightly in her chair, weeping uncontrollably. She was oblivious of anything except the hot redness in front of her eyes and her panting breaths and the wetness which coursed through her fingers. But gradually, as her sobs began to die down, she began to feel a gentle lifting in her body. The strains and tensions which seemed to have been building up inside her for months, very slowly started to ebb away. She felt her shoulders begin to loosen and her neck begin to relax and her taut constrained brow gently begin to expand. And inside her mind she began to be aware of a gradual lightening, an easing, a slipping away of the shadowy, looming, permanent edifice that had been part of her every thought and dream since the whole thing had started.

'It was just there all the time!' she suddenly wailed. 'It spoiled everything. All we could think about was the case! Oh God, Barnaby! What were we doing? We were mad!'

Barnaby's head jerked up.

'Do you mean . . .' he said hesitantly, studying Louise's wet, red, tear-streaked face. 'Do you mean you definitely want to call it off? I mean . . . I mean, a minute ago you were all in favour of it. You can't have changed your mind that quickly.'

Louise took a couple of slow shuddering breaths and rubbed her cheeks. Then she looked up at Barnaby.

'I haven't changed my mind,' she said. 'I've just opened it up and looked at what's really inside.' She paused. 'If you hadn't said anything, then, yes, I would have gone along with the case, but only because I didn't see any other option. I felt trapped. I just sort of assumed we had to go to court, whether we wanted to or not.' She gave a shaky laugh. 'As though it wasn't up to us all along. And now . . .' She pushed her hair off her wet face. 'Now I feel as if we were mad to keep going with the idea for so long.'

'But what about . . .' Barnaby shrugged helplessly. 'Oh, I don't know . . . the money?'

'The money,' said Louise flatly. 'No amount of money would make me go into a witness box and tell the world that Katie's a walking disaster.'

'What?'

'That's what they said, those lawyers. They said', Louise's voice trembled, 'she wasn't injured enough. They said we'd have to play up the personality changes; make her sound like a monster; unbearable to live with.'

'Bastards!' Barnaby stared at Louise.

'Either that or forget about half a million,' said Louise. She looked down. 'And anyway,' she added softly, 'what do we really want with half a million pounds of Hughs' and Ursula's money?'

There was a long pause.

'We don't,' said Barnaby.

'No,' said Louise, 'we don't. We don't want any of it. I can't even bear to think about it any more. I suddenly feel . . .' She ran her fingers shakily through her hair. 'I feel liberated. As though I've got rid of a disease that was poisoning me and making me sick.'

'That's a bit how I feel, too,' said Barnaby.

Louise smiled tremulously at him. For a few moments they looked at each other silently in the still garden air. Then Barnaby took a deep breath and said, 'What about Cassian?'

For a moment Louise stared at him, as though she didn't know who he was talking about.

'Cassian,' she echoed weakly. 'Oh, God. I don't know.' She took a sip of wine and winced. 'He'll be furious; he'll be absolutely furious.' Suddenly she gave a strange, almost hysterical little giggle. 'He'll go completely mad,' she said and giggled again. 'He'll probably explode.'

Barnaby stared at her. He opened his mouth to speak, then shut it again.

'I don't know how I'll tell him,' said Louise. Barnaby licked his lips nervously.

'Do you think . . .' he began. 'Do you think he'll try and make you change your mind?'

'Never,' said Louise determinedly. 'Let him try.' She sighed and sipped at her wine. 'The trouble with Cassian', she said in an almost conversational tone, 'is that he takes everything so bloody seriously. I don't think he even knows what a sense of humour is.'

Barnaby stared at Louise, unable to reply.

'All he thinks about', continued Louise, 'is his career, and his political prospects, and winning this stupid case. He wants to move to London, you know.' She looked up at Barnaby. 'He wants us to move there with him; the girls, too.'

Barnaby felt a jolting pang in his chest.

'To London?' he said weakly.

'Yes,' said Louise airily. 'That's what he says.'

'And . . .' Barnaby swallowed. 'Are you going to go?'

Louise put her drink down and looked straight at him.

'Barnaby,' she said gently, 'do you really think there's any future for me and Cassian now?'

Barnaby stared back at her for a moment, then he

looked down and shrugged. He felt unhappily confused. Louise drew breath to speak again, but she was interrupted by the sound of the telephone ringing.

'Oh, God,' said Louise. 'That might be about the girls. Hang on a minute.'

She hurried into the house and Barnaby leaned back heavily in his chair, trying to make some sense of this conversation; trying not to let himself draw the wrong conclusion; trying not to allow the insidious, corrupting, unstoppable emotion of hope to take root in his chest.

As Louise came back again he was frowning hard, and he looked up to speak. But she spoke first.

'It was . . .' Her voice was trembling slightly, and Barnaby felt a sudden thumping panic. He stared anxiously at her. Had something happened to the girls? To Katie?

'It was Cassian,' said Louise. 'His meeting was cancelled.'

The fearful beating in Barnaby's chest began to subside and he gave a small sigh of relief. Louise licked her dry lips.

'I told him we were calling off the case,' she said. 'I thought it would be easier that way. I thought he was miles away.' She gave a strange giggle. 'But he was calling from his car. He's going to be here in about five minutes.'

Daisy and Alexis stood at the corner of the square of grass in front of Linningford Abbey and waved. On the other side of the Crescent a gleaming red BMW signalled, then smoothly turned and disappeared through the narrow stone gateway. Daisy dropped her arm and sighed.

'I'm so glad you've met my parents,' she said happily. 'I think they really liked you.'

Alexis looked down at her innocent face and recalled,

in spite of himself, the expressions of suspicion and incredulity which had greeted him in the vestry. The mistrustful probing questions from Daisy's mother; the alarmed frown on her father's forehead; the looks of surprise from the others. All covered in a civilized veneer of friendly politeness.

The only one who had completely failed to conceal his hilarious astonishment had been Daisy's brother. He had stared agog at Alexis, then at Daisy, then back at Alexis. Then he'd sidled up to Daisy and said in a penetrating whisper, 'This your fella, then?' Daisy had blushed and smiled. 'Isn't he a bit past it?' continued her brother cheerfully, and Daisy had blushed even harder, and her mother had hastily asked Alexis, in a loud distracting voice, a question about his work.

Now Alexis smiled at Daisy and said, 'I hope they did. They certainly seemed very nice people.'

'Oh, yes,' said Daisy vaguely. 'Yes, they are.'

'They were talking about the Academy,' continued Alexis. 'You didn't tell me you'd won a scholarship there.'

'Oh,' Daisy shrugged, 'it wasn't anything much.'

'That's not what your parents seem to think, nor that conductor chap.' Alexis looked seriously at her. 'You know, Daisy,' he said, 'you have something very precious. I don't think I realized before today quite how precious it was. And how important it is that you make as much of it as you possibly can.'

He walked a few steps, sat down on the grass, still warm from the day's sun, and patted the ground next to him. Daisy sank down in a dark billowing cloud of taffeta, and nestled up to him.

'Today was lovely,' she murmured. 'Doing the concert, and seeing my parents, and them meeting you and everything.' She looked up at Alexis. 'This has been such a perfect summer.'

'I know it has,' said Alexis softly. 'Perfect.' He paused

and ran a hand through his hair. Daisy nestled closer.

'But, you know,' continued Alexis slowly, 'the summer's nearly at an end. And then you're going to move to London and start your new life at the Academy, and things might . . .' he swallowed, 'might be a little different.'

'What do you mean?' Daisy turned her head to look at him, wide-eyed. 'What do you mean, different? Do you mean us?'

'In a way,' said Alexis. He put up a hand and cradled her chin.

'Your life is just beginning,' he said gently, 'and it's going to be a very exciting life. You must make the most of it.'

'I know,' said Daisy. She stared at him. 'But we'll still be the same, won't we? I mean, I'll come down every weekend, and we'll still see each other nearly as much as we do now, that's what we said.'

'I know that's what we said,' agreed Alexis, 'and of course we will see each other, but . . .' He broke off.

'But what?' Daisy sat up, suddenly agitated. 'Wh-what's wrong?' In her distress she began to stumble over her words, and Alexis felt his heart squeeze painfully.

'Nothing's wrong,' he said. 'It's just . . .' He broke off and briefly closed his eyes. What was he doing? What the hell was he doing? Why was he torturing himself and Daisy like this?

'D-don't . . . don't you want to go out with me any more?' said Daisy. Her lips were quivering and her eyelashes batted nervously. Alexis stared at her, almost unable to reply.

'Of course I want to,' he said at last, his voice thick with emotion. 'Daisy, I love you.'

'And I love you, too,' said Daisy in a trembling voice. Alexis looked away. He could hardly bear to say what he was about to.

'But sometimes,' he said, forcing himself to speak,

'sometimes just loving each other isn't enough.' Daisy drew breath, and he carried on quickly before she could speak. 'When you get to London, you're going to meet a lot of new people, all your own age, and you're going to have a lot of fun. And, I hope, you're going to work very hard at your music.' He paused. Daisy was silent.

'And all I wanted to say,' he continued, 'was that you mustn't come back down here every weekend. You must go out and have fun, and join in with all the others. And if,' he swallowed, 'if you happen to meet someone – a boy – who's a bit nearer your own age . . .'

'I won't!' said Daisy passionately. 'I wouldn't ever . . .'

'You might,' said Alexis gently, 'and if you do, you mustn't feel bad. You mustn't feel guilty.' He somehow managed to smile at her. 'We've had a perfect summer together, and nothing can ever change that, but now you're moving on.'

'I don't want to move on,' whispered Daisy. She bit her lip. 'I want to stay here with you. I wish I wasn't going.'

'I know you do,' said Alexis thickly. 'God, so do I.' He suddenly pulled her close to him and buried his face in her soft, white, scented neck.

'Let's not think about the future,' he murmured against her skin. 'Let's just enjoy the next two weeks. And then, when you move to London – well, we'll just see how it goes, shall we?'

'OK,' said Daisy in a shaking voice. She pushed him away slightly, and he saw, with a small shock, that her cheeks were stained with tears. 'I'll always love you, Alexis,' she said. 'It wouldn't matter if I was in London or here or . . . or on the moon. And I think,' she hesitated, 'I think you're wrong. I think that's all that counts. We love each other, and . . . and nothing else matters at all. That's what I think.'

Alexis stared back at her for a few trembling moments.

'I'm an old fool,' he said at last. Daisy gave a surprised giggle.

'No, you're not!' she said.

'I am,' said Alexis. 'I don't know what I've been thinking of. I should be wining and dining you, sweeping you off your feet. We should be celebrating! What are we doing, sitting here?'

He got to his feet, and held out his hands to Daisy. 'Now,' he said. 'You're the star, so you can choose. Red wine, white wine, or . . .'

'Champagne,' said Daisy, 'of course!'

'As much as we can drink,' said Alexis. He looked at her ruefully. 'Daisy, don't ever again listen to a word I say,' he said. 'Please.' Daisy giggled.

'OK,' she said, 'I won't.'

'Good,' said Alexis. 'Now, let's go and find some champagne worth drinking.'

Louise and Barnaby sat, in silence, in the kitchen of Larch Tree Cottage. They had neatly folded up the garden chairs, brought the wine inside, and sat down to wait. That was five minutes ago. Now every little sound from outside made them start and glance towards the door, then look sheepishly at each other and back down again.

Barnaby stared miserably into his glass of wine. He felt as though he had been on the brink of something outside, on the edge of a new understanding, a new beginning, even. If they'd just had a bit more time to talk . . . He glanced covertly at Louise and her words floated through his mind. 'Do you really think there's any future for me and Cassian?' Barnaby clenched his fist tightly. He felt like smashing it down on the table. What did she mean? Was she asking him a question? Was she trying to tell him something? Was she teasing him? He couldn't stand this roundabout talk.

Suddenly there was the sound of a key in the

lock. Louise jumped, and looked at Barnaby.

'I feel like hiding under the table,' she whispered. 'Don't you?'

But there was no time for Barnaby to reply, as into the kitchen strode Cassian. He looked office-smart, and swung his briefcase jauntily. To Barnaby's amazement, he was smiling.

'Hello,' he said. 'Hello there, Barnaby. Nice to see you.'

'Oh,' said Barnaby, taken aback. 'Yes.' Surprise made him sound gruff and ungracious, and he suddenly felt a bit unsure of things. Had Louise really made up her mind about the case? Why was Cassian looking so cheerful? What was going on? He watched as Cassian sat down and poured himself a glass of wine; he looked completely unperturbed. Barnaby glanced at Louise, who was looking down pensively. He couldn't tell what she might be thinking, and in spite of himself, his heart began to beat nervously.

'So, I gather', said Cassian smoothly, 'you've been having second thoughts about the case.' He spoke to Barnaby, as though Louise were not there, or didn't count. Or as though she didn't agree with Barnaby.

'Well,' said Barnaby, glancing at Louise, 'yes. We've decided we don't want to go any further with it.'

'I understand completely,' said Cassian kindly. 'It's a very daunting prospect, going to court, but don't worry, you'll be fine. So what I suggest is that you have a careful think and sleep on it, and don't rush into any decision yet.'

'Well,' began Barnaby doubtfully. He looked at Louise again; she wasn't saying anything. What was wrong? Had she changed her mind about the whole thing? He looked up at Cassian, who was politely waiting. Someone was going to have to say something. Barnaby frowned.

'The thing is, Cassian,' he said, 'I really think we've

made up our minds already.' He glanced at Louise and, when there was no response, ploughed on. 'We think the case is going to be too much of a strain, both on us and on Katie,' he said, 'and there's no guarantee of getting any money, and even if there were, the Delaneys . . .' He tailed off feebly.

'The Delaneys are your friends,' suggested Cassian.

'Well, yes,' said Barnaby, 'something like that.'

'Yes,' said Cassian. He didn't sound surprised. 'Well, as I say, have a good think, and I'm sure you'll come round to the idea again.' He smiled at Barnaby. 'You know, you owe it to Katie.'

'Don't say that!' Louise's voice interrupted him like a whiplash, and both men jumped. 'Don't you dare say anything at all about Katie,' she said in a fierce deliberate voice. 'You have no idea at all. This case isn't going to help her! It's going to label her as some kind of helpless head case! It's going to tell the world that her whole life has been ruined! What kind of help is that?'

'Louise,' said Cassian in soothing tones. 'I realize it's difficult to face up to Katie's needs . . .'

'I face up to them every day, thank you!' exclaimed Louise. 'I know exactly what her needs are. She needs a normal life and support and encouragement, not a bloody legal battle to screw her up!'

'Oh, right,' said Cassian in scathing tones, 'and I suppose all this comes free, does it? All this support and encouragement?'

'Most of it, yes!' said Louise. She folded her arms and looked straight at Cassian. 'Katie is not a victim any more,' she said. 'She's just fine. We've been incredibly lucky, and I think it's time for us to start appreciating that a bit more. All of us.'

'Well, great,' said Cassian sarcastically, 'that's a lovely romantic vision, but what happens, I wonder, when Katie grows up? And she realizes that she could have had half a million pounds, but her parents were too lily-livered to go to court? What are you going to say to her then?'

'For a start,' said Louise furiously, 'I think you should just stop talking about this famous half a million pounds. I'm not stupid, I saw the way those other lawyers were looking at each other. We would never get that much in court, never!'

'That's not . . .' began Cassian. But Louise interrupted him.

'And even if we did! Even if we did! What do we need it for?' She paused and glanced at Barnaby. He was gazing at her, mouth open in shock. She gave him a quick grin and looked back at Cassian. 'We're OK for money,' she said slowly. 'We're more than OK. And when my father eventually dies . . .' She swallowed awkwardly. 'Well, then we'll be even . . . even more OK. And for us to go to court and fleece Hugh and Ursula of all their life's earnings, just because Katie happened to be in their pool and not someone else's . . . well, it's immoral.' She took a sip of wine and both men eyed her warily. 'You can say what you like, Cassian,' she continued calmly, 'but we're not going ahead with this case. We should never have got into it in the first place.'

'Louise,' said Cassian smoothly, 'I can tell you're a bit upset.'

'Oh, shut up, Cassian!' shouted Louise exasperatedly. 'You can't tell anything! You can't tell when a case starts to look weak; you can't tell when someone really does change their mind.' She paused. 'You can't even tell right from wrong.' Cassian glared at her.

'This case is *not* weak!' he shouted. 'It's a very strong case, backed up by some of the finest legal minds in Britain, and if you pull out now, I can tell you, you'll be making a big mistake!'

'Fine!' cried Louise. 'Let us make a mistake. At least we'll be able to sleep at night!'

'And actually,' pointed out Barnaby in a low gruff

voice, 'we could always sue later on, if we wanted to. We've got up until Katie's eighteen.' Cassian shot him a look of pure loathing.

'How very clever of you, Barnaby,' he said in a voice which quivered with anger. 'Any more top legal tips from Farmer Giles?'

'Leave him alone!' shrieked Louise. 'God, you're a shit, Cassian.'

'Well, you're a fool!' retorted Cassian. 'You're both fools! This case could be a gold-mine!'

'We don't need a gold-mine!'

'Yes, well, I do!' Cassian suddenly yelled. 'I fucking well need this case to happen! Everyone knows about it; everyone's involved in it. I mean, the London office is helping to draw up the writ. The London office! Do you know what that means? Do you know how important that makes it? Do you know what a fucking *disaster* it'll be if I have to turn round and say, Oh, sorry, the clients have changed their minds?' He stopped, panting slightly; Louise and Barnaby exchanged astonished glances.

'I should have known,' he continued in slightly more controlled tones, 'you fucking well haven't got a clue, have you? Either of you. Bloody peasants.'

There was a thunderous rasping as Barnaby pushed the kitchen table forward by about three feet. His face was bright red and he was breathing heavily.

'That's enough!' he bellowed. 'That's enough! Now get out, and don't ever dare to talk to my wife like that again, or I'll kill you!' He stood up, a big rough giant. Cassian raised an eyebrow.

'Of course,' he said, 'now we move on to physical threats; the last bastion of the cerebrally challenged.'

'Shut up!' commanded Barnaby.

'Oh reall . . .' began Cassian, but he broke off into a yelp as Barnaby's huge hand grasped his shirt by the neck.

'Now,' said Barnaby, breathing heavily, 'either you go, or I throw you very hard against that door. And then I pick you up and throw you again.'

'Louise!' squawked Cassian. 'Tell him to stop! This is assault. I'm warning you,' he said furiously to Barnaby.

'Take me to court,' said Barnaby, throwing him back down into his chair. 'See if I care.'

Cassian smoothed his hair down with trembling hands and straightened his tie.

'Louise . . .' he began. But she cut him off with a raised hand.

'If I were you, Cassian,' she said gently, 'I'd go. Now.' Her mouth twisted into an unwilling grin. 'You don't know what these peasants are like when they get really angry.'

Cassian stood up. He looked from Louise to Barnaby and back to Louise again; his face white; his features distorted with anger.

'You'll be hearing from me,' he said curtly and picked up his briefcase.

'Goodbye, Cassian,' said Louise.

'Oh, fuck off,' said Cassian.

Louise and Barnaby listened as he walked furiously out of the house, slammed the door, and started up his car. Then, as the sound died away, they looked at each other.

'Well,' said Louise, 'I wonder if he got the message.'

Chapter Twenty

The next morning Meredith woke at seven o'clock. She looked at the clock on her bedside table, cursed, and flopped back onto her pillows. The night before she had taken a herbal sleeping draught, to give herself the chance of a good night's rest. But now, although her body felt heavy and sluggish, her mind was racing, as alert as ever. Impossible to go back to sleep. She turned over angrily, and tried to remember a Buddhist chant she had successfully used before in moments of anxiety. But even as the words formed in her mind, she was remembering, with a pang, Hugh's pale face and frail form as they'd led him out of the hospital the evening before.

Before leaving, she'd spoken with Hugh's consultant, trying desperately – irrationally – to get a promise out of him that this wasn't going to happen again. But instead of giving her the blank reassurances she craved, the consultant had taken the moment as an opportunity to explain to her exactly what changes Hugh must make to his lifestyle, exactly what state his arteries were in, and exactly what all the family could do to help. He'd pressed on her a cheerful educational poster depicting food groups in bold cartoon characters, and suggested that she put it up on the fridge. She'd stared back at him, wondering how he could be so obtuse. It's not the fucking food! she'd wanted to shout. It's the fucking court case!

They'd had a cautious evening at home, trying to act normally. Ursula had carefully prepared supper out of a recipe book given to her at the hospital, and they had all exclaimed with forced cheerfulness over the poached salmon without hollandaise sauce and raspberries sprinkled with orange juice instead of cream. Hugh had automatically reached for a bottle of wine, then stopped, hand still outstretched. And Meredith had wanted to weep. Not because of the wine, or the hollandaise sauce, but because, behind the jollity, behind the united pretence that they all suddenly felt like drinking lemon squash instead, loomed an unspoken fear, an unforgettable, permanent shadow.

Abruptly, she pushed back the covers and got out of bed. From behind the curtain were peeping tiny dazzling rays of light; the promise of another bright day. She pushed up her window and breathed in the fresh air; still summery, still mild, but with a hint of autumnal bite. Meredith didn't know whether this made her feel sad or relieved.

'What a fucking awful summer,' she said aloud. She leaned out and squinted down at the silent, dewy, glistening grass. She took a few deep breaths, closed her eyes and felt the breeze on her face, and suddenly the heavy torpor seemed to leave her legs. She turned back into the room and began quickly to get dressed. Before breakfast; before the beginning of the day and the return to real life, she would go for a walk. A long, fresh, cleansing walk.

At half-past eight the phone in Louise's bedroom rang. She picked up the receiver, listened for a few seconds, then said, firmly, 'I don't think so, Cassian. I think we both know it's a bit late for that.'

She listened for a few more moments, then, with deliberate care, she replaced the receiver. She lay back and stretched luxuriously.

'That's the first time I've ever done that,' she said. 'Cut

someone off mid-flow. I have to say, it's a wonderful feeling.'

'What did he want?' said Barnaby sleepily.

'My body,' said Louise.

There was a rumpling sound from next to her, and Barnaby's head appeared from under the duvet, tousled and still half asleep.

'Are you serious?' he said.

'No,' she said, in regretful tones, 'I don't think so. He was just generally grovelling. I think he was hoping we'd changed our minds about the case.'

Barnaby regarded her for a moment, then flopped heavily back down onto his pillow with a thump that made the whole mattress quiver.

'I don't understand you,' he said. 'I thought you were in love with him.'

'I know,' said Louise. 'I thought I was, too.' She sighed. 'I realized something was wrong when we started talking about calling off the case. I found myself thinking that it would probably mean the end for me and Cassian, and instead of feeling upset, I felt . . . relieved, more than anything else.' She shrugged. 'I don't really understand it.'

'Well, it doesn't matter,' said Barnaby contentedly. 'What matters is that we're back together again.'

'Are we?' said Louise sharply.

'Aren't we?' Barnaby sat up abruptly and looked at Louise with a puzzled frown. 'I mean, after last night, and . . . and everything . . .' He gestured vaguely around.

'I know,' said Louise patiently. She sighed. 'Look, Barnaby, I'm not saying we can't get back together, but you mustn't think that just because Cassian's out of the picture, everything's suddenly rosy. We had problems way before he came on the scene.' She pushed back her hair and pulled her knees up under the duvet. 'The thing you've got to get straight', she said deliberately, 'is that I wasn't having an affair with Cassian behind your back. I wasn't. I used to go and see him, yes. But we used to talk, that was all.' In spite of herself, she could feel a note of resentment creeping into her voice. 'When I tried to tell you, you wouldn't listen. You just listened to your own suspicions and the village gossip.'

'Well, you shouldn't even have been talking to him,' said Barnaby gruffly. 'The creep.'

'Barnaby!' exclaimed Louise angrily. 'You still don't get it! I'm allowed to see and talk to whoever I like, whether they're a creep or not. God, if you still don't understand that . . .'

'I do,' said Barnaby hastily. 'I do understand it.'

'Do you?' said Louise.

There was silence in the little room.

'I think', said Louise eventually, 'that it would be a good idea for me to take the girls to London next week as planned. We'll go on our own, and have a good holiday, and then we'll come back and . . .' She looked at Barnaby. 'And then we can talk.'

'Yes,' said Barnaby seriously. 'Good idea.'

'I really need to get away,' said Louise, 'and I think the girls could do with a change of scene too.'

'Yes,' said Barnaby again. 'Good idea.' There was a pause. 'Louise?'

Louise raised her eyes. Barnaby was looking yearningly at her.

'I don't suppose I could come with you?' he said. 'To London?'

'Oh, Barnaby,' said Louise. She began to laugh. 'But you hate London.'

'I know I do,' said Barnaby, 'but I'd like it if I went with you. I could take the girls to the zoo, and show them Big Ben, while you go shopping in Harrods. It'd be great. What do you think?' He looked at her eagerly, a huge entreating smile on his face. Louise couldn't help smiling back.

'Maybe,' she said at last. 'Maybe.'

*   *   *

Meredith walked quickly, feeling the morning air filling her lungs and a pink tingling glow spread over her cheeks. The roads were empty of cars this early on a Saturday morning; most people seemed to still be in bed.

Without really noticing, she headed towards the church. The graveyard was silent and the headstones damp with an early morning moisture. She sat down on the single wooden bench, closed her eyes and tilted her face towards the gradually warming sun. She waited for a calming relief to spread through her body; for the natural power of the sun's rays to channel her energies in a positive direction; for her mind to achieve a balanced position of acceptance. But when, a few minutes later, she opened her eyes again, nothing was different. Unless she concentrated very hard, she could not rid her mind of all her background whining worries – about Hugh, about Ursula, about the case, and shrieking loudly above the rest, her bitter, fruitless, constant feeling of anger.

Her mind flicked to Simon, and away again. She had been thinking of Simon more and more over the last few weeks; on the night of Hugh's heart attack she had dreamed a long and happy dream about him, and had awoken to the realization that he was dead with a shock that almost reduced her to tears. But in her waking moments she was well used to fielding emotions about Simon. Now, in an automatic reaction, she got to her feet and thrust her hands in her pockets. It was way past nine o'clock; time to head home.

'Of course', said Louise, 'the first thing we must do is tell Hugh and Ursula.'

Barnaby stopped in the middle of buttoning up his shirt and stared at her.

'My God,' he said, 'I hadn't even thought of that; I

hadn't even thought what it'll mean to them.' He looked down sheepishly. 'All I've been thinking about is us.'

'Yes, well,' said Louise, 'that's important too.' She gave him a little smile. 'But I think we ought to tell them as soon as possible, don't you? We ought to go round there this morning.'

'Or phone them, maybe?'

'No,' said Louise decisively. 'We've got to tell them face to face. They deserve it.'

'OK,' said Barnaby. He looked at his watch. 'Let's go round there straight away,' he said enthusiastically.

'Now? Before breakfast?'

'Why not?' said Barnaby. 'Good news can't wait for breakfast.'

'What if they're not up yet?'

'They will be,' said Barnaby confidently, 'and if they aren't, we'll wait.'

'Well . . . all right then,' said Louise. 'All right. Just let me get dressed.'

She reached behind her neck to fasten her dress and frowned, as she missed the button.

'I'll do it,' said Barnaby at once. 'Let me.' He bounded over, seized the fabric from out of her hand, and attempted to fasten it.

'Damn,' he said, breathing heavily, and grasping the fabric harder with his huge hands. 'It's tiny.'

Louise automatically opened her mouth to say, Oh, for heaven's sake, Barnaby, give it here, I'll do it. Then, thinking again, she closed it, and found herself gazing silently, with a fondness bordering on love, at his serious frowning reflection in the mirror.

On the way home, Meredith took a different route from the way she'd come. She was walking briskly along, her mind full of abstract floating thoughts, and just beginning to feel hungry, when something ahead of her made her stop in her tracks, take a sharp inward breath, and clench her fists inside her pockets.

There, unmistakably, in front of her, was Alexis's car – smooth, green, and parked at a skewed angle to the road, carelessly, as though its owner had been thinking of other things as he parked it.

Before she could stop them, Meredith's eyes moved from the car to the wrought-iron gate swinging casually open nearby, to the charming orchard garden and, only a few yards away, the front door of a pretty little cottage, stout and thick and shut tight against the rest of the world.

Daisy Phillips's cottage. Behind that cosy front door, in some bloody cosy little bed, Alexis lay with Daisy Phillips, with a dumb teenager young enough to be his daughter.

Meredith didn't quite understand her own reaction to this affair. When Frances had first told her about it, she'd been astounded at her own nonchalant attitude. 'Damn!' she'd said carelessly, swigging back her vodka. 'Looks like I missed the boat.' And ever since then she'd tried to maintain a semblance of cool indifference. She even thought she'd managed to fool herself. But now, seeing Alexis's car parked so casually, so, so . . . *familiarly*, outside Daisy's cottage – as though that was where it belonged – Meredith began to feel a raw hot feeling of hurt rising through her. Her cool, calm, sophisticated veneer felt as though it were being melted in patches, and her breaths began to come more quickly. Why did he choose Daisy? she found herself thinking, like an aggrieved five-year-old. Why didn't he choose me? She felt suddenly exposed, vulnerable and, uncharacteristically, close to bursting into tears.

'I've had enough,' she muttered aloud, walking past Alexis's car, looking away and trying to ignore the painful pangs below her ribs. 'I've just about had enough.'

As she entered the drive of Devenish House, her stride

slowed down. She felt a sudden dread of seeing Hugh and Ursula; of having to summon up a smile and a cheery greeting. She took a few deep breaths and tried to focus her thoughts on something positive, but her mind batted relentlessly between disturbing images of Hugh, Alexis and Simon. Emotions surfaced in uneven, uncontrollable waves; there was no room for anything else.

She couldn't face Hugh and Ursula while she was in this state; couldn't face seeing anybody. For a while she stood completely still on the gravel of the drive, trying not to panic, trying to work out what to do, where to go. The friendly face of Frances Mold flashed through her mind, and for a moment she considered taking refuge in the unquestioning vicarage. Then she remembered that it was Saturday morning. Frances would be in church, busy with the flower ladies.

An unfamiliar, unwelcome feeling of loneliness began to spread through her. Where was her self-sufficiency? she asked herself furiously. Where was her independence? Where was her sense of humour? She bit her lip and pushed her hand through her hair, and wondered whether she should simply turn round and go for another long walk. And then the answer came to her: she would go to her studio and paint. She would paint until she had worked out of her system the anxiety, the hurt, the grief. She would channel the destructive feelings pounding round her body into something positive. She would make use of the moment.

Quickly she headed for the back of the house and towards her studio, then she remembered she didn't have the keys on her. An uncharacteristic white-hot annoyance flashed through her body.

'Fuck,' she said aloud, and quietly opened the conservatory door. She would quickly get them from her bedroom and hope that no-one heard her.

But as she moved silently through the conservatory, she heard voices from the hall. She paused, mid-stride, and wondered whether to back out again, into the garden, but that would leave her stranded. So, taking a deep breath, she pushed unwillingly forward into the hall.

What she saw made her stop still and draw in breath sharply. There, by the door, talking to Ursula, were Barnaby and Louise Kember.

Meredith felt herself recoil slightly and her heart begin to beat more quickly, in anticipation of a confrontation. She glanced quickly at Ursula, but Ursula looked unperturbed. She was standing near the stairs, dressed in her pretty blue and white dressing-gown, actually smiling up at Barnaby. As Meredith came in, she turned and beamed at her.

'Meredith, dear,' she said. 'I'm so glad you're back! The Kembers have come here with some wonderful news.'

Meredith stared blankly at Ursula. Dimly she registered that Louise and Barnaby were holding hands.

'They're calling off the case,' said Ursula. 'They've decided not to go to court after all. Isn't that marvellous?'

Louise smiled hesitantly at Meredith, who looked back numbly. Her throat felt constricted; she was unable to speak.

'We suddenly realized that we just couldn't go through with it,' said Louise, in a rush. 'For . . . for several reasons. We're pulling out completely. And we just wanted to say how sorry we are, for all the trouble it's caused, and everything. I hope you can forgive us.'

She smiled again at Meredith.

'Well, dear, isn't that lovely?' said Ursula, beaming at Meredith. 'Hugh will be so pleased.'

Meredith stared back at her with a white, taut face. All the emotions that had been pounding separately through her body seemed to be coming together in one huge rolling tidal wave of anger.

'Lovely?' she managed to whisper. 'You're saying this is lovely?'

She stared at Ursula's smiling face for a few seconds, trying desperately to keep on top of it, trying to keep her head. But then, suddenly, the wave broke, and through her body surged a terrifying fury which she couldn't begin to control.

'You've ruined our lives!' she screamed, rounding on Louise and Barnaby like a killer tigress. 'You've ruined our lives, and you have the nerve to come here, like Mr and Mrs fucking Happy Couple, and expect to be forgiven! Well, it's too late! You should have thought of that before you decided to take everything away from us. You should have thought of that before you gave Hugh a heart attack!'

She swooped on Louise, so that their two faces were only inches apart.

'I will *never* forgive you', she said savagely, 'for what you did to Hugh. Do you think you can take that away by saying sorry? Do you?' Her voice rose to a scream. 'Because if you do, you're wrong. Our lives will never be the same again, and it's your fault! It's your . . . your greed which did it all. You don't ever deserve to be forgiven. Ever!'

Louise took a step backwards. Her face was white and trembling and there were unshed tears in her eyes.

'Meredith!' said Ursula in an almost sharp voice. 'You don't know what you're saying, dear.'

'Don't defend them, Ursula!' shrieked Meredith. 'Don't let them get away with it that easily!'

'It's not easy!' cried Louise suddenly. 'OK, we made a mistake, and we're sorry, but we haven't had it easy!'

'We'll do anything we can to make up,' said Barnaby gruffly. 'We'll pay your legal fees, and we'll visit Hugh . . .'

'We don't want your fucking money, and we don't want you in this house!' Meredith's voice lashed across the hall.

'Meredith!' said Ursula. 'You really mustn't talk like this! I'm sorry,' she said quietly to Louise. 'She was very upset by Hugh . . .'

'Don't apologize for me!' yelled Meredith. And suddenly, to everyone's horror, she burst into huge, pent-up, shuddering sobs. Barnaby caught Louise's eye. She looked aghast.

'Don't apologize for me!' Meredith shouted again, furiously wiping her eyes. 'If I'm embarrassing you, Ursula, then I'll go, but I'm not going to forgive them. Not now, not ever.'

And abruptly, without looking any of them in the face, she turned, and half walked, half ran up the stairs. As she rounded the corner of the landing, she gave another huge sob.

Barnaby relaxed his grip on Louise's hand. He looked shaken.

'I'm so sorry,' he began in a low trembling voice. Ursula looked up at him.

'Yes,' she said simply. 'Yes, so am I.'

'I didn't realize', he said, 'how destructive this case was. I didn't realize how much damage we were causing.' He gazed entreatingly at Ursula. 'I just don't know what we can do to make up,' he muttered in a hopeless voice. 'I just don't know. I just wish we could start again. I just wish . . .'

He broke off, and there was a long miserable pause.

'We ought to go,' said Barnaby eventually, 'we've disturbed your morning enough.' He took Louise's hand. 'We'll be in touch.'

'No, don't go yet,' said Ursula. She drew her dressing-gown more closely around her and looked thoughtfully at them both. 'We all need some fresh air, I think. Let's go outside.'

The morning air felt clean and pure as they stepped out of the warm dank conservatory. As they walked, Barnaby took several deep breaths, then glanced at Louise; she still looked pale and shocked, and seemed unable to return his tentative smile. Through his head rang Meredith's bitter screams, and he winced. Then his eyes swivelled over to Ursula; her face was collected, composed, almost serene.

Suddenly, with a shock, Barnaby realized where she was heading.

'Here we are,' said Ursula softly. Louise and Barnaby looked at each other. In front of them, glistening bright blue in the pale sunshine, was the swimming-pool.

They watched numbly as Ursula sat down by the water's edge, and obediently did the same when she gestured to the ground next to her. Louise stared ahead blankly, shrinking at first from the gleaming silent pool, from the memories and the horror and the danger. But the water had a strange compelling power. After a few minutes, without quite meaning to, she found herself slipping off her shoes and, one by one, very slowly, lowering her feet into the pool. The clean chilling water rose gradually up her calves until her legs were knee-deep; vague mushroomy limbs floating in the blueness.

'I always knew', said Ursula in a soft, almost dreamy voice, 'that you would decide against going to court in the end. I knew it. I tried to tell them,' she smiled at Louise, 'but no-one would listen to me.'

'We didn't know ourselves until last night,' said Louise.

'I knew it,' repeated Ursula gently. She lowered a hand into the water and trailed it along the shiny surface. 'I knew you would come round, eventually.' She looked at Louise with a faintly complacent expression.

'It was my letter, wasn't it?'

'What?' said Louise, startled.

'My letter,' said Ursula happily. 'I was so sure that when you read it – when you understood – you would change your mind.' She beamed at Louise. 'Wasn't I right?'

Louise looked at Ursula's innocent face. Into her mind came a vision of pale mauve paper covered in foolish, incriminating, loopy writing, now filed away as evidence in one of Cassian's files. She bit her lip.

'Well,' she said eventually, not looking at Barnaby, 'I suppose it did help, yes. In a way.'

'I knew it would,' said Ursula. She sighed contentedly and smiled at Louise. 'And you were never really in love with that young man, were you?'

Louise glanced at Barnaby. She felt herself turn pink.

'Well,' she said, 'no, not really.'

'There,' said Ursula in a satisfied voice, 'I knew that, too.'

Louise leaned back on her elbows, closed her eyes, and felt the water lapping gently, soothingly, against her legs. They floated aimlessly, weightlessly, in the cool supporting depths; she felt almost as though she might float off with them. Without thinking, she said, 'I must take the girls swimming.'

She broke off abruptly. A tiny tension ran through the silence like a silvery thread.

'Before the end of the summer,' she carried on bravely. 'Just so that . . .' She paused uncertainly. 'So that they don't . . .' She tailed away and bit her lip. A breeze rustled the leaves in the trees nearby and she felt goose bumps rising on her bare arms.

'I think', said Ursula at last, 'that's a very good idea.' There was a pause, then she added in hopeful, hesitant tones, 'Is it true . . . is it really true that Katie is going back to school?'

'Yes,' said Louise eventually. 'Yes, it is. She's going

to start off part-time and see how she does. She's . . . she's much better.'

'Oh, I'm so glad,' said Ursula in a voice that trembled slightly. 'I'm so, so glad. We all hoped and prayed so much . . .'

For a long while nobody said anything. Then Barnaby asked in a hoarse voice, 'How's Hugh?'

'He's much better, too,' said Ursula. 'Much better.' She smiled at Barnaby. 'Everything's much better now.'

Louise's lips quivered and she began to cry softly. Tears streamed like warm raindrops down her face.

'I'm so sorry,' she said hopelessly. 'I don't know what else to say to you. I'm so sorry.'

'Don't,' said Ursula gently. 'Don't cry . . . and don't be sorry.' She reached over and put a warm papery hand on Louise's. 'Be glad,' she said. 'Be glad that the worst is over now. For all of us, the worst is over.'

Louise gave a huge shuddering sigh, and gratefully clasped Ursula's hand. She looked up at Barnaby and gave him a hesitant, tearful smile. And the three of them sat together in a gentle silence, staring ahead, watching the deep blue water glinting in the sunshine.

THE END

F   Wickham, Madeleine,
WICKHAM   1969-

            Swimming pool
            Sunday.

DATE			

PLEASE NOTE

To save dollars . . .

No overdue notice(s) will be sent on this
material. you are responsible for returning
by date on card in pocket. Otherwise you
will be billed.

Board of Managers
East Hampton Library
159 Main Street
East Hampton, NY 11937

BAKER & TAYLOR